THE METAL WITHIN

THE METAL WITHIN

A CYBERPUNK NOVEL

LEN GIZINSKI

Polestar Press

Cover art copyright © 2023 by David Triplett
ISBN: 979-8-9878613-0-1 (Paperback Edition)
ISBN: 979-8-9878613-1-8 (Hardcover Edition)
ISBN: 979-8-9878613-3-2 (epub)
ISBN: 979-8-9878613-6-3 (Kindle)

Library of Congress Control Number: 2023903743

DEDICATION:

To the Seven, Who First Read:
Jack and Emery Miller, Aidan and Gabe Taylor, Michelle Slater,
Gunther Johnson, and Vince DeBellis

To the Six, Who Imparted:
Jerry "Hawk" Hawkins, Bill Stone, Len Eller,
C.S. Lewis, Dave Minton, and Sung Han

To the Five, Who Inspired:
Lorie, Amber, Jon, Bethany, and Chris

To the Four, Who Wrote:
J.R.R. Tolkien, Frank Peretti, Stuart Jackman, and William Gibson

To the Three, Who Live:
Father, Jesus, Holy Spirit

To the Two, Who Encouraged:
Charles & Kate Ritz

To the One I Love –
My Heart, My Parallel, My Soulmate, My Wife:
Ruth Marie Gizinski

And, Humbly,
To You, Dear Reader
My sincere *Thanks* to you all.

ENJOY THE RIDE!

TABLE OF CONTENTS

"So, WE CAN see how the corruption of the United States Congress, plus the general lack of concern of their peoples by governments worldwide, led to several global crises. We also noted how the short-term profit-taking and lack of funding for alternative fuel resources led to the depletion of oil reserves, again on the global level. Question, Tom?"

"Yeah, I thought the electric power plants were used even back in the early '90s."

"True, electric cars were used, attaining the speed, reliability, and performance of six-cylinder internal combustion engines. But oil companies sabotaged the attempts to support the recharging requirements. We can go about 200 miles plus without having to recharge, but if we had to go 800 miles until we hit the next auto stop, we'd be dead in the water. Even then that was a risky situation at best, and they could only go about 100 miles before needing a full recharge that would take about eight hours, so who would buy the electrics?"

"So, with the oil crunch the oil corporations finally switched over?"

"The ones that survived did. Judy?"

"But there was still oil. I mean, there still *is* oil—and Lubric was still part of the United States back then, right?"

"Right again, on both points. Louisiana, Arkansas, and northeast Texas were still in the United States at the time. As we know, however, it *was* the oil crunch, which led the United States to launch the attempt to nationalize the Texarkana oil wells. In response, those states seceded and formed Lubric International Corporate Conglomerate, or Lubric ICC for short, as the first of the true nationally-independent megacorporations. The secession, of course, then led to the Southeastern Oil War. But tanks don't run without fuel. 'All the king's horsemen,' so to speak, ran out of oats in the Ozarks, and they couldn't keep the already fragile Humpty together anymore. The notion of international corporate conglomerates was novel in its day but soon other major corporations and organizations followed suit to create self-governing corporation states of their own.

"What other event did the secession of Lubric ICC lead to? Jim?"

"The secession of Utah?"

"Good guess! How?"

"Well, according to the book, a lot of people in Utah saw the secession and the general deterioration of the United States' moral quality as a sign that the great destruction they said would come was here, and that the time had come when they would have to 'save' the Constitution, which they thought was divinely inspired, by stealing it from Washington, D.C. When the attempts failed, they claimed they interpreted things wrong, made their own constitution, and seceded from the U.S. The U.S. was too weakened by the oil war to risk another defeat, so they let them go…"

PART 1

PARALLEL PROGRESSION

And there is the headlight, shining far down the track, glinting off the steel rails that, like all parallel lines, will meet in infinity, which is after all where this train is going.

— Bruce Catton
Waiting for the A.M. Train

1

PREACHER JACK

THE OPPRESSIVE HEAVY heat of the July air somehow both stifled and aggravated the inner-city denizens, like putting an elastic muzzle on a rabid dog. Overbearing high temperatures and teeming humidity threw the city under a blanket of fetid moisture, transforming the urban ghetto into a concrete oven that somehow dripped.

Thirty-three-year-old Jack Mathews was wrapping up a phone conversation with Rita Williams, one of his favorite neighborhood personas in this urban ghetto turned tepid sweat-house. Phone to his ear, he stood in the doorway of his run-down tenement and looked out into the darkness. Several people sat out on porches, trying to catch the ghost of a breeze that might waft through the maze of brick, macadam, and debris. It was nearing midnight, but still they maintained their almost hopeless vigil. Downing their beers and homemade liquors they waited, wishing for that cool breeze, trying not to hear the sirens, fights, or any other evidence that they were in a dying, dead-end ghetto, which it seemed even the air itself wanted to avoid. But still they held on, drinking on their doorsteps and street corners, yearning for some break from the stifling mugginess. Holding on, wishing, was the only thing they could do. Anyone who could afford an air conditioner could afford to live somewhere else.

A rat skittered across the darkened alley on the opposite side of the street from his apartment. His attention drawn, he observed three hoods trying to spot a mark for some quick credits. Most of the people out tonight preferred to be out at night, when the darkness might give them an extra edge by covering up their equally dark activities. The night made them feel more powerful because they thrived inside this tough and hostile world, yet somehow at the same time braver because they dared to come out at all. Jack was feeling neither particularly powerful nor especially brave. His only intention was to visit someone now in need of a friend.

Rita hung up the phone, and Jack smiled. The love and appreciation he felt for her softened his gaze, if just a little. Yes, of course he'd go to see her tonight. It was Friday night after all, the first night of the inner-city weekend. Though everyone still called her Mrs. Williams, her husband had died several years ago. She was alone, and being alone, a lot of little things tended to frighten her. Besides, she spent more than her share of time hearing him out. She was the backbone of his church before anyone else would listen to him at all. *She was pretty good at listening, herself,* Jack thought with a warm smile.

Yes, Jack would visit her tonight, keeping her company as long as she wanted. He enjoyed the evenings they spent together, passing the time in conversation and friendship. He was alone, too. Had been on his own for more than he liked to remember. So, he agreed and got ready to go to her apartment building for the night's visit. He found he regarded her like she was his own grandmother, which she really could have been. Rita Williams was eighty-six years old.

He stepped out of his apartment building and into the dark urban street. Heat, humidity, and sense of threat combined to mute both thought and voice, creating a palpable aggravation that few could do more than scowl at. The collective animal that the urban zone often became shrank back on its haunches and tensed. Jack sensed that animal was fully alert, hunting, ready to spring in fury at the first victim it could ensnare. Violence would meet many tonight before dawn would pry open the vestige of the darkness that freed muggers and street gangs to feed on the city's remains. Countless criminals and hoods waited, hiding just behind the cracks, in the shadows, salivating over the rotting leftovers of civilization the ghetto could still scrape out. They were like half-crazed, malevolent beasts feeding on the dark, the fear, and now the pervasive heat.

The irony was not lost on Jack. The beast they wished to become a part of to feed upon others would eagerly turn on these would-be predators, consuming them as well. In the concrete and plasteel jungle full of carnivores, often enough the predators became the prey. After all, Jack thought, the cracks of the streets didn't care whose blood they gulped, as long as they were full. The morning would reveal most of the victims to the survivors. Others would never be found. Many would only be missed by a few, yet each night also brought good lives to a bitter end; the passing night was indiscriminate in its feeding.

More would be driven to hopelessness and despair by the very dawn that was supposed to bring comfort and hope. Jack grimaced and continued, distancing himself from his own thoughts. He shrugged his shoulders against the darkness, the heat, and the fear. He shrugged against the city itself, trying to forget where he was for the moment and focus on whom he was going to see. He hoped she would be okay when he got there.

He walked on through the litter-covered neighborhood where few outsiders would venture even in daylight. Two men silently approached him from behind and began to walk alongside and slightly behind him, one on each side. Jack tensed, waiting for their next move.

"Yo, Preach, what you doin' out on a night like this? Your little halo startin' ta slippin' or somethin'?" It was Fearless, a member of the Razors. The gang held this section of the city, and over time Jack had rubbed shoulders with almost all of them one way or another.

"No, I'm still on track," Jack replied, letting himself relax. "Mrs. Williams asked if I could stop by, so here I am. How about you? You ready for *your* halo yet?"

"Not yet, Preach," Beast replied. "Scissors got word that you were out and about tonight, and he wanted us to keep escort for you. So here we are, ridin' your shotgun. You know how Scissors is."

Jack knew how the street gang's leader was. He'd met all five feet, eleven inches and 215 pounds of muscle of him a couple days after the minister first moved into the city. Scissors asked the new preacher what he was doing there in his territory, and Jack answered that he was planning on planting a church on the hoodlum's turf. Scissors was furious. Then Jack told him that he needed Jesus, whereupon the young warlord proceeded to hammer on Jack's jaw and take what credits he had. Jack had been praying for Scissors ever since, and except for Mrs. Williams, everyone kept their distance from "that crackpot preacher."

Two years and countless Razor beatings later, Jack sheltered a little kid called "Not-Nuff" from a couple of street hoods and later led the kid to the Lord, saving him from the gang violence that claimed so many young lives of the neighborhood. Not-Nuff turned out to be Scissors's younger brother, and Jack had made a friend of the gang leader for life.

Now the Razors didn't hassle Jack at all, and even listened to him from time to time. Word was out, too, that anyone messing with Jack or his church would be "found." Jack didn't like their threatening, but he had to admit his church was safer due to the strange guardian angels the Lord sent his way. Even the rest of the neighborhood noticed the change in the Razors, and with that came a flicker of hope to the otherwise dead-end slum. Yes, Jack's church was growing, his emergency calls lessening now because of his labor of patience and nearly unimaginable love for the people in the run-down dying remains of what was once an inner city. Over time, "that crackpot preacher" eventually got shortened to the favorite Razor buzz name for him: "Preach."

With Fearless on his left and Beast on his right, the rest of the walk was uneventful. Jack stopped at Mrs. Williams's building and started going up the steps. He stopped halfway.

"You two want to come along?" he asked.

Both gang members smiled but declined. "Not tonight, Preach," Fearless responded with some amusement. "We'll wait out here."

"Okay, your choice. But don't wait too long, guys, okay? Every day we get closer to not having another chance." Jack then finished climbing the steps and went inside as both men nodded.

"So whatcha thinkin'?" Fearless asked after Preach left them, noting a concerned expression on Beast's face. "You worried about Trickz cuttin' out on ya?" he asked, grinning.

"Nah, she'd never leave," the ganger replied. "We're gold, man. She's gold."

"Dude, I know. Like seriously, you two are lookin' good. So, what's eatin' you?"

"Somethin' Preach told me once. I know he means best, but y'know, he's...*different*. That bro' got game goin' we just don't. Drives Trickz nuts.

"Anyway, we're talkin' one day, and Preach tells me that him an' me ain't so different, but he's got connection to God somehow. Says I could, too."

Fearless laughed out loud. "Beast! You *really* think this God stuff is for real? Let me ask you somethin'. Look around you. If there is a God, he has *surely* frakked us over this time. Do you see anything in this dump of a hole that gives any slightest clue that there's a God? Bro, think 'bout it an' answer me." Fearless jeered. "C'mon, just *one* thing. I'm serious."

"I see Trickz," Beast admitted, almost shyly.

"Ha! Oh man, you are so lost! Because of some wh—" Fearless stopped, catching the glower crossing his friend's face. There were reasons the guy was called Beast, and Fearless was exactly one half of one syllable away from being reminded just what exactly those reasons were.

"Sorry, Beast. Trickz was a good call. Ya got me," Fearless quickly offered. He glanced away, into the night sky, the pattern of the urban skyline tattered as a pair of old sneakers. "I sure as hell don't see no god, not here."

7

"Preach does," Beast threw out, then thought for a second. "Hey, Fearless?"

"Yeah, Bro?" Fearless asked, obviously uncomfortable with how the conversation turned.

"Think about it for a second. If we really could see God…I mean, with the way we live and all the drek that we're into…"

"Yeah? What's up, Bro?" Fearless asked again, wondering where his friend was going with all this.

"Do you really think we would *want* to?"

The unanswered question hung in the air, like the smell of sweat and garbage decaying on a hot July night.

… …

Inside, Mrs. Williams greeted Jack.

"I'm sorry I called so late. I just felt this gnawing feeling that something was going wrong, and I felt so lonely that I wanted you to pray for me, but you certainly didn't need to come out on a night like this!"

"That's okay, Mrs. Williams," Jack assured her. "After all, the Bible does say, 'For we know that all things work together for good to them that love God…,' and maybe God is working right now," he said, motioning towards Fearless and Beast.

"Yes," Mrs. Williams agreed, "that very well could be."

"Now," Jack stated, "let's pray."

2

CAMP-OUT INBOUND

"GOD, GET US *out* of here!"

Another blast sounded, this one close by, augmented by the staccato chopping sound of M-16A2's firing on full automatic.

"How could I have been so *stupid*?!" screamed Corey, grabbing his shotgun and pumping several rounds into the area where he thought the firing was coming from.

"Sue! Get to the car! Hurry!"

Sue was sobbing openly now. "It's them again, isn't it?" she cried.

"Yeah, but we don't have time for that now. Move!"

She may have tried to add something more, but the cracks of bullets hitting nearby trees drowned out whatever it was she had been trying to say. Corey tried to return fire, but he was hopelessly outgunned. The motorcycle gang was far better armed, and they had caught him sleeping. *How could I have been so stupid?* he thought again. Their only hope was to get to the car.

Suddenly, the firing stopped; an eerie, dreamlike quality settled over the roadside woods where they camped. A public-address system screeched, then Corey heard the <PUFF PUFF> of someone blowing into a microphone—and Corey knew who that someone was.

"How could I have been so stupid?" Corey almost audibly cursed to himself again.

"Hellooo, out there!" an amplified voice amusedly called. "It's us again. And how are *you* tonight? I know you're still alive, 'cause you fired back, but we'll soon fix that…"

The voice went on, but Corey was trying hard to pay more attention to hear the sounds of any bikers trying to creep up on him through the brush under the cover of the bullhorn. It wouldn't do to get himself killed so pointlessly right now. Susan needed him, and he was sure that thought alone would see him through Hell and back again.

"…You lis'nin', son? Iron Mike himself comes all the way to the old border, and you're not even goin' to answer to what I have to say?

"Okay, look. I'm sorry about your Old Man and all, okay? We're all sorry, ain't we, Jackals?"

Various cheers and whistles assured Corey that not a single one of them was. "Well, maybe not *all* of us, but what do you *want*? Your father was a pain in the neck, you know that? We could have just rode into town peaceably and helped ourselves to what we needed in that cesspool of a town of yours, but *your* old man had to play 'Cops and Robbers' and get the locals all stirred up. So, we lynched him, is all. After all, since he was so hot to play the Cops, *somebody* had to be the Robbers!"

Corey translated to himself what Iron Mike was telling him. The Steel Jackals would have rolled into and looted the town, kidnapped the women, and literally tortured them to death without any resistance. His father, Thomas Martin, wouldn't let that happen.

Since the government had failed back in '28, Thomas Martin had headed the local militia, and his bike-breaking tactics were very effective. Thomas taught his son Corey everything he knew, until one night the gang managed to catch the town off guard. Waynesville, Pennsylvania died that night, and Thomas Martin was forced to face the wrath of Iron Mike and the Steel Jackals. Their house was burned down, and his whole family was literally butchered that night. Only Corey had managed to escape, surviving by hiding in a junk lot until they had left. They stayed for a week, killing and maiming for sport, then left for some other nearby town.

Corey returned to his former house and retched when he saw the remains. The bike gang took a special interest in the leader of the town's militia force. Corey spent the remainder of that week burying the remains of his family. At the end of that week, he checked his dad's car.

The car had been his father's pride and joy, but it was reduced to a wreck from the gang's violence and the burning of the house. Corey spent the next month working on the car, each day filled with memories of him and his dad working on it together. Grimly the weeks passed, and after Corey had at last closed the hood, he drove off out of Waynesville to make his father proud.

"Sorry, Dad. I didn't mean to be so stu—"

Just then Corey heard the padding sound of a footstep in the leaves just ahead to the right. He threw a rock into the area screaming, "Sue! Frag out!"

A large figure dove to clear the blast of the "grenade," but instead he met the blast of Corey's shotgun. The biker rose high into the air after the first shock of the pellets hit him. Corey fired a second time at the now aerial target, and the biker never moved again. Corey rolled right to avoid a burst of automatic gunfire.

"*ALL RIGHT, THAT'S IT!!*" The voice on the PA was now hysterically screaming. "You think you've had your fun and games? *No more* of my men will die by a member of your family!! You're *dead*, man, and after we get done with you, your little girlfriend Susie's gonna be mine, and there won't be any more little heroes runnin' around to screw things up! You got that? I just thought I'd leave you a little somethin' ta think about while you're bleeding to death!"

Corey froze at the mention of Susan. What was taking her so long? *Did she make it to the car?*

"CARVE 'IM UP!!" roared Iron Mike over his PA, and a murderous volley of machine gun fire opened, threatening to shatter his eardrums as the guns blasted away. Corey cringed and lay flat behind a tree, but then he noticed most of the noise was coming from a pair of .30 caliber machine guns behind him. The dull whump of a recoilless rifle sounded, the shell blasting the area where the PA system had been sounding from. He then heard a door open behind him and a female voice yelling, "Hurry up, Corey, and get in!" His 6'2" muscular frame lumbered into the passenger seat, and the door closed just as about a hundred rifle and shotgun shells started rattling against the armored body and windshield of the vehicle.

Sue had made it to the car.

3

SABRETOOTH

"We're not out of here yet," Sue stated. Corey knew that without her having to tell him, but he still felt glad that at least they had a chance.

The car was a midnight black Sabretooth, a descendant of the previous century's muscle cars, modified by Corey and his dad. The engine was a reworked Haze 437, superconductor and racing suspension added. The car was fully armored, had puncture resistant tires to resist bullets and fragments, and his father went to the expense of hooking up a vehicle PA system for directing dismounted town defense forces. Corey now used the system mainly just to broadcast his favorite music during a firefight to keep his attitude sharp. He also thought it might confuse the enemy's communications—anything for an edge.

The Sabretooth was designed a few years after the government collapsed for a special group of people called Wheelmen. After the Iranian missile strikes, most areas had little to no police protection of any sort. Gangs and rioting broke out in most cities and towns large enough to have crowds. Large corporations, already having their own static armed security forces, were sometimes able to survive the riots, but they didn't really care about the devastation unless it directly affected them. If it ever did, they would bear their "corporate assets" to bring swift justice upon whomever offended them. Corporate wars took on a new meaning that only two generations ago, few could have ever imagined. The smaller companies and local governments usually succumbed to the violence. Society itself had been dying.

Most of the outlaws took to motorcycles as fast-moving, light, and easily hidden vehicles. Townspeople then started arming themselves to protect against the new bike gangs, and then the gangs started arming and armoring their bikes. Since nobody else was either willing or able to help the common citizen fight against the outlaws, people started arming their own vehicles to combat that threat.

With the miniaturization of electronic control devices, development of high-performance electric engines, and arms building technology, the desire for more heavily armed and armored vehicles increased. This brought certain corporations, which had already begun arming their own executive vehicles for their protection, and some auto design specialists together to develop factory-produced vehicles for the commercial market. Eventually they designed and equipped cars, buses, tractor trailers, boats, and even helicopters (for those who could afford them) with firepower almost equivalent to 20th century tanks, with tractor trailers sometimes even surpassing them.

Corey's Sabretooth's punch consisted of twin .30 caliber machine guns and a vehicular grenade launcher that fired front, with the recoilless rifle mounted on a top turret. His dad mounted various anti-personnel mines on the sides of the vehicle, and a very special weapon to the rear. It was expensive, but Corey's dad was one of the best Wheelmen in western Pennsylvania, and he knew when to spend for quality. Nicknamed "The Dragon's Droppings," the principle it operated on was simple. The device held a rack of ten metallic canisters suspended in sealed gelatinous sacs to avoid jostling. When triggered, the device would simply break the seal and drop a canister. The kick was that the gel would ignite when exposed to air, melting the canister and half dumping, half spraying the compressed phosphorous and napalm contents into the still

14

burning gel. The canisters would typically melt through in three to five seconds; the resultant explosion and fireball most described as nothing less than horrifying.

Susan saw a large flash off to her front left and braced herself. A shell punched the car hard and pushed it right. She heard Corey grunt, and he almost landed in her seat after flopping against the turret rail overhead.

"You okay?" she asked. He had really been thrown against the vehicle hard.

"Just get us *out* of here!" he replied with a grimace.

She noticed him feeling his right elbow, trying to strap on his harness. Then he checked his various weapon gauges as he took control of them from his gunner's seat.

Susan emitted a "Roger," then noted several bikers on foot approaching the vehicle. At least one carried another LAW rocket. Without waiting, she threw the Sabretooth into reverse, hoping not to hit a tree on her flight back to the road. As the car started to speed backwards, she almost reflexively hit the thumb switch on the steering column that triggered the rear weapon.

The next four seconds slowed to an eternity. The car continued dragging itself backward, almost ignoring the summons for speed that Susan, putting all her weight on the accelerator pedal, urged upon it. They ran over a little hill with its front left tire, then settled back to the ground. Susan saw a couple of Jackals float to the ground in slow motion—the one with the rocket launcher lowered himself gently to one knee, and two or three dirt bikes entered her view from the front. Lights of tracer streams flashed from their fronts, and chips of the car's front armor spun slowly past the windshield over the roof of the car. She then somewhat offhandedly observed that the "little hill" was a chunk of the front left fender armor, which had been blasted completely off by the rocket that hit when Corey had first gotten into the car.

She fired a twin burst of her own tracers that, in her heightened state, seemed to casually ribbon out to the dirt bikes. Her last sight was a small metal cylinder that appeared from under the front end of the Sabretooth as the car slowly inched its way backwards to the road. Knowing what was coming next, she squeezed her eyes tightly shut, braced herself, and pushed even harder on the accelerator pedal.

She saw the bright lights flash all around her despite her tightly closed eyes. A muffled explosion filled the air, and in half the time it took a heart to beat the temperature inside the car jumped 142.38° Fahrenheit. Corey screamed, but not as loud as the dismounted bikers. The white phosphorous cloud of flame very visibly hurt one of them, transforming him in that single moment from a human being (if she could really consider any of them human) to little more than an animated marionette of living flame. Soon both human and flame would die out.

"Sue, why didn't you warn me?" Corey demanded, snapping her back into real time.

"There was no time," she answered, still trying to make it to the road in reverse. She knew that Corey's night vision was completely gone, as was (she hoped) the Jackals'. Moreover, the intense heat and light of the flame cloud was sure to defeat any infrared or night vision equipment the bikers may have trained on them. She completely dismissed anyone actually caught *inside* the cloud. Unless they were wearing fireproof body armor and insulated underwear? Well, Puppet Man had just gone out.

She finally ran up the embankment and bounced onto the roadway, firing a burst from a single machine gun into the area where the confrontation had just taken place, hoping to scatter anyone left. Not waiting to stop, she slammed the car forward and away from the bikes that were sure to follow shortly.

"Well, my knight in black cryoplast armor," Susan asked, "where to now?"

"East, then South. We gotta get away from Pennsylvania, go someplace where we've got some friends left," he said, his ears still ringing from the explosions and gunfire. "But as soon as we can, the car needs to be fixed, fueled, and restocked with ammo."

"What about after that?" Susan asked.

"Well," Corey responded, "by that time the heat from the Jackals should be off of you. If you want, I could leave you at the next town. I'll keep heading south." He drew in a breath, then risked it. "You're welcome to come along further, if you want—but you don't have to," he blurted at the end.

"Well, outside of having some distant relatives in Asheville, North Carolina, I don't have anywhere to go anymore. Besides, do you honestly think, after all we've been through, that you can just drop me off at the next recharge station?" She paused, smiled, then asked more softly, "How's your arm?"

"It's okay," Corey answered. "Anyway, serves me right for being so off guard back there. I'm really sorry, Sue. I could have gotten you…"

"Hey, you have nothing to be sorry about," she softly told him. "You had a long day, you've been driving ever since six this morning on very little sleep, always on guard, staying alert—it's okay. I wouldn't have ever made it this far if you hadn't rescued me back…home." She felt her eyes beginning to tear. "Besides," she said, trying to snap herself out of the emotional black hole she had just opened, "you drew cover for me so I could get to the car. Thank you." She peered at him so intensely he felt the sincerity of the words.

"You're welcome," he returned so wholeheartedly she felt the genuineness of it resonate through her.

4

PRIVATE EYE/PUBLIC EYE

THE PHONE WAS on its fourth ring when Melissana hit the answer button. Josanne was grateful that she could share her news with her friend live, if not in person, without having to dump it on her recorder. It was rare to find Melissana on the first try, either at home or in the office. If she wasn't at either one of those places, it may have been days before Josanne could reach her friend again. An excited Josanne noted the cheerful smile on Melissana's face as she recognized her friend's digital image.

"Hi, Josie! What brings you to call? You'd better tell me quick before you explode. With all your bouncing around, I can barely keep you on the screen."

"I got the job!"

"Really? That's *great*! When do you start?"

"The day after tomorrow! Can you believe it? Just out of college three months, and already I'm starting out in photo layout at the Roanoke Review!"

"Wait a minute. Photo layout? I thought you were majoring in journalism."

"Well, Mr. Lisben told me I didn't have enough experience to qualify as a reporter, but he noticed from my resume that I was a camera buff, so he asked me if I could show him some of my shots because they needed a layout assistant. So, I showed him my photos and some of my vids, and he said I could have the job! According

19

to him, this will give me the perfect opportunity to rub shoulders with the reporters in a way that won't be competing against them, so I should be able to learn a lot more from the experienced ones. Usually, they're pretty closed-mouthed about their trade secrets and sources. Anyway, he also said the experience will show me more about how an article is assembled after the reporter has submitted it. I can watch the 'big picture' unfold as I do a piece, and be better able to adapt my own articles to the newspaper formats when I am reporting. Do you realize how much that can help speed up my piece publication?"

"Trigget," Melissana interrupted, referring to Josanne by the reporter's favored street handle, "are you sure this guy isn't just selling you a line with a song-and-dance routine thrown in for free?"

"Well, that might be," Josanne considered, "but I really don't think so. Even if it is, the department is really intriguing enough on its own. Besides, Mel, it is a start."

"Well, all right, Josie, but you just watch this Mr. What's-His-Name."

"Melissana! This isn't some case you're on, so you can tone down some of your sneaking-suspicion hunches! For crying out loud, I got the job!"

Josanne was angry now, but she caught herself yelling at the best friend she had in Roanoke, and probably anywhere else. Shocked out of her uproar, she suddenly felt a flat pang of guilt.

What her friend had told her could be right. One of two children (and the only daughter) of Harris Sinclair, president of SyncTech Incorporated, she grew up in the rather isolated estate her father was wealthy enough to afford (and need). *Extensive* self-defense training was *expensive* self-defense training, and the wealth of Harris Sinclair was applied liberally to that end. Josanne and her brother James had some of the best hand-to-hand and firearms tutors available. In fact, Josanne was one of the few non-military personnel who could say she had actually trained with a real laser pistol. Even for 2048, the weapons were relatively rare.

The estate insulated the young Sinclair's from the effects of the food riots, and for that matter, most of life in general. This worked well for her security and happiness, but the downside was that she was a bit naive at times. Perhaps that was why the hustle-and-bustle, down-and-dirty industry of journalistic media attracted her so much; she could bask in the feverish involvement of investigative reporting that was teeming with human character and drama.

She didn't consider herself very pretty—not enough to attract Mr. Lisben's attention. With her medium-length sandy hair, light green eyes, slim figure, and ready smile, though, she admitted to herself she usually got noticed entering a room. In fact, that was how she and Melissana had met. New in town, she asked some jerks for directions. They started hitting on her, and then it progressed enough to get really scary. Street-worn Melissana showed up from out of nowhere and sucker-punched one of them. It wasn't enough to end any fight, but it sure started one! Josanne's training kicked in, and the two girls ended up besting the four guys they were up against. Out of thankfulness and to celebrate their victory, Josanne treated Melissana to lunch, which eventually developed into a deep and long-lasting friendship. All these thoughts passed through her mind in one of those moments known as awkward silences. In the end, she still just felt guilty.

"Sorry, Mel." She then added, "But if he is trying something, I hope he gets to it soon; he's actually pretty cute." With a smile that told Melissana she was sincere with both the apology and the boss's flattery, she asked, "Will you forgive me?"

Melissana smiled. "For the yelling or for your drooling over some guy you just met a couple days ago who's probably gonna sexually harass you until the day one of you dies?" she joked back.

All was forgiven, so Josanne just flashed another quick smile.

"Why, the drooling, of course."

Both girls burst into laughter.

5

HIGHWAY DUEL

THE BURST OF the near miss caused the car to skew sideways and launch into a counterclockwise spin. Corey silently swore and attempted to regain control of the 3,500-pound conglomeration of metal, plastic, circuits, and rubber between him and the ribbon of cracked macadam whirling by, sideways now, at fifty miles per hour.

"Incoming!" he yelled to Susan. If he had the time, he would have laughed at himself for so dramatically and still so uselessly announcing the obvious. The steady slamming of machine gun fire walking the length of his vehicle's driver's side added to his present need for concentration. Corey didn't laugh.

Susan Blakeslee was moving instantly. Snapping on the helmet of her MetaRace body armor, she slid out and up the vehicle's weapon's controls, locking them into place and activating the car's various weapon systems. By the time they had spun a 3/4 circle, Sue had transformed herself from a mere passenger to his somewhat formidable vehicle gunner.

"Three bikes, behind us again!" Corey announced, knowing Sue would interpret "behind us" to mean that the bikers had fired the initial shot from behind them. At the exact time he called their positions, they had been directly in front of them, sickeningly rushing by sideways in his counterclockwise spin. They were to his right when he finally got the car stopped. Flashes of light from two of the approaching bikes announced more volleys of machine gun fire were inbound.

He heard the muffled <whufft> of his own turret-mounted weapon firing and watched as the shell Susan had fired landed just behind the moving bikes. Two of the bikers quivered but somehow managed to stay up. The leftmost was picked up from behind by the blast and thrown airborne to the side, bouncing once off its front tire before smashing into a roadside tree. "Got 'im!" Susan yelled into her helmet's microphone.

Corey responded by punching his accelerator hard, the 2048 equivalent of a 13th century cavalryman giving his steed a forceful spurred kick to make his animal give its all. The car did just that, with all ferocity spinning its four independently powered wheels forward, mirroring the fervor of a horse going into a charge at full gallop. Another near miss from the bike's recoilless rifle sent shrapnel into the car's now almost unarmored driver's side, but the car kept moving. Corey could almost hear the car's whinny of approval. He felt its instantaneous response to his call, evoking a bond that further united him with those ancient riders: the feeling of love and pride for his mount....

...   ...

Griff's head was still slightly spinning from the blast of the car's turret gun, causing him to fire a quarter-second too late for the direct hit. This car was supposed to be an easy take, all by itself on this isolated stretch of two-lane highway. He thought for sure the first shot was going to drop the car, but the driver maintained control and quickly brought the car to a spinning stop. Okay, if the driver wasn't that good, Iron Mike would've had him by now.

His second mistake was not expecting the car's gunner to be able to play the turret that fast, what with her being a girl and all. If she had been any more accurate, she could have knocked out all three Steel Jackals. As it was, only Itch went down. Well, they would pay for that, too.

His bike also mounted a recoilless rifle. That was partly why Iron Mike had sent him as leader of the three-bike raid to catch up to and destroy them. Well, outright destroyed wasn't quite right. Ol' Mike, he wanted the girl as a permanent souvenir. If possible, he wanted the guy alive, too, so the guy would know and watch the certainty of it. Griff's reward would be that he could keep the car's unexpended rounds, whatever else he could fit onto his bike, plus seconds on the girl. The beat-up car had seen better days, and Griff didn't see the need for the three veteran bikers to ask for help to pick off this harmless pile of slag that was once a vehicle. That was Griff's first mistake.

Griff and Harbo were now weaving around the vehicle. Harbo was keeping the gunner busy trying to sight on him long enough to fire. This freed Griff from having to worry about the turreted weapon. His job now was to try to stay out of the path of the front machine guns long enough to fire his own recoilless rifle into the damaged side of the black Sabretooth. Technically he could fire one of the explosive rounds per second, but a full motorcycle rack only held seven of the shells, and Griff's rack wasn't full when he started the chase. Also, the reality of actually making a good shot moving at forty miles per hour required at least a second or two of aiming when shooting at another moving vehicle, all the while trying not to get shot yourself. In a highway chase, one shot per second was possible; vehicular infighting with the risk of hitting a brother Jackal on a second bike was different.

Griff could only helplessly watch as the next scene unfolded before him. In what had to have been a well-coordinated plan, the Sabretooth's recoilless rifle fired into the path of Harbo's machine gun-toting bike. At first it appeared he had avoided the blast by cutting right, but the maneuver brought him right into the fatal twin stream of machine gun rounds. The bike's heavy front and rear armor may have withstood the car's .30 caliber rounds, but at the nearly perpendicular angle that armor was useless. The first few rounds of the car's powerful machine guns tore Harbo's flak vest and cryoplast leg armor to shreds. With the rounds that followed, Harbo had completely vanished in a burst of crimson spray.

Three armed and armored motorcycles against one beat-up car was a good bet for the bikers. One biker against a car that may have been in better shape than it appeared and crewed by a highly organized driver and gunner was suicide. Griff was no longer up to taking chances.

True, the bikers had definitely damaged the car in the dogfight. The armor on the driver's side was hanging, almost dragging. The puncture-resistant tires had taken a terrific hammering. The tracks left where the machine gun rounds had hit laced the entire vehicle. Finally, Griff noticed that the turret in the Sabretooth was becoming sluggish in its turning, and this gave Griff his plan to fight his way out of this nightmare he himself had so willingly begun.

Griff fired one of his last rounds into the path of the now approaching Sabretooth. He hoped to force the driver to swerve so he could avoid the deadly front guns. Grinning at his success, he then swerved right and unholstered his Uzi, preparing himself for a final drive-by pass at the driver of the car. The car's turret pointed front and could not track him fast enough now that it was damaged. Besides, if the gunner's shot hit too close to the vehicle's now nearly armorless side, the explosion would take out the car's own driver.

If he took out the driver, the passenger would pay dearly for the loss of his "brothers." If not, he would distance himself from the vehicle as fast as possible, avoiding the machine guns that had caused so many of his own to fall. Either way, he reasoned to himself, he was out of there.

He gunned the bike's electric motor and raced towards the Sabretooth, executing his plan. It was Griff's last mistake.

As the vehicles closed to within thirty-five yards of each other, the car's driver gunned his engine and jerked his wheel hard to the right. Griff panicked as the resulting tailspin slid the driver around straight into the path of the oncoming bike. The helmeted driver, laughing to be sure, was looking straight at Griff. Caught, the biker had no way of stopping himself, and he could only stare helplessly on. The driver must have toggled a switch, detonating one of the anti-personnel mines mounted on the side of the car. For a moment, even Griff had to admire the driver for pulling a stunt like that with so little vehicular armor on that side of the car. Then the comet of shotgun pellets and sprocket washers from the mine exploded at such a short range it devastated his bike's front armor.

The sudden rush of agonizing pain in Griff's now shredded left arm and bleeding legs screamed to him that his bike's armor was penetrated; he suddenly realized he was going to die. In the remaining instant of time before colliding at 40 mph with the jagged edges of the car itself, Griff noticed the militia patch on the Sabretooth driver's body armor. His very last thought was that maybe if they hadn't been as hard on the town that kid was from, he would still have another day to live. He never had time to fire his Uzi.

······ ······

Corey brought the car to a stop and locked away the vehicular weapons. Susan soon climbed out, removed her helmet, and stood by him, toting her shotgun and scanning for any more bikes. She only shook a little.

"Is it over?" she asked.

"Yeah, it's over," he responded weakly, causing her to check to make sure he was okay. When she saw the punctures in the armor and the effects of the collision on the side of the car, she turned white.

"Geez, what hap—*are you all right*?" She started to run around the car to get the medkit, panicked that Corey had been hit.

"Susan, it's okay. The blood's not mine, mostly."

"So then, whose is it?" she started to ask, but upon observing the bike lying almost underneath the driver's side of the car, she had seen all she needed for the answer.

Corey sighed. "Well, come on. We've got some fixin' to do. I'll patch up the armor as good as I can until we can get to a shop. Why don't you see what you can find for us that we can use, or at least salvage? We're gonna need some credits bad."

"Well, for starters, maybe we can put *this* to good use," Susan replied, prying an Uzi from the dead biker's hand. "I wonder what else you left here for us." With that, Susan Blakeslee began scavenging the battlefield with a strangely absent air similar to that of a debutante's shopping excursion at a mall.

Corey watched her start towards the machine gun bike, then with a shrug he reached down to the crushed and bloodied bike he'd slammed down only a few minutes ago. *So what?* he thought to himself. They were the ones who'd attacked him, and after this firefight they would need something to salvage to pay for repairs and parts. Confiscating the various salvageable parts from the bike, he willed his mind onto the need to glean a few recoilless rifle rounds and a couple hundred credits' worth of parts.

Suddenly, he shouted and jumped as a vision of the heavily bearded face of the biker again came lunging at him from the motorcycle, Corey's own face too horrified to turn. Sue stopped and turned to him, checking to see if he was okay. After watching him for a moment, she slowly turned back to her task.

She had been pretending she was in a dream, but she couldn't maintain that illusion anymore. Reality pushed itself onto her, ripping her illusions aside, tearing hope from her, just as Iron Mike tried to. Iron Mike had failed, because of Corey, but reality didn't fail. Even Corey and that car of his couldn't fight reality. She went down the road into the woods, hopefully appearing as though she were looking for the third bike. She was able to get ten feet into the wood line before she dropped to her knees. She started crying softly to herself at first, but the reality of the trauma of the last few weeks kept pushing at her, pulling her for more. Soon her open crying was echoing the waves of pain and grief rising up and washing over her again and again.

Corey heard Susan's crying, but he decided he should just let her get out as much as she could. He didn't mean to lie to her, but it was far from over. Her recurrent nightmares, and his own flashbacks of that fear-struck face coming towards him, would be there for a long time to come.

6

THE URCHIN QUEEN

AFTER WHAT SEEMED like a long time, Melissana picked up the phone on the fourth ring, hoping to give any potential client the impression that she was busy. In fact, she was completely caseless, and her office rent would soon be due.

"Focus Investigations," she declared when she got the phone. The woman on the other end was female and civil, yet tired and flat—an almost Shakespearean example of hopelessness.

"May I speak to Ms. Trellan, please?"

"Speaking," Melissana answered. It was not unusual for someone calling to think they would reach a secretary, but Melissana couldn't afford one yet. "What can I do for you?"

"If you can, would you please meet me at the Golden Chalice Tuesday at 12:30 for lunch? I know it's short notice, but…"

Whoa! Melissana did not completely fail to catch the "If you can," implying this woman must have really needed her, and the place mentioned was one of the most exclusive restaurants in the city. They even served real food! Melissana almost forgot to respond. When she did remember, she hoped the delay would communicate to her caller that she was checking a busy calendar.

"Yes, I believe I can make it," she said, trying to sound important, and the details of the meet were finalized. Melissana hung up the phone, wondering why someone who could afford to eat at the Golden Chalice would call a fledgling private investigator in the lower end of town rather than one of the hotshot expensive firms. Well, she had some work to do, and Melissana mentally hired herself to find out who this mystery caller was.

In a way, it was most natural that she became a detective for hire. She grew up in the ghetto sections of Roanoke after running away from a broken home (and a father who liked to do the breaking). Life was never easy for a seventh-grade girl of any time period, and it didn't take Melissana long to learn everything she'd ever need to know about betrayal and rejection on the streets. Burned at almost every turn in life, in those first couple months in the alleys she learned street survival. After that, she learned street *biz*. In a very real way, she had as much of an education as her wellborn journalist friend. She just got hers from a different school.

Part of what Roanoke's school of the streets taught her was that the more you knew about people, places, times, and happenings, the more likely you were to survive. Two different people saying the exact same words to describe an event could have two exactly opposite meanings. Eventually, she got really good at finding out— *things*. Over time, people started asking her to help them find *things* out. Of course, there was a price. Sometimes it was money, but in those earlier days very often for other bits of information, some return service, or some goods that were more easily exchangeable, like the guy who coached her for three months on how to use a computer to find even more *things* out. She was amazed at how much information she could obtain just by asking the right questions and building proper relationships between what seemed to be unrelated facts. Melissana wasn't very good at building human relationships, but she certainly knew how to ask the right questions. She became a small-time but competent amateur hacker by the handle of Queen Vixenn, and although she was getting quite capable at dancing the 'net, her conscience bugged her too much to resort to a career of thievery. As time progressed, she decided to utilize her talents as both a survivor and a personal data collector to open what was to become a fledgling one-woman private investigation company.

In true slewfoot form, Melissana started collecting even before hanging up the vidphone. The caller was slim, average height, well-mannered, and apparently wealthy. Her hair was probably fake, and the makeup overdone—on purpose, Melissana thought. The lady obviously (to Melissana) wanted her privacy; Melissana just wondered how much. After a moment of consideration, she decided to find out, and Melissana Trellan, private investigator, was on the case.

Private eyes normally worked on the shadowy side of the law. Sometimes there was just no other way. Melissana wasn't the kind of person to flagrantly spurn the law for the most part, but she needed ways to find out what was really going on—and the best way for her to do that, she found, was for Queen Vixenn to take a walk in the data.

Her first act was to place her own call through her computer's com-link and access Roa-Comm's billing services. Next, she entered the data code for Roa-Comm's collection agency and retrieved the phone company's billing records. Skipping through to the last couple minutes of today's date, she scanned the records for the phone that had just accessed her vidphone. She then accessed the billing code for that phone and came up with a pay vidphone. Further checking showed the address of the pay phone to be in an uptown shopping district, where nobody would notice the five foot seven, thirty-five-plus, petite but slightly tired-looking blonde calling her. Queen Vixenn downloaded the information, deleted her own calls into Roa-Comm, and as an afterthought deleted the records of the original call to her. If the lady wanted privacy that badly, she would have it.

For a moment, the Vixenn scolded herself. A *pay* phone, she thought. She should have known that a woman who had gone through so much to disguise herself would use a pay phone. Suddenly Melissana had an idea and brought the data from Roa-Comm back to her screen. "YES!" she exclaimed, almost jumping out of her chair. Melissana got up from her office desk and walked around the room, still exulting in her discovery. Again, she should have thought of it before, but usually people came into her office or called her less mysteriously. She took another stroll around, then poured herself a cup of coffee. Finally, she settled herself back into her silicon-circuited nest.

"Not bad, Shadow Lady," she said, "but you left a little trail, you did, when you didn't use a credit chip for the phone. You paid with a card. Now let's see who you are." Melissana loved shadows. You could hide in them, and sometimes they made things seem different from what they really were. She enjoyed the thrill of discovery, and shadows provided a place for her to explore. Even more, they allowed her a place to *operate*.

Vixenn accessed Roa-Comm again, this time searching for the account numbers of Roa-Comm credit cards. When she finally got in, she entered the number the woman used when she called Melissana earlier. She had to wait about 38 microseconds. It was not enough time for her to prepare herself for what she would see.

Melissana stared down at her computer screen, lost in thought. She was completely stunned. After a time, she let out a low whistle. The mystery caller was Elaine Martinez. Elaine Martinez, as in the wife of *Justin* Martinez—and Justin Martinez was the Deputy Director of Research and Development at FoodTech ICC.

The revelation almost caused her to fall onto the floor. She sat still; it wasn't often the street-raised private investigator was caught off guard. Somewhere in the back of her mind she was grateful for her recent lack of business. The office silence waited, giving her a chance to process the thoughts that her mind, now in overdrive, was sending her.

The Grain Blight hit in 2029. As a result, some 70%+ of the grain, first in the United States, then all over the world, had just withered and died from the inside out. Though the exact cause was still unknown, the results were all too familiar. Livestock that used to feed on the grasses died out, then food reserves dwindled.

Mass starvations, food riots, and civil wars followed, as people lost confidence in their governments' abilities to keep them fed.

Between the missile strikes, the blight, and the oil crises it was a miracle that any civilization survived at all. Melissana shuddered as she realized that, as bad as it was, it could have been much worse. The corporations already experimenting with high performance electric vehicles dramatically alleviated the oil crises. FoodTech, International Corporate Conglomerate (just plain FoodTech then) was one of about a score of companies that saved the human race from extinction.

Discovering a method to synthesize and process foodstuffs from algae, FoodTech and those other corporations began to market a whole new food type. Artificially colored, shaped, and flavored, it became the staple of almost every diet in the world, and people had to eat. Of course, there were a few dissidents who complained. There was, for almost a year, an upsurge of a nuclear-fearing cult dedicated to a late 20th century actor, constantly plugging the ancient movies about corporations turning people into foodstuffs. After a time, however, they either starved themselves out or converted to the inevitable. After all, the algae substitute would in no single area of comparison match up to any of the natural foods it was created to replace except one. It was available.

Most of these companies grew dramatically into larger corporations better able to manage worldwide algae-based food relief. By the end of the initial growth spurt, FoodTech (now FoodTech ICC) was near the top of the food chain. Its subsidiaries ranged from manufacturers of algae farm equipment to the orbital facilities necessary to maintain its somewhat successful space borne hydroponics research station. FoodTech acquired the station and its support vehicles from the old NASA program of the all but defunct old U.S.A. national government. After all, the government had much more important matters to attend to, and it made the then President look *very* good. Donating the theoretically nice but by then completely useless Space Agency to a food corporation solving the world starvation problem seemed sensible. It freed up that federal budget money formerly poured into the program. It also brought 18.5 billion *new* dollars (credits, after the dollar collapsed) into the government coffers to help its citizens in a very real way: the additional funds provided military and law enforcement assistance in a country that was unraveling faster than it was originally created.

Though she was not familiar with the FoodTech corporate structure, Deputy Director of R&D for a company founded on research had to be near the top. Melissana realized that if it wasn't for this woman's husband, the food—the very *real* food—they would be eating would probably not even exist. She suddenly had a new appreciation for the meal, and she pledged herself to approach this whole experience more carefully. Melissana's last realization from this flurry of thought was that Elaine would probably not have to pay a single credit for the showy luncheon. She picked up her coffee, wondering what to say, and again wondering why Elaine had called her, and why the elaborate show. She could hardly wait for the day of the meeting.

7

RESPITE

"THANK YOU FOR waiting," the synthesized voice intoned. "Welcome to the Fortress Town of Hagerstown, Maryland. Please ensure you obey all traffic and weapons regulations. We wish you a pleasant visit."

The recorded voice stated almost verbatim what was said at the main gate of every fortress town. On approach you were told to stop, then came the questions of: 1) Have you engaged in vehicular combat activity within so far of this city, and 2) Are you carrying any wounded? If you answered yes to either you would be escorted to either a local militia leader or local hospital after a quick ID scan. If not, then a computer voice (usually female-sounding) gave you a rundown of the various traffic and weapons laws of the city, which must be obeyed pending swift and severe retribution by whatever means of enforcing the law the local population had.

Following the legal briefing, the visitors were required to offer handprints, retina scans, voice pattern samples, or combinations thereof into electronic devices that would record both the visit and the voluntary compliance to local law. They would then have the option of purchasing a map of the town for a few credits, and the fortress gates would open to admit them.

The walls of the city varied from a few inches of steeloy metal to three car lengths or so of concrete/steeloy mix. Sometimes the walls inside the gates were solid, but often they were hollow to garage the town's ready reaction units, forcing any hostile vehicles to maneuver through a gauntlet of anti-vehicular weaponry fired from within hardened firing points.

Driving into Hagerstown was like driving into most of the other fortress towns Corey had been in before, but he was glad to be here regardless, especially with Susan safe. They were both exhausted. After getting a couple algae burgers, they placed a call to the police to report the attacks they had undergone, and where they occurred.

Though the attacks of the motorcycle gang occurred well outside the town's usual sphere of influence, bike gang activity always interested fortress towns, especially if it was as large a gang as the Steel Jackals. The war on crime, long ago merely a political buzz phrase, had come into its own. The desk sergeant dutifully thanked them for their report. Due to the size of the gang involved, and since whole towns were being swallowed up, he invited Corey and Susan to the station for a follow-up interview with the local Hagerstown Defense Militia garrison representative. They agreed to do this the following day. Their adrenaline rapidly ebbing, they almost numbly decided to get a room to stay for a couple days while they tried to get the Sabretooth repaired.

After calling around, the worn duo finally found a place to stay and wearily began to make the drive to the motel. They barely observed the stares they got as the local citizens watched the shot-up and torn car drag itself down the road. The hanging driver's side fender and gaping hole punched through the door exposed the occupants to view and drew a crowd of spectators as the heavily damaged vehicle made its way to the lodge. The townspeople cleared a way for the black Sabretooth as word of the vehicle spread, and the street took on an almost parade-like quality, the car being the main float. The crowd stared as it passed, not out of scorn or condemnation, but out of wonder, empathy, and even pity.

Too exhausted to notice the attention, the couple made their way to the Hagerstown Motor Lodge. Corey drove as though he were in a shadowy tunnel, fixing his mind on the task of keeping his car on the road. Susan focused her mind on mentally commanding herself to stay awake at Corey's side until he, too, could rest. The beat-up Sabretooth, almost sympathetically mirroring the pained expressions of its occupants, obediently crawled on.

... ...

Susan showered first, then prepared for the 2:00 P.M. bedtime her body and mind were demanding as Corey took his turn. The water had been hot and seemed to wash away at least some of the immensity of the bike gang ordeals along with the road grit, July heat, and the continued wear of her armor. Sue felt herself relax, exhaustion beginning to claim her.

So, Iron Mike called Corey a hero? she thought, her eyelids beginning to flutter. She smiled, allowing an inner warmth to soothe her even more. She surveyed the room, seemingly a lifetime away from the ambushes of the last couple of nights. *My very own knight in cryoplast armor, a prince who rescued me from evil incarnate....*

Susan found herself once again at the awards ceremony in her hometown of Elizabethville, PA, where she received her trophy for gymnastics. In her dream she could change focus, allowing her to watch the scene unfold from angles that weren't possible in real life. She once again saw her father, a well-to-do businessman, and the rest of her family cheering for her. Tall for a gymnast and attractive with a medium complexion, golden-blonde hair that flowed to her shoulder blades, and green eyes, she had always had a variety of suitors whom she neither took advantage of nor spurned. She enjoyed her popularity and got along well with almost everyone she met, and they were all there for her special event. Then the dream shifted, and the Steel Jackals showed up.

Practically everyone in her home town was trained on how to defend it. Yet, painfully mirroring real life in her dream turned recurring nightmare, it just wasn't enough. She once again relived most of her friends and family succumbing to the raids of the bikers in only two weeks. Then the pillaging began. She once again re-endured in dreamtime another week of hearing the wailing and cries of pain and anguish before she was caught, again reliving the terror she felt; she had known all too well what capture meant. Sue held out as long as she could but was eventually seized before she had a chance to shoot herself. Because of her looks, the bikers who grabbed her brought her before Iron Mike, the leader of the Steel Jackals. Now the dreamtime slowed unbearably, each second taking an eternity of its own. In the motel room, she fitfully tossed on the bed.

Iron Mike was big. Standing over six feet, four inches and weighing almost 275 pounds, his very appearance was frightening to her, especially since she knew of his sadism and wanton violent streak. He stank. He immediately grabbed her, shaking her violently, and began to scream into her ears for resisting them when they came into town. Then he punched her in the side of the head, knocking her down despite the fact that she was being held by another biker at the time. She fell against his heavily armored reverse trike, earning her another blow that knocked her unconscious for a moment.

When she was brought to, her armor was roughly stripped from her. Though she was still fully clothed, she nearly fainted from panic when she saw how he was ogling her, the leer shared by a number of the surrounding bikers. Grinning, he ordered the company to form a circle around her, both trapping her in and allowing the entire group to see the open shame he was about to inflict upon her. She started crying then, but it only brought mocking sobs from the crowd jeering at her, especially, she found to widen her dismay, the female bikers. Almost all of the gang members focused rapt attention upon her like the animals they claimed themselves to be. This was where the dream-turned-nightmare usually ended, with Susan waking in a tormented panic after reliving the memories once again. But this time she sighed to herself in her sleep, allowing the dream to continue.

Echoing the events of real life, the gang's ravaging focus on her gave Corey his chance to approach as close as he did without being detected. Her dream replayed the rest of the story. After several sniping shots into the ring around her, he fought his way through the circle on foot under the cover of two smoke grenades. The Jackals shouted orders to each other in confusion—evidently, they didn't anticipate a direct attack on so many of them without a vehicle, which they would have heard in time for them to mount their bikes. Corey grabbed Susan just as Mike was going to beat her out of rage at being interrupted. In a blind fury, Corey kicked Mike's extended hand down and swung his M-16A2 rifle butt in an upward arc against the bike gang leader's face. The blow shattered the plastic stock of Corey's weapon but stunned the Goliathan biker long enough for the pair to escape. With Corey there, her dream had stabilized, and Susan's physical body calmed as the history lesson of the dream continued.

Knowing the gang would be listening for the sound of any vehicle, they circled through the town on foot, hiding out the next two nights in the midst of the gang. In this way, Sue re-outfitted herself in some new body armor while Corey retrieved a resupply of personal weapons. Though the hiding out was necessary, it was difficult. Several times, especially at night, Corey had to stifle screams of remembered horror from the victim he was trying to rescue. He was a stranger and could have left her any time. It would have been far safer for him to do so, but that seemed to be beneath him. Susan had never seen any braver act of compassion, made all the more endearing because he'd risked his life like that to help somebody he didn't even know, just to help someone in need. The dream began to fade as Corey, now mounted on some enormous black stallion, smiled and reached for her, gently scooping her into his arms. Safe and now carefree with her knight, they rode off together, heading for a castle in the distant sunlight....

Susan awoke to the sound of the shower and sighed deeply. Ever since her original rescue from the Steel Jackals, she and Corey had been together, cautiously moving from camp to camp, trying to evade the motorcycle gang more than 500 members strong. Susan had some family in North Carolina, but the pair travelled randomly for a while so the bikers would have a hard time trying to determine which direction they were really going. Now, for the first time since she'd met Corey, they could truly rest.

She considered the room's bed and sighed. She inwardly appreciated the excuse for the two of them to sleep close to each other, this time not because she had cause to be afraid, but just for the security of knowing he was going to be beside her when she awoke.

Over the weeks they had been together in their escape they talked often; he ended up exposing almost everything he knew about himself. She was relieved to find that her rescuer was actually a very tender person who didn't enjoy the violence—she'd initially been afraid he was just another Iron Mike type who justified his actions by just *claiming* to be a good guy. Sensing his need for someone close to listen to him so he could talk out what he had been through, Susan listened to him, held him, and sometimes cried with him. Turning down the sheets, she realized that she very much cared for him.

The shower stopped, and Corey exhaustedly shuffled out to see Susan sitting on the bed. He paused and hung his head, suddenly embarrassed, and started reaching for his armor.

"Hey," Sue called softly, "where are you going?"

"You go ahead and sleep, Sue. I'll keep watch," he answered, almost falling over in his exhaustion.

"What do you mean? Against whom?" she asked, then caught the sadness and disappointment in his weary eyes.

"Sue, a couple nights ago we were ambushed because I let my guard down. It was my fault, and I came too close to losing you. I don't want anything to happen to you, you know what I mean?

"And now this!" he declared, with a frustrated sweep of his arm to the hotel's bed. "You're probably thinking I'm no better than

Iron Mike…" He let the thought hang, at first unable to complete it, but he had to let her know. "I'm not trying to take advantage of you! You've just gone through this trauma with the Jackals, and last time I let my guard down at that campground they almost caught us. I won't let that happen again." Corey turned his attention to the front door, making sure he had a weapon within reach. "I'll guard the door. You go ahead and rest."

Susan's eyes teared, and she was too drained to do anything but let them silently fall. She reflected on how Corey had driven for almost a month straight, so concerned for her safety he wouldn't quit even though he seemed he was about to pass out. She regarded him again, almost collapsing in his chair, and something did happen. Corey had tenderly, unassumingly entered right into her heart, and she wouldn't let anyone stop him if she could.

"Corey, please don't do this to yourself. You need sleep." Patting the bed next to her, she continued. "You saved my life over and over again. If it wasn't for you…" she let the thought trail off. She wasn't ready to think about *that* again.

"Come here, okay?" she asked, and this time he sleepily made his way to sit on the bed. Kneeling upright in front of him, her eyes searched out his as she continued. "We're out of danger now, Corey. We're safe. *I'm* safe, and it's because of you. You got me out of that nightmare, and now it's gone, okay? Corey, it's all right."

He silently nodded agreement, and she hugged him hard, allowing the fullness of all her emotions—fear, relief, exhaustion, concern, and now newfound love—to be expressed and drain from her. "Thank you for caring for me," she quietly affirmed in their embrace. Corey held her softly but close, clinging to her for his own lifeline, and yet at the same time afraid he might hurt her. Then Sue moved to sit at the head of the bed, and drew him, now too tired to resist her slightest tug, down to rest his head on her lap. He lay quietly, watching her watching over him, her light honey-colored hair framing her face like an angel's. In his exhaustion, he suddenly had a flashback, and another face flashed in place of hers: the heavily bearded biker came screaming again at him from the motorcycle. Corey jolted. Sue saw he was too worn, shaken, and exhausted to talk about his start and decided to let it go.

"Shhh, rest now," she said, lulling him back down as he was finally drifting to sleep. Corey simply smiled, too tired now to even open his eyes, let alone reply. Sue felt herself warm to him even more, and allowed herself to bask in the smile he wore as the last of his consciousness faded. She softly kissed him, then started drifting back to sleep herself. Corey was here; her dreams would be quieter this time. She lay down alongside him, wrapping her arms around him like a blanket. She felt him unconsciously take and hold her hand, and with that, Susan fell into calm slumber.

··· ···

He stirred, then woke softly. He didn't remember where he was, and he surveyed his surroundings through sleep-filled eyes and a dream-filled mind. Then he saw her sleeping beside him, peacefully ambling through dreams of her own. The twitch of a smile played across her lips, betraying some joy that somehow she was able to store in her subconscious mind. Then *he* smiled, to her, tenderly smoothing her hair. He would have given her a quiet kiss, but he didn't want to risk disturbing her. Unbeknownst to either of them, their hearts shared a secret game across the dimensions. For in her dream, they walked together, and she smiled at him, and he had smiled back. He watched her for a few minutes more. Slowly, inevitably, he succumbed to his need for more rest, and was treated to his own visions of them walking a secret pathway together. And so Corey Martin and Susan Blakeslee slept on, in repose and dreams taking the first steps towards the healing of them both. It was a night of peace, and innocence, and bliss.

··· ···

They both awoke to the sound of the hotel manager knocking on their room door.

"Eh, excuse me," he stammered somewhat apologetically. "Listen, I know you two kids just got in yesterday, and I gotta admit it looked like you both went through hell wearing gasoline underwear." The weakness of his feigned smile projected guilt. "I'm sorry about this, I really am," he continued.

"There's a 'but' coming in here, somewhere, isn't there?" Corey interjected.

"Well, yeah," agreed the manager. "Y'see, we're a business, and well, you kids don't have what we call 'visible means of support.' We let you kids stay yesterday an' last night, and we want to work with you, we really do. But you're gonna have to work with us on that. So, we normally charge 130 creds a night for two. Due to your circumstances, we can drop it to 115 credits per night for the first week, or 100 credits a night if you commit to a month. I'm really sorry I have to bring it up, I really am.

"Here's what I can do. I can let ya's stay another night on us, but after that, well, I really am sorry."

Corey glanced at Sue and sighed. Paying that kind of money just for the room, he saw no way he'd ever get the car fixed, at least not in any way that they could leave town on. He was just now beginning to realize that there had always been more to survival than living past the end of a gunfight. Up until now, his future had always included doing something with his dad; somehow the pressure of having Susan with him made him feel even more isolated.

He sighed, searching around the room for some writing on the wall to tell him what to do next. Then he spotted that same helplessness reflected in Sue's eyes, saw that she was still depending on him, trusting him to somehow do the right thing despite their newness at all of this.

"We really appreciate all you're doing for us, and we do want to work with you." Corey sighed again and examined the face of the hotel manager, trying to nurture a hope suspended by a spider string. Corey finally let the breath out he wasn't even aware that he was holding.

"You know of anybody hiring? I guess my getting a job would help solve a lot of all our problems."

8

GLORY AND FEAR

"...AND NEVER HAS it been clearer that man's government cannot solve all our problems and deliver us from the crime, poverty, and violence, now all around us. Yet Jesus said, and still calls out to us, for us to cry out to God, 'Deliver us from evil! For thine is the kingdom, thine is the power, and God, thine is the glory.'

"For too long we've been trying to claim that we, through our governments, our programs, our technologies, our corporations, and yes, even our churches, that we have the power and the glory. It's time we give this glory back to God! Paul wrote to the Corinthians, and I believe also to us, 'You're glorying is not good.' Get rid of it! Give it back to God, and let Him make it good again!

"God truly has the power. He is still the resurrection and the life. Thank Him for that, and let Him live—in you. Give Him the kingdom of your heart, the power to use you for good, and give Him the glory and thankfulness when He does.

"Let's pray. Holy Father in Heaven, thank you for all you have done for us. Thank you for allowing us to be here today, and God, thank you for letting us know You personally, even in this, and especially in this evil day. I give You my own heart this day, Lord, and I pray that You receive all of us unto Yourself, as many as call upon You in truth. Those who do not come to you this day I pray You draw them into Your everlasting love. Bless them all, Lord Jesus, for You do make Your Sun to shine on the just and on the unjust, and Lord, please remember your servant here, to strengthen and bless me also, for I so deeply need You myself. Thank you, God. Amen."

Jack usually tried to greet and bid a good week to each member of his small congregation. Chyleena brought Jubilee and Angie, a couple of her friends from the street to visit today, so he spent most of his time meeting and talking with them. Jubilee was couch surfing, Angie worked as a waitress at the diner about three blocks away. Jack was well known in the gritty neighborhood for genuinely liking the people, and all three girls felt a sense of peace, talking to this man who seemed to have no hidden angles to fear. They also enjoyed his interest in what they wanted to talk about, almost as if he shared their interests in the latest music and vids. To their modest surprise, he wasn't pushy with them, not giving them the hard sell, the buy-now-into-my-product-line routine they had expected. In short, they saw he respected them, and though it was new to the three ghetto-raised slum-teens, they knew it was something they liked. Maybe they were worth a little bit after all. Maybe there was a little more to life than the streets.

Jack, for his own part, was just being Jack, just talking to Chyleena and her two visitors. They had so much to say, so much newness of life, even in this slum. He truly loved the youth of this area and wanted the best for each one of them. He could see their need for something to believe in, someone who wouldn't use them—again, he thought, remembering Chyleena's crying to him about the "boyfriend" she had when she was ten. Jack never prayed so hard in his life as he did that night, crying to God half the night on her behalf. New tears started to coalesce in his eyes as he listened to these girls talking and laughing together with him, absorbing the once-again renewed realization that yes, God truly does hear. *Thank You, Lord!* he thought, as he struggled to contain the joy that flooded him, a joy he could not help but reveal by laughing and talking right along with the three girls.

Most of the congregation had left by now, and Jack started walking the girls to the door. Along the way he asked them a couple questions. No, the other girls had never been in church before. Yeah, it was okay if you believe in God and all. Yeah, they think they might come back sometime, maybe next week. Yeah, it's okay for him to pray for them as long as he doesn't do it too loud, so everyone won't hear it and know.

Jack thanked them for coming, wished them back again, and bade them a good week, adding that if they needed someone to talk to, they could call him, and that he knew a good lady they could talk to for personal confidences if they'd like. At first, they laughed at his being so old-fashioned, but then realized he was making sure they knew he wouldn't manipulate them, so they said okay. He again bade them goodbye and watched them walk back into the shadows of the streets for about half a block. Then he turned back inside to his small urban church, closed the door to the sound of the outside activities, and sat down in the front pew.

In the quiet stillness, he thanked God for this, his third, congregation. He hoped he had not offended the girls by escorting them out once the church started emptying. His congregation wasn't a collection of scandal seekers, but he was still responsible to represent God in as pure a manner as possible. In his mind, that prevented him from talking to them inside alone. Plus, while it was certainly okay for the girls to respect and like him, he wanted them to be drawn to Christ, not him. He had always maintained a close guard on his congregation's purity, and to his knowing, had never failed.

Even now, both of his prior pastorates had high words for this aspect of his character, remarking on his fervor and integrity. "Couldn't be questioned," both church boards basically told him, "but we can't have you in the pulpit anymore." And so, with that, Jack had been fired on the spot twice before when the congregation he was pastoring found out about his "dirty little secret." He despaired at the injustice behind it, but he didn't want to cause division. There was nothing for him to do but move on to where nobody had ever heard of him before.

Jack approached the church's small altar, with nicked wood and faded carpet. He paused and knelt to pray off the bitterness that once again swelled over him as he unwillingly recalled the memories. He clung to the desperate hope that God had led him here for a reason, that his life was really not as much of a dead end as the rest of the ghetto seemed to be. Now that he was alone, he was free to pray as he felt....

"God, Holy and powerful Lord of all, please keep my past behind me…"

9

HANDSIGHT

COREY, TIRED AND discouraged, shuffled past his Sabretooth back to their hotel room home, trying to leave his bad day behind him. "My third day drudging for work was as fruitless as the first two," he mourned to himself.

Susan met him at the door and, seeing his sagging shoulders and the worn expression on his face, immediately assessed how his day had gone. "Corey, it'll be okay," she offered.

"I don't see how, Sue. I don't know how we're going to get out of this. We started with 638 credits but had to spend almost all of that for the first month at the motel and other basics. We spent the rest of that first day going through our options. We need credits to live on if we stay. We need credits for more clothes to get a job so we can get credits so we can stay. We need credits to fix the car if we leave. We need credits for more clothes to get a job so we can get credits to fix the car so we can leave. We need credits to stay to get credits to leave. We only have about 87 credits left, which isn't nearly enough to do any one of those things! So, things are *not* looking like they'll be okay!"

Just when they thought things couldn't get any worse, they heard a tow truck inching its way through the motel parking lot, brakes screeching with a metallic wheeze as it stopped outside their room. A few seconds later, there was a knock on the door. Peeking out the window through the curtains, they saw the tow truck was dark blue with a gold star emblem on its driver's side door. As they peeked, a grinning, sunglass-wearing cop approached the curtain gap, tapping his badge against the windowpane.

Corey concluded that the hotel manager had called the cops to haul the Sabretooth out of his lot, and that the cop was a totally asinine jerk with a star who enjoyed harassing disconnected travelers who came into *his* town. Sue tried to calm Corey down, but in the end, it was she who opened the door.

"Yes, officer? What is it?" she inquired, being as polite as she could be.

"Good afternoon, ma'am," he said in a professional cop voice. "You two Corey Martin and Susan Blakeslee?"

Corey paced up to the doorway starting to breathe a little faster. The pressure of the last three days, the battles it took to get here, his town, his family, and now this cop—he was barely keeping himself together. He approached defensively, hopefully intimidating but not openly hostile. The cop didn't even seem to notice.

"This your vehicle?" the cop asked, thumbing to the Sabretooth.

Corey sighed in defeat. He could see it coming. His car that he and his dad had worked on, that had saved them so many times, the car that got them *into* this town, was now an eyesore to the owner of this second-rate motel. His shoulders sagged as he looked down and sadly uttered a "Yes, sir."

The cop removed his sunglasses and smiled. "Easy, kid. Your mind is travelling westbound, and I'm heading east. I can tell where you're going, kid, and this ain't what you're thinking."

Corey glanced up, confused.

"We checked out your report; I reviewed it myself. What you and your dad did in defending Waynesville, what the two of *you* did, just to get here..." The cop looked Corey straight in the eye, blew out a breath to square his own emotions, then offered his hand. "Well, kid, we're really glad you made it, and we would be honored to take your car in to our shops and fix it back up for you, if you'd let us. By the way, we also heard you're trying to find work. We can take you on as a temporary hire at our shop while we're fixing your car up, if you want. What do you say?"

Corey's mind was trying to catch up to his ears, and he was too stunned to speak. Sue's mind was thinking she'd heard wrong.

"I don't understand," she began. "You guys came to help us out? How do you want us to pay for it all?"

The cop really smiled this time. He genuinely liked this couple. A lot of the Wheelmen that wandered in were bounty hunter types, arrogant and bloodthirsty in their own right. Many of them were only slightly different than the criminals they got paid to drag in. The way these kids handled the Jackals, he expected them to be a couple of bitter punks who would just as soon tear up the town before moving on somewhere else. Relieved, he saw they were just a couple kids who had the skill and determination to survive, and the luck to have somehow found each other along the way.

"Not too much out of pocket for us," he admitted. "We've got a reward system for tips regarding threats to civic safety, a bounty system for bringing this kind of scum to justice. We all figured that what you two did qualified a couple times over." He grinned. "Besides, our mechanics would love to get their eyes on the modifications you and your dad did—they're really into that kind of stuff. Like I said, you've earned it, the hard way. *We* owe *you*, and are really sorry you had to go through what you did. So, we got a deal?"

Corey's mind caught up, grateful for the time afforded by the cop's explanation. Beaming, eyes laughing out loud at the relief that somehow this was all coming to an end, he stuck out his hand.

"Deal," he agreed, with Susan starting to squeal in euphoria and relief.

The cop laughed and shook hands with Corey.

"The name's Jenkins, kid, but my friends call me 'Handsight.' You call me anything else but 'Handsight,' and we'll have words, understand?"

"Y—yes, sir. Handsight."

"Great," Handsight continued. "Your car will be at the municipal garage. Things are a little busy in there at the moment. We got all our regular municipal vehicles in there. Also, the Cryo-Jaegers, our local militia led and commanded by Gerald 'Wolfram Knight' Jefferson, are there as well. He's got them inside retrofitting all their rigs right now. But you'll still be able to find a place to fix up your ride."

"Sure," stammered Corey.

"By the way, I'm presuming you don't exactly have plans for dinner. My wife's a good cook, can do a few things with that algae stuff that almost makes it taste real."

Sue smiled. "Thank you, Handsight. We'd like that."

"All right, then, I'll come by and pick you guys up at about 5:30, okay?"

The tow driver had finished loading Corey's car onto the truck. "Well, I have to get going," the cop said, turning towards the truck. "I don't normally do tow duty, but I'm in charge of the rewards program and wanted to ride along to tell you myself," he explained as he climbed into the cab.

Just before closing the truck door, he turned once more to them, adding, "By the way, I almost forgot. Welcome to Hagerstown!" Then the truck left Corey and Sue, hugging each other and waving their goodbyes.

As they drove away, Handsight caught the sideways glances the tow driver was giving him.

"What?" Handsight demanded.

"You didn't tell them, did you?" the driver asked.

"Listen. We checked the story, it all fits. It would all go down anyway, and at least this way we have a chance. We're going to need them on our side—would you stick around if you didn't feel connected? And besides, we're *their* only chance."

"You sure about all this, Hand?" the driver pressed.

Seeing the driver's head shake, Jenkins continued. "At any rate, he's going to need that car back to do us the most good. I like 'em,

Jimmy—they're good people, and I'm glad they came here. You know yourself a lot of other towns would've turned them over to those Jackal pukes. Those kids sure as hell will need *us*. But they're exhausted right now—they need a break from it all. The last thing they need to hear is that Iron Mike swore a blood vendetta against them; if they knew that as we speak, he's gathering for an all-out assault on us just for taking them in, they'd probably try to bolt just to try to draw them off."

The tow driver masked his shudder by pretending to roll his shoulders. "How long until they get here?"

Handsight fixed his eyes squarely on the driver, concern etched into his face, and sighed. He suddenly felt very tired.

"A week and a half to two weeks, Jimmy—about a week and a half to two weeks." Then he got on the radio. "This is Captain Jenkins, inbound with the car. I want a *full* team on this bird the second we get the thing unloaded. I want you guys to examine what it has for armor, weapons, *all* of it. Fix it up right proper. These kids and this car have been one of the very few things that have ever survived this Mongolian horde of a biker clan, so *learn*, people. I want this car back in prime, and I mean *prime* condition when those two-wheeled savages show up.

"I remind you, we got about two weeks to get ready until the devil comes calling."

10

THE PAINS OF PARADISE

WAITING IN THE spacious seating lobby of the Golden Chalice, Melissana spotted Elaine, still in wig and makeup, as she entered the exquisite restaurant. The P.I. was grateful Elaine hadn't gotten a table yet, as that would make their exit more noticeable. Melissana didn't know what the high-class caller wanted to talk about, but she didn't want to take the chance of someone eavesdropping on them. As much as she really wanted to eat here, she knew they couldn't.

"Mom, there you are!" she stated, approaching a startled Elaine. "Really, I know you want to celebrate Mike and me, but we can't afford this!" Turning to the host, she added, "Mom's really such a romantic, and this is such a beautiful place, but," turning back to Elaine, she continued with, "I really insist that we don't eat in such an expensive place. You and Dad work too hard to get your credits without you breaking yourselves here. I really thank you for the gesture, Mom, but please, let's go somewhere…" Melissana let her voice trail off into a whisper, "more affordable."

Elaine's focus wavered between Melissana, who wore a warm smile of sheer gratefulness, and the host, who wore the polite smile of a patronizing restaurant host.

"We can still make a day out of this," Melissana added. "And we won't have to spend so much money. Come on, Mom, okay?" Melissana waited for a response, wondering how quick of a thinker Mrs. Martinez was.

"Okay, dear," Mrs. Martinez finally responded. "It's your occasion. I'll let you pick the place we eat, but you'll have to drive if you name somewhere I don't know. I guess I just have to get used to the fact that I'm just the grandmother now; but I'm so proud for the two of you!" With that, Elaine surprised Melissana by clasping the private eye's hand in her own. Mrs. Martinez then turned to the host, and said, "I hope we haven't caused any problem here by our little scene. You really do have a wonderful restaurant here! Thank you for everything." With that, they left.

Outside, Melissana took the cue to drive and led Mrs. Martinez around the corner to her car. Her natural curiosity was well piqued, and for Melissana, that meant the world was still a good place to be. Elaine's smooth lie had the street-raised sleuth both slightly amused and also concerned. If Elaine could lie like that at the drop of a hat, Melissana wondered what she could spew with a practiced story. She decided to size up everything she could with each word uttered by Mrs. Martinez. The woman seemed to be a bit nervous, or maybe something else, but just what, the detective couldn't name. Additionally, Melissana caught enough air of tacit scrutiny from her potential client to know that Elaine was evaluating her just as carefully.

She opened the door of her red Zimata sports car. Zimata's were equipped with light armor and two linked machine guns, plus a ram plate mounted in the front bumper. Her strategy, if attacked, was to avoid a long and heavy gun battle, relying on speed and maneuverability to avoid and outrun any serious trouble. She started the car and drove several blocks, purposefully speechless, allowing Elaine to begin the conversation. The street investigator was about to say something, anything to break the developing silence, when her potential client spoke.

"May I ask you something?" Elaine hesitantly asked.

"Of course. I may not answer it in a way you'd like, though," Melissana replied, observing again the woman's politeness. She didn't exude the cold civility of most of the wealthy, and none of the arrogance Elaine easily could have displayed. Instead, Melissana just felt a genuine and sincere desire to show respect to another human being. *Kind of like Josanne,* Melissana thought, and immediately tried to dismiss it. The stranger in her car was a potential client, and Melissana had to remain detached and unbiased towards the woman regardless of her starting to empathize for her already.

The woman went on. "I have heard that you are—discreet?"

"I'm sorry," Melissana replied. "I'm afraid I'm not qualified to answer that question. I'm too biased. You would do better by trusting someone who has relied on me in the past. If you know anyone who has." Melissana hoped what she offered would bring in the client. If she proclaimed her confidentiality too loudly the client wouldn't trust her, yet if she said nothing or too little her caller could perceive that as a silent admission of guilt. The first meeting of a potential client was always a one-legged juggling act, and if Melissana blew it here, there would be no second chance. Whoever this lady was, with her makeup job and careful calling procedure, she must have checked Melissana out pretty carefully already, or else she wouldn't have called in the first place. Let her trust her own sources. Besides, Melissana *was* quiet, and conscientiously so. She would never give up a name of a former client, even if it landed a wealthy contract with Elaine Martinez. For all Melissana knew, this whole meeting may have been just an attempt to find out a name of someone she had helped in the past.

"Well, I guess I have to trust somebody, and it at least appears you're pretty careful about names," consented Melissana's passenger, drawing in a deep breath. "Here goes...

"My name is Elaine Martinez. My husband is Justin Martinez of FoodTech ICC," she declared, her voice cracking slightly at the mention of her husband's name.

Melissana relaxed a bit now, pleased that Elaine had told her the truth about who she was. Another silence ensued, and Melissana saw that Elaine was waging an inner struggle to keep control of her emotions. She silently wondered what might trouble someone who had the whole world at her feet.

"Mrs. Martinez," Melissana offered, "what would you like me to do for you?"

"I—I'm not sure, really," she stated, puzzling Melissana. "That is, I don't know that if you do what I ask it will help me. But at least I'll have an answer." Seeing the quizzical expression on Melissana's face, she cleared her throat to steady herself, looked squarely at Melissana, and hurriedly explained. "I think my husband is cheating on me. I have no direct proof, so I can't openly confront him with it. If he isn't, my suspecting him could really hurt him, and if word gets out that he's having problems at home, he could be labelled a risk personality, and he could lose his position."

It was another shock for Melissana. The Martinez marriage was one of the most celebrated success stories of the day. They were both publicly noted and even respected for their love and devotion to each other.

Melissana now realized why Elaine had avoided using FoodTech's detective firms. Due to Justin's position, any of those firms may try to further themselves at the Martinez's expense by leaking information about her case. Almost any senior FoodTech exec, a rival employee, or even another conglomerate could be willing to pay for that type of information. In any event, the information would find its way into the FoodTech personality profile most ICCs kept on their employees. The next time the computer reviewed the records, it would detect the new data and immediately flag the file. That would alert their Human Capital department to review the employee, especially if he was a senior management type. Human Capital could then ask Justin to step down from his position for a number of reasons ranging from an evidenced disloyalty (if he would cheat on his wife, what would stop him from cheating on his company?) to destabilizing emotional pressures, to simply lack of confidence. FoodTech was big, but it did not have room for burnouts and emotional suicides.

If Elaine was even suspected of going to any investigative agency other than FoodTech's, the ICC's own firms would dispatch resources to find out why she didn't confide in a Food-Tech detective—and they would have found her out, because as a matter of course the various upscale cloak-and-dagger firms tried to keep tabs on each other. That left Elaine completely alone, suspecting her husband but still trying to hold on to some hope, with no way of finding out either way. Melissana appreciated the beauty of the trap. *If Justin is cheating, her life is emotionally ruined and she is secretly protecting him, yet if he's* not *guilty, then he could still lose his job because he's faithfully married to a paranoid.* Melissana may have been the only hope Elaine had. *So much for having the world at your feet,* she thought, as she considered Elaine's trouble. Melissana might just be keeping Elaine from going completely over the brink to despair.

Still, the sleuth in her was a little disappointed. A child of the streets, she enjoyed the action, the biz, the street work. She enjoyed detecting, and she enjoyed the thrill of mixing in rough company from time to time. To her, this was like a 20th century cop getting traffic detail. She also had another reason to hate a case like this; it reminded her too much of her own father. Yet, she needed the money, and it wouldn't hurt to connect with Elaine. Playing hide and seek with a loose husband was dull and unpleasant, but it would bring in the rent. Besides, Elaine really did need her. Melissana couldn't think of anyone Elaine could safely trust as much as her. Most other PI's would take Elaine's credits and sell the story to the highest bidder. She decided she would take the case. Then, as her street schooling demanded, she started accumulating the information she needed to work with.

"Mrs. Martinez, this may sound terribly blunt, but who do you think he started running with?"

"That's easy," Elaine decisively responded. "His secretary, Monica Powers."

"You sound pretty positive. Any idea how this started?"

"No, I really don't know. He's always been a wonderful husband. Even when we first met, he was so kind and gentle towards me. We were very much in love. After a storybook courtship, we married. Everything was so wonderful! At least that's what I thought."

"What happened?"

"I honestly have no idea. All I know is that about a month ago he got a phone call at home. He took the call in our living room phone at first. Then he spotted me still standing there, and his face changed. He seemed sad, or guilty, or something. Then he quickly turned his back to me and started talking quietly for a minute or two—only long enough for him to switch to our den phone.

"I knew something was wrong, so when he hung up the phone, I asked him what the call was about. He looked down and said he had to go in to work. He then called his secretary and told her to meet him at the office. Then he gave me a quick goodbye kiss, told me he loved me, and left. It's not unusual for him to have to go in after normal hours, but he was gone for a while, so I called to see how everything was going.

"It must have been 'going' pretty good by the time I called. His office answering service said that neither he nor his secretary had come in at all that night. Now he's hardly ever home, and when he is, he's distant and—tired.

"And now this!" Elaine cursed herself as she started to cry openly. "I *swore* to myself I would not start crying like a schoolgirl, but there's no stopping it! I've been trying to figure this out, trying to be brave. I've really tried to be there for him, really went out on a limb to be more, available to him—you know, charge up our relationship. He tried to be polite about it, but he didn't even seem interested. Melissana, what am I going to do?"

… …

Melissana had some research to do, so she locked up her office and got ready for her online burial. She poured herself another mug of coffee, sat back down at her desk, and adjusted her keyboard. Queen Vixenn was about to check in.

"It's 6:05 P.M. Are you quitting for the day?" the synthesized female voice of her computer queried. Melissana grinned and shook her head no. "Just goin' in." She smiled and clicked onto the net.

One of the problems of doing an in-depth information search on Martinez was the probability of detection. Ever since the turn of the century, a moderately-priced computer program could track a given corporation's or individual's press releases, publications, etc., searching for small pieces of information. It could then store the data, linking the files to other files already created on the target. A slightly higher-end version of that same program could compare the data with its linked files, analyze the data, and extrapolate possible corporate moves, progress on a product line, or even predict when a company was about to make a new technological or service-related breakthrough.

For this reason, most corporations—especially ICCs—were extremely careful concerning information accessed about their company, including their star Research and Development personnel. Any of the sources she would normally use could be regularly scanned by an ICC to try to detect someone attempting corporate espionage. A private detective trying to snoop out Martinez would trigger every flag in the FoodTech system. Yet a few queries here and there by a couple of your average random everyday Joe's would be no cause for concern. Some corporate suit going to a meeting might need some cursory information about whom he would be meeting with, a newspaper might routinely check on corporate high-ups for a bit of news, or even a schoolkid might do a report on "The Man Who Saved the World from Extinction." As a matter of fact, she was counting on it. The Queen chuckled aloud at the cleverness of her idea. "Okay," she said, mostly to her computer, "let's go."

First, she hacked into a middle school in a far western state. The hardest part was finding where she could look, where she would be the least suspicious. From there she launched a small daemon program to scan the net and log any schools doing any projects, papers, or contests involving the business, technology, or history of the algae food industry. The school net addresses were saved in a file. Next, she scanned each of them (there were always at least several dozen) to find out how many were doing biographies. Martinez's name was bound to show up in all three categories. She then compiled a list of the names of the students doing any biographies, along with any net handles of their own they might be using. By the time she was done, she had 150 names—names that would arouse no suspicion. She could now check out almost anything she would want to know, and leave only scant little footprints, all of which headed to different areas of the country, all of which belonged to feet that were less than fifteen years old.

Satisfied so far, Queen Vixenn turned her attention to the various social online magazines. Using a sub-account she had created with a travel agency, she again built up a collection of articles—this time on the marriages of fifty different celebrity couples. She checked to see when and where each of the couples had vacationed over the last three to five years. She then made a second query to see when and where each of the couples had honeymooned, and for how long. This would appear completely innocuous to anyone who noticed that the files had been accessed by a travel company. She then downloaded all of the articles on each couple and organized an electronic payoff into the Online Data Accounts Dept. of the agency to pay the exact amount for the information accessed and retrieved. This made it highly unlikely that anyone would ever notice her access had ever taken place.

After that, all she had to do was log off. It took her almost no time at all to delete the data on the forty-nine other couples that she had no interest in whatsoever. She again arose, stretched, poured herself another cup of coffee, and sat back down with her electronic collection of social data, rumors, and tidbits on the Martinez family. Sipping her coffee and rubbing her eyes, she bent herself to the task ahead of her. It was time to read.

11

WHAT YOU SEE IS WHAT THEY GOT

HEAT AND SWEATY humidity radiated off the ghetto street, filling the air with an aroma not unlike the smell of a day-old coffee spill on a musty shag carpet. Coming back to his rundown apartment after a morning run, Jack decided to stop and pay Angie a visit at the diner where she worked. Jubilee had attended his church every once in a while, when she was flopping at Chyleena's, but Angie, evidently the more stable of the two, had become a regular attender. In addition to enjoying the visit and encouraging Angie, he hoped to grab some relief from the tepid conditions of the ghetto. Besides, even he needed to eat sometimes. At one time, he would have had breakfast in a five-star hotel restaurant. Now the algae food product at the local diner would have to suffice.

He caught himself absently chuckling to himself, thinking of his latest congregation. He thought of their times together, relaxing in each other's company, just blessing each other and working together to help their community. His church was easily worth the high living tradeoff, even if the members never knew that the tradeoff had been made. After his visit, he paid for his breakfast, bought an extra bag of ice, and headed back into the street.

The pavement population turned especially dour from the oppressive heat and humidity of the inner city. The archologies were climate-controlled, but the exhaust and other detritus of their filtration systems were unceremoniously dumped into the adjoining ghettoes, accentuating the already sweltering early July conditions.

After the missile strikes, much of what used to be the United States (actually, all civilization) had first fragmented, then dissolved, into a nearly feudalistic society of fortress town havens. Jack lived in an urban sprawl formed by the merging boundaries of three major corporate archologies. While each megacorporation provided aggressive protection of their own assets, any areas outside of the archology border were for the most part ignored. Many non-archology areas did have privatized police protection in the form of contracted security, but they very rarely ever showed up in the urban DMZ Jack now lived in. In a very real sense, his sprawl zone was not much different from the outlands of the Wheelmen. For both, the primary security was often left to the local populace having to fend for themselves as best they could. The only difference was that in the city, the gangs were mostly on foot.

Looking over the crowd, Jack paused. He wasn't sure why he noticed that one particular youth out of the rest of the crowd. He couldn't place the kid, which was not unusual given the size of the zone's ghetto population. Nothing about his torn and ragged clothing really made him stand out, either. The young teen's dress and appearance seemed fairly typical as he nonchalantly meandered through the heat-oppressed mob around him. Still, something about the boy drew Jack's attention. The kid just glided through the sullen crowd, aggravated as it was by how the effects of the sweaty air, already thick from the corporate exhaust vapors that were further compounded by the prolonged heatwave.

Jack scrutinized the face further, and then he saw it. In the living maze of humanity enshrouded by climate-inspired tension, the expression on this kid's face was completely blank. His walk was more of a loose-stepped shuffle. Except for his mindless navigating through the crowd without incident, the kid's eyes were so vacant that he could have been blind.

Jack had seen high before. He'd seen people drunk, strung out, doped up, and trashed on ups as well as downers, but he had never seen such absolute blankness by anyone not already passed out. Yet except for the hollow shuffle, the kid appeared to be functional. Got to be a new drug on the streets, he thought to himself, and a bad one. He'd have to keep his eyes open for this one, and try to get word out for people to avoid it, whatever it was. He'd seen plenty of street drugs before, but this one reeked of inevitable, painful death.

He decided to have a talk with Scissors about this. Lately something seemed to have changed in Scissors. The gang leader had become more distant, more reserved around Jack. He knew the Razors used as well as sold some chems, but this stuff somehow seemed below them. He caught himself. Had he gotten too friendly with the Razors? He thought he was having an impact with the gang despite their differences, but maybe he was just being deluded by a false hope that he was being more of an influence on them than he really was. Had they been fooling him this whole time? If so, he had really fallen off his game.

"Crud," he swore to himself. He went home to deposit his groceries, changed, then went to the church to pray about what to do.

12

HOME FRONTS

"THANK YOU, SAMANTHA, for such a wonderful dinner," Susan offered again. Dinner with Handsight and his wife proved to be quite therapeutic. Susan decided his wife, Samantha, was adorable—quaint, fun, an excellent cook, everything she wanted to be for Corey, everything she—had…at…home. She couldn't help it. The memories of home, what she went through, were too much. She tried, hard, but…

"*Damn* it!" she yelled at herself. She grabbed her head in her hands and started openly crying.

Corey was more than a little embarrassed, and when he looked up at Handsight, the cop could see that Corey was silently pleading for some advice on what he could do. Samantha was up in a moment, glancing at her husband, who nodded. With a gentle, "Come here, Susan. Go ahead and let it out, it's okay," Samantha guided the survivor from Elizabethville, escorting Susan into the living room.

As soon as they had left, Handsight looked to Corey. With Susan gone, Corey visibly sagged, his own emotional toll of the terror, the rescue, the dedication, the flight, the newfound love, the pressures of life, even the elation of the financial bailout by the Hagerstown police and militia—the cop saw Corey's will and emotions being twisted back and forth like a wire, trying beyond all odds not to snap. Handsight stepped back a little and allowed Bill Jenkins to replace him. Right now, the kid needed a human, not a hero.

"Hey, Corey," he began. "First of all, about Susan just now—it really is okay. I honestly have no idea how the two of you survived, but somehow you did. To be honest, I have no clue how you're surviving right now. Hell, even good news adds stress. But you are surviving, Corey, and those emotions you're trying to hold back are proof. When I first met you two this afternoon, I was afraid, y'know? I was afraid you two would be some kind of idiot punks with an attitude, feeling like we owed you something for showing up on our doorstep."

A dry chuckle, then Bill continued. "But you're not. Somehow, against it all, you two have kept each other from turning into one of those bikers. The urge to hate and revenge is strong, I know. When we lost our kids to a raid, well, let's just say that's when I started earning my nickname. But no matter how many outlaw barbarians I killed, it never got us our kids back.

"Hey, Corey," he gently commanded. Corey, starting to lose his fight to keep his emotions under control, looked up at the cop, who was himself showing the strain of keeping his past memories in check. "We know what the loss is like, and we didn't go through as much as you did.

"You did yourself good, Corey. Yourself, and that young lady in the other room with my wife. Now I don't know what exactly my Sam is telling your Susan. I mean, yeah, I got a general idea, but I don't get half that emotional 'What are your needs' stuff." He smiled at his own joke, and was glad that Corey also let out a little breath of a laugh.

"But I do know what I want to tell you. Ready?"

"Yes, sir."

"You are doing a fine job, son, and I thank God we're able to be here for you. I would wish that if my boys were alive, they'd be doing as good as you. I know for a fact your father would be busting buttons if he were aware of less than half of what you've accomplished. You done good, Corey."

"Thank you, sir," was all Corey could think of to say. Handsight—Bill—was the closest thing to a father he'd had in what seemed a very long time.

"The poor girl's asleep," Samantha said gently when she quietly returned to the room thirty minutes later.

Bill looked at Corey. "Well, what do you say I give you a ride back? Sue can stay here—if that's okay with you. Sam here can take care of her in the morning, maybe try to help her unload—Sam's really good at that sort of thing. Of course, with all you been through, I'd understand if you weren't ready to trust us yet…"

"No, that's fine," assured Corey. "You guys are great, and she needs this more than a motel room somewhere—she'll probably sleep good."

"Yeah, probably," Jenkins affirmed. "But the morning's coming, and we've got some work to do. We've got us car to work on. Mind if I help you work on her, Corey?"

Corey smiled, loads lifting from him. Bill Jenkins wasn't his dad, but Corey could see he was trying, and more than anything right now he needed a dad to be there for him. "You can do that?" he asked. "I thought you were like a regular cop."

Now it was Bill's turn to smile. "Nah, funny thing happens when you do some of the things I've done around here. A regular cop? Nah, I'm the *boss* cop."

And with that, farewells were exchanged between Corey and Samantha, and Handsight gave him a ride home.

… …

It had been a week since their first dinner with Handsight and Samantha. Sue was still grieving, as was Corey. Still, the older couple did much to help them both get through it all.

At the station, though, things seemed different with the other cops. Even the mechanics were pretty tense, working with an argumentative attitude Corey couldn't understand. It was like they were trying to meet some impossible deadline that Corey didn't know about, but he couldn't get anyone to talk about it with him when he asked. There was constant murmuring, tension, and bickering. The pace of the shop was tremendous. Besides working on his own car, it seemed to Corey like the mechanics were repairing, restoring, or refitting every vehicle they had.

The mechanic next to Corey suddenly shouted out, swearing in anger and pain as he kicked against the Sethura Motors Nightking he had been working on. Tired and short-tempered, he dropped his wrench. Bending down in a huff to grab the tool back up, he scraped his arm against one of the side-mounted body blades that ran down the length of the Nightking driver's side. Fuming, he was now holding his sliced arm in one hand, blood seeping through his fingers, looking for gauze and a medpatch kit.

"Hey," Corey asked, "want me to help you out with that gash? How about if you take a break for a while, maybe we can take a look at it?"

"No time, just get back to work," was the mechanic's terse reply.

"What do you mean?" Corey asked, starting to get annoyed. "What's going on that all of you are so ramped up about? I've been in garages before and seen militias before, and yeah, sometimes they were busy, but you guys are nuts! What's going *on* around here?" Corey yelled.

The entire shop stilled, deafened in silence. Corey saw *everybody* stop and just stare at him. Another mechanic across the far side of the garage slammed a hammer down onto a workbench. Dripping with sweat, he approached the injured man and carefully inspected the wound, then turned to Corey. The mechanic's shirt had a name tag on it, one of those old-fashioned patches of a white oval with red script that read simply, "Jimmy." Jimmy glared long at Corey, breathing hard. Corey had a hard time reading all of Jimmy's current emotional bogeymen, but anger, exhaustion, and maybe even fear were at the top of the list. Nobody else in the garage moved, only stared darkly at Corey like they were members of an inquisition about to convict the guilty. Corey quit caring.

"*What?!*" Corey exclaimed, throwing his hands up in the air. "What'd I do?"

Jimmy took another breath, then sighed. "Nothin', kid. You ain't done nothing. It's not your fault, it's just that you're just as caught up in all this as we are. More, actually. But I ain't gonna be the one ta fill you in. That's Handsight's job." Jimmy walked over to the shop phone and started almost literally punching buttons, the frustration showing in the sharp jabbing motions Jimmy inflicted upon the device. "And it's about time he did it."

Nobody else really moved. They just stopped, hung their heads, lit up some cigarettes, and waited. Forty minutes later, Handsight entered the dead silence that was once the busy garage. He surveyed the room and its occupants, sized up the situation, and cleared his throat.

"Stretch, you okay?" Handsight asked the guy who cut his arm.

"Yeah, it'll be all right. It'll slow me down some, though."

"Don't worry about it—you're doin' fine." He lit a cigarette and looked at all the men, worn, exhausted, almost beat. "You all done good. I'm proud of how you're all kickin' the stick to get this done. I know what you're doin', know how hard you're trying. We'll get this thing. It can be done, and by God it *will* be done. But only if we don't let this thing beat us before it gets here. You men are exhausted, and it's showing.

"Wrap up what you're doing and take the rest of the day off. Spend some time with your families. If any of your spouses are working, tell 'em they got the rest of the day off, on my executive order. Try to relax, breathe, and be human again for a while. You, too, Jimmy—those are orders! Come back tomorrow, but if I see any one of you back here before noon, we're gonna have words, got it?" Heads nodded around the room. "Now go on, we'll all be here tomorrow."

The men slowly started to file out, forming into a groggy line as they got to the doorway. Handsight glanced up at Corey, who was still standing next to his Sabretooth. He was numb from the experience, Jimmy's remark about him being more involved than the rest of the mechanics, and now this speech. "Hey, Corey, can you come here a minute?"

"Sure," Corey said, stepping away from his car. He took another appreciative stare at the pride and joy of both him and his dad, amazed at how far along the other mechanics and he had already come in the restoration process. Sighing, he patted the front fender under-plate and left the car to approach Handsight. "So, what's going on?" Corey asked apprehensively. The activity, the urgency, the growing tension—the pattern was starting to register. They were getting ready for an attack—a *big* one. They were worried. The fact that nobody was willing to talk with him about the reason why, the stares of the other men over the last hour, and the silence, it didn't take a nuclear engineer to figure out that they were on a death march, and at least some of them blamed him for it.

"So, you figured it out, eh kid?" Handsight stated more than asked, blowing a cloud of the cigarette with such force Corey thought the stream would have broken something if it was close enough.

The young driver had enough left in him to nod his head. "It's Iron Mike, isn't it?"

"Yeah, it sure is. I meant what I said when I told you I was glad you were here. A lot of other towns would have handed you and Susan over. Well, they'd have to hand me over, too, and a lot of others of us as well. Even Jimmy. He's not mad at you—he's mad at me, for not telling you sooner." Another cigarette cloud. "Fact is, I knew you needed a break, so I let you have it as long as I could. But listen to me, kid. This ain't all charity. You and Susan are the only ones we know of who have gotten away from that cloud of two-wheel trash. We're in this thing every inch of the way for you and Susan, but we are for damn sure gonna need every inch of help from you to do it. So right now, we're needing you just as bad as you need us. Iron Mike and the Jackals have declared a Blood Vendetta on you, and on us for helping you. By all our recon, they'll be here in about another week and a half. Those men you just saw leave here are putting their families on the line for you, son, and we're gonna need whatever you got left to help us make those barbarians wish they'd never left the crib. Can you help?"

Corey was already so numb it sounded like he was hearing Handsight speaking to him straight into his skull. Flashes of Waynesville's death melded over recent memories of Hagerstown. The memory of that night in the woods, Iron Mike's taunts about his dad playing Cops and Robbers melded with Handsight, a.k.a., Bill Jenkins. Susan once again under threat by that sadistic freak. Corey wanted with all his might to look Handsight squarely in the eye and respond with a classic, "Whatever you want me to do, I'm on it." But he had been brave too long, seen too much, heard too much, smelled too much of burning houses, burning cars, burning oil, burning flesh. He tried to be tough, but he had nothing left. When he looked at Handsight, his mind's eye saw his dad's remains grossly juxtaposed over the cop's frame. It was just too much to keep restrained any further. Under the burden of the overwhelming helplessness and guilt, the son of Thomas Martin had a breakdown, collapsed to his knees, and cried.

Handsight had a lot to do. He had a town depending on him. He had to come up with a strategy. He had to make sure the canons on the walls were perfectly aligned. He had to make sure all the ammunition magazines were full. He had to double check the perimeter defenses. He had to double-check that the town's supplies would all be there before the bike gang was due. He had to double check the ammo printers were working. He had to double check his checklist to make sure he didn't miss adding anything that needed to be done. But somehow, deep down, he believed that somehow none of those things would matter in the end without Corey. The young driver was the key to the whole mess. Handsight knew it; he just hadn't figured out why. Corey was the sole survivor of two town desecrations and had pulled off a rescue in the middle of the second one. Yet, if he didn't allow Corey to come to emotional grips with what was going on, he would lose the kid, and in doing so, he would lose Hagerstown. So Handsight knew that at the top of his priority list was to simply do nothing except be there for Corey until he was ready.

… …

Thirteen minutes later, Corey's emotions were spent. To his bewilderment and embarrassment, Handsight was still there, just waiting. Ashamed of himself for bawling like that in front of the tough but kindly cop, Corey stood up, and through tears and sniffs, started to apologize. The cop cut him short.

"Kid, I told you before, you been through hell, and now it's comin' back after you. There ain't one of us who'd want to trade places with you, and like I said the other day, we're damn proud to have you next to us. I believe you got what it takes, or Iron Mike wouldn't have chased you this far.

"Now he thinks he has a good thing going for him, but I promise you we have something far better, and he's gonna break himself trying to get it. You know what that is, son?"

"What's that, sir?" Corey asked.

"You're addled, so I'll let you get away with that 'sir' this one time…" he began, trying to restore some sense of normalcy in Corey. "But I digress. The other towns were taken by surprise. We know he's coming. We faced gangs before, big ones. We've been through some stuff ourselves. We got the wall canons about ready to go, we got our own force training up, plus we've been mobilizing and assisting the local militia to get their cars ready. We got walls, perimeter bunkers, and the will to kick his sorry butt back up to Ohio. But most of all, what I am absolutely counting on," Handsight paused, fixing his stare on Corey to fully convey the truth of the statement to come, "is *you*. You're the secret weapon. Somehow you beat this punk twice on his own turf, after he had already won. I stated it before, but you're the only one who's survived one of his massacres—only you did it twice, saving a hostage right out from under him.

"You're the key, and now I know why. You beat him, Corey, in front of his own gang. Twice. *That* is what I think this is all about. It's come down to he has no other choice than to take you out, or he maybe loses his gang over it—and from what I understand of that culture, you don't want to be the guy who was fired because he couldn't handle one little kid from a washed-out town.

"So, I'm asking you, kid. I know I ain't got the right—you been through more than most of us even want to think about. You and Susan can light outta town if you want, the gates are open. But we need you. Will you stay and help us rid the planet of this scumbag and his cretin followers?"

Corey wiped his eyes one last time with his gloves. He inhaled, deeply, then expelled the breath from his lungs in both resignation and final commitment. He looked Handsight squarely in the eye and responded with a classic, "Whatever you want me to do, I'm on it."

"Thank you, Corey, thank you. We got until noon tomorrow before the others get back. Here's what I have in mind…"

… …

It was 9:30 P.M. before Corey got back to the motel. Handsight showed Corey their defense systems, their vehicles, the numbers of militia, and an outline of the fortress town's perimeter defense system. At each point he asked Corey about his own town's defenses, Sue's town's defenses, and anything he could think of that might be helpful for the Hagerstown defenders to know. Corey filled in as much as he could. Hagerstown was definitely better defended than his own hometown had been. Waynesville's defenses consisted of a maze of low walls, defensive trench-works, and mobile defenses, whereas Hagerstown had wall-mounted anti-vehicular canon and heavy machine guns. The wall itself was durasteel-plated concrete, which was thick enough that at the gate a tractor trailer could pull up completely under it to get checked into the town. Not all of the wall was that thick, but it was still impressive. High enough that no vehicle could jump it, the outside of it was overhung with coils of concertina razor wire supported by serrated metal pipes hanging at a downward angle. A six-foot-wide platform circuited the inside edge of the wall, allowing dismounted citizens the opportunity to amass and fire through gun slits at any bikers that got in range.

In preparation for the upcoming onslaught, all exposed flammable materials had been removed from the areas outside the perimeter, as well as a cleanup campaign of all debris or burnable materials inside the town. Handsight explained all of this to Corey, and Corey recounted as many details as he could remember of the assault on Waynesville and Susan's town. All in all, it had been a long day.

As he walked through the doorway of the motel, he hesitated. The familiar room had somehow been transformed into a scene from some vid. The soft glow of a single candle lit the room with a shimmering glow, the warm scent of roast—some real meat—wafted about the room. Most enticing of all, Susan stood near the middle of the softly-lit room wearing an emerald green dress she had either gotten from Samantha Jenkins or picked up from a store that day. It wasn't expensive by any means, but she was at that moment the most beautiful thing he had ever seen. She fingered the hem of her dress, timidly, vulnerably, waiting for him with a shy yet hopeful expression in her green eyes.

"You like it?" she asked in a tone that implied her heart was hanging on his response.

"It's, it's—you are absolutely beautiful," he stammered. He took a step towards her, drawn, entranced. "I thought you were going to be staying with the Jenkins's tonight," he said softly.

"Come here, Corey," Susan said.

He took another step, then she closed the distance, holding him in her arms, closely, tightly.

"I saw some of the workers and mechanics coming home early." She felt him stiffen at the mention of the imminent threat, but she held him tightly as she continued. "So, I asked Samantha what was going on." She leaned into him some more, arms draped around his shoulders, not letting him go. "She told me about what's happening, told me about the Jackals, and how the town's going to fight for us. She told me how Bill is convinced that you're the key to them winning this thing." She embraced him tightly now.

"Then she told me how Bill sent all the men home to be with their families. And I thought about how you don't *have* any family, and I don't have any family." At this point, Susan pulled away from Corey, just enough to search his eyes with a passionate intensity he had never seen in her before.

"And that's not really fair to you, Corey. It's not fair to either one of us. I mean, after all you've done for me—after all you're going to do for all of these people. I know how you feel about me, and you already know how I feel about you, have felt about you since before we got into this town. Once we got here, you could have left me—I was afraid you would, you know that? Because I was safe, and you could let me go and move on with your life. But you didn't. You stayed, and even those first couple days you stayed with me and protected me. I see how you look at me, and you've been giving me my space, but I've seen it. On top of all that, you're being patient for me because you even want to protect me from yourself."

Her eyes seemed to be darting back and forth into his, searching him out, as if she were trying to penetrate to his very soul.

"And I've been thinking all this through, and Corey? I really, really *want* to be your family. I want to be the family that you can come home to. I want to be the family that helps all of this make sense. I want to be the family that makes all of this worthwhile. You have given me my life back, Corey, now please let me give you yours. I'm really new at a lot of this, and so I ask please forgive me for the mistakes I know I'm going to make, but I will do my very best for you. Because I'm with you, Corey. I am with you all the way with this, until neither one of us is breathing. Because I promise you, Corey Martin, as long as I am breathing, I swear before God that my every breath belongs to you."

And Corey hung on, squeezing her as hard and as softly as he could, just stroking her hair, breathing her in. He wept silently for a moment, just holding her close. She didn't withdraw, only held on to him. He then closed his eyes for a moment, and his mind's eye watched as they stood together, in a timeless eternity, their two hearts enlarging beyond galaxies as they stood together, alone as one. After several minutes of the two of them just standing there, he in his street clothes and she in her dress, he slowly broke the embrace, held her at arm's length. In the candlelight, he could see the tears drifting down her cheek, her eyes hoping, trusting him but now unsure of his response. Never taking his eyes off hers, he slowly bent to one knee.

"You're right, you know," he began. "I have wanted you, and felt guilty because I had. You were right about me protecting you from myself. In my mind, if I moved on what I felt I might have been manipulating you, taking advantage of the 'protection' I was supposedly providing you.

"But the truth is, Susan Blakeslee, I would spend my whole life watching over you, if you would let me. So, I vow before God Himself that, if you will let me, I will be your family, and watch over you, and take care of you as best as I possibly can. I'm really new at a lot of this, and so I ask please forgive me for the mistakes I know I'm going to make, but I will do my very best for you. Because I am with you, Susan. I am with you all the way with this, until neither one of us is breathing. Because I swear before God that as long as I am breathing, my every breath belongs to you. Will you have me?"

Then she lowered her head to his, and barely whispered, "With all my heart."

Corey stood then, cupping her chin in his hands as gently as he could. "Then I am yours," he promised her, "with all of my heart." So together they stood, the complete earnestness of his spirit and the complete opening of her heart melding them together. They both stood, alone in their togetherness, and embraced into eternity.

In some quiet point during the night, the candle silently dimmed, fading to join the evening's ambience it had helped to create. Neither Corey nor Susan noticed, though, mutually enraptured in each other's love, dancing slowly together in a starlight that was all their own.

13

A GIRL'S BEST FRIEND

"Coming!" Jack yelled, making it to the door on the fourth set of beating knocks. He had heard police raids go quieter! He opened the door to find Chyleena, eyes wide with fear, in tears and breathing fast and hard, ready to start banging on the door again.

"Chyleena, what's wrong?" asked Jack.

"Pastor Jack, it's Phant. He's gone all crazy, real bad! We was just talking, and all sudden he just jumps up and starts yellin' and shoutin' 'bout some crazy war or somethin', then he just stops for a second and starts laughing all crazy.

"I ask him what's goin' on and can he stop it 'cuz he's scaring me, and he just look at me wi' crazy eyes and tells me to let him be and stop bossin' him. It's like he do somethin', but he ain't like that—he my best chummer, that boy! Preach, you know Phant!"

Jack had only rarely run into Phant, but he remembered seeing him outside the church a couple times. Jack had only really talked at length with the youth once or twice, but he seemed to be a genuinely good kid. It's not like it was totally unheard of for a kid in the neighborhood to go bad on him, but Chyleena would have known if Phant was "doing." *Dear Lord, help us,* Jack silently prayed.

"Chyleena, where is he now? We need to go find him."

"Thank you!" Chyleena exclaimed, relieved that Jack would help. "Last I saw he's at my place, but he started actin' all ape an' I just got scared and ran over here. Pastor Jack, I'm real scared, and I don't know what to do!"

"It's okay, Chyleena, but we need to go back there."

Eight minutes later, they entered what was left of Chyleena's tenement. Pictures were smashed and knocked off the walls, cabinets ransacked and trashed, furniture shredded and overturned. Chyleena was too terrified to even scream. As they tried to take in the damage to the living room, they heard the "thump! thump! thump! thump!" of a solid blunt object repeatedly striking against something heavy and equally solid.

Jack urged Chyleena to stay where she was and went around the corner to investigate. Entering one of the bedrooms, Jack saw Phant swinging a wooden baseball bat with all his might at what used to be a stuffed animal. The thudding sound came from the bat striking against the carpeted floor of the bedroom through the tattered remains of what used to be the animal's face.

Phant then spotted Jack standing there. He stopped, slinging the weapon over his right shoulder. His body was sweating and panting from his exertion, but otherwise he seemed to be acting like everything was normal, like Jack had just bumped into him at the local market.

"Uh, Preach? Hey, what you doing here?" he asked, seemingly out of sheer curiosity.

"Hey, Phant," Jack said, his own mind racing to make some sense out of all of this. He noticed immediately that Phant's eyes were dilated so big his irises seemed almost nonexistent. "Uh, what's going on?"

Phant smiled a dreamy smile. "Oh, nothing. I just came over to watch some TV with Chy." His smile broadened widely, jaw agape, teeth showing, his tongue poking just beyond the middle of his lower lip. "I think she likes me."

Tread careful, Jack, the preacher thought to himself. "That's real cool, Phant. Chyleena's a beautiful and really sweet girl." Jack smiled as naturally as he could.

"So, Phant, I thought you were working earlier. You come straight from work?" he asked, stalling for something better to say.

Again the smile. It was now so wide and dreamy-eyed that it made Phant look like a cartoon spoof of himself. It would have been almost funny if it wasn't so horrific a setting. "Well, I pretty much came right over. I did make one stop along the way," Phant offered after some amount of concentration, appearing oddly proud that he had actually remembered something.

"Oh? And where was that?" asked Jack, exceptionally interested in what Phant would say next.

"I ran into some brothers who said they were in real tight wi' Scissors."

"Really? Wow, how cool," Jack said, trying to sound encouraging. "What happened?"

Phant started coming out of his slack-jawed stupor, his sense of pride renewed with his recalling his meeting, feeling important about being noticed by friends of the leader of the Razors. "I mean, it was some bros tight with *Scissors*! And the chummer comes up an' says, 'Yo, Phant! Scissors wants me to show you some haul.' An' I was like, 'What? Scissors don't even *know* me!' And this guy jus' grins an' says Scissors knows everybody, 'cuz it's like his 'hood, y'know?? An' he says he's got some diamonds to show me." As Phant was narrating the story of his meeting, Jack noticed the youth's energy level continuing to climb.

"An' he says, 'Yeah, c'mon I'll show you' and opens a drink and takes some, then wipes the bottle and offers it to me—to *me*, drinking with one of Scissors's bros! So, we drink a little, and he says it's time I see how diamond hit a man. Then he opens a bag, but all I see is a couple pieces of glass."

Phant was starting to go manic now, beginning to pace a tight circle around the room as he talked. "And I say, 'Yo, bros, that ain't diamond jus' glass,' and then he jus' laughs and says, 'I'll see diamond soon 'nuff now go home.'" Phant was yelling now, the bat leaving his shoulder. Jack was able to watch his pupils contracting to the size of pinheads. "And that null-brain was right. The diamond was in the glass, and I am *frakked*!"

With that, he threw the bat with all his might at Jack, who ducked the projectile. Meanwhile, Phant had bolted out of the room, past a now hysterically screaming Chyleena, and up the tenement hallway stairs.

Jack sprinted off after him, but by the time he caught up with him, Phant was on the roof running to the edge.

"Phant! Stop! What are you doing?" Jack cried out in desperation.

Phant stopped, panting, pupils again expanding. "Why did Scissors jack me up like this?" he wailed.

Jack slowly, calmly began to approach the confused youth, trying like mad to figure out what to say next. "It's okay, Phant. Let's go to my place and try to get this all figured out somehow, okay?"

Phant relaxed, the calmness beginning to claim him again, pupils expanding to about half over their normal size. *What the heck is he on?* Jack thought to himself. Whatever it was, it was twisting the kid back and forth like it was bent on breaking him in two.

Suddenly Phant went blank. "I'll be over right away, Preach," he stated vacantly. "But first I'm gonna let Chy know." A half-smile started to play across his face, then sickeningly contorted his face back into the cartoon. "I think she likes me." The goofy horror smile blossomed to full bloom for a full three seconds before his expression went totally blank. "I'll let her know," he said in a near monotone.

And with a finger-curl of a wave, he turned, and before Jack had time to reach him, Phant stepped over the thirty-fifth floor roof ledge to his death.

Jack had seen enough. He angrily marched down the stairs, not stopping to talk with Chyleena. He had nothing to say at the moment. Not to her. Storming past the front doors of the tenement, Jack headed back out into the exhaust-laden heat of the dead-end neighborhood to find Scissors.

… …

The Razor spotters allowed Preach to approach the entrance to their compound. That he got that far was a sort of minor miracle. Most people avoided the place and everything around it in a two-block radius. Almost anyone who would have *wanted* to approach wouldn't have made it to the sidewalk. The bouncers were used to seeing Preach near the compound, though he had never tried to enter before. As Preach approached, however, they noticed he wasn't the carefree street pastor they had come to know. Even in the thrashings they had given him, they had never seen this side of him. His face grim, set with determination, they wondered to each other what he was up to. They had never seen him mad before, and they weren't sure how to handle it.

"Scissors in there?" asked Jack, as he approached.

"Yeah," they answered, "but he's busy."

"Fine, then," he declared, as though he hadn't heard them. Or maybe he was just ignoring them. "This won't take long."

Preach entered the Razor compound. Since he was tight with Scissors and saved his kid brother, they were just going to let him in anyway, but he entered with such a sense of assumed authority that for the first time they wondered whether they could have stopped him if they'd tried.

… …

The inside of the compound was dark in comparison to the smothering haze of the July sun outside. Jack stared into the relative darkness of the compound interior and took in the scene before him. The amount of activity surprised him. Most of the commotion was centered on a table in the middle of the main room, where a map of the city lay flattened, various details scribbled and pinned to the decaying fabric of the paper scale drawing. Something big was going on, but just what that was Jack had no idea. Still frustrated that he had allowed Scissors to play on his sense of hope the way he had, Jack didn't really care what that something was. A chorus of different voices were talking all at once, each vying for the attention of the gangers at the table. Two girls were updating the map, and three gangers were busy feeding as much data as they could into mobile computers. That, too, was a surprise to Jack, who up until now had only seen the street side of the gang. Scissors, of course, was in the center of it all.

Of course they're organized, thought Jack. He again felt the nagging jab that Scissors was more ruthless than he had given the gang leader credit for, that Scissors had somehow played him, and that they were laughing at him behind his back.

"Scissors?" asked Jack, just one more voice in the din.

"Scissors?" Jack repeated a little louder, but the leader's attention was drawn to one of his block managers saying something about—the addictiveness of the new drug? So, there it was. Jack had seriously misjudged the gang leader, giving him far more credit than the man had ever truly earned. Oh, maybe he left Jack alone after the pastor had helped his little brother, but that hardly meant that Jack had been any more of an influence on the ganger than becoming some sort of sense of debt. Evidently, even after all this time, Scissors had no trouble ruining the lives around him as long as his own close ties were not immediately affected

Then Jack thought of Chyleena and the other kids in his church morphing into that street zombie he had seen a couple days earlier. That thought was too much, and Jack was done waiting.

"Scissors!" Jack yelled over the crowd, defiant of the busy activity in the room. All activity stopped, the sudden silence deafening as all eyes turned to where the sound had come from. They all saw Jack, and yet even though they all knew who he was, he somehow seemed different to them, as though none of them had ever really seen him before.

"Yo, Preach," Scissors began, then saw the hard glare the pastor was giving him. Scissors didn't get and hold on to his status as the gang leader by neglecting challenges to his authority, and he suddenly realized Preach was giving him one. Scissors instantly went on guard.

"What you doin' here, Preach? I don't like that look you're giving me, in my house," Scissors said, a little unnerved and already getting annoyed. "Who does this choob think he is?" he voiced to the crowd. Then, glancing around to the other Razors, "Who let him in here?"

"It was Raymaz and Back-Fly," someone offered. "They's guardin' the fron' door. They let him in."

"Bring 'em in here," Scissors ordered.

"Yeah, Boss, what up?" Raymaz asked when they got in. It was unusual to get called inside while spotting.

"You two let Preach in here? How come?"

"Well, it's Preach, man, like he's tight wit' all us. He's practically one of us," Raymaz replied.

"Y'see?" Scissors smiled, but Jack could tell there was more behind the gesture than goodwill. "Practically one of us…. But he ain't really *one* of us, is he? So, you two both just let some passing lowlife bum we happen to tolerate into our home—into *my* home? What was the *one* thing I gave the two of you to do during this whole time we were planning, and tryin' to take care of biz, huh?"

"Guard the front door," Back-Fly admitted nervously, not liking the sound of how things were going. None of the gangers knew exactly why, but all knew that the dynamic between Scissors and Preach had somehow shifted, and not for the better.

"Guard the front door," Scissors repeated, as though recalling a distant memory. He slowly nodded to himself, like he was vaguely remembering something, ruffled his hair with a sheepish smile, then hammered in a perfect sucker punch to Raymaz's breadbasket. Raymaz, not expecting the blow, crumpled. Back-Fly's impulse was to help his comrade up, but he checked it out of fear. Scissors started a kick at the downed Raymaz but stopped himself. Instead, he grabbed Back-Fly by his hair and yanked his head to within four inches of his face, which had become a mask of fury. "Then tell me why you let him in here!" he bellowed.

"Sorry, Scissors, we thought he was cool!" was all the terrified Back-Fly could manage. Raymaz was still on the floor, just catching his breath. *Dag!* Back-Fly thought to himself. *Don't let your voice crack or he might* kill *you!*

Scissors disdainfully grimaced, as though he had contaminated himself by holding the ganger's hair. "Why am I even letting myself touch you?" he said, jeering. "Preach *was* cool. Until you two let him in here, even though he's not a Razor!" He then pushed his hand forward, still holding Back-Fly's hair, jolting the young ganger's neck and letting go. Back-Fly stumbled backwards and tripped over Raymaz, who was just starting to get up, and fell backwards, toppling both of them back onto the floor.

Scissors pointed at the unfortunate pair. "Back-Fly, get it?" he said to the rest of the gang who were there. The other gangers were quiet, not sure what to make of Scissor's outburst, but too cowed by the assault to speak out.

"Get up!" Scissors ordered the two fallen gangers. "You let Preach in here, you throw him out! We got biz to take care of, an' I don't want *no* non-Razor interrupting again, got it?"

Without complaint, without understanding, without question, without any expectation of mercy, Raymaz and Back-Fly gained their feet. They then grabbed Preach by each of his arms and literally threw him through the doorway and into the street.

"C'mon, Razors, we got biz," Scissors said to the others inside. "Where were we? Oh yeah. *You* two guard the front door!" he ordered, pointing to Raymaz and Back-Fly. "The rest of us got some figuring to do."

The other Razors silently went back inside. They liked Preach, but they were loyal to the Razors—and as leader of the Razors, they were loyal to Scissors most of all.

Jack's interrogation of Scissors was over.

14

QUEEN ON THE HUNT

LOGGING IN TO her computer, Queen Vixenn reviewed the data she had retrieved from her previous data expedition. Justin had been a smart kid, but economics had been against him ever since becoming more than marginally successful. Then a high school counselor took an interest in helping him, and young Justin Martinez eventually won a full ride scholarship to University of North Carolina, which was at the time spearheading research into global food problems. Majoring in Foods Research and Agricultural Sciences, he not only graduated summa cum laude, but he was able to complete his doctorate with a 4.0 GPA in only seven years. By that time, he had become somewhat renowned in his field for his research into alternative food sources for third-world countries. It was then that FoodTech first approached Justin, offering the young prodigy a position in their Research Division. He refused that first offer, preferring to teach and continue his research from U.N.C.

Then came the Iranian missile crisis. From what Melissana had learned, once Iran had access to nuclear technology, extremists within the government were able to make good on all the threats they had been proclaiming against Israel, the United States, and almost everyone else they had a grudge against for either having more than they did or for not believing in their flavor of religion. Evidently in their minds Allah didn't care all that much for people, leaving the group with quite the complex regarding their individual sense of identity and self-worth. Whatever their motives, a few hundred ballistic nuclear missiles were launched against approximately thirty-five dozen targets around the globe. Most failed, either by failing to reach their targets or by failing to go nuclear where they did hit. Even so, the devastation was catastrophic.

Those responsible undoubtedly had counted on a worldwide fear of harming the Iranian citizenry and the Earth's oil reserves to stave off any retribution, but the response was globally unilateral. For a period of nearly forty-eight minutes, there was a tense global silence. On the forty-ninth minute, nuclear facilities from around the world launched a colossal coordinated counterstrike. So much ordinance was launched in that pulverizing retaliatory storm that to this day, approximately 68% of Iran's ground cover was still a blackish glass. The combined nuclear detonations had triggered an oil vaporization. The cumulative effects of the massive tremors had been further intensified by sustained concussions from additional bombardments, setting off a chain of seismic events.

Eventually that section of Earth had given up trying to maintain its stability. The evaporated oil, sandy terrain, and shock waves caused an enormous sinkhole from Tehran to the Namak Lake area, the entire region collapsing and turning into a massive concave crater. Approximately 275 miles in diameter and one fifth of a mile deep, it was now globally known simply as The Bowl. A completely unforeseen natural phenomenon had occurred as a result. The black glass of The Bowl naturally collects and focuses the Sun's energy, reflecting a beam of heat and slightly visible light through the stratosphere. Street rumor has it that some government or corporation now has a satellite system in geosynchronous orbit that can capture and redirect the ray back to Earth, in essence a weapon of mass destruction that can be focused on a whim and fired any time the sun was up in Iran. Melissana glanced upwards and involuntarily shuddered as the memory passed through her mind.

The oil vaporization led to the oil crisis, and once the crisis was at its zenith, machinery started grinding to a halt. Corporations that had invested heavily into developing GMO's could no longer control all of their experimental strains, and in 2028, a grain blight broke out that wiped out over 77% of the Earth's remaining grain crops. Without the crops, the cattle and other meat products also quickly dwindled.

FoodTech, like humanity itself, was desperate. This time they begged Martinez to join them, offering an enormous benefit package and more importantly, a carte blanche budget for his research. Within a few months after he signed on, he had engineered his world-saving algae processing method. A few years later, FoodTech purchased NASA for his space-based hydroponics program, and the world was eating again.

He had been in a relationship with Monica Powers through some of their school years, having met via some school and sporting events. The two had become fast friends who made a formidable team. Melissana laughed as she read some wild account in the school gazette about how the two had actually won some sort of underground demolition derby together! Shortly after that, the pair separated. Elaine somehow entered the picture, surfacing from out of nowhere—she had never attended the college. Tabloids picking up the story at the time said she was a waitress at some local restaurant before the two had met. Two years later, Justin and Elaine married, and Monica seemed to disappear for a while. Monica returned a few years later when Justin hired her as his secretary.

"Interesting," the Queen mused to herself. She looked for evidence that they'd had an affair for another hour. She eventually gave that up, though. She was an unwilling expert on betrayal—knew all the signs and hints of it. There was simply no evidence Justin and Monica were romantically involved, either before or after the hire.

Justin and Elaine loved each other deeply, that much was clear to anyone who ever saw them together. This now included Melissana, who had just spent the last several days poring through every vid, pic, and article on the pair. By the time she was done, she was more than just a little sad, jealous, and well, *lonely*. There were absolutely no signs of him being disloyal to Elaine. Melissana wondered if maybe Elaine *was* starting to go paranoid on her. But then, Elaine herself showed no signs of paranoia, jealousy, or even housewife boredom. There must have been something, then, for Elaine to go to all those lengths to find out what was causing Justin's and Monica's behavior.

So Melissana would have to dig deeper. For as much as she wanted to know what was going on with Justin Martinez, Melissana knew she couldn't just walk in through FoodTech's front door without a corporate pass. She also knew better than to try to apply for a job at FoodTech, but without some sort of pass, she doubted she would get within one of the city block-sized exterior ground approaches before one of their security teams would have apprehended her. After that it would only be a matter of time before the corporate HQ interrogators cracked her.

FoodTech was a benign megacorporation on the surface, but they were still an ICC, which meant they took their security as seriously as a small country with big neighbors—and if FoodTech knew one thing really well, it was exactly how human anatomy functioned, what made it tick, and what made it sick.

Trying to hack the FoodTech network would be just as foolish as trying to kick in the ICC's front door. What had begun as network firewalls and antivirus software in the late 1900s had since evolved into elaborate intrusion counter-electronics, or ICE as it was referred to by the technologically aware. Melissana was technologically aware enough to recognize that, while she could hack Roa-Comm and other smaller companies, utilities, local governments, and school systems, she wasn't *ICC* good. The ICCs could afford to pride themselves in ICE that not only defended the network, but would actively trace where the intrusion came from. If the signal got back to the point of origin, it would trigger a current that could override the user controls, download the hacker's machine in a counter-hack, or even fry the CPU's of the assailant system. In the process, it would also alert the corporate security teams, who would have no trouble gaining the support of whatever local law enforcement was in existence to bust the hacker. While some local jurisdictions might actually sympathize with the poor slob caught hacking an ICC, jurisdiction would undoubtedly pass to the corporations.

Once the extradition to the megacorporation was complete, the hacker would in most cases never be heard from again—unless the corporation would want to use the hacker as an example to others. That got ugly, and most people preferred that the corporations kept their darker secrets to themselves. Melissana knew that by the time she tried to spoof the ICE, the security teams would be breaking in her office doors.

"Can't get in by myself, so I just gotta find another way. C'mon, Mel, *think*!" Then the Queen had an idea. She readily admitted not even the mighty Queen Vixenn could hack directly into the FoodTech database to get directly into Justin Martinez's records. So, she would have to do the next best thing.

··· ···

The go-to's on Monica Powers yielded similar if less than fantastical results. First, the urchin Queen had engineered a persona at a hiring agency Monica had used when she first graduated college. Then, she fabricated a cover story of updating records of several prominent former clients. Finally, she conducted several calls and interviews with agencies and individuals that knew Monica when she and Justin had been an item. They all came up blanks. Monica herself had never married after Justin, but by all accounts, was living contentedly. She was currently seeing a guy, Adam Stellman, who worked at a construction company that had nowhere near the clout or wealth of an ICC. Queen Vixenn had no trouble hacking that company's network and downloading some of their personnel database records regarding Stellman, his job performance, medical records, or anything else that may have been an indicator of problems Monica might be having with him. She found none.

"Next layer...." The Queen sighed. What did Mr. Stellman think of Monica's night rendezvous? She would prefer not to involve him directly, but if she didn't find something solid soon, she wouldn't be able to help it. So, what was next?

Monica's number was unlisted, and due to Monica's own position at FoodTech, Melissana did not want to risk hacking the account attached to Monica's name to search for a number. Too obvious a hacker ploy to get celeb numbers, the attempt would probably alert Roa-Comm that one of their higher-profile customers was attracting sniffing activities. Reviewing the data from Stellman, she hit unexpected pay dirt with the construction company. Evidently, things had been going very well between Monica and Adam—he used her as his emergency contact, and...*voila!* Melissana finally got Monica's number.

"So, let's see," the Queen said to herself, so pleased with her success that, in her mind, she almost purred the words. "According to Elaine, you called Justin on May 29 around 9:30 P.M., and... hello, what have we here?

"You *didn't* call Justin—and you two hadn't talked privately until he called you, about two hours after receiving that first call. So, where did Justin go? And it seems that all of this started with that first call, so what was that first call *really* all about? And what exactly is going on between the two of you, anyway?

"Well, I got your number, lady—literally—so the next time you two get together you're going to have a chaperone."

... ...

Melissana didn't have long to wait. Within thirty minutes, Monica's phone chirped with an incoming call from Justin. By the time Monica answered her phone and got past the initial greetings, Melissana had bored a side vent into their encrypted secured communications tunnel and was streaming the transmission packets to her office computer. The computer just caught the packets; they would be decrypted and reassembled in their original sequence offline. The technique didn't reproduce the message in immediate real-time, but it did guarantee almost zero latency between Monica and Justin. There would be no warnings or delays that might trip alarms or tip off the couple that their conversation had indeed been hacked.

As it was, about forty-five seconds after the pair had disconnected, Melissana remote-called into her office computer and listened to both sides of the dialogue as if the conversation had occurred with all three of them in the same room.

"Hello, Justin?"

"Yeah, Monica, how are you doing?"

"Tired tonight, but ready. Any idea when this will all be over?"

"Soon. He said to get the money together by the end of the month."

"That's only three weeks away. You think we're ready?"

"Well, we've been hitting the arenas pretty hard. <Justin chuckles> Kind of like being back on the college off-road circuit again."

"And Elaine doesn't know, she really has no idea?"

< Justin sighs> "Monica, if Elaine knew I was being blackmailed because of her past...I mean, it would ruin her. I don't care what the world thinks if they find out, but I know she'll never forgive herself. It's taken years just to get her to see herself 1% of how I see her. <anger rising> This would kill her."

"Well, I'm with you, Justin. I hope to God we can pull this off."

"Thanks, Monica. You've always been there."

"Hey, no worries—we're good. I just love what you're doing for her."

"Monica? Elaine can never know."

"I suppose you might be right. Justin, thanks for taking such good care of her."

"Yeah—actually, thank you for helping! I don't think I can do this by myself, and I don't have anyone else I can go to that I trust with this."

"Well, we had better head out. Night Track opens in a half hour, and we still need to work on the spin shots."

"Okay, see you in about twenty."

< CLICK>

The click of the disconnection closely mirrored the nearly audible sound going off in Melissana's brain. Stunned, she sat in silence, not moving, saying nothing, thinking nothing. She had nowhere to go with her thoughts.

15

STEEL JACKALS AND CRYO-JAEGERS

KAREN SAT, AGAIN feeling dry tiredness etching the whites of her eyes with streaks of red. Each second that her eyes were open, the air pressed against them like puffs of cotton balls, lifting the moisture that by rights was theirs. It was 4:30 A.M. A mother of three, she had once been accustomed to sleepless nights. The tension and anxiety of the last two weeks at first intensified but then later drained her body and spirit of any energy she had. All was quiet, but she continued to push to maintain her vigil. She frowned, then resignedly smiled. Annie, her five-year-old, was sick with a slight fever, so either way she would have been up tonight. But Karen wasn't home with her daughter. Her husband, Vance, was monitoring the kids. Karen was monitoring the Hagerstown radar displays. She had two-and-a-half hours before she would be relieved to go home.

She yawned, stretched, and got yet another cup of coffee. Then she returned to her watch, staring at the familiar pattern of blips and contours as the screen refreshed itself once again. All was still, quiet. Again wearying, she squeezed her eyes shut for a few seconds to massage some life back into them, even if the relief lasted only for another few minutes—and in those few seconds, one of the blips moved.

At 4:45 A.M. she heard the wall sentries call in several reports of rocket fire. A few seconds later, their voices died to static just as Karen's entire screen flashed in an incandescent bloom of lingering,

99

twinkling white. Wireless communications useless, fatigue replaced with a sense of urgency and fear, Karen was on a hardwired landline.

"Handsight? This is Karen Waverly, on radar. They're here, sir—hit us with a ton of chaff. Clouds of aluminum and charged particles are killing the radar, radio transmissions are out—and they'll stay out until the cloud clears."

"Okay, Karen.… Use the message system to let the sentries know to use the landline phones. But we need eyes, and we need 'em now. Hit the button, get our people up on the walls. And Karen? Good job. I hate to say it, but you'd better call Vance. You're gonna be working late."

< CLICK >

In another twenty minutes, the wired landline systems were fully employed. There was little to report, however. About two minutes after the chaff rockets were fired, a heavy barrage of smoke was laid around the entire town. The sophistication of the fortress towns was rendered effectively useless. The defenders couldn't see a thing.

… …

"Hell, son, you never mentioned they had this stuff before," Handsight began, as Corey entered the town's command post.

"I never saw them use it before!" Corey said defensively. "Maybe they just never needed it?"

"Answers, people!" Handsight demanded. "What do we have to see through this? Karen?"

"Radar's out, the aluminum clouds are either lingering or being refreshed. Smoke is killing visual and severely crippling infrared. The ionic particles from the chaff are also refracting laser targeting and sonar pulses. The short of it is, beyond about ten yards of the wall we're blind and deaf, sir."

Jefferson looked up from the map he'd been studying. "I think I figured out where they got this stuff from, but you're not going to like it, Hand."

Handsight sighed, lighting a cigarette. He silently vowed to himself he'd quit smoking, again, when this was all over. "Wolf, I already don't *like* it—where'd they get it from?"

"The kid was right—they didn't have it before. See this?" he asked, tracing a route on the map. "This was the route Corey used to get here. We know he had contacts with the Jackals on northbound on 209, here on I-81, then lost them here on old 419. So, Iron Mike was trailing him, eventually taking it to old 78 westbound back towards I-81. I figure eventually the swarm skirted south around the Harrisburg wastelands, caught 76 westbound, here, then circled south again down 81 to pick up Corey's trail again."

"*Very good*, Detective Jefferson," Handsight said sarcastically. "But it doesn't answer the question. Where'd they get that stuff from?"

"Right here," Jefferson said, stabbing the map with his index finger. "They must have hit the Gap."

"Fort Indiantown Gap? You been hittin' some serious squeezin's yourself, son! That place closed down back in the last century sometime!"

"Well, yeah, but that whole area had been a supply center for the military for I don't know how long. They reactivated during the blight; I think they opened up the stockpiles. Or maybe they just left some behind, or the Jackals scored a convoy along the way. I think they found the place and raided it."

Karen interjected, setting a phone on speaker. "Hand, I think you guys should hear this. Any idea what it is?"

Muffled through the clouds of chaff and smoke, the silence began to dissipate. Sounding far away, the whines of hundreds of electric motors murmured through the dense manmade fog. The high-pitched buzzing grew in intensity, becoming louder as more bikes joined in the revving of their electric engines. Still the din grew, growing ever louder as more bikers joined in, eventually filling the air with their metallic shrieks and whines. The Steel Jackals maintained their barrage of chaff and smoke clouds, blinding the eyes and eventually making breathing difficult for those on the walls.

The droning continued for almost two hours, grating on the ears and wearing on the spirits, overwhelming those on the walls. Still the clouds and metallic whines continued. Then suddenly, the noise stopped, lingering in the air as a dying echo fading back into the stillness of the manmade fog. From several places around the surrounded town, out of sight in the smoky haze, a public-address system loudly screeched against the predawn night, then relayed the <PUFF PUFF> of someone blowing into a microphone. From Corey's briefings, everyone knew what was coming next. Whether they were prepared for it was another question.

"Helloooo, out there! Anybody home? I can't really tell for sure right now—I'm kinda havin' a hard time seeing if anyone's payin' any attention, y'know?" The voice chuckled at its own joke.

"Well, this here's Iron Mike—maybe some of you heard of me... Anyways, I brought along some of my friends. See, we was wonderin' if you 'uns had taken our offer ta heart. I heard a couple weeks ago there was a kid who came into your town here with my wife. Now surely you good people ain't gonna harbor that kind of sweet-talkin' fugitive an' let me have my wife back. Oh, and honey? If you can hear this, don't you worry 'bout nothin'. I forgive you, honey, an' I promise I'll treat you just as nice as I ever have, okay, sweetheart?

"Now, I came all this way jes' t'get her back, and maybe ta teach that wife stealer that good people don't tolerate that sort of behavior. I'll give you 'uns another chance—you can either hand 'em over, or you and your families might feel just like ole Iron Mike feels right now, wishing you had jes' one more day with your wives and kids. It ain't a pretty feelin' when someone else grabs 'em and does Lord knows what with 'em when you can't do nothin' about it to defend 'em! But hey, I don't want you good people ta feel rushed about all this. I'll give you 'uns another hour or so ta think about it, okay?"

Then the PA system cut out, the buzzing of a thousand whining electric motors resuming, adding the honking, ringing, and blaring of their motorcycle horns to their shrieking cacophony.

The time was 6:38 A.M. The sun was just beginning to reveal itself across the eastern horizon, muted as it was by the dense cloud of oily smoke that continued to permeate the air. Handsight took another hit off a second cigarette, held it for a few seconds as he contemplated what they had all just been told. They had been completely blinded, and now they were deaf as well. Then he blew out the cloud of his own making with a forceful sigh. It was going to be a long day.

… …

At exactly 9:00 A.M., the noise ceased, replaced by the characteristic screech of the PA system broadcasting across speakers deployed around the perimeter of the town.

"Okay, everybody—Now I ain't heard nothin' yet outta ya's, but juuuust to be clear, you got seven seconds ta bring that wife stealer and my bride out to me, or I'm gonna come in there and get 'em myself. An' I guess if I gotta do that, then you 'uns ain't the good people I thought you were. No takers? I gotta be fair, I know you can't tell where we are, but it ain't likely y'all have moved your city much over the last couple hours. Y'all sure you ain't gonna throw that trash out for me?" He allowed himself a brief pause to wait for a response, but none came. "All righty, then." Any trace of friendliness in Iron Mike's voice was now gone. "We do it the fun way. *HIT THESE DREKS!!*"

The speaker cleared just as several volleys of rocket fire were heard through the fog of the clouds. Some fell short of the wall, many hit the wall, some overshot the town completely. But while Hagerstown was never very large, some fell within the city perimeter. While many of the construction materials were fireproof and buildings were constructed for durability, not every building could be hardened against the high explosives. Homes and shops blasted apart and vehicles detonated. The dense smoke was only now beginning to dissipate; airborne chunks of concrete and plasteel blasted away by the multiple explosions were still largely invisible. Many unfortunates outside hardened shelters at the time of the attack were literally torn apart by the unseen secondary shrapnel.

"Whoo-EE!" Iron Mike called out over the PA system. "Did you *see* that, people? Like the old Fourth of July!! Betcha you'd like to hand 'em over now, wouldn't ya's? Well, too late! *HIT 'EM AGAIN!!*"

Another volley of rockets and mini-missiles rained down upon the town. The wall held, but inside flames roared and buildings lay in ruins. Emergency crews that had begun to respond to the carnage of initial volley drew back, not wanting to be killed in another round of attacks. They were wise, as a third, then a fourth, then a fifth wave hammered against the town. The Hagerstown defenders had withstood assaults before, but never anything like this.

… …

"Hand—what are we gonna *do* about this?"

"Well, Wolfram, what exactly would you want me to do about it? Our perimeter guns are blind, the guys on the wall are barely able to breathe with all that electronic confetti they got floatin' around out there. You know it's suicide to open the gates and go out after 'em. They know where the main and side gates are. Even if we risked using the sally gates, we have no idea where the Jackals are. *And* we can't just sit there doin' nothing! So, I know all about the problems—give me ideas!"

"Sir?" Karen called, hesitant to be the object of attention.

"*What*, Karen?" Handsight barked. Then he sighed. "Sorry, Karen, we're all in this, and you longer than any of us. Whatcha got?"

"Perimeter defenses triggered at Alpha-13, Bravo-39, Delta-17, and Echo-23. Wall-mount machine guns laying suppressive and interdiction fire in reported areas. Guys on the wall also reporting mines and napalm traps going off in the same areas."

"Anybody hear the bike engines?"

"Verified, no. Kinda hard for them to hear anything at this point, but outside of a couple one-off's, no bikes."

"Excellent, Karen! Something's actually workin'! They're getting' impatient, or maybe they think they hit us harder than they actually have. They're tryin' to sneak in. Karen, tell the emergency crews to get back on the job. They'll cut their bombardment while their own troops are assaulting the walls. The wall guns should slow them down. Tell the men on the wall in those sectors to brace themselves and shoot anything moving out there that gets inside the perimeter.

"Hmm," Handsight wondered while reviewing the map of the town defensive sectors, "everywhere but the main gate sector. Wolfram, I got fire orders for ya. Have the wall cannon open up on Charlie Sector. Have 'em shell every square foot along the path, starting ten yards outside the perimeter defenses. You can bet they didn't magically send their bikes home.

"*Finally*, ladies and gentlemen, something to *do!*"

... ...

It had been a long day. Both sides scored heavy losses, both sides suffered heavy losses. After the initial shelling, Iron Mike assaulted the walls with foot soldiers to thin out the defenders at the main gate. Once the defenders were stretched thin, the Jackals would hammer the gate with the vehicles. Handsight had guessed correctly; the cannon fire had devastated the forces that had attempted to assault the main gate. The problem was the sheer number of vehicles coming against the town. Fifty motorcycles and other assorted vehicles would get shredded by the cannonade, only to have twice as many take up rank behind them.

In the meantime, the defenders on the wall were getting thinned by the constant peppering of small arms fire, rockets, and mini-missiles from the bikers assaulting the walls. The attackers could spread out their forces, but the wall turrets and heavy guns were large targets. Even though the turreted weapons of the defenders could withstand a beating, concentrated fire from the assault forces whittled away at them.

By the end of the day, the north wall lost four of their ten main support weapons and the south wall lost half their number. The eastern wall, opposite the main gate, received most of the shelling not only from the fire actually directed at it, but also by the overshooting of the morning rocket attacks concentrated against the main gate that missed their target.

··· ···

The second day started to play out pretty much the same as the first. By the end of the day, the Jackals sensed the oncoming destruction of the eastern wall. Along that wall, Golf sector took so much damage from both sides of its foundation there was actual risk of that section collapsing entirely. Just before nightfall, the Jackals threw everything they had against it, hoping for it to collapse. That final assault was repelled by The Wolfram Knight and his Cryo-Jaegers. He sensed the move, and as the gang forces drew to the eastern wall, the defenders on the wall opened a massive volley of fire to cover the opening of the town's main gates. Before the Jackals could regroup, thirty-five well-armed and armored Cryo-Jaeger sedans, coupes, and SUV's roared out of the main gate. Led by The Wolfram Knight in his red and black Dragontooth, the Cryo-Jaegers circled behind the path of the bikes. Spreading in a wide staggered rank, the cars chewed away at the bikes in the assault force from behind. To protect the Jaegers from the Jackals surrounding the town, the two outermost vehicles had additional armor plates and fixed machine guns mounted on their right. As the vehicles circled around the town counterclockwise, the outer vehicles fired a continuous stream of .30 caliber fire into the crowd of bikers. With their primary weapons facing front, the bikers trying to assault the wall could only return weak fire at the heavily armored vehicles now pursuing them.

Any support for the biker assault group was severely hampered by both the Cryo-Jaegers and the town's defense forces on the wall. The bikers couldn't turn around to return fire without exposing their vulnerable sides to the already withering gunfire from the Cryo-Jaegers. The Jackals were packed around the city in a concave phalanx so tight the assault force was blocked from fading back into their own. All they could do was try to race around the town to their pre-planned return point in order to escape their own attack.

As the remnants of the assault force melted back into the biker horde, The Wolfram Knight called his Jaegers to return to town. Again, the wall guns opened up to cover prearranged fire patterns so the vehicles could break formation and return to the city via three of their sally gates. As the last of the Cryo-Jaegers returned, the city let up a wild cheer. What had begun as a day of dread had a strong and encouraging ending. They could still fight. Despite the Jackals firepower and numbers, their Cryo-Jaegers were still capable of punishing the city's attackers.

But "Wolfram's Charge," as it was hailed by the townspeople, only offered a brief respite. On the late-night wall inspections, several cracks were revealed in Golf sector's wall construction. It wouldn't hold against much more pummeling.

Neither would the townspeople. It didn't seem like the bikers cared about their losses, or maybe they just fueled the rage of the horde. The defenders, on the other hand, were getting tired. Vance left the kids with a neighbor, and Karen was fearing for how Annie was faring. All over Hagerstown people had lost loved ones. Wolfram's Charge did much to restore the people's morale, but with no other hope in sight, the resolve of the townspeople would soon begin to weaken.

... ...

Predawn of the third day opened differently than the previous two days. Handsight decided it was time to start taking the fight to the Jackals. Wolfram's Charge showed him what he had already suspected—the bikers were tough and well-armed, but they lacked the discipline and training to stand against a well-disciplined force. Fifteen minutes before the bikers began their rocket attacks the previous two days, Handsight opened all of the town gates and issued out another massive raid by the famed Cryo-Jaegers. A full seventy Wheelmen formed up in ten wedge "V" formations that consisted of seven cars each that raced out toward the surrounding ring of bikers. Except for the last two vehicles of each wedge, every vehicle had front-mounted vehicular shotguns and either forward-facing rocket pods or recoilless rifles. Underneath the ranged weaponry, each car mounted a spiked bumper ram plate. On the outward front fender of each vehicle were mounted two anti-personnel mines, angled slightly forward.

The plan was viciously simple. Firing the explosive weaponry on the approach, each wedge would pierce just inside of the biker line at different points and rotate to the right. For the next quarter mile, they would drive through the biker forces at full speed, firing the heavy shotguns and ramming anything in their path. At the first quarter mile mark, all vehicles would fire their first of the two anti-personnel mines into anyone on the sidelines. After a second quarter mile, each would fire its remaining mine. Once each wedge fired both sets of mines, it would perform a second right flank wheel maneuver and return to the city.

Once they broke clear of the Steel Jackals, each group would reform into a reverse wedge. The last two vehicles of each group's reversed wedge had rear-facing extra heavy armor plating to protect the vehicles from return fire. Flamethrower and smoke generator nozzles jutted out through heavily armored plates like crossbows from medieval castle arrow slits. These would cover the teams and cause further damage to the Jackals as the defenders returned to the safety of the town. If any wedge got into a particularly perilous situation, they were to fire off their remaining mines and get back to town immediately.

The Wolfram Knight led the first of the wedges, Jimmy led the second, and Corey and Sue led the third in their Sabretooth. It wouldn't end the fight, but Handsight hoped it would weaken the Jackal horde at least a little bit.

"Besides," Corey heard Handsight tell Jefferson as they were getting into their vehicles, "it does a man good to take the fight to the enemy for a change." The Wolfram Knight smiled, shook hands with the iconic Handsight, and climbed back into his Dragontooth, refitted overnight for this morning's counterattack.

The plan was simple, quick, unexpected, and executed with a vicious precision. In the darkness and chaos of the maddening chase, untold damage was done to the bikers in the vicinity of each wedge's strike zone. For the Cryo-Jaegers, three vehicles were lost. People mourned for the six crew members, but overall hearts were lifted at the telling damage the wall sentries reported from their posts when the sun rose. Unlike the previous days since the assault began, no shelling occurred that morning. Either the Jackals were licking their wounds, planning a new strategy, or waiting for something. The people of Hagerstown spent the rest of the day trying to repair their city from the damage already done and shoring up the wall in Golf sector.

The Jaegers attended to their vehicles, and the regular city police forces used the gap to try to gain some intelligence on their enemy. Finally able to pierce through the clouds at a time they were not busy ducking fire, they discovered there still remained over a thousand bikers. They were also able to spot the source of the merciless shelling. The Wolfram Knight must have been right when he assessed they'd hit a military facility. They counted no less than seventeen tractor trailers and five old military grade tanks. The big vehicles were constantly on the move and screened by their own escorts, making it difficult to effectively fire back at the gang's big guns.

Even Handsight had to admire Iron Mike's tactical mind and sheer tenacity. *Iron Mike might win this,* he concluded silently to himself. He would have to be careful. If he started saying that to anyone else, the town could lose what heart they had left, and it took heart to have hope and courage. Yet without either hope or courage to face the days still ahead, the Jackals would surely win. He had to do something to keep the momentum going his way. Maybe he could draw Iron Mike into making a mistake, but how? It seemed like the gangers had all the time in the world.

At 9:00 A.M., the public address systems Mike had set up around the perimeter of the town once again opened up with the classic screech, followed by the now familiar sound of Iron Mike puffing into the microphone.

"Hey, in there! Anybody home? Oh yeah, y'all can't get out! I mean, that was some really great driving y'all did last night. Oh, and this mornin'? Wow! Who knew you guys would try somethin' like that? I guess I got a little predictable—y'know, start the shelling at 4:30, get the blood flowing a little. But you guys pulled a good one there! We didn't know what the frack you guys were up to, so we moved our vehicles around a little. Well, we've tightened up our lines a little now, so next time we start the shellin', we ain't letting up until that wall of yours is reduced to rubble.

"Now, y'all been real good at hanging in there. I mean, I swear we ain't never had so much fun goin' down on the town like we're gonna do with you 'uns. But just think about it—y'all can still just throw the kid outta yer little hick village, with that little girl he's got, and we'll leave y'all alone. I do solemnly swear! So y'all just think about it. I mean, really. Y'all surprised us once, it ain't gonna happen again. I'll let y'all think about it the rest o' the afternoon. Sleep on it, if y'all want to. If y'all can."

<CLICK>

Handsight felt the impact. Even some of the people in his command center were starting to reconsider their decision to shelter Corey. How would the townspeople reply? Then he thought about it further—this was the first time Iron Mike had addressed the town since before his assault had begun. Thoughts began to fly about throwing Corey and Sue out to the gangers. Others, horrified at what the town would become if they started going down that path, argued against it. Still others began to join in, that at this point the Jackals would ruin the town anyway. The arguing grew in volume until it became a din, then got loud enough that others down the hall heard some of the commotion, which would take a life of its own through rumor mills and grapevines. Handsight just gazed into a vacant point in space. At length Corey and Susan, hearing about the arguing, entered the command post.

At first nobody noticed the couple. Corey tried clearing his throat. Susan started asking, "Excuse me…" The arguing continued and Handsight remained fixed in abstract concentration. At last Corey couldn't take it anymore, and mainly to protect Sue from hearing any more about the townspeople turning them out to the gang, swung his rifle in a wild butt stroke against a metal filing cabinet, yelling *"HEY!!"* as loud as he could. The crash and holler jolted everyone except Handsight to silence. Suddenly, Corey was the center of attention of everyone in the room but Handsight, who was apparently lost deep in his own thoughts. Corey shrugged at the man, not knowing what to make of his inner distance. He decided to continue on with what he planned to say.

"First of all, Sue and I would like to thank you for taking us in, and even helping me fix up the Sabretooth. You guys are all awesome. But we've brought you a lot of grief, a lot of loss. Fact is, Sue and I have already seen this twice, and it's not pretty—at all. Our homes have already been destroyed, our families…" Corey let that thought hang—there was no need for him to say more.

"Anyway, we were honored you guys took us in, and we are grateful you even tried. Handsight here," Corey said, motioning to Handsight, who seemed to shift his stare a little towards Corey. "Handsight told us most towns would've just turned us in outright. So, I'm not blaming you guys for rethinking that decision now. Iron Mike is after us. I've seen what he does to towns that resist him. Maybe if he gets what he wants, he'll leave you alone.

"And we're not going to put that on you guys. You've stood by us, and we appreciate it. You have sacrificed greatly for us, and now it's our turn. Give us a couple minutes to get ourselves together, and we'll go."

Susan hadn't uttered a word, just stood there, blankly staring out at the group of militia commanders and defense force leaders. She felt her heart breaking. She was afraid, but also committed. If she started to say anything she would lose it completely, so she just stood there, next to her knight in black cryoplast armor, afraid for them both, immensely proud of Corey, and in love. For as long as they both shall live, they had promised each other. Who knew it would be just days? So, she stood there, quietly, trembling just a little as she squeezed his hand for all it was worth.

Karen started crying. Some of the men who were the strongest opponents of turning Corey over grimaced in poorly concealed rage. Those who were just a moment ago arguing to throw them over to the Jackals hung their heads in shame. Corey stood resolutely grim, every bit the statuesque hero Susan saw him as, unflinching while facing the same fate the rest of his family had faced. Nobody said anything more. Nobody had anything more to say. The pause continued for a full minute.

Then Handsight looked up at Corey and Susan and did something that surprised everyone. He *smiled.*

       … …

At 2:30 P.M., the town gates opened again, allowing Corey's lone Sabretooth out from the city. Twenty seconds later, six other black Sabretooth's identical to Corey's emerged from the besieged city.

Wary and defensive, the bikers just watched. They had overwhelmed towns and small cities before; however, between the townspeople's resolve and the stalwart driving of the defending Cryo-Jaegers, for the first time on this entire crusade, they were stalled. Each time the town gates opened death poured forth, and the bikers were bracing for another counter-assault or trap of some kind.

Instead, the seven Sabretooths drove away from the town walls about 500 yards. Maintaining their wedge formation as they wheeled right, they drove around the town in a clockwise circle at a leisurely, almost lazy, thirty miles per hour. The turreted recoilless rifles were pointed at the bikers the entire time, but they didn't fire a round. On the second lap, they maintained speed but edged towards the bikers another hundred yards. They were now actually between the bikers and the PA systems Iron Mike had ringed around the perimeter of the city. At this point they were closer to the bikers than they were to the town. They began swerving in and amongst each other, displaying precision driving skills and talent that was worthy of a media event. The bikers, still fearing another death trap but being drawn into the performance, just watched. Even Iron Mike got curious to see what they were up to. He was coming to the conclusion that the town was offering Corey and Sue to him, and making a sacrificial show of it to appease him.

"Okay," he remarked to those around him. "It's about time they start showin' some respect!" He was already planning on what he would do with Corey before starting to go in on Sue. Both would bring him pleasure, and he began to grin at his victory. "Too late for the townpeople, sure!" he said, slapping one of his lieutenants on the back. "Don't worry, Zike, there's plenty more where these two came from. Their people are weak now. Soon they'll be turning each other out just so we leave them alone."

Zike grunted in satisfaction and pleasure. A sadist to the core, he had tastes of his own to fill, and it would not be pretty when he sated them.

Another lap had begun, but two of the Sabretooths drifted off and returned back inside the town. The remaining five continued their lap. By the end of the third lap, the bikers were growing tired of the game and beginning to grow restless. For the fourth lap, two more Sabretooths returned to town, leaving three of the vehicles still outside the town. Of those three, one of them stopped directly in front of the town main gate facing the bikers, engine idling as the other two cars accelerated to 55 miles per hour in a tight side-by-side driving drill. The outer vehicle kept its explosive turret gun pointed towards the bikers, while the inner vehicle rotated its turret obliquely front.

As the pair of vehicles began to approach the first of Iron Mike's PA systems, the driver and gunner emerged from the Sabretooth in front of the main gate. With dauntless flair, Corey Martin and Susan Blakeslee removed their helmets for all to see. Their boldness was not what the bikers expected. Some actually cheered and applauded. A moment later, the circling Sabretooths each fired a round from its front-facing vehicular grenade launcher into the first of Iron Mike's PA systems. The blasts exploded the communications equipment and speakers apart. The bikers, completely drawn in by the bold performance and the boldness of the presentation of Corey and Sue, had been trying to figure out what the riders were up to. They were all genuinely surprised when the weapons fired. Almost as a whole, they jumped at the sound of the impact detonations. Then both vehicles floored it, circling the town, knocking out each of the eighteen public address systems the gangers had set up around the town. Then they, too, returned to the safety of the city, leaving the solitary Sabretooth outside the front gate facing down the horde of gangers by themselves. Iron Mike was 200 yards directly in front of them both, glaring.

Corey raised his right hand to his mouth. The sound system on Corey's own car screeched, and Corey performed a double puff on his vehicle's microphone. The bikers were still too stunned by the turn of events to respond. Iron Mike was panting heavily, almost salivating in rage.

"Hello, out there!" Corey began. "You guys are a long way from home. You've had a good ride, got some impressive loot. Seventeen trucks, the tanks, you guys scored some impressive bangs.

"Why though? Shouldn't you guys be partying it up, celebrating all your success? Is one guy and one girl really worth all this? Are the two of us really worth the lives you have lost? I mean, after a while you guys just gotta ask what this is all about, right? After all, if this is a personal score between Iron Mike and me or something, then fine, let's settle it. I'm right here. But how many of you is he going to get killed just to boost his ego?

"We're done here, going back to our town. You guys, you all think about it. But these people want me to let you know—this town's tight as a pack, their tuff, and you're on their turf. So, think about it. Iron Mike? Why don't you earn your name? I'll be out here at 2:30 tomorrow afternoon. We finish this. You want me? You'll have your chance then." And with that, while the bikers just watched, Corey and Sue got back in their car, turned around, and drove back into town. Handsight was there to greet them as the gates closed behind them.

"Kid, you sure can give a speech!" he exclaimed, clapping Corey on the back and grinning ear to ear. "Some of those bikers actually cheered you!"

Corey just shook.

··· ···

Day four began at 4 A.M. with a screeching microphone and the double puff of Iron Mike.

"Haaaayyyyygers-*town*! Good morning, y'all! Now, I just wanted t'let y'all know we considered pretty-chummer's speech. An' let me tell you, it was a fair set of words! But y'know, you 'uns still protected that choob, and a fair sight of our brothers were killed by y'all. Now, what kinda family would we be if we just let you get away with that?

"So, here's the deal, Hay-for-town. We'll see if you 'uns last until 2:30 this afternoon. If this little anthill of a town is still standing, I'll consider your offer."

<CLICK>

Seven chaff rockets puffed against the predawn sky, spraying their radar-jamming contents as they went. Handsight was sure the Jackals were now setting up their trucks and tanks, preparing another rocket and artillery attack against the town. He figured they had maybe thirty minutes left until the shelling resumed. So, Mike had won. Despite the counter-attacks of the Cryo-Jaegers, despite all his planning, despite Corey's stand the day before, Iron Mike still had enough control over the Jackals that he could sway them into maintaining their shelling. Jefferson and Corey approached grimly.

"Hand, the Cryo-Jaegers need to go back out there. We're dead if we just sit here," The Wolfram Knight proclaimed.

Handsight sighed. "You'll be dead if you go out," he said, disgusted. He had failed them all.

"Corey and I will go out in two teams. They can't handle wedge formations. We'll try to get through the lines and take on those trucks."

"Jeff, that's at least partial suicide!" Handsight said, reprimanding him. "And even if you do get through, then what? We'll be out our best forces. Besides, what are you guys planning to do against the tanks, anyway? And if Corey buys it, then…"

"Then I would have done my part," Corey interjected.

"Damn it!!" Handsight swore, loudly. "I thought I was done losing family!" When neither Jefferson nor Corey backed down, Handsight sighed in resignation. "Well, all right. On *one* condition."

Corey didn't know what that condition was, so he glanced to the leader of the Cryo-Jaegers to see if he would ask. Jefferson had known Handsight for many years, though, and he knew exactly what that condition was. The Wolfram Knight actually bowed. "We'd be honored," was all he replied.

Handsight got on the landline, punching a memorized number. "Jimmy, get on up here in five minutes, I need you. Karen will brief you." He then dialed a second number. "Hey, Sam? Mornin', angel. I just wanted to talk to you again. Might not be coming home tonight. Yeah, me, too. Love you, honey, more than I can say, but I gotta go for a ride. I love you, hon. Thanks for, y'know, everything. Yeah, I know. I love you, too."

<CLICK>

Handsight met Jefferson, Corey, and the remaining Cryo-Jaegers in the town's garage seven minutes later. Jefferson was addressing his riders. While they only lost a few in their raids, the group was getting worn down by the shelling and wall attacks. The air was tense. Holding up his hand, The Wolfram Knight motioned for their attention.

"*CRYO-JAEGERS!*" he bellowed. "The day of the enemy has come. They have destroyed all in their path. *This* day, they seek to destroy Hagerstown as well. Us. Our wives. Our children.

"We have fought well. We have met the enemy and inflicted many losses. But this seems to be their day. We can stay here, like badgers trapped in our holes. Death will be certain. But we will not do that, my hunters. On this day, the day of our enemies, we *ride*. For Hagerstown. For us. For our wives. For our children. We will let the enemy know, on this, their day, that they have met the Cryo-Jaegers. This day, there are no grand strategies. This day, there are no clever tricks. This day, there are no great plans. This day, there is only the ride. This day, there is only the *hunt*. But this day, there is not only us. Corey Martin and Susan Blakeslee, rise and be present!"

At the pronouncement of these words, all sound in the room ceased as every Cryo-Jaeger in the room snapped to attention. Corey and Sue looked at each other. Neither knew what was happening, but the importance of the occasion was obvious. Corey and Sue stepped up to Gerald Jefferson, the famed Wolfram Knight, who now actually held out a sword.

"Corey Martin and Susan Blakeslee," he began, "you and your families defended your hometowns with both honor and courage. Together you have defended Hagerstown with both honor and courage. Today I dub you members of the Cryo-Jaegers. We are honored to have fought by your side." Then, to the gathering, "My Brothers and Sisters, I present to you Corey 'Hardcore' Martin, and Susan 'Lady Blackwolf' Blakeslee. Does any object?"

Not a single voice was heard.

"Hardcore and Lady Blackwolf ride with us. Handsight rides with us. So, if this is to be our final ride, then my Brothers, I would have us remembered. So, my Brothers, my *Jaegers*—this is our enemy's day. *LET US RIDE, THEN, AND BRING IT TO THEM!! FOR HONOR AND COURAGE!!*"

"*CRYO-!*" Jefferson thundered.

"*JAEGERS!!*" was the response, roared in unison.

"*CRYO-*" Jefferson repeated.

"*JAEGERS!!*" the team roared again.

"*CRYOOOOOO-*" Jefferson held this one out, building up the frenzy.

"*JAEGERS!!!!*" The men now cheered, the resounding ovation almost deafening in the municipal garage.

Corey and Sue joined in with the cheering. In their minds, they knew about the charge to come. They knew about the odds of survival. They knew all about the risks, and the tanks, and the tremendous improbability of success. But in their hearts, none of that mattered, for honor and courage had taken residence there.

··· ···

By 7 A.M. the Cryo-Jaegers had just barely gotten through the enemy ranks. The fighting was fierce along all fronts. The sheer numbers of the bikes hemmed in their movements, but it also allowed the bikers the luxury of fighting in a near phalanx position. The Jaegers were more mobile and better armored, but to get to their targets they had to pierce through the wall of armored bikes. Rather than leading a wedge, Handsight seemed to be everywhere. His vehicle mounted what Corey and Sue could only describe as a vehicular sniper rifle. The devastating single-shot slug-thrower weapon fired a shell that would punch through the front armor of any of the bikes it connected with.

Stretch's wedge finally broke through, but on the way to the coveted tractor trailers they discovered that the bikers had laid out spike plates across the paths en route to the trucks. After a few minutes of trying to negotiate their way through the plates, the bikers were able to swarm the vehicles completely, and they were lost. The most that could be said of their progress so far was that they were able to keep the chaffers from overlaying the town. As the chaff still ringed the town and blocked the ability to lock on to the trucks and tanks, however, that news brought little comfort.

At 10:45 A.M. the shelling began, albeit without the immediate intensity of the first two days. At least the Cryo-Jaegers were slowing the bikers down.

… ……

Jimmy, now defense coordinator for the town in Handsight's absence, quickly entered the room. "Yeah, Karen, what is it? I know they're starting their bombardment again. What—" He stopped, seeing Karen with her head in her hands, crying. "Karen! What is it?"

"Those *monsters*!" Karen cried, slamming her desk. "It's not enough that they're laying us all out. The chaff wasn't bad enough for them! Now they're toying with us—playing *games* on our networks while we're dying! Look!"

Jimmy and Karen just watched. Karen's computer screen perimeter defense graphics flashed a pixelated picture of a smiling

Robin Hood. The screen flashed several times, then the following words appeared on the screen:

> "Hey, Karen! Hope the kids are all fine. I know this probably has you creeped out, and all, but try not to worry."

> "Get off our system!!!" Karen demanded in type.

> "Yeah, sorry about this, but I really am here to help. I'm a little busy right now though, so I gotta run."

"No, no, no, no, NO!!!!!" Karen yelled. Then, to Jimmy, "He somehow took over our entire perimeter system! I have no way of accessing our gates, wall cannon, or anything else, for that matter. Now he's, oh Lord, no! He's powering up the cannon!"

What in the world am I doing in here? was all Jimmy could think. He was in way over his head, and he knew it.

> "Hi Karen! Me again. You're not listening. I'm here to help, remember? We called for backup. More help is on the way, it's just easier for me to get here first."

> "Get off our system!!!" Karen again commanded in type.

"How did he know what you said?" Jimmy asked. Then, with dawning horror, he shouted to the others in the room, "Cover up those security cameras! They can see us!"

> "Yeah. Except I don't know how else to say this, but I really am here to help. Tell the guys on the walls to cover their ears."

> "Who are you, and what are you doing?" Karen demanded, pounding the question into her keyboard.

"I'm going to help you with your truck problem. But you need to trust me."

"Why should I trust you? You've hacked our system, and it's protected!"

"All right—Fair question. One, because if I wanted to hurt you guys, I could have done it by now. Two, I can see their trucks and you can't. And three..."

"Yes?"

"Simon says. Now tell your guys to cover their ears."

And with that, Karen decided to tell the guys to cover their ears and brace themselves.

"Thank you, Karen. It's a shame you can't see your screen—I pride myself on my archery. Tell you what, just for you.... Tada!"

Karen's screen went blank for three seconds, then flashed twice. Jimmy was watching the dialogue the entire time. "What on Earth is he doing?" he asked incredulously. A moment later, Jimmy saw his answer, and Earth had little to do with it.

"I don't believe it..." was all Jimmy could say.

Karen's screen was replaced by a satellite image of the North American eastern seaboard. The image zoomed to Maryland, then in on Hagerstown. Superimposed over the satellite image there was a series of twenty-three red circles in a ring approximately three quarters of a mile outside of the town. Each circle contained either a tractor trailer or military vehicle with a screen of escort vehicles.

"There's your problem!" the hacker proclaimed.

One half second later, before Karen could even think of a reply, all eighteen remaining cannons under the city's computerized control adjusted their aim. Some raised their barrels, many swerved to the right or left. After each gun was re-aligned, every wall cannon fired in unison. By the time the first shells had landed, the guns had been auto-loaded, re-aligned, and fired a second time. By the time those shells had landed, each of the town's wall guns had been auto-loaded, re-aligned again, and fired a third time. A few seconds after the blasts shook the earth, a new satellite image appeared on Karen's screen. Within each of the rings there was nothing left but craters. The effect of the fifty-four cannon shells fired with pinpoint accuracy was instant and final. In less than twenty seconds, Iron Mike had lost his shelling capability as well as their escort screens.

"I don't believe it," was all Jimmy could say.

"Karen? Nice talking with you. Thanks for trusting me."

"Wait! Who are you?" Karen typed.

"Name's Iylothien, Barde de la Nêone. Just call me Iylo. Dang good speeches you guys give around here, by the way! There, I said it! All right, Gotta go! Have a great day—you'll be going home today, I think!"

And with that, a pixelated picture of Robin Hood hopped on a giant pixelated locust and flew into the distance of the screen. A second or two later, Karen had all her systems back under her control. Bewildered and shaken, Jimmy kept the security cameras covered.

... ...

The Cryo-Jaegers received a strange warning over their secured communications channel to brace themselves just before the

122

artillery storm from the town hit. Every one of them cheered as the telltale explosions repeated themselves in triplicate. By the intensity of the blasts, the riders all knew their targets had been neutralized. But if not by them, then by whom?

The bikers nearest the eruptions finally routed. The town's defenses were definitely tougher than what they were led to believe. Now with their big firepower gone so quickly, they just saw no point in staying. By noon, Iron Mike was down to about half of the fighting members he had started the battle with.

The Jackals had made their share of enemies along the way. Now over the hillside from the north, two groups of vehicles rolled into sight of the bikers towards the outer edge of the ring. The first group wore the rust-on-black logo of Alloys Incorporated, the tough steel corporation's security forces. The second was the dark blue, gold, and green of Penn's Rangers, remnants and descendants of the former Pennsylvania State Patrol. At the sight of the reinforcements, the demoralized bikers routed. The remaining Cryo-Jaegers, receiving the news that the cavalry had indeed arrived, took new heart, drove off the now scattered remnants of the horde, and returned to town. The siege had been broken, the invaders repelled, but still the returning riders mourned.

The Wolfram Knight was not among them.

16

FRIENDS AND ENEMIES, OLD AND NEW

"Preach—yo, Preach!"

Jack turned, recognizing one of the Razor mid-level gang members calling him from the street corner he had just crossed.

"Shank—how you doing? Need a Word?" he said with a smile. Behind the smile, he was still trying to hide himself fighting off the bitterness that would not help him or this kid. Shank had been there when Scissors threw him out of the Razor house, but that didn't necessarily mean Shank agreed with what had happened. Putting on his service face was the only way Jack could think of to get past his internal struggle with the gang's leader. It was rare but not completely unknown for a Razor to ask Jack for some counsel or even sometimes prayer.

"Not this time, Preach—this time Scissors has a word for *you*."

"And what might that be? He wants me to leave? Some threat?" asked Jack, trying not to appear as angry as he now felt.

Shank furrowed his brow, trying to follow. "Huh? Preach, what you talkin' about?" Then the light clicked on. "Whoa, the other day! Preach, what you goin' talkin' like that for? Man, you gotta know him better than that by now."

Now it was Jack's turn to be confused. "I'm not tracking, Shank. He made it pretty clear he didn't want me around. By the way, how's Raymaz and the other guy doing?"

"They're good—but you got it all wrong. Scissors got major drek goin' down all around him, so he was holding a war meeting. Someone's trussin' the hood, and Scissors thinks they're targeting us. We don't know where it's comin' from, so he wanted the building locked down tight so we could try to figure out what's goin' on. He wasn't mad at you, least not 'til you started goin' all off on him for who knows what."

"Wait—so you're saying Scissors is trying to—what's 'trussing'?"

"*Don't* tell Scissors I told you. Somebody is trying to infiltrate the area. Got some outsiders setting up some crazy-chems. Not regular pushers, though—we'd know about that."

"Yeah, I bet you would," Jack said, the frustration starting to get the better of him.

"Dag, Preach, what's up with you? I'm tryin' to help you out an' you start goin' all 5-O on me."

Jack sighed—Shank was right. Jack was talking and not listening, attacking the kid. He hated the drug trafficking, but he wasn't going to be a help if he alienated the Razors now. "Sorry, Shank—I really am. How could you tell they're not regular pushers?"

"Null sheen. First off, chummers gotta set up a local place to do regular biz. If customers can't find ya, they can't keep comin' back."

"Makes sense," Jack assented. "What else?"

"They ain't sellin'. They're giving, or something. The people who are getting it would only buy from us. They'd know better, and we would know if they did. Creds flow in currents, Scissors says. There ain't no currents here."

Jack was starting to get a better appreciation for Scissors's abilities. He had no idea Scissors had the slightest kink for economics. If the young gang leader was onto tracking currency flows, though, it seemed he had a pretty adept understanding of the subject, at least on a practical level.

"Anything else?" asked Jack, now curious.

"Yeah," Shank answered, turning dour. "The stuff is killer, and they're only giving it to people we're tight with. Scissors figures we're under some kind of attack. So, Scissors is thinkin' you're goin' down on him, but he was just tryin' to figure out what was goin' on."

"Wait—you said Scissors knows nothing about a new drug coming into the area?" asked Jack, hope renewing in him.

"Believe me, Preach. If Scissors knew who was punkin' that drek into our turf they'd be dead by now. We got Jangin', Not-Nuff's best friend in the basement now, trying to keep Jangin' from killing himself. Not-Nuff's freakin', and Scissors sent me to see if you would come help."

At the mention of what was happening with Jangin', Jack put his fears and frustrations away. He was needed.

…… …

"Scissors—how's Jangin'?"

"Not sure, Preach. Figured it wouldn't hurt to have you here."

"Well, thanks. Lemme see him," Jack almost commanded. This time Scissors backed away, not out of fear, but just knowing somehow that Jack knew what he was doing.

"Null sweat, Preach. By the way, about the other day…"

"Forget about it. I came in with an attitude and challenged you in front of your gang. I get it. How are Raymaz and the other kid?"

"Back-Fly? Yeah, they're okay. Caught us at a very bad time." Scissors shook his head, spat. "Jangin' got nothin' to *do* with us!" He emphasized the statement by punching at a target board set against a basement wall. The board cracked.

Jack glimpsed up from checking Jangin's eyes, traced the patterns of the dust particles jarred loose from Scissors's blow. Scissors was obviously taking this more personally than Jack would have ever given him credit for. Jack's remorse at his attitude towards the leader ran deep, hitting a hollow piece of him with the taste of dripping grease draining from an old frying pan.

Jangin' stirred, then began to convulse. Jack peered deeper into the boy's eyes, watching them contract despite the low level of light in the basement. He threw himself over the boy to keep him from spasmodically jerking against the basement floor, yet allowing for the boy's movements to be taken out on himself. *God, not another one. Not again,* he pleaded, as the thrashing grew in intensity. After six minutes the spasms subsided, the body going limp like a doll.

"Hey, Preach—you okay?" It was Scissors. "That was one hell of a beating you just took."

Preach looked up, seeing the obvious concern over the face of the Razor gang lord. "Yeah, *null sheen,*" Preach said, smiling a little. "Had a lot of good training in that department."

Scissors grinned. "Hell, yeah, we're good teachers," Scissors boasted, offering Jack a hand to help him up. "Y'know, you're pretty intense for a preacher."

Jack grunted. "Actually, Scissors, I owe you an apology. I was convinced dead to rights that this stuff was coming from you. That's why I came into the compound the other day. Sorry, I have really misjudged you. Seeing you in here, I've been seriously underestimating you as well."

"Preach, I'm a street mongrel. We got nowhere to go. Streets are tight and tough, and these guys would've gotten eaten alive if we didn't do the toughness to the others first. Yeah, we do stuff a lot of people are too scared to do. We fight back. Sometimes we fight first. An' sometimes it's fun, and a blast, but after a while it gets old, but you just got nowhere else to go.

"An' then you see your friends get stomped, cut, shot all to drek. An' you want to quit, but who's gonna take you?" He sighed. "An' then you start to think, 'Hell, if I quit, some of *them* won't stand a chance.' And that's when you know that you're stuck. You jus' end up hopin' it's for the right reasons."

It was like a whole new universe of Scissors was opening up to Jack for the very first time.

… …

It had been a long four days. Jack sent one of the Razors to the congregation for prayer, and they held vigil at the church while he was in the compound basement. Over the course of those days, Jack saw a side to Scissors he had never seen before. Pacing and brooding like a cat, Scissors spent every spare moment he had working alongside Jack, trying to help care for Jangin'.

"So, why'd you think it was me?" Scissors asked Jack as they were taking turns watching the boy.

"Sorry, what?"

"Y'know, the other day you said you came into the compound and thought I was pumping this stuff into my own hood. Why?"

"Well, you own the streets, and commerce is commerce."

"True that," Scissors agreed. "'Cept I have no idea where this stuff is comin' from. We're watchin', but so far we're empty as a chemhead's wallet."

"Well, by now you heard about Phant," Jack began.

Scissors got agitated. "Yeah, another one! Lynch's brother. Found him in an alley outside where Chyleena lives, the day after…"

Jack nodded. "Bingo. He was over at Chyleena's, busting up the house. I think he would have killed her. She got out, came over to my place for help. Same thing, but he was talking. I don't know, maybe because he was older than Jangin'."

"Yo, Preach, that don't make sense. Ain't nothing woulda gotten Phant to tweak, an' that boy was crazy for Chy."

"Well, it happened. He mentioned some brothers told him you wanted to show him a haul of diamonds. Guy took a drink from a bottle, wiped off the mouth of the bottle, and passed it to Phant. I figured they either dropped it into the bottle or rubbed a dose onto the bottle's lip while passing it to him."

"Yeah, maybe like that," Scissors assented.

"And yeah, he was absolutely crazy for Chyleena." Jack stiffened at the memory. "So, I figured since you're 'Bros' were so set on jacking him up, you were making customers. I was wrong, dead wrong. But

I was there, watched him walk off that roof, and I couldn't do one thing about it.

"So yeah, you saw it right. I was going to call you on it." Jack noticed the stare Scissors was giving him. "What?"

"So the chem has a name—'Diamond.' That's a start." Scissors nodded. "And from what you just said, someone is specifically targeting Razors. Trying to get us to turn on ourselves. Which means someone outside, 'cause if someone was buying from inside, one of us would have heard about it by now, and nobody's mentioned Diamond to me before."

Jangin's stupor ended. A few moans in the background quickly turned into giggling, then belly laughter. It might have been funny, except the whole time the expression on Jangin's face reflected not humor, but pain and horror. It took both men to keep him from choking and smashing his own head against the floor. Thirty minutes later, Scissors summoned some of his lieutenants. After sharing some information, he gave them some instructions and sent them out. Then he approached Preach.

"Told them about your conversation with Phant. We'll know by tomorrow night if any Razors are involved in this. If there are, I promise they'll need your prayers before we're done with them."

....

After six days of constant watch, prayer, and intervention, Jangin' started to stabilize. The kid was by no means ready for prime time, but they were able to bring him upstairs and wash him off a little. Scissors had another conference and came back somewhat less edgy than he had been the last day or so.

"The Razors are all cool," he announced, rendering his verdict. Calling outside, Scissors yelled, "Gigz! C'mere." Gigz entered the room, a five foot nine, 130-pound kid with very alert eyes. One of the gang's hackers, Jack concluded, as Gigz carried a computer in with him.

"Gigz, listen to this, and listen good," Scissors pronounced. Then, to Preach, "Gigz knows a lot of stuff, kind of like a street encyclopedia. It's weird, but Gigz can sometimes connect dots we don't even see, make more from a story than we can. So, Preach, tell me an' Gigz *exactly* what Phant said."

Jack repeated the story, almost verbatim. Once or twice Scissors nodded, or grunted, or shook his head. When Jack finished, Gigz asked Jack to repeat the story, word for word, twice. On the third time, Scissors closed his eyes and listened, intently, to every syllable. The entire time Gigz was tapping at his keyboard. As Jack was relaying the flight up the stairway, he was interrupted.

"Wait a minute!" interjected Gigz, holding up a hand like he was trying to mentally focus on something.

"Go back to where you first asked him what happened. Use exact words, if you can."

Jack again began to narrate the tale but was again interrupted by Gigz. "Tell me about when Phant saw the bag—exact words, but talk as regular as you can."

Jack again repeated the description of Phant's narration, and Gigz nodded. Then he told Jack he could stop.

"You got something figured, Gigz? Let's hear it. Preach is in on this, however it runs."

Gigz nodded, glanced sideways at Jack, then shrugged. Evidently Gigz was not used to rendering his conclusions to anyone but Scissors.

"Phant wasn't saying Bros, as in 'Brothers.' Preach heard him wrong."

"What do you mean? I was there when—" Jack's denial was cut off by Scissors.

"Don't interrupt him," the gang leader ordered. Then turning to Gigz, "Go ahead, what did he say?"

"Well, you hear all the references to the Brothers? Then there was Bros."

"Yeah?" Scissors asked dismissively, "So, Brothers, Bros." The shrug of Scissors openly showed he didn't know what Gigz was getting at, either. At least Preach felt like he wasn't the *only* one who wasn't understanding what Gigz was getting at.

"Yeah, that's what I thought at first, too. But that wasn't what he was saying. They did lie about bein' tight with you, Scissors, but they are *Brothers*. When he was either talking about how many or talking to however many there were, it was always Brothers. It was never 'Bros,' 'cause 'Bros' was only used when he was talking to one guy."

"It wasn't 'Bros'…" Gigz continued.

"It was *Broze*," Scissors finished, glowering. "Crack City Brotherhood." Scissors was seething, still—except for the darting movements of his eyes as he assimilated and contemplated what he had just learned.

"*DREK!!!*" he suddenly bellowed. He jumped up and grabbed a bat that had an edge filed into it, smashing it against one of the practice dummies supported by a beam that ran from the floor to the basement. Blow upon blow fell against the dummy until nothing remained but spent cloth strips and piles of sawdust. Still the enraged, Scissors set his aggression against the remains until the beam itself gave with a loud crack as it splintered. The noise caught the attention of everyone in the house, who came down to see what was going on.

"Get everyone, and I mean *everyone!*" Scissors commanded, breathing in heavy gasps after venting his fury. "We got a name on what they're doing, and we got a name on who's doing it. It fits.

"As of now, Razors are at war. First thing we do is meet up together, then come up with a way to hunt down the ones on our turf, and remove 'em," he said, still breathing hard. Then he looked purposefully to Jack and continued. "Pass on to everyone that Preach is *in* with us, he needs to know what we know. They are specifically targeting civilians, and he needs to be able to get word out to them what's going on." Then, to Preach, "Listen, you seen what this does, and you chat up with people who don't give us the time of day. You let us know if you see anyone who shouldn't be here. Help us try to spot them!"

Jack had watched Diamond already begin to tear at his congregation. First Chyleena, then Not-Nuff, and their friends. *Lord, how does a pastor get caught up in a gang war?*

"I don't want you to kill them, but they need to be off the streets," Jack replied. "We also need to talk with anyone you pick up so we can find out where this stuff is coming from, okay?"

Scissors nodded. "Can't promise, but we'll try to have it so you can talk with them."

Jack nodded, a terse nod from years gone past, just like the old days. The motion triggered a memory of a response he used so frequently in his past that it became one of his signature lines. The memory was so strong he knew he was going to say it, just like the old days. He really didn't want to say it, but the force of the old habit gnawed at him like a rat on an old bone. He couldn't resist it, despite himself…

"I'll keep my eyes open," he responded.

Suddenly Jack felt a connection to the gang on a level he had never felt before. The feeling was as old as the habit, alien and familiar in equal degree. It was…*camaraderie.* Jack paused, wondering if that close of a tie to the street gang was a good thing.

Jack turned from his own thoughts to the other Razors in the room, who seemed to be in a state of, well, he couldn't tell. It didn't really feel like anyone knew *what* state they were in, but he could see their questions and confusion easily enough. Among their several unvoiced questions was whether or not Preach had just joined their gang, whether or not that was cool, and why would Scissors even do that after the confrontation just a few days earlier?

Scissors didn't have time to explain. In his mind, the only reason they knew about this enemy was thanks to Jack. He wanted to return the favor. The gang lord and Jack had gotten close after the last several days, and Scissors wanted Jack to be aware of the threat to his congregation.

133

"We meet back here in four hours. Move!"

…… ……

"Yo, Preach!"

Jack turned, recognizing Shank calling him, like a *déjà vu*.

"Shank," Jack returned, "how you holding up?" The search for the Crack City Brotherhood was on its fifth day, with no results.

"I'm holdin'. Scissors wanted me to pass some word onto yo. Been by your building, but ain't seen you there for a couple days now."

"Yeah, I let the congregation know what was happening, told 'em not to hang around or out with anyone they didn't know personally."

"Preach? Cancellin' church?"

"Yeah, well, I've now seen three kids on Diamond, and with everything in me I never want to see a fourth. At least some of the members are potential targets, so we decided to cancel services for a time. I still meet with the couple of home groups we have within the congregation, but other than that I'm spending most of my time with you guys. If ever you needed me, it's now. This guerilla drug war is beginning to take its toll. Fatigue and trying to smoke out an invisible enemy are starting to wear on all of your nerves."

"Whoa, Preach, deep. You really care about us? I just thought that was some kinda commercial you had goin'."

"Sorry." Jack grinned. "You're stuck with the B-Team, but I'm really here for you guys as much as anyone else who lives here. So anyway, whatchya got?"

"Oh, yeah—stats and' updates, and somethin' else," Shank began. "First, Jangin' seems to be doin' okay, finally startin' ta sleepin' normal, but you prob'ly figured that.

"Second, we ain't seen nothin' o' the Brotherhood. Gigz 'n' the other hacks say Brotherhood begun doin' quite well for themselves. Guess our boyz hacked some transactions, traced down some Bro biz, and they sudden got more creds than a rat's got fleas. Guess we also hacked some street cameras, the Brotherhood also seemed to be able to get corp playland toys and bang-bang that most gangers never hear of, let 'lone get a chance ta pack... *We* sure can't get that kind of pack. We don't even know where to get it *from*. If we did..." Shank let a wolfish grin escape, and Jack caught it instantly.

They're gangers, *Jack,* he reminded himself. *Who's affecting whom? Lord, am I getting in too deep? Just what am I doing here?* he asked, not for the first time. Yet even as he asked, he knew. The answer came to him when he first asked back in the house basement how pastors get caught up in gang wars. They get there by *caring.* He was their Pastor; his call was to serve them. No, he didn't agree with them in a lot of ways, in a ton of ways. But they were under attack by an enemy who was willing to kill totally innocent kids just to try to get to them. Whoever it was killed someone who came to his church, injuring Chyleena in the process. Had almost killed an eleven-year-old kid just to hurt Not-Nuff, who wasn't even a member of the Razors. Now they supposedly have some kind of financial backing? Jack wasn't sure of what exactly was going on, but he felt like he had to do *something. Love is a verb,* he thought to himself. *Love* does. His brand of Christianity wasn't always easy—in fact, it seldom was *Look around you, Jack!* he thought, grinning in spite of himself. It was exhausting, it was dirty. But it was real.

"Okay, thanks, Shank," Jack said, grimly smiling. "And thanks for keeping me up to date with Jangin'." He gave the ganger a pat on the shoulder and turned to leave. "But for now, I need some decent doze. I'll be home crashing. If you guys need anything, though, I'll be there."

"Null sheen, bro," Shank offered. "Ya been with Scissors an' Jangin', you prob'ly ain't been home in over a week. Scissors called up a guard on your crib while you were out. Grab some doze. Y'know, thinkin' 'bout it, I can send some sister your way—help you sleep *good,* my man. Know a couple who've been right impressed with what they see in you. I think a couple would really like to…" Shank offered with grinning wink.

Jack started at the suggestion, even knowing the young ganger had not meant offense. Yet even he had to admit—"No. That would *not* be okay. Don't throw something like that at me again," Jack emphatically, forcefully stated.

"All right, man," Shank retorted. "I mean, wow, jus' tryin' to be nice."

"Yeah." Jack sighed, wondering if he was ever making any real headway in this city. "I know. But God don't roll like that, Shank. He's got better in mind than a temp rush with a lead bag of aftermath on the other side."

Jack let it go at that. He turned and walked away, shaking his head, leaving Shank on the corner. *Walkin' the bear,* Jack thought to himself. *Sometimes it's just two steps forward, one back. Lord, help all of us understand what in the world we're all doing here.*

… …

He was about to round the corner to his building when Fearless tapped him on the shoulder, leaning in and quietly talking into his ear. "Preach, we think you're a target. Keep walkin' straight," was all he said. Knowing the Razors had someone scouting his door, he obeyed. After passing the block, Jack turned. "What's up now?" he asked, tired and now impatient.

"We got a line on two out-of-towners that dropped into the hood a couple days ago. We started tagging 'em, thinking they might be connected to the Diamond flow. They're askin' about you, stopped by earlier lookin' for ya."

"Why would they want me?" asked Jack. He already knew the answer as Fearless explained.

"Well, they're targeting friends and family of the Razors," Fearless answered. "Guess it's your turn."

"Then why am I here? Let's go confront them," Jack offered, eager to gain some information on what was going on.

"Well, these guys are different," Fearless began. "I mean, they seem like they can handle action if they find it, but they're not wearing any colors. Scissors want us to just watch them, keep him informed. Turns out they don't really seem to be connected to either the Crack City Shove-her-hood or Diamond."

"Great," Jack said. "Nice to see some people might be just people," Jack started to offer, then saw in the somber expression in Fearless's face that there was more. "So, what's going on with these two? You don't think they're just two regular guys, do you?"

"Nope, we do not. We did some follow-up with some of the people we saw them talking with. It felt like they were fishin' for buzz. Each person we talked with told us the same thing. They were asking questions, trying to find info on someone."

"And you think they're the ones coming after you. Well, okay, you want me to go meet with them to find out what they're about?"

"Again, nope we do not. Personally, Beast an' me think you already met. They are asking questions around the turf. Questions specifically about *you*."

Jack's blood froze. Time stopped. Objects. People. Fearless's mouth poised, framing the eternal syllable of "you." Sound waves. The slide of molecules inside their elements. The flow of electrons. All stopped. Absolute zero formed in his soul. From somewhere far away, across an infinite expanse of forever, it began. In the silence of the blackness not even he could see into, Jack heard the primal scream of a man trapped. Caught. In that darkness of his mind's oblivion, the resonance of the silent scream echoed in his mind. One thought, one emotion, one primal fear, united in scope and focus. His one raw emotion, beyond any thought he might have tried to conjure, his one silent scream welling up from nowhere, from everywhere:

"Dear God, No!"

"What did they look like?" asked Jack, after the timeless stretch of several eons of eternities lived through the few microseconds that had actually lapsed. "And what kind of questions have they been asking?" Jack silently searched his memory through most of his adult life while he waited for Beast to respond. He could not obtain one possible answer to either question that ended well or brought him any relief from his sudden sense of ominous foreboding.

"Well, like I said," Fearless replied, "no colors we know of. Definitely not suits, but they smelled corporate. Joe-boys, for sure, but no telling where from—though it's not like those types always wear logos. Some cross between corp and Yak, maybe. Anyway, two guys, one light-build Spanish guy with a 'fro, the other a heavy muscle with a blonde, tight-crop wearin' a black t-shirt. Muscle always has shades on. Spanish guy easy enough to talk with; the other guy seems he wants to fight.

"As to what they're askin', their story is they heard you were around here somewhere, an' they're saying to pass the word they just want a chance to talk. Scissors told us to lay back and observe, so we ain't scrambled with 'em yet. But Scissors wanted you to know. He's offered to flick 'em if they're not friends of yours. Gotta admit, a few of us would enjoy a go-to with the muscle-boy. We asked who was askin' so we could pass the word. Their tough guy's tag was Chrome, and the Spanish guy was—Ronnie?"

Jack sighed, outwardly releasing on a nano-molecular level the groan of despair that was now escaping his soul, trying to find any trace of grace in what he'd just heard. Out of all possible answers to either question he had asked, Jack had just received what was probably the two worst answers to both.

"You want us to off them?" the Razor asked suddenly, noticing the expression on Jack's face. The last couple weeks had been weird for everybody, but he had never seen Preach shaken like this before.

"Gotta admit, my life would probably feel a whole lot easier if you did, but no thanks. Besides the wrongness of it, even if it did work—there'd just be more firestorm than anyone here would be willing to buy. Especially me. Try to stall them for me to get me some time to pray and think about this. Tell Scissors I said thanks for the heads up."

Fearless nodded a "You got it," gave a little head duck in farewell, and drifted back into the street.

... ...

It had been about four days since Jack had heard Chrome and Arañé were looking for him. But why had they followed him here? Why now? He thought he'd put enough distance between him and his past to bury himself forever, but evidently the third-world ghetto wasn't quite far enough. He allowed himself a mirthless laugh. "Not like anyone can stay hidden for long in this day and age. Not if someone wants to find them."

He had been spending most of his days visiting his congregation, checking in with the Razors, trying to find Crack City Brotherhood activity, and visiting with Jangin' and his family. Between every stop, he kept a special eye out for the pair that were searching for him. Chrome, with his burly physique and a demeanor that would compel most people to back away from him, would by far be the easier to spot. Arañé (Spider) could be almost anywhere.

Jack was just leaving the tenement of Mrs. Williams. The late July heat and humidity were unabated, and eventually turned to an August promising an entire month of dog days. People's attitudes were again beginning to match the mugginess of the humid air. The neighborhood seemed unusually quiet, like the pause of a growling dog just before it bites.

"Pastor Jack! Pastor Jack!" a young male voice breathlessly cried out from outside Jangin's house. The voice belonged to Not-Nuff, the younger brother of Scissors.

"Hey, 'Nuff," Jack said in greeting. Then he noted the scared look of his young convert. Between his faith in God and his older brother being the leader of the Razors, Not-Nuff didn't have a lot of reason to get scared about anything. Now the kid was almost panicked. "What's going on?" asked Jack.

"Pastor Jack, it's Vinnie—Scissors. Krellick from the Crack City Brotherhood called them out to rumble at the old freight warehouse tonight, and he's getting the Razors together to go. Pastor Jack, I know Vince means well and wants to protect us all, but the Brotherhood's got crazy stuff we don't, and the Razors will get themselves killed. Pastor Jack, please pray that God'll do somethin' to save them from Crack City!"

17

PUZZLES SOLVED, MISSING PIECES

IT HAD BEEN a few days of the same routine. Each night, Melissana got inside her Zimata to check out Justin and Monica at the track. Each night, she just sat in her car for a while, tapping her keys against the steering column. Then she would get out of the Zimata and go back to her apartment. She knew about the Night Track, had even gone there a couple times to check it out. In a world where vehicular combat was a way of life, the Night Track was classified as entertainment. It started out as an amateur arena where kids and people who didn't have much to lose came to bet on their skills in mock combats. Local contestants could enter the gladiatorial events for gate shares and bet winnings. While none of the duels were officially to the death, Night Track events were dangerous enough that not everyone walked away.

The ticket revenue was sizable enough that there was always a steady stream of entrants. Word got out, crowds grew, as did the prizes, which drew in more competition. Eventually vehicle, armor, and weapons corporations heard of the events. Over time, they began sending local talent scouts to watch the combat events, looking to discover particularly skilled drivers and teams. In the world of corporate warfare, there was always need for good wheelmen, whether as couriers, interceptors, or the ever-necessary executive bodyguards. After that, some corps began using the arenas as a kind of beta-testing grounds for new ideas, weapons, and vehicles.

Once they saw the idea could work, corporations began to officially sponsor arenas in other towns, even organizing tournaments. Arenas were starting to pop up in many cities, and even fortress towns large enough to hold an arena had at least one for militia training. Night Track, though, had been one of the first, and remained one of the nastiest she had ever heard about. Now featuring amateur animosity coupled with corporate professional interests and prototype debuts, combat arenas were growing to be popular media events. She had lost a couple friends there—good friends, who were just trying to get a break. The night they died, they were driving a corporate-sponsored rig from a company that decided crowd sympathy was more important than immediate winnings. Putting the pieces together afterwards, she discovered the corporation her friends freelanced for had shorted their weapons feeding systems, making them an easy kill. Additionally, an agreement had been made that the three nobodies couldn't be left alive to spill the story. They were gunned down as they exited the vehicle. After that, she had no real desire to return.

Still, if Justin and Monica were working all day and then lighting up Night Track, they must be dead serious good at dueling, and dead-to-rights serious about whatever they were planning to do. She wanted to provide an overwatch for them, see if she could spot anyone following them. Finally, on the fifth night, Melissana started her car. She had pledged to chaperone them, so she headed to the Track. At least she wasn't wasting all night eavesdropping on the intimate conversations of two adults promising undying love to each other by poisoning the relationships they were already in.

… …

Though they both used an alias, it didn't take Melissana long to figure out who Justin and Monica were. After all, how many male/female teams could there be at this particular track, whose first appearance was on or shortly after May 29? Watching the excitement of machine guns and rockets, ramming and spinning, Melissana saw that as a team they really were pretty good. He had evidently augmented his previous amateur college experience by going through corporate executive protective combat driver training, and she was a focused and quite capable gunner. It was hard not to root for them, and even harder not to get involved by betting on them.

Melissana was relieved Justin wasn't cheating on Elaine. She decidedly liked Elaine, and was glad she could honestly tell her that her husband was not cheating. But then, what was really going on? She had done her job, so she could justify removing herself from the situation. Most professionals would simply stop there, and leave the rest behind, uncared for. She was trying to tell herself to just let the rest go. Take the creds, move on. The problem was she felt she was leaving something unresolved. As Justin and Monica won another round against two motorcycles, Melissana decided she had had enough for one night. It was now 2:15 A.M., Tuesday. This was the last week of the month. If whatever was going to happen was going to happen this weekend, she had little time to put the pieces together before then. She would have to think about it in the morning.

She had two choices. She could try to find out just what in Elaine's past was bad enough and worth enough to risk retribution by someone who was as significantly powerful as Justin Martinez. Whatever it was, it had to be evidence of something that the FoodTech executive wouldn't risk renting a mercenary force to get back; and whatever it was, it worked. She also noted that whoever was trying to blackmail him. Martinez didn't necessarily expect the payoff to go smoothly, so he involved his trusted friend and former gunnery partner as insurance. To make matters more complicated, and despite her respect for Elaine, Melissana was starting to get really curious about just what exactly that evidence was.

On the other hand, she could try to I.D. and track down the mystery caller who had started all this on the 29th. While maybe not as immediately gratifying, Melissana recognized that mystery was a little more relevant to the immediate situation. Getting the Martinez home number would not have been easy for a common street thug. Finding something worth turning Martinez into a blackmail mark had to have been harder still.

And if it really was that bad, she suddenly thought—whose side should the young detective be on? Blackmailers were commonly regarded as some of the lowest most cowardly scum, but maybe it was just some hacker who found out something that would cast a whole new light on "The Man Who Saved Earth." It all depended on not only what the score was, but the motive of who it was who was trying to score. That thought decided her—she had to know exactly what was going on, and since she only had a few days before the payoff, she decided to go for the caller. For now, it was time to sleep.

…… ……

Back in the Roa-Comm network Queen Vixenn paused, concerned that a direct number query on Martinez's number would trip an ICE alert. She then had an idea and started in earnest. The time was 10:40 A.M., Tuesday. She held her breath as she scanned all the incoming local line call logs in Martinez's sector for May 29, within a ten-minute timeframe of when Elaine said the original call came in. There were only 1,457 calls that matched. She breathed—it could have been a lot worse. Filtering out all calls by the duration of that phone call narrowed the list to 386. This time she sighed— the next steps would be tedious, but necessary to gather the data she needed without tripping any alarms. She logged out of Roa-Comm, then to completely clear her machine's cache, she deleted all browsing history, RAM, swap files, temp files, and any other system cache she could think of. Then she logged off her system, rebooted with another registry and cache cleanse, and logged back in to her system. Step One was done.

Over the next several hours, she repeated the process of bouncing a set of intermediary jumps to different remote hosts, re-hacking

Roa-Comm, capturing two or three of the 386 calls, screenshotting them to avoid direct data downloads, logging out of Roa-Comm, and cleaning up the link trail so the hacks wouldn't be traced back to her. One hundred fifty virtual trips and not a few coffees later, Step Two was done.

She got up, stretched, and ate. After a few calisthenics and a fifteen-minute stint of shadow kick-boxing to pump blood through her system, she went back to work. Step Three was waiting for her. That next step was to manually key the data from the 150 screenshots into a spreadsheet on her computer. By the time she was done, she had started singing to herself, but Step Three was now completed. Now all she had to do was filter by the Martinez's number as the recipient, cross-indexed with the incoming call ID list, and there it was—the number of the caller. Done! Stretching her neck, Melissana saw it was dark outside; it was 11:35 Tuesday night.

… …

The vid-phone rang, and Melissana checked the clock. 10:45 A.M., Wednesday.

"Focus Investigations," Melissana stated somewhat groggily.

"Melissana, is that you?" a familiar voice asked.

"Elaine? Why are you calling? That's kind of risky."

"I'm sorry, but Justin wasn't home last night. He's at work now, but I—I—I need to know if you've found anything."

"Where are you calling from?" the detective asked.

"I'm downtown. I traded something for someone's phone, I'm calling you on that."

Melissana almost let out a whistle. First the quick lie, now a trace-proof call. Again, she found herself asking just who Elaine really was.

"Elaine, please listen to me. I have stumbled onto…something. I'm not sure exactly what yet." *That* was safe enough for Melissana to say without tipping Elaine off to anything (she hoped!). "But I can say with absolute certainty he is absolutely *not* cheating on you, not a doubt in my mind."

Melissana was going to continue, but Elaine was openly weeping.

"*Thank you!!* Thank you! I can tell in your voice you're telling the truth! Thank you!" Sobbing and laughing so many thank you's, so profusely, Melissana could not find the heart to go on, and almost started to laugh herself. Elaine finally broke the call with a proclamation that Melissana had truly saved her marriage and her life. Her last statement was that on her own life, Elaine would fully pay Melissana a queen's ransom for the work she had done. Melissana was totally bewildered. What on Earth could anyone possibly have against Elaine, she wondered?

······

Melissana tried to get a lead on the number but found out that the caller had used a stolen phone. It was now Thursday morning. Melissana's phone rang, and Elaine was on the other end. "Melissana, you've been great to work with, and if I may, I would like to consider you a friend. You have certainly earned my trust when I really had nobody else I could turn to. I'd still like to keep our contacts discreet, if you don't mind. The reason I had to come to you in the first place was to keep all this a secret. Now that it's resolved, I would like to meet with you openly, but I can't afford to risk that just yet, if you don't mind."

"Sure, that's understandable," Melissana agreed. "Where would you like to meet?"

"How about downtown on the corner of Elm and Parkway?" Elaine suggested. "There are enough people randomly bumping into each other that we shouldn't be noticed. By now you know I was disguised; I'll wear that same disguise so you will recognize me." She laughed. "What a world we are in, wearing a disguise so someone will recognize me?" Elaine then continued. "I'll drop you an unregistered credstick with what you may consider as a down

146

payment on the debt I owe you for my life itself. Is that okay with you?"

"Yeah, that's great! But really, I didn't do all that much" Melissana stated, almost embarrassed.

"Not at all, I'm looking forward to being able to really show you how much I appreciate your service."

"Okay." Melissana smiled. "I'll see you at 2:30 P.M., then." The smile on Melissana's face remained as she hung up the phone, but then her expression changed. Something was bothering her about this conversation.

... ...

Not ten minutes after returning from her meeting with Elaine, her phone rang again. Picking up the receiver she greeted her caller, "Focus Investigations!"

"Mel, I finally got you!"

"Josie? What's going on? How are you and Lisben getting along?"

Josanne smiled. "What's going on with me? How about what's going on with you? I've been trying to call, where have you been?"

"Working." Melissana smiled, thinking about the last couple days. She called herself Focus Investigations for a reason—when she was working, she tended to lose contact with friends. Sometimes, just every once in a while, Melissana would have a case that just felt good when it was over. She still had sticker shock from what was on the credstick Elaine passed her. She had been worried that expensing the price of Night Track would set the relationship with Elaine on a nose dive. There hadn't been enough time to converse. Other than Elaine smiling at Melissana so genuinely and giving the detective an impromptu hug, the handoff had gone off without incident. They just more or less passed by each other. But she was glad she waited to get home before slotting the credstick. Because of Elaine's joy, Melissana had expected maybe 900 credits on the stick, but she was wrong. The balance was 18,000 credits. Melissana started, knocking her purse off her counter, spilling some of the contents. Picking up her belongings, she spotted two more credsticks.

"Ahem." Josanne cleared her throat, snapping Melissana out of her reverie.

"OH! Josie! How about you?" Melissana quickly replied, catching her own mind wandering, caught up in staring at the other two credsticks she was now holding in her hands. "Hey!" she cheerily offered, thinking of the small fortune now in her possession, "I have an idea! Can I take you out to dinner—if you don't have plans?"

"Great!" Josanne replied. "But come on, Melissana, I'll buy."

Melissana beamed, suddenly knowing how Elaine felt. She really enjoyed being able to be generous with her friend. "Not a chance, sister. I'm picking the place, and I'm buying," she declared.

Josanne agreed, noting the cheer on Melissana's face. Whatever she was working on must be paying good. "Okay, then—let's go!"

Melissana had an hour to kill before she would leave to meet with her friend, and she decided to use that time to check in again on Justin and Monica. The payoff would happen sometime this weekend, but exactly when and where they still didn't seem to know. She saw the two did have a conversation; decrypting it revealed the payoff would occur at a nearby quarry somewhere. Somehow that reminded the young P.I. of her meeting with Elaine, and again she thought something wasn't quite right. She drove the feeling off; she was going out for a good time with her friend.

··· ···

It wasn't the Golden Chalice, but the food was great, and the atmosphere was exactly what Melissana and Josanne needed to get caught up. They were both basking in the luxury, the food, each other's company, and every once in a while, a guy or two. This was *exactly* what Friday nights were supposed to be like!

"Well, things have been going great, but we had a problem yesterday," Josanne was telling Melissana. "Chance, one of our photo op journalists, got hurt. He was banged up by a bunch of bikers."

"In the city?" Melissana asked, surprised. Roanoke had its share of sprawl ghetto zones, but cops were still around in the city. They didn't get into the inter-archology ghetto zones much, but they patrolled the green sectors that were not quite archology, not quite slum zones. A journalist in a ghetto zone would get jumped by guys on foot, and archology security forces would be the likely choice for someone nosing around ICC business inside the archologies. Bikers inside the city didn't make much sense.

"No, not in the city. He was just doing some old historical stuff on some of the pre-strike industries. He really got it bad, though. He gets in a lot of tight situations, so he had a chip implant that monitors his vital signs and puts out an alarm signal if things get too crazy out of norm. Fortunately, the chip worked. He'll survive, but barely."

"Wow, where was he?" Melissana asked.

"He was just doing some quick shoots all over the place for an ad campaign. Then he went out to a scenic overlook by the big quarry north of town, and then it happened."

Something clicked in Melissana. She dropped her glass, causing those in the vicinity of their table to stop and see what was happening. Melissana didn't care, in part because she didn't notice. Martinez had mentioned in his conversation with Monica that the payoff would be at a quarry. Leaning forward, Melissana intensely, desperately, interrogated her friend. "Josanne, *where?*"

The newswoman repeated her story, confirming what the detective thought she'd heard. After Josanne finished, Melissana checked her watch as a sickening feeling came over her. The time was 6:59, Friday evening. With a rushed and minimal apology to her friend, she bolted from the table. She had work to do.

…… ……

She had to move fast. The streetwise sleuth preferred subtlety, taking her time gathering data from only the slightest twinges of the information network. She would rather not risk drawing attention to her darknet work, but there was no time for that now. She still had the number of Justin's mystery caller. The phone had been stolen, so she knew she could not conclusively I.D. the caller from the phone's account, but urgency drove her to new thoughts and ambitions she hadn't considered daring before.

The young Queen first hacked the email account of a cop she knew and got the email addresses of several cops from his contact list. She then hacked some of their accounts. Eventually she worked her way up high enough the chain of command that she could impersonate a Captain of Detectives and gain access to his remote connection to the Roanoke Police Database. She then ran a daemon program to watch for the blue ICE of the law enforcement agency's IT unit. After that, she queried the database phone fields and crime description text narratives for the report of exactly when that phone had been stolen. She came up with May 26, three days before the call to Martinez. *Good and bad,* she thought to herself. Good because she only needed to go through three days of Roa-Comm phone logs, bad because it appeared the phone was stolen specifically for the blackmail.

She paused, once again thinking of her meeting with Elaine earlier that day, resurrecting the feeling that something was not quite right. It wasn't that she mistrusted Elaine, but something about that meet was really starting to irritate her. The time was 10:54 P.M., Friday.

Cracking back into Roa-Comm as her cop persona, Vixenn now searched for any phone logs either in or outbound associated with that phone number. She hoped that, at least for the time she was hacked in to the phone company, a cop searching through phone logs of a stolen phone wouldn't seem too far out of place. There was a total of sixty-three phone conversation logs recorded since the reported theft. Only six were outbound—all to Martinez.

She smiled. "Hello! You're from today!" she observed, noting the timestamps of the last two calls. She decided to focus her attention to those last two calls. One hundred forty-seven seconds later, she had retrieved Roa-Comm's voice recording transcripts of the last inbound call. The call came in at 1:57 P.M., just about the time she'd left her meeting with Elaine. It was only about ninety seconds long.

"Yeah?" a gruff, low voice, spoken quietly answered. Sounded tough.

"Meet's on, at the old quarry in what used to be Staunton, off I-81 North," pronounced a second gruff voice.

Melissana thought she was overhearing a soundtrack from an ancient gangster movie.

"So, the Road Ragers are coming?"

"They're already there," said the caller, with a guttural grunt that could have served for a laugh. "Some reporter stumbled into 'em, but they took care of 'im. Only a miracle if he's ever found."

< A chuckle> "Heh, we're not in the miracle business."

< Return chuckle from caller> "No, we are not."

"All right, I'll call and tell him."

"You sure he'll show?"

"Target'll be there. He's saving his wife."

< Another chuckle> "Yeah well, if this goes well, maybe he'll get to tell her all about it."

< Barking laugh> "All right, I gotta go. I'll phone target and see you tomorrow."

Nine, then. Good work."

<CLICK>

Melissana fumed. On top of everything else about that call, the mention of Elaine plus the nagging feeling about that meeting was driving her nuts, and she still had to try to get some sleep tonight!

As she lay tossing, she thought about how Justin and Monica felt. Maybe they were sleepless tonight as well. She hoped *somebody* got some rest that night, because those two voices on the phone sounded like they were professionals. Plus, somehow Josie's bike gang was involved in this? She almost growled, but instead just stole a glare at her clock. The time was 1:45 Saturday morning. Eventually her tiredness took over, and Melissana somehow drifted off to sleep.

PART 2

CONVERGENCE

"A human being becomes human not through the casual convergence of certain biological conditions, but through an act of will and love on the part of other people."

— Italo Calvino
Letters, 1941–1985

18

BREAK JOBS

IT HAD BEEN a week since the attack on Hagerstown. The fortress town was still a mess, but the residents weathered the storm with the same tenacity they wielded during the actual assault itself. They had taken a brutal pounding, but they would continue on. Handsight once again seemed to be everywhere—helping with the reconstruction of the defenses, checking in on the populace, helping Jimmy clean up the wreckage that was everywhere. Samantha also seemed to be everywhere—rendering assistance to those in need, helping with food distribution, helping parents organize childcare, just visiting with families. The work seemed to be endless.

When not towing cars and wreckage to be salvaged or just moved off the roads leading to the city, Jimmy was busy organizing teams to clear the town of the damage caused by the shelling. Though he tried not to show it, the brief time he had led the town's defense changed him, left him with the impression he was not up to the task of being Handsight's second in command. He appreciated Handsight more than ever; that hour or so he was filling in for the man showed him he was in way over his head. He'd have to talk with Handsight about that. For the immediate present, he'd keep his mind busy with what was at hand.

The Cryo-Jaegers were burying their dead. Based off reports turned in by his wedge, The Wolfram Knight's Dragontooth was found about 100 yards from the group that had been overrun by the bikers. From all appearances, Wolfram tried to rescue the cut off wedge, but the bikers recognized his vehicle as he headed towards the group. Realizing he was leading his own wedge into a trap, he ordered them to retreat. What his wedge did not know was that The Wolfram Knight continued his charge so the rest of his element would have a chance to make a break for it. His ploy worked. Enough bikers had noted his hated Dragontooth that nearly every one of them went after him. Eventually, during the weave of the chase, his Dragontooth caught one of the spike plates strewn about the battlefield by the bikers. They buried their leader as he had trained them to fight—as a unit.

Over his grave was a cross-shaped headstone bearing an eagle engraved over an emblazoned shield, the eagle's outstretched wings spanning both arms of the cross. The eagle held an unfurled scroll that curled down the length of the post. On the scroll were the words, "Here lies Gerald Jefferson, commander of the Cryo-Jaegers. He died as he lived, defending those he loved. Always hard, never melting, ever a shining light in the darkness—forever The Wolfram Knight." Engraved on the eagle's left wing was the word "Honor," and on the right, "Courage." Corey and Susan both cried. Nobody judged them for it; they were not alone.

For her part, when Karen was not at home she was glued to one spot—in front of her computer screens. She of course called for the IT teams to run full security scans on all the town's systems, scanning for lingering vulnerabilities, how the hacker had gotten into their systems in the first place, and any signs or clues the hacker may have left behind that might lead her closer to him. As she expected, despite the team's expertise, nothing was found except the satellite images he had left for her. Who was Iylothien? Who in Hagerstown had the hacking capabilities to do what he had done? The IT team wanted to send the report to the creator of their network security and ICE providers, but Handsight wouldn't permit it.

"He saved our lives," Handsight had said. "We owe him our skins. He's obviously on our side, whoever he is. Don't hand him over to them." That was all he needed to say on the matter.

··· ···

On the final day of the battle, the combined forces of Alloys Incorporated and Penn's Rangers linked up with the Cryo-Jaegers. Together, they were able to fight their way through the remaining forces of the Steel Jackals. Finally, the last vestiges of the Steel Jackals broke. The path to Iron Mike's camp headquarters was now wide open. The town defenders closed the distance with prejudice.

They didn't need to hurry. Iron Mike was there waiting to greet them. He would've waited all day, all week. Evidently, Handsight had read the group correctly, and his strategy paid off after all. By the time the defenders and their allies had arrived, most of Iron Mike waited sitting in a chair that must have been his command throne for the siege. Whoever was now in charge of the Steel Jackals had Iron Mike's head impaled on a pole. When Corey definitively identified the body, Handsight pronounced the final verdict.

"It's over, kid. The fact that they impaled his head proves it. Either his head or yours—those are the terms of a Blood Vengeance. They admitted defeat—you beat your death sentence."

··· ···

Both Corey and Sue were suddenly exhausted, and only dimly aware that the threat of the last four months was finally over. They had peace, but they were still in the war zone of the city that they had helped to create. Everywhere they turned, everywhere they looked, all they could see was the carnage that had been caused by their existence. Even the Jensen's, Handsight and his wife Samantha, were barely hanging on, finding their only comfort in the solace they were able to offer others. So much had been fought for them, so much had been sacrificed. Finally, they could take it no longer. They had to leave and get a break from it all.

Late Friday afternoon on the day they were to leave, they met with Handsight and Samantha one last time before heading out of town. "You sure you want to leave now?" was all Handsight asked. "I mean, you're of course free to go, but this town took a serious beating for you kids. You're leaving us now?" The expression on Samantha's face was heartbreaking, especially to Susan. The older pair had meant a lot to her and Corey, and they had helped a lot in their healing process.

"We're just reminders now," Susan offered. "We're still trying to get past all this ourselves. We don't know anybody. How can we possibly be able to even say anything, other than we're terribly, horribly sorry?"

Samantha's eyes started to tear, knowing Susan was right despite her wishing she was wrong. Handsight just grumbled a, "Well, maybe that's all you'd need to say."

"We'll be back," Susan gently offered in encouragement. "We promise. We just need to get away from all of this for a couple weeks to recuperate. I'm sorry. I really, *really* am." At that point, she could say no more.

"We're going to North Carolina for a little while," Corey chimed in to fill in the gap. "Let her get re-acquainted with her family. I'm sure we'll be back in about a month or so."

"It's okay, kid," Handsight admitted. You guys been going through this for months now. We've just been hit for one week. I said it before, I'll say it again. I have no idea how you kids did this, but we all owe you our thanks."

"There's no way we would have possibly made it without you, sir," Corey confessed, starting to choke up. "Thank you for everything."

With that, Handsight was on the radio. Now that the chaff had dissipated, the frequency was again clear. "Jimmy, open up Garage Three and show Hardcore his rig. We couldn't keep 'em, but I can't say I don't agree with their need to get away for a while, either. Let's let 'em know how Hagerstown shows our appreciation."

Jimmy emitted a "Roger, Handsight," and the door to Garage Three opened. A team of five mechanics rolled out a fully restored, good as mint condition, reworked, restocked, and freshly repainted midnight black Sabretooth. Across the hood was an emblem in gold of an anvil with lightning bolts coming out of it. Mounted on a rearing medieval warhorse on top of the anvil was a knight in black cryoplast armor holding an extended lance. The word "Hardcore" was emblazoned across the top. On the left front fender, in gold, was the word "Honor." On the right, "Courage." Nor was Susan left out. On each door was a running black wolf with Susan's face half-morphed onto the wolf face. Corey was speechless. Mouth agape, he just gawked back and forth from Handsight, then to Jimmy, then to Susan. Sue just smiled, delighted the secret had been so skillfully executed.

"I—I don't know what to say…" he finally admitted.

"You're welcome, kid," Handsight declared, as he approached Corey, shook his hand, then embraced. Samantha and Susan laughed—the most emotion Handsight's wife had publicly expressed since they lost their sons in the attack several years ago. Jimmy then approached, extending his hand. "Been a pleasure to get to know you two. We'll miss you both. Hope you guys come back real soon."

To add to the moment's emotion, every remaining Cryo-Jaeger formed a double parade line that extended to the city gates. In an almost ghostly reminder of how they had first entered Hagerstown, Corey and Sue left as much a center of attraction as when they had first arrived. Only this time, as they passed each Cryo-Jaeger, each citizen defender, each man, woman, and child in the crowd came to a standing salute.

Corey and Sue paused just before going through the exit gate. They looked at each other, smiled, held hands for a moment. Then Corey took a deep breath. "Ready?" he asked.

"We're alive, we're together. Corey, at your side, I'm ready for anything!"

"Okay, then, let's go," he said.

"With Honor and Courage," she responded with a smile.

Passing through the gate, they held hands tightly. Once outside the walls, they paused again. Then Corey exhaled, declaring, "Asheville, here we come." He hit the accelerator, and the pair headed off to find I-81 south.

19

MEETINGS

JACK STOOD IN the old industrial warehouse parking lot, praying silently while staring out into the blackness just beyond the illumination from the single working lamp post. In its day, the lot had been host to countless tractor trailers hauling machine parts to destinations all over the country. Now, like most of the industry itself, many of those cities probably didn't even exist anymore. Jack waited in the spot of light, praying he could negotiate a gang truce between the Razors and the Crack City Brotherhood.

Shivering, Jack thought he noticed a sudden chill in the August night air and wondered if it was real or just his nerves going on edge. Turning up the collar on his coat, Jack continued to pray silently. *Lord, here I am. I don't know exactly what You want me to do. I don't even know what I* can *do, but I'm here.*

The meet was set for midnight. After he'd heard about the upcoming rumble from Scissors's younger brother, Jack called up the leaders of his church's prayer groups. First, he advised them of the situation, then he asked them to get their prayer chains going. In minutes, each of them called the people on their group lists. Within a half hour, the entire church was praying about the gang war soon to occur. Jack was not the least among them.

While he was praying in his apartment, though, Jack began to feel as though he should do something about it. The only problem was he didn't know what exactly it was he was supposed to do. At first, he dismissed the notion. As he prayed, though, he became more and more annoyed that he *wasn't* going. Pretty soon, he gave in to the only idea he had. He would meet with the rival gang and try to talk them into leaving.

He knew it didn't make any sense, but he also knew that he had to at least make the attempt. He got up and put on his long overcoat. Despite the August heat, it at least appeared to offer a little protection against blows and knives. He made one phone call to Rita Williams and explained to her what he was doing. After receiving a special prayer of blessing from her, he grimly smiled against some resurrected memories. Inspired by those memories, he donned a seasoned fedora to complete his outfit for old time's sake and headed out the door.

Jack expected each of the gangs to show up about an hour or so early to set up traps and ambushes. He arrived about 9:00 P.M., leaned on the solitary working lamp post, and waited. It was now 10:30 P.M. He waited.

Though he heard footsteps approach from behind him, Jack continued to face forward, studying the darkness in the direction from which the Crack City Brotherhood would approach.

"We have to talk," a low, grim voice quietly spoke from behind him, almost under its breath. Jack closed his eyes and inwardly sighed, choosing not to answer, hoping he was having a nightmare. He shrugged his shoulders against the chill he now knew to be his nerves. The bad night had just gotten a lot worse. The voice spoke again.

"Nice night for stargazing," the somber voice said. Jack closed his eyes and again sighed, then renewed his vigil.

"Yeah," Jack somberly replied. "Only it's not stars I'm looking for. How've you been?"

"Busy," replied the voice from behind, closer now. Jack felt the owner's approach, the voice coming up behind him and to his left, entering the halo of the lone streetlight. He knew the other one would be behind and slightly to his right. Jack maintained his scan of the darkness ahead of him.

"You?" asked the voice.

"Busy," Jack replied, not relaxing.

"So we heard."

Jack paused. "How's Rick?" he asked at last.

"Still rollin'," the grim voice answered.

"He here?"

"He's tending biz up north a little. Sends greets." A pause, then: "You ready for this?"

"Yeah, I guess. I want to talk to them, try to keep this from happening. The kids have families, and those families are scared. The Razors really aren't as tough as they used to be, and…"

"And it's 'cause of you, isn't it? These are tough streets, and wars happen. They're a gang. They've got their fights. It happens."

"No, this isn't normal. The Razors have been getting easier, but this other gang has a supplier somewhere. They're not just a street gang anymore. They've got backing, and that backer is giving them weapons and gear that are impossible for normal streets to get hold of."

"So, what are you going to do? Ask them to just put down their toys and leave?"

"I don't know! I'm going to try to talk to them, get them to—"

"Repent?" the voice asked with a sneer.

"Yes," Jack soberly affirmed. Though he really hadn't intended to say the word, the thought now spoken offered the focus of the vague reasoning he'd had since deciding to come out. Still peering into the darkness, he continued. "I can't just sit back and watch all this happen. I have to at least try."

"You still got your spit," the voice approvingly judged. "You know, I guess you really haven't changed all that much after all. You sure there's no way we can peaceably talk to you somewhere else for a while?"

163

The compliment found its mark, and the ice was finally broken. "No," Jack stated, hopefully sounding more assured than he felt. "I've got to at least try. You know how that feels. Right now, I belong here, and I'm staying."

"Yeah, us, too." With that, the two figures stepped up to Jack's side into his peripheral view. Jack glanced at each of them, and already found himself drawing strength from them. He smiled, adjusted his jacket lapel, and stood fully, removing himself from the streetlight he had been leaning on. For all his anxiety about his past, and the tension of the night, he was now grateful he had some friends beside him. Oddly enough, now *especially* these two. Memories came to him, and he had to make a conscious effort to focus his mind on the present. After a few minutes, the voice on his right spoke. It was not as deep, but softer, and had a Hispanic accent.

"Just like old times, eh *Jefe*?"

Jack nodded. "Yeah."

"You want one of these?" A brown hand held out to Jack what appeared to be a tiny hearing aid.

"I guess it wouldn't hurt, but we're here to talk, okay?"

"Suits me fine," said the forbidding voice on his left. "But this thing may not go how you want it to."

It already hasn't, Jack thought, as he slipped the earpiece into position. It had been years since he had last used one of these, and he was surprised at how quickly and easily he had inserted the device. Instantly he became aware of several inner body noises stirring within him. Almost immediately he automatically filtered these out, adjusting his hearing to focus on the Hispanic voice now inside his head.

- *"Testing, testing. Do I have you?"*

- *"Yeah," Jack stated under his breath, answering through his sub-vocal transceiver. He even used throat control to project his speech through his Eustachian tube rather than vocally. The skill took about four solid months of training to obtain; Jack used it, even after all this time, without even needing to think about how. All that was on his mind was the pure irony of his response:*

- *"Yeah, you got me."*

…… ……

"Movement," Arañé quietly announced after another fifteen minutes had lapsed in silence. They were standing under a streetlight, and the approaching gangers were out of earshot; there was no need to use the sub-vocalizers at this point.

"Got 'em," Jack answered, still peering into the darkness. "I got five or six coming around the stack of crates."

"Oh boy…party time," Chrome murmured.

"Remember now," Jack said, "we're here to talk."

"Correction," Chrome responded. "*You're* here to talk. *We're* here to back you up—for old times' sake, if nothing else."

"Yeah," Jack grunted, then added, "Hey, Chrome? Arañé? Thanks." Jack paused, then continued. "Listen, in case anything goes real wrong here, I want you guys to know now that I appreciate all you've done for me."

"No problem, Jefe," Arañé said, with his usual grin. "It ain't like we don't owe *you* a couple."

"Yeah." Jack smirked. "Thanks again, though."

By then, about fifteen members of the Crack City Brotherhood assembled at the stack of crates on the opposite end of the warehouse lot. The trio knew there had to be more in the area, probably occupying some of the abandoned buildings. Points and gestures revealed to Jack and his friends that the Brotherhood group at the crates had also spotted them. The fifteen spread themselves out into a vague, concave rank. They then advanced about half the distance to the three men. Three figures emerged from the center of the loose line of the Brotherhood and approached the streetlight.

Here we go, Jack thought, sizing up the three as they approached.

The central figure had to be Krellick, one of the principal leaders of the Brotherhood. Not especially tall but with a bulldog build, he radiated hatred, fear, and *disgust.* Jack could see in his eyes the flat appearance of bored disregard for the life of anyone not immediately connected with his gang. Those eyes might flicker to life at the sight of another Brother, or to rage at the sight of an enemy, but would disgustedly regard anyone else as nothing more than an ant to be stepped on and crushed at whim. Jack had seen eyes like that before, and the memories almost made him shudder. Maybe life had been cruel to Krellick, but Jack could see in the ganger's eyes that Krellick was also cruel to life.

The head belonging to those eyes had brown hair just longer than shoulder length. It seemed like it hadn't been combed in a month. He wore a denim jacket that looked like it had plates sewn into the body of it. His jeans also sported ragged pieces of heavy leather and metal on the fronts and sides of his legs. Complementing this, he wore boots with razors attached to the soles, sides, and toes. Leather gloves with a bowie knife strapped to the top of each, and razors along the outer side of each hand, completed his macabre outfit. He held a piece of chain that had sharpened bolts fastened on along its length, and Jack knew he must have had other weapons as well.

To Krellick's right was one of the tallest men Jack had ever seen. An easy six feet five inches, Jack concluded immediately he must have worked out lifting cinderblocks. His head was completely shaven except for a high orange, green, and purple Mohawk that only added to his height. He wore a plate-lined leather jacket similar to Krellick's, but except for a spiked knee pad, heavy boots, and a metal plate taped on to shield each hand, he was comparatively unarmored. He openly carried a large, ham-shaped club with spikes driven into the business end. Jack also knew that was probably not his only weapon, either. His eyes were not as completely disinterested in all non-gang life forms. Instead, they openly jeered at them. He wore an undisguised smirk of contempt as they approached.

The one on Krellick's left was about Chrome's size but with a slimmer build. He'd painted his face in honor of the night's festivities. His entire face was bone white, with the exception of a black band, like a mask, around his eyes. Random streaks of dark green had been added. He, too, was dressed to kill, wearing a full-length coat similar to Jack's. Similar, Jack noted, but not identical. The bulk underneath indicated that it, too, was armored, Jack thought at first, and then he almost visibly started. The coat wasn't lined with leather or plates after all. Underneath his coat the guy, was wearing a full suit of—

- *"Cryoplast," Jack heard Arañé declare with disgust inside his head.*

So, the rumors were true, Jack thought. A street gang may have their hands on a few odds and ends of the tough, bulletproof, hyper-frozen ceramic and plastic polymer, but in no way could they have gotten a perfectly tailor-fitted full suit of the stuff. The Brotherhood definitely had some backing. But why them? Jack almost cursed. Why *here*?

Currently Number Three wasn't carrying anything, but Jack knew that wouldn't last long.

Lord, is there any *way I can talk to them?* Jack prayed silently. *Did You really want me here?*

When the three figures approached to within twelve feet, Armor-man swung an eighteen-inch shotgun from under his coat. Jack also saw at least three other weapons. They got to within five feet before they stopped, Armor-man fully training his shotgun on Arañé. For a moment, there was a tense silence.

… …

167

Reigis and Zip occupied the catwalk of an old billboard overlooking the parking lot. Zip began laying out the duo's rifles while Reigis scanned the area with his binoculars. They were the gang's sniper team tonight, but first they had to locate targets.

The glow from the lone streetlight drew Reigis's eyes, so naturally he started his coverage there. He immediately rechecked with his binoculars what he thought he'd seen with his naked eyes. He was on a headset radio instantly.

"Scissors? Reigis here. I know you're pretty busy on the ground now, but you'd better get up here, quick." A pause followed, then, "You'll see when you get up here."

Two minutes passed, then an angry Scissors stormed onto the catwalk.

"All right! What's so important tonight that you're distracting me from the ground?"

To his surprise, both Razors urged him to be quiet, an extreme outrage to the gang's leader. If not for Reigis's rep for his loyalty and judgment, Scissors would have had them both beaten for their insolence. As it was, his outrage gave over to curiosity when Reigis, still watching the warehouse lot, extended his binoculars over his back to Scissors, along with a single utterance. "Check it out," he whispered, pointing down to the streetlamp.

"What's *he* doing here?" demanded Scissors upon recognizing Jack. "What's he think he's doing?"

"I don't know," Reigis responded. "Looks like those two guys finally found him. They were standing there when we got up here. You think they're sellin' us?"

"No way," Zip inserted. "If he wanted to do that, he would have done it years ago, right, Scissors?"

"Yeah, null sweat, Zip," Scissors answered, remembering the way he'd treated Preach at the compound. "Well, well, they've got company," he added, seeing the Brotherhood approach.

"You want us to lay some cover fire for them? Those two guys he's with might be pretty tough, but they're not even armed, as far as I can tell."

Scissors considered it for a moment, then decided.

"No, let's wait and see what they're pulling. Set up the Sounder, and let's just sit back and see what happens here," Scissors said, with grim curiosity.

Zip and Reigis began at once to ready the portable parabolic microphone. Normally there wasn't much of a need for them in a war, but now they were glad they had it. They would hear everything the groups would say to each other.

…… ……

"Move," Krellick ordered disinterestedly.

Lord, here goes, Jack prayed, as he began to exhale his response. "I'm here to talk," Jack declared.

Mohawk contemptuously eyed up Chrome. Armor-man grinned at Arañé. Krellick didn't budge, save to drop the chain from his left hand, letting it jingle as it loosely swung from his right.

"You a Razor?" he said, glowering at Jack.

Jack thanked God for his success so far.

"No," replied Jack. "I'm a minister in—"

Krellick raised a hand to his mouth, poorly choking back a laugh and insultingly pointing at Jack. "Wait—I heard about you. You're Preach?" Krellick asked, amused. "*You're* Preach? You tellin' me those altar boy Razors of yours sent you out here? What'd they do, ask you to come out here and fight for them? Or let me guess. They want you to bore us to death!"

Chrome shifted, his jaw tightening as the insults spewed out against his friend. Arañé's eyes moved back and forth from Armor-man to Krellick to Jack.

169

"Easy, Little Man," Mohawk said to Chrome. "You ain't nearly big enough." Armor-man just giggled a little, keenly eyeing Arañé. Suddenly, Krellick turned his attention to Jack's left.

"But you're no preacher, are you?" he said, taunting Jack. His eyes appraising the muscular crew-cutted man wearing jeans, a black t-shirt, and sunglasses. Chrome just returned his stare.

"No weapons, no armor. Oh, you're a tough one, all right. But you're not a Razor, are you? I don't recognize you. Besides, not even Razors are stupid enough to come out here without weapons and armor.

"Okay, so we know who you're not. So, humor me, tough man, who are you?"

 - *"Go ahead, Chrome," Jack transmitted.*

"My name's Chrome," he said, almost threateningly.

Mohawk jumped in. "Oooh, that's scary!" he said, mocking him. "And who's the dirt—Tinsel?"

"No, not Tinsel," Arañé somehow lightly replied. "My friends call me Arañé—you know, like Spider," he said, somehow managing an easy smile.

"Kill the clown act, dirt-boy, or we kill the clown. We ain't your friends, dirt-boy, and we ain't likely to ever be," Armor-man retorted, again giggling, fingering his shotgun.

"Now hold on here," Krellick calmly ordered. "Come on, Preach," Krellick continued. "Come on and do your thing. Come on, you came to talk. So, talk." Suddenly sobering, Krellick's eyes glared at the so-far silent Jack.

"I know that you might feel like the more violent you are, the more power you have, but you're wrong. The more you rely on the power you wield, the more enslaved you become to it." Jack, given his chance, began with a confidence he didn't completely feel. "Why start this war? It'll only enslave you further. Allow God to—"

170

- "You still got your spit, Jack," he heard Chrome say in his transceiver.

The sudden voice caused Jack to pause. Krellick's eyes almost glowed red.

… …

"Scissors, they're in trouble. I guess he was trying to head off the war. Do we go now?"

"No, hold on. Preach isn't that dumb," Scissors responded.

"Remember when he first moved into the 'hood? Didn't he try the same thing with us?"

"Yeah, but those two guys he's with? They know streets. No, something's happening. I wanna see what Preach is up to. Let's wait a little while and see."

… …

"Slaves? *Us* slaves? Choober, we own this town now. As a matter of fact, we own *you* now. I'll tell you how much of a nice guy you've made me, though. When we get through trashin' the Razors, I'll be nice and intimate with you, and show you how much I appreciate this chat of ours. We all will. Now, like I said before. Move, you—"

Chrome's jaw tightened as the insults again poured forth. Maybe Jack could handle that, but how was something Chrome could not understand. Mohawk cut in on his thoughts.

"Watch it, Little Man. You're gettin' jumpy," he said, sneering. "You move once, and I'll split your side from your ribs to your throat," he coolly threatened, grinning.

Chrome calmly looked up at him.

- "Arañé?" he asked over his throat mike.

- *"Your guy has the club, three knives, and a pistol inside his jacket: standard slug thrower type, .45 caliber. Mine has a pepper gun in his sleeve and three slug pistols of various calibers. Mouth has the chain and a pistol, Gauss from the energy cell. Jack was right. These guys are definitely fed by somebody.*

- *"Right building, second floor, third and fourth right windows, slug rifles. Left building, first floor, second window, slug rifle.*

- *"In the line-up: Man # 2, 5, 7, 9, and 11 have pistols; 3 and 14 have shotguns; 15 has two grenades and an autorifle. All the rest are normals—various armors like your man. There's also some movement behind us, and somebody in the area is using a Sounder."*

- *"Jack?" Chrome sub-vocally asked.*

- *"I came to talk," the street preacher electronically answered.*

"Come on, Little Man," grinned Mohawk. "You look like you're going to wet your diaper. What's a matter? Didn't your mom ever train you? Come to think of it—"

- *"Jack?" Chrome again asked, trying to sound patient.*

- *"I'm here to talk, Chrome."*

- *"This might not work your way this time, Jack."*

"—left, too, if I'd have had a kid as ugly as you," Mohawk finished.

Chrome raised his head and stared through his sunglasses into the face of Mohawk, who now prepared his massive club for a swing.

- *"Chrome..."* Jack *called through his transceiver, trying to keep his man from losing his temper.*

"Don't move," Armor-man grimly ordered, as he tightened his grip on his shotgun and watched Arañé.

... ...

"Now?" asked Reigis, aiming his rifle at the person with the shotgun.

"Wait, wait just a little longer," Scissors patiently commanded.

"I've got Broze, too, Reig," Zip confirmed. "We won't both miss."

"You two just hold until I say. I wonder what they're up to..."

"That's easy," Reigis said. "They're up to over their heads in Crack City."

"Okay, get ready to shoot. But if Preach and his friends make it out of this, I want answers from him!"

... ...

Chrome turned and looked at Arañé.

- *"Chrome..."* Jack *said again.*

"What's the matter?" Mohawk menacingly grimaced. "Your mother dead or something?"

Chrome again looked up at his tormentor, who was obviously enjoying his own sense of humor.

- *"Chrome..."*

Chrome sighed. "You don't know my mother," he finally intoned flatly. Then he looked up into Mohawk's eyes, smiled, and added, "I doubt you know yours, you drek-faced sorry excuse of a govek."

Ten years before the missile crisis, government bureaucracy was at its zenith. In its somewhat-less-than-infinite wisdom, a federal government think tank came up with a program that offered a cash-for-your-child program to buy off welfare recipients. In theory, their government boarding schools would teach the children how to grow into respectable citizens, thus breaking the welfare cycle. One of its more visibly evident problems was that, in an effort to achieve cost efficiency, the young students were often ignored, underfed, or treated like hardened criminals. Additionally, since they were brought up by the government, they actually learned to become even more reliant on welfare-type government programs than ever before. This placed even greater strain on the shrinking tax base. In the end, the program and most of those who participated were deemed utter failures. The program failed so miserably that govek, or government kid, was now a deeply stinging insult implying helplessness, laziness, worthlessness, and almost any other stigma society had. Chrome's remark hit home.

"*Die*, Little Man!" Mohawk screamed. A flick of his muscular forearm snapped the huge, spiked club into an upward side-arc that would have punctured, uplifted, and knocked over a file cabinet.

Chrome's left arm swirled even faster in a counterclockwise arc that impacted against the massive weapon, both slightly splitting it and causing the force of the club's swing to jar the handle out of Mohawk's grip. Chrome wasn't even off balance.

Everyone was tensely still, watching as the heavy club clattered to the pavement. Trailing wood fragments hung suspended in the lamp-lit air between the two men like they had gravity fields all their own. Chrome looked down at the fallen weapon, now cracked, then back up to the tall man. All Mohawk was doing at the moment was staring, slack-jawed in dismay, soothing his sore wrist.

"Oh, I almost forgot," Chrome added after a moment. He stared squarely into Mohawk's eyes without flinching and smiled again. "Ouch."

... ...

"How did you do that?" Mohawk asked, nearly whimpering.

"I told you that you didn't know who my mother was. I'll explain this to you in tiny little words so you can understand it.

"You see, there's been a marriage of man and machine," Chrome said, grinning, "and I'm its first spawn." With the closing of his proclamation, Chrome brought his right arm back, stepped forward, and in a blur hurled a fist into Mohawk's plate-armored leather jacket. The force of the blow penetrated Mohawk's chest plating and, from the crunching sound within, probably broke a few of Mohawk's ribs. The impact launched the giant airborne; but with unprecedented speed and strength, Chrome opened his fist and grabbed Mohawk's leather jacket as he began to speed away. The sudden jerk from the catch whiplashed the ganger further, and the giant, once fierce, now hung limply suspended in the air by Chrome.

"I have an idea," Chrome said to the now beaten and shaken gang member who had been so full of taunts. "Since we seem to be such good friends, let's play a game.

"I know," Chrome continued, now grinning maliciously. "How about—*Paddleball*?"

... ...

"*HOLD FIRE!*" Scissors commanded.

"What the he—*what happened?*" Zip asked, dumbfounded.

"I don't know, but I *know* that guy with Preach ain't wearing any armor. That swing should have leveled him even if he was!" Reigis responded.

"Shut up, both of you!" Scissors demanded. "I gotta think. Zip, watch Broze and that shotgun of his; Reigis, pick a new target, or something." Raising the binoculars back to his eyes, he renewed his study of the confrontation below.

"Wolfman," he spoke into his headset, "forget about meeting at the light. Circle your group left, around to the factory buildings. Watch for traps and ambushes, the place is already crawling with Brotherhood. Also, Preach is down at the light. Get ready to cover for him and the two muscles that were looking for him. They're together. And Wolf—don't let Preach leave without saying goodbye."

 ... ...

Armor-man screamed with murderous intent as he returned his gaze and his shotgun's aim back onto Arañé. Spider moved. His right arm shot out in an outward circle, deflecting the shotgun and its blast outward and up. He gripped the barrel, then spun into a crouch like an ice ballerina on a good day. A half second later, when his spin was almost complete, he kicked out his left leg. Armor-man, already off balance from having his weapon almost skewed out of his arms over Spider's spinning body, had his legs swept out from under him and was heaved over his assailant's shoulders. He fell heavily, almost as fast as Spider had spun, discharging another blast from the shotgun as he hit the macadam. Spider, still gripping the barrel, now sprang to his feet, breaking Armor-man's fingers as he tore the weapon away from him.

Hearing a shot from the Brotherhood lineup, Spider quickly rolled backward over his right shoulder, obtaining a crouch position almost immediately behind the stunned Armor-man's head. He nudged the weapon into the base of Armor-man's skull to make that point known.

"Be very still, my friend," Arañé warned him with a smile. "I won't miss."

Broze, fingers broken, rang out with a maniacal laugh like the caged animal he was. In a rage, he wildly began scissor-kicking his legs, trying to trip Arañé up, but whatever Broze seemed to be on, he wasn't fast enough. Where Chrome was built for raw strength, Arañé was wired for reflexes and speed. Jack had seen Arañé do speed drills before, but even he was having a hard time tracking Arañé's movements. Like a football player running a tire drill, Arañé just picked up his feet to avoid the kicks. Finally, he bound to the other side of the fallen Crack City Brother and hit him over the head with the shotgun, knocking the ganger to unconsciousness.

With Jack temporarily distracted, Krellick swung the chain in a tight circling snap that could have smashed Jack's skull had it connected. Jack spotted Krellick twist his left side back to add more power and speed to the right-handed strike and ducked low to avoid the deadly instrument. Whirling inside the arc of the chain, Jack maneuvered into Krellick in a low spin. Once close enough, he shot his arm straight up into Krellick's chin while snapping to a standing combat stance. Krellick's head popped back, taking the rest of his body with him. Before he hit the ground, Jack caught him in a judo hold and tumbled over him, using his inert form as a shield against the rest of the Brotherhood lineup.

"DROP 'EM RIGHT NOW!!" Jack yelled with an authority the Razors had never heard come from their docile, pushover preacher. Crack City Brotherhood was better funded, equipped, and armored than the Razors, but they had just seen their gang leader and two of his toughest lieutenants taken out in a few seconds; their best just took a dive from some wuss preacher and a couple of his unarmed friends. The remaining Brotherhood melted back into the shadows, disappearing like roaches when a light's turned on.

Jack himself couldn't believe it. He watched the Brotherhood members go, filing out in silence, beaten. Arañé's voice was again in his ear, audibly grinning.

- *"Just like old times, eh, Jefe?"*

Even Chrome smiled. Then he looked at Krellick and Mohawk.

"Well," he said, taunting them, "maybe you little boys won't mind letting us know where you get your toys now." Jack absently glanced up at the night sky to thank God for the victory He had let Jack have, against all possible odds. The gangers were all leaving, the battle never fought. Then Jack noticed a flicker of movement in a darkened window in the factory building across the lot. In the seconds he had, he focused in on the window. A man, older and better dressed than the rival gang members, was aiming a heavy-barreled rifle into the circle of light. He braced, thinking the man was aiming at him until he traced the line of fire and realized he wasn't the target—Krellick was. Evidently, whomever was funding the Brotherhood was not doing it for the gang's welfare. They had someone there monitoring the Brotherhood's activities—someone who would terminate the caught gangers before they could talk.

"*SNIPER!*" Jack yelled, again rolling into Krellick, pushing him away just as Arañé registered the silenced shot ring out. Jack had saved Krellick's life.

By yielding his own.

· · · · · ·

"*PREACH IS DOWN! PREACH IS DOWN!*" Scissors shouted over his radio.

"Reigis, he pointed to that building right before he got hit!"

"Only like five windows the shot could've come through, or maybe the roof. How'd Preach know?" Reigis questioned.

"Don't care, Reig," Scissors said darkly. "Light that frakker up!"

"Pleasure," Reigis replied, training the heavy barrel of his rifle and firing a shot at one of the possible windows. Glass shattered and something splintered from within the room.

"I can't even tell which windows are open—how'd Preach know where the shooter was?" he asked again as he chambered another round. He and Zip were now both firing rounds into the various places the shooter could be. Scissors was still on the radio.

… …

Arañé saw Jack take the hit that had been intended for Mouth. Normal people would have either panicked or instantly swarmed the victim in an attempt to help. He had given up on normal a long time ago.

- *The guy's gonna do a move and a bugout,"* he announced over *his comm device. "I'm quicker, I'll run him to ground. You stay with Grey."*

- *"I got Greyscale. Move!" was Chrome's reply, silent to all but Arañé.*

Spider moved. Extending his right arm and flexing his hand down, he fired a microfilament line with a stiletto grapnel shard into the stack of crates half the distance to the building. A rotor embedded in his forearm then rewound the line, pulling him to the crates at a speed that proved too difficult to trace. Another aim, another shot of his grapnel, and Arañé had made his way across the 120 yards to the warehouse building where the shot had come from. He closed his eyes for a second to focus; the thumping of sneaking steps revealed the location of the shooter. Then the thumping stopped. *So, I was wrong,* Arañé thought. *The shooter's not bugging out yet. He must be moving to—*

- *"Another shot coming your way,"* Arañé warned Chrome. *"Watch over those gangers Grey was covering. I don't know why, but we both know he's always got his reasons for what he does."*

… …

Chrome then looked at the two remaining conscious Brotherhood leaders and grinned wickedly. "Won't do to have you two run away," he reasoned, hitting Krellick and knocking him out instantly. Then he turned his attention to the near giant who only a few minutes earlier had been so full of taunts for Chrome. The giant whimpered, feeling the glare Chrome was giving him through his shades. "And now it's just the two of us, and one of my closest friends just got shot protecting you goveks.

"Now," Chrome said menacingly, leaning into the large man's face, "how do you think that makes me feel?"

Mohawk passed out just after hearing the crunch of his jaw resounding in his skull. Chrome didn't have much time. He didn't need the govek conscious with his back turned.

"Jack, Jack, Jack…" Chrome lamented. "What are you doing here with these sewer rats?"

… …

"Wolf, Fearless, you met those two friends of his before," Scissors began. *"Get to the light and get them outta there. Axis, you see the building Reigis and Zip are hitting?"*

"Working my way to it."

"Light it up!" Scissors commanded. *"Nothin' above the third floor, got it?"*

"Got it!" was the reply.

"Hey, Scissors, Wolf here. The others are all here, but the Spanish guy is gone."

"How's Preach?"

"He's out. That Chrome guy popped Anchor near dead, Krellick and Broze are out. Damn, I wish it wasn't Preach…I wish could have had the time to think this was funny."

Scissors was focused on the activity around the lamppost. Wolf, Fearless, and Skint met up with Preach and company, and were starting to gather everyone back to the Razor side of the abandoned lot. The sniper's silenced rifle barrel spat a tiny flick of light as the shooter fired a second time. Chrome was hit in the back shoulder. He staggered and dropped to one knee. *Oh, that sniper will fry but good!* was the one thought Scissors had at that moment.

"Razors! Lay down some cover fire on that building 'til Skint and the others get outta there! Where's that Ronnie guy? His friend just took a direct hit from the sniper—What the...? That ain't possible!"

Chrome, stunned for a second, lifted himself up off his knee and stood. He then tore through Krellick's gear until he found a sidearm Krellick had been carrying. The weapon appeared tiny in the large bulk of his hands. He fired off about ten shots in rapid succession while the Razors dragged the others to safety. Then he himself withdrew to be with the others.

... ...

"I see 'im!" Reigis declared, unaware of the stand at the lamppost. "That Ronnie guy! He's outside the second floor of the building!"

"That's impossible, Reig! How'd he get there—teleport?" demanded Scissors. The night was getting to be too much for him—Krellick's challenge, the setup, Preach and his two friends, Preach shot—who would have thought Preach would go so quick? And now that other guy takes that hit like it was a BB gun, and the other guy?

"No, he flew." It was Zip, one of the most reliable sets of eyes Scissors had, which was why Zip was spotter on the sniper team.

"Oh—well, then," Scissors said, throwing his arms into the air, mentally giving up, yielding his sanity over to the night. "Then there you go. He flew."

"Axis, take the whole frakkin' building down! Hell! Better yet, light the whole frakkin' block."

"You got it, Scissors."

<CLICK>

Arañé heard the transmissions, saw one of the Razors near the base of the building setting some explosive of some kind.

Razor bullets were starting to fly all over the building. Armor was Chrome's thing, Arañé was all speed and dodge. Eager Razors on full auto, building set to blow in about another minute, he had to move fast if he was going to catch the shooter. Throwing another ping, he electronically spotted him two floors above him and down the north hall.

Quietly racing up the stairs three at a time, he bounded down the hallway and kicked in the door where the shooter was lining up his next shot. Hearing the door collapsing, the shooter spun and aimed the deadly rifle at the door's center of mass. Arañé burst through the door to face the waiting rifle barrel.

"I don't know how you got here," a calm voice intoned quietly. His accent was odd, Arañé thought, almost sounded German. "But I do know how you are leaving. Raise your hands and tell me, who are you?"

"Spider," he answered, "but I don't think I'm leaving the way you think I am."

"Oh? And how is that, my arachnid friend? I will shoot you, I will carry you out, and then we will dissect this spider and see how you got here so fast."

"Actually, I'm carrying you out," Spider announced. By the time the sniper's finger squeezed the trigger of his rifle, Arañé snapped his right arm down, firing the microfilament line's shard through the gunner's skull. The grapnel's functionality was not limited to transportation.

After a cursory scan for any additional evidence, Arañé picked up the rifle and fallen sniper, ran to the far window, and jumped to the second-floor fire escape of an adjacent abandoned office building. Still carrying the shooter, he jumped to the ground, racing for the corner. He dodged around the building just as the warehouse went up in a roaring boom, throwing brick and burning timber fifty feet from the blast center. He shook his head at the destructiveness of the Razors, then circled the conflagration to rejoin Chrome. He caught the rifleman, but that was no solace to losing his friend.

20

MIND-SHADE AND DRIVEN THOUGHTS

"*Drek!*" Melissana swore to herself as she slammed her clock. "It's 7:04! How could I have slept through the first four minutes of the alarm, today of all days? I gotta get going!" She paced herself through a shortened version of her morning workout, hit the shower, dressed in her street clothes, and ate a quick breakfast heavily augmented by coffee. By 7:45, she was ready to suit up. Something with this whole thing was off, out of place. She still didn't have all the pieces put together to know exactly what it was, but she felt it. The familiar nagging doubt had become a shrieking ghost trying to get some message through to Melissana, but like being stuck in a bad dream, she couldn't make out what that message was. But she felt the tension, as tangible as the uneven patch jobs in her apartment walls. She suited up into her body armor, very conscious of each chip, nick, crack, and tear in the faded black leather.

Except for the occasional visit to Night Track—it's not like she normally ran with the racing crowd—her style was to distance herself from any attackers as quickly as she could. Today, though, Melissana wouldn't be racing her Zimata out of a fight; this time, she was speeding into one.

She checked herself in her mirror and sighed. The thin, worn collection of plated leather offered only minimal to moderate protection at best. *I guess it's better than nothing,* she thought to herself. *But until Elaine passed me those credsticks yesterday, I couldn't afford anything better—and at the time all I wanted to do was hang out with Josie.*

She stopped at the thought of her friend. "I might not ever see her again!" she said out loud, struck by the thought. She checked her watch. "I can't afford more than a minute or two, but after the way I ran out on her last night, I have to at least call."

"Hello? Josie?"

"Mel?" Josanne asked, waking sleepily.

"Hey, I just want to say that I'm really sorry I cut out on you last night."

"Wha-? No, that's okay. But what happened?"

"You mentioned something that might be tied to the case I've been working on."

"I thought you were done—they paid you already."

"Yeah, but there's one thing left. Josie, I don't know how this thing's gonna turn out."

"You okay? Wait, you're suited!" Josanne suddenly observed. She was wide awake and alert in an instant. "What are you doing?" Josie asked, alarmed.

"I don't know. What I gotta do, I guess. The only thing I know I can do. Anyway, I really wanted to say that I really appreciated your friendship, that it's meant the world to me, that I couldn't have made it this far from my past, and that I love you. In case things don't trick out proper out there, you take care of yourself, all right?"

"Mel!" Josie called in near panic. "Wait!"

"Can't, Trigget. If I don't get on the road like now, I'll be too late."

"Is there anything I can do to help?"

"Nothing I can think of. This gig's not your cut. Damn it, Josie! I gotta run. Miles to kill, and all that."

"Take care of yourself, Mel. You're the best friend I've ever had. Come back."

"I'll do my best," she declared with the best grin she could muster. Then, Game Face. "Gotta run, Josie."

<CLICK>

....

Josanne worried for her friend. It was all too true that Melissana, raised out of the streets of Roanoke, was tougher than her. But Josanne had come through some stuff, too, albeit with the street detective's aid. Now it looked like her friend needed help, but what could she do? Mel was right. Though Josanne had self-defense training from her father's security forces, she was not a street fighter. She didn't even know where her friend was off to. She had no idea what the case was or for whom the young private eye was working. *But wait,* she thought to herself. *Mel said something I mentioned might have been connected to her case.* What set her friend off the night before was the story of how Chance got busted up by the biker gang. *No, Josanne, that isn't quite right, either. Come on, think!*

"It was the *where* that caused her to flip!" she announced out loud. A plan started to flicker to life like a candle trying to decide if it was going to light for real. She began to get dressed. There was little time to lose.

....

The stretch of road from Roanoke to old I-81 had some spots that were tricky to navigate. Traffic wasn't the issue—with the exception of truck convoys and some business travelers, intercity traffic was almost non-existent. The problem was the roads themselves. With constant skirmishes, duels, piracy, raids, and retaliations, the vehicles (and the people inside them) were not the only things ever damaged. Weather and rockslides had been surpassed by bullet fire, rockets, collisions, and land mines. While local law enforcement and militias generally maintained patrols of the main roads within their areas of control, ambushes and banditry in between patrol zones were always threats motorists had to consider, if not actually contend with.

She had about two miles before merging onto 81-North when she hit an actual traffic stop. "What the—" Melissana exclaimed, jamming her brakes.

She had never seen anything like it. Cars, several trucks, even some bikers were stopped on the highway in front of her, all lined up, idling. The inter-vehicle radio traffic was outrageous, but nobody was shooting. Two heavy police cruisers patrolled up and down the shoulder of the road, making sure nobody started to. A procession of vehicles came from the north, flowing past the stalled line heading the opposite direction. Helplessly stuck in the jam, Melissana just watched the strange parade. After an assortment of vehicles passed, a corporate limo, complete with an escort of two motorcycles and three sedans slowly drove by. She didn't know who it was, but that kind of protection meant upper corporate exec. The shade of her doubts resurfaced as though occupying the seat next to her. It seemed to sigh in delight; she wished she'd gotten more sleep. A few trucks later, she had a *déjà vu* moment. Another couple motorcycles in front of another limo, but this was just a casino limo toting some mark inside—probably letting him bask in a win or two in order to set him up for the fleecing he'd take once he got into their den. She shivered, the specter inside of her somehow approving of her noticing. Then just more cars, all unremarkable.

The line of vehicles cleared, and her lane began to inch forward. It took a few minutes, but when she reached the cause of the slowdown, the line stopped again. She had to admit to herself that she was impressed; Melissana knew about road maintenance crews, but she had never seen one in operation before.

The lanes in her direction were blocked off by a series of concrete barriers and spiked tire traps. A platoon of men and women in full heavy body armor lined the barricades at hard-points armed with bipod-mounted heavy machine guns and rocket launchers. Where the lanes shifted was a military grade mobile field artillery anti-tank canon. Two dump trucks that Melissana could only describe as massive flanked the gun, their own vehicular canons lowered and apparently prepped to fire. They packed a *ton* of hardware on those guys! If one of those construction vehicles opened up nobody would even notice the heavy cruisers of the cops. No wonder everybody was behaving—*nobody* messed with the road crews.

Melissana's thoughts strayed as she waited. After the governments collapsed, it was the megacorporations that, however unforgiving, were able to preserve any semblance of society at anything beyond a local level. That society, not bound by any national allegiances, required order. Contracts were to be honored, deals were to be made. Competition was both aggressive and fierce, but the order itself, though shaken, was maintained. That order required commerce, commerce required a flow, the flow required deals, and deals required the dance of biz. Biz itself required both communications and the means to move materials across land masses, seas, and occasionally, air.

Eventually the surviving corps started working together to either fund or directly provide for the infrastructures formerly supported, if not sometimes limited, by governments. Road and highway crews armed and armored their vehicles to the teeth and had local police and militia support—commerce needed the roads.

Communication company personnel and equipment were similarly required and, after a while, pretty much left alone when they were working. The capability to immediately uplink and broadband any attacks was more effective than most may have thought. A simulcast could broadcast an attack on a network crew over television, radio, and data network channels, potentially identifying the aggressors to local law enforcement and any bounty hunters in the area—and net and communications corps paid *big* on their bounties for people messing with their techs! They could afford to. The simulcast would not only boost ratings from the live feed, it also drew sympathy from the captive audiences watching the fight from the perspective of the defenders—crowds of spectators tended to get emotionally connected with their local guys fending off a bandit raid. It was rumored that every once in a while, a corp struggling for ratings would try to take advantage of this by staging a raid against its own staff, but the tales typically faded away after a short period of dis-accreditation of those spouting the spurious and malicious hearsay.

Besides, for the media-habituated public, attacking communications corporations was self-defeating. One of the more popular urban legends circulating was of the biker maniac who blew up a couple LinkWarez Corporation techs working on the local broadcast grid. The biker reportedly went back to his gang bragging about the loot he'd hauled in from the attack until the gang's leader heard him and shot him in the mouth. Evidently the gang leader missed his favorite TV show because the transmission was lost when the poles blew.

"Television programming" didn't solely apply to the media itself anymore; it also applied to the people watching it, consuming whatever the broadcasters suggested. Everybody wanted their phones, but everybody *needed* their TV.

Melissana's line started moving again. She had lost about fifteen minutes, but she was through the construction. Relieved, she was now passing the stalled line of vehicles on the other side. *Weird,* she thought, *another motorcade.* Two black motorcycles with riders clad in black armor followed by a hearse, followed by two black sedans.

Did you miss me? asked her mind-shade as she once again took her seat next to Melissana. Melissana nearly growled as she entered 81-North. She knew there was something she was missing, but for the life of her, she just couldn't fit the pieces together—and she felt like even *that* was a clue. Then, merging onto highway 81-North, she passed a road mile marker sagging after being used for target practice. Maybe nobody messed with the highway crews themselves, but the markers were often used as targets.

"*Drek!!*" she shouted, suddenly seeing red and beating her steering column.

"*Drek! Drek! Drek! Drek! Drek!*"

"DREK!!!" she screamed, then finally forced her mind to grasp the truth of what was really happening. *That's* what was bugging her. Justin would have rated at least the level of protection of the exec motorcade she'd seen earlier. Justin wasn't a mark—the guys on the phone called him their *target!*

The wraith within her mind squealed with glee. Melissana finally understood the message, releasing the shade from her subconscious mind back to its own ethereal plane of existence.

It all made sense to her now. A simple blackmailer would have traded the package either at a public drop—like Elaine passing the credsticks to Melissana on the crowded street corner—or a dead drop that the blackmailers could monitor to pick up the payoff when they felt it was safe to do so. The crowds would mitigate potential retribution at the hand-off. These guys were drawing Justin out. The biker gang imported into the quarry area proved it. They thought they kept their presence a secret by jacking the journalist, but they didn't know about the implant that alerted Roa-Comm about his condition and location—and she was running right into it. She checked her vehicle's clock. The time was 8:45 A.M., Saturday—she had fifteen minutes to get there.

"DREK!!!" she swore again, flooring the pedal and kicking in the afterburners. She would get there with five minutes to spare.

… …

"Lisben here, what's up?" the media manager stated as he answered his home phone. Seeing her media-conscious boss unkempt and groggy could have been funny, but she didn't have the time.

"Mr. Lisben, this is Josanne."

"I can see that, Josanne. By the way, today's Saturday—my one day to sleep in! Do you have any idea what time it is?"

"Sorry, but I can't help it. I've got a legitimate scoop. I want to be the one to cover it, but it's happening this morning, fast."

"I'm listenin', kid. You're suddenly sounding an awful lot like a reporter. Whatcha got?" Lisben asked, now fully alert.

"Live auto-combat is going to break out. Pretty girl, a local, up against a bunch of bikers. I have photos of the girl. We can also work in local sympathy for the news show as well. I'm sending the photos now."

"Wow, she's not bad lookin'. But sympathy's ratings, kid? Where's the sympathy cut?"

"It's the same bikers that hit Chance this week. It's going down at the quarry about twenty miles north of here."

"You *found* 'em?" he asked, now intensely interested. "How'd you do that?"

"The girl found them, called me before she left. They're going after some friend of hers up there, and she's going to try to help out."

"You sure this is for real, kid?"

"Yes, sir." Josanne grimaced as the reality of the danger her friend was rushing into hit her. She nodded, responding with a suddenly cold tone, "Beyond any doubt."

"Yeah, I can see it on you. This girl, she's a friend of yours, isn't she? This is *personal* for you, isn't it? You'd risk yourself and our show's resources, just for your vendetta to help your friend?"

No! she screamed in her mind. He saw through it. Nothing for it now but to just fess up and tell him the truth.

"Y—yes, sir," she admitted.

"*Excellent!*" he exclaimed to her surprise. "I've known Chance for a long time, kid—we've been through quite a bit together. I would absolutely love nothing more than to spend this fine morning explaining that to those mongrel savages who jacked him up. Meet me on the roof of the news building in twenty-three minutes. Oh, Josanne?"

"Yes, sir?"

"Have you ever flown before?"

"Yes, sir, a couple times."

"Good—you'll ride with me." It seemed that he'd just had an idea of his own. Then, after picking up and dialing a second phone, he turned his attention back to her. "And by the way, stop by makeup on your way to the roof." With a wolfish grin that almost made her feel sorry for the bikers, he added, "This is *perfect*, kid! When we go out there, we're not only going to *get* the news, we're going to *be* the news!"

<CLICK>

21

QUARRY GATE

MELISSANA PULLED OFF the road and snuck down on foot in time to see two bikers erecting a chain and spike plates across the quarry entrance. Martinez and Powers must have already entered, she thought to herself, so these guys were blocking off the exit. It was time for her to go to work.

She removed her helmet and returned to her car. Then she tousled her hair and smudged on some makeup. Vaguely approving of the overall effect, she flipped two switches on her car, then started back down the road towards the bikers.

... ...

J-Bone and Flatch were guarding the gate, not at all happy about missing the action that was going to start in about the next ten minutes. The ambush would be easy—some guy thought he was doing a trade or something and didn't even know the gang was in the area. Both saw the target's gunner was a girl, and they knew what *that* meant when they were captured. Cursing their luck, they fumed. They'd hardly get anything out of this job.

Just then they heard a car having some engine problems lurching down the road in a series of hiccup movements. Rounding a corner was a red Zimata convertible, hood smoking. The driver was a hot, black-haired beauty, waving at the smoke to clear her vision.

193

Possibly best of all, it looked like she was already crying. Maybe she was breaking up with her boyfriend, or maybe she was lost, her car breaking down here of all places. Flatch nodded to J-Bone and grinned, feeling every inch the predator. They both had the same idea, suddenly not feeling so bad. They'd be able to get some action themselves. Their cut would be fresher than the girl down in the quarry, by the time they'd be able to get to what was left of her. This one was all theirs. They wouldn't even have to battle the car below. Elated at their change of fortune, they quickly split up and hid on opposite sides of the road. She'd be easier for them to grab at when she drove by.

"Hey there, sweetheart," Flatch called, suddenly appearing from the right side of the roadway. "Car giving you some problems?"

As if on cue, the car stopped completely. The black-haired girl looked up at him. "Can you please give me a hand?" she asked, her brown eyes as big as moons, pleading—the rest of her was a good sight, too.

With a laugh at their good fortune, Flatch wickedly declared, "Oh, baby, I'll give you more than a hand. J-Bone, get over here, you have *got* to see this, bro!"

J-Bone sauntered over to the car, laughing as Flatch was leaning over the passenger side, grabbing at the girl who appeared like she was trying to retreat into her driver's seat. "Hey, there, darlin'," he said, leaning on the driver's side door. "Tell me, what is an absolutely drop-dead gorgeous girl like yourself doin' way out in a god-forsaken place like this?" J-Bone then just laughed and began a bestial howl to terrify her more. He expected her to scream. He wanted her to scream.

... ...

Instead, she just focused a cold stare upon him, all traces of the damsel in distress gone. "Hunting," Melissana replied, while flipping the switch in the driver seat console. Before the bikers could react, a jolt of 25 amps ran through the entire outside surface of the vehicle, instantly stunning and paralyzing both. It would take an hour of nonstop driving to fully recharge the capacitor, but Melissana managed to catch both bikers actually touching the car. Given their size, their body armor, and grounding, she figured she had at least two minutes to silently dispatch the pair of deviants before the effects of the shock wore off. She did it in twenty-three seconds.

··· ···

"Justin, I don't like the looks of this," Monica protested through her helmet link. "We are really cut off out here."

"Yeah, I'm starting to feel sorry I dragged you into all this, Monica."

"Well, forget it. We had a blast, and I'm glad we're doing it. Elaine's been through enough. She doesn't need this kind of hassle now."

The duo was winding down the gravel road leading into the quarry. Scattered wrecks and debris littered the landscape, ghostlike reminders they were not the only ones who had ventured through the quarry since the latest oil crisis. If Wheelmen had a sacred "Elephant's Graveyard," this place might have been it.

Monica hummed to herself, trying to distract herself from the macabre scene. Finally, she turned to Justin. "Justin, if we get out of this, you, Elaine, me, and Mike are *definitely* going out on the town—on *your* dime!" Then she smiled and added, "And I promise you, Mike and I are going to do our best to break your bank!"

"Deal, Monica—sounds like *exactly* what we all need!"

Then Monica pointed, suddenly grim. "Up ahead—there they are."

"Okay, we got this. You stay in the car. I'll get out and make the trades. Anything starts to go south, you just get out of here."

"Right, boss—but you get yourself back here. Elaine needs you." Then, after giving him a hug for luck, she closed the remaining distance to the meeting site. Two armed men wearing jeans and leathers flanked a third, who was wearing a half-open business suit. Behind the trio waited a black sedan, its trunk facing Justin and Monica as they pulled up to the meeting place.

"Well, well, well, well, well!" the man in the suit began. His hair was overly oiled, his tan looked fake—and those were the positive statements of the guy's outward indicators of his character. His over-emotive gesturing and cheesy-nice smile displayed his utter enjoyment of the situation.

"Mister Justin Martinez himself! To you, sir, I say *Thank You*, for saving us *and* this planet. And now, please forgive me, but I just *have* to ask you a question I have been waiting to ask you since the very first time I heard about you and Elaine."

The voice drifted off into the air. Justin grimaced, then put forth the obvious question just to get the conversation over with. "And what is that?"

The man leaned in to Justin's face, all pretense of a smile gone, replaced by a cold ruthlessness. "Do you have my money?" he said, jeering.

… …

The Zimata edged closer to the edge of the quarry pit. Melissana tried to take in the entirety of the biker forces. From her vantage point, she spotted several heavy bikes and a few more lightly armed ones, but she also saw enough of the quarry layout to know she would not be able to see all of the vehicles. So, it was her, Martinez, and Monica Powers against more than she cared to think about. She paused as she factored in that her car wasn't exactly built for off-road fighting. She didn't want to give away Martinez, but she didn't want to die mauled to death in a quarry, either.

....

"Do you have the videos, negatives, and discs?" Justin replied, much cooler than he felt.

"Oh yeah, it's all there, in the trunk. Let's see the credits," replied the suit bum.

"Here's a sample. The rest I have in the car," Martinez said, trying not to get in too much of a disadvantage. As he reviewed the terrain further, he became more and more aware of just how desperate his situation truly was.

"Ah, very nice, Mr. Martinez. Hey, you mind if I call you Justin? I mean, I knew your wife so well…"

"Don't push it," was all Martinez could think to say.

"Oh, no problem, Mr. Respectable Citizen. It's just that, you know, she was one of my best girls."

"Where are the videos?"

"Oh, right here," he said, tiring of his game. "Come on, you're boring me anyway."

As Justin neared the trunk of the car, one of the other men began to move forward just a little too quickly. Justin, now defensive, blocked the man's hold attempt and gave him two quick jabs to the kidneys. Out of the corner of his eye, he saw a briefcase in the trunk of the car. He warded two more blows from the other muscle as he grabbed the briefcase, then evaded the suit bum and ran to the car. Monica slid over and let him get in the driver's seat.

He shifted gears and hit the accelerator as Monica powered up the weapons. Racing the car in a reverse spin, they heard several bike motors starting up. *"Ambush!"* he shouted angrily.

... ...

Melissana saw some of the bikers start to move, and there was no time left to think. From somewhere deep within her, the street kid who had very few friends saw the strongly devoted husband of

197

her new one threatened by death-dealing thugs. It didn't happen often, but Melissana cut that street kid loose. With a scream, she punched the accelerator hard, racing down the quarry road like a twin machine gun-wielding banshee.

"Justin, Monica!" she called over her vehicle radio. *"No time to explain. You got six bikers on your right flank waiting for you to come around the rock pile!"*

Justin cut into a right-hand power slide around the rock pile, Monica firing a stream of .30 caliber machine gun fire and a rocket into the waiting bikes. The machine gun fire was mostly deflected by the front-facing bike armor, but the rocket impacted just under the front tire of the middle bike, blasting the formation in five different directions at once.

"Thanks, but—who are you?" It was Monica. *"And how do you know who we are?"*

"Not now—I'm in the red Zimata convertible. Everyone else is hostile. Let's get outta here!"

"We see you, Red."—That was Justin. *"You can get out. We got a slalom gauntlet to run down here before we can even think about making a break for it."*

"Hear you, Grey, but I came to help—damn it!" Melissana found herself taking fire from some other bikers. *"Where do all these creeps keep coming from?"* she asked.

She led the bikers away from the quarry's main roadway, then hit a switch on her steering wheel that triggered the release of two dozen caltrops behind her. One of the bikes hit the caltrops, tearing its front tire to pieces. That bike flipped, causing it to collide with another of the closest riders. The two other bikes slowed and inched around the dangerous spiked traps.

Justin and Monica were demonstrating the skills they had polished in Night Track, weaving between the bikers, lighting up one here, one there. Still, though, the bikers were starting to nip away at Martinez's vehicle. Try as they might to escape the trap, the bikers kept Justin and Monica hemmed in among the lower pit levels—and Melissana's Zimata was built for running away from fights, not engaging in full vehicular onslaughts. If they couldn't make the break for it soon, they wouldn't be able to break out at all.

22

HANDOFFS AND HANDSHAKES

It was a bright Saturday morning, perfect for the peaceful drive to visit family. They had camped along I-81, just enjoying each other's company, letting their newfound love and commitment to each other grow in the time they finally had to themselves. They had found love in a crisis—now they were both taking new joy in the knowledge that they liked each other even more in this time of peace. It was a time of delight and of healing. Traffic was scarce, and Corey and Sue were both enjoying being carefree.

The sleek angles of a heavily modified yellow and black Dominator passed them by, heading north on I-81. A deep voice hailed them on their vehicle radio.

"Hey, South-bound, Rickshaw on the north side. Nice marks on that Sabretooth—Hardcore, is it?" Susan beamed, Corey's chest inflated.

"Aye, that's us, Rickshaw—not bad yourself on that Dominator!" Susan responded. *"How are the roads ahead of us? You're clear through Hagerstown."*

"An' thank ya, Lady."

Susan threw Corey a puzzled look on that one. They guessed he'd seen the "Hardcore" on the hood, but calling her Lady? She thought to herself, *Weird coincidence,* but then dismissed it as just radio manners.

"You're clear the next several miles, but there's some bike gang activity down by some quarry. Bunch of gangers against two cars—a woman and two friends of hers. Best you stay clear; the bikers are winning."

Corey pulled over. He and Susan just stared at each other, stunned. Hagerstown was a battle won, not a war. In both their minds, someone else was going through exactly what they had just gotten out of. "Corey, those poor people…" Her heart sank. Corey felt like mud. "What should we do?" she asked him. Corey continued his stare, searching her eyes, her heart. "The only thing we can do," he finally decided. "We just got out of that mess." Then he resumed his course.

"Rickshaw, this is Hardcore," Corey radioed. *"Can't let that happen, not while we're alive. Sure could use your help."*

"Hardcore, this is Rickshaw. Ya got heart and guts. Sorry though, kid. Ain't my fight."

<CLICK>

…… ……

Corey and Sue were both puzzled as they passed the two unconscious and bound ganger types just inside the quarry gate. Inching towards the edge of the quarry pit, they surveyed the state of the battle below them. By all evidence, the bikers had won. They were dismounted, their bikes in a few scattered groups. There was a grey Talon knocked out of commission, and a red sports car was being towed by several bikes towards the center of the activity. Zooming in with a monocular, Corey spotted a woman, bound and staked to the ground. Near her was what they could only presume to be her partner. He was talking to a man from a third vehicle, but judging by the sagging body language of the partner and the swagger of the man from the third vehicle, it was clear they were not friends. Some hoots from the pit echoed against the walls—evidently, the bikers had spotted something in the sports car they were savagely excited about.

Sue spoke her mind first. "Corey, they're dead meat as soon as we make our move. We can't get them all out on our own. Even if they can't help, we need to try to free them."

"Agreed," Corey said. "Drop me off, then get up the road."

"Not this time, Corey. By the time you get up, they'll be blasting you to pieces."

"Have a better idea?"

"Yeah, I do. This time, you drop me off..."

... ...

Corey hit the Play button as he inched his Sabretooth up to the lip of the quarry, and the car was filled with some modded old chant sung by a choir. The track was one of his dad's favorites, and Corey knew it by heart. In a few seconds, there would be a held pause, then the music would break into a fast-paced anthem that was perfect for what he and Susan were about to do.

The bikers were starting to hammer on the sports car to dislodge its occupant. As the chant continued, Corey hardened himself against the battle just seconds away, reassuming the edge and persona that had seen him through the siege of Hagerstown. He aimed, then almost silently fired a single vehicular grenade launcher just as the chant faded. As the slow-moving projectile sailed over the quarry airspace, Corey flipped the switch to the PA system, now set at full volume. Hardcore smiled, remembering his dad repeatedly listening to the tune. *Anything for an edge*, he thought, reminiscing.

His aim and timing were both perfect. The grenade hit the center of one of the main groups of bikes, blasting bike parts and systems outward in all directions just as the opening blast of the anthem started blaring from across the quarry. The bikers were completely surprised by the suddenness of the explosion and the confusion of the music echoing off the quarry walls. The newly appointed Cryo-

Jaeger gunned the Sabretooth, sailing over the lip of the edge and down the rocky wall, heading for the group of bikers near the staked victim. *This one's for you, Dad,* he thought, firing a steady stream from his machine guns at various targets of opportunity he spotted while heading down the quarry rim.

Sue was holding on for dear life as the vehicle half-rocketed, half-plummeted down the canyon-like walls of the quarry, resisting the urge to line up targets for the turret gun. In any other fight she was the gunner, but now she had to steel herself for an entirely different battle. As the car roared down towards the main group of bikers, she held her M16-A2 tightly to her chest and double-checked her gear. She wondered if Corey had been this scared when he had rescued her. She borrowed his courage from the memory, and then she was ready.

... ...

The bikers were already beginning to recover by the time Hardcore made it to the quarry floor. Three separate groups of bikes were starting up as he fired another grenade into a fourth group. Instead of maneuvering around the packs of bikes, though, he plowed straight through one of the groups, continuing to fire the twin .30 caliber machine guns in a steady stream of ribboning mayhem. The Sabretooth roared right through the area where the captives were held, not even slowing down. The main group returned fire but held a loose perimeter around their captives. The mounted bikers gave chase, and Hardcore drove on.

A hundred yards past the hostage point, he slowed, allowing the bikers to near. As they closed in for their kill, he spun a hard U-turn and charged the bikes, now at point-blank range. Two went down, two others crashed in side-skids to avoid the Sabretooth's charge. Again, he raced to the location where the victims were being detained. The captured guy tried to make a break for his vehicle, but before he could make it, he was tackled by two thugs. The good news for Hardcore and Sue was that now their line of fire to the group of hoods in the center was clear.

Firing both machine guns, they approached the group. Beyond where the victims were being held, another group of mounted bikers was heading straight for him. Still another group of bikers was closing in on him from behind. Upon approaching the victims, he jerked the wheel hard right, power-spinning the Sabretooth until he could take off away from the victims in a new direction perpendicular to the line of merging biker groups. Both groups of bikes veered off their paths to maintain their pursuit, followed by a few more from the group guarding their prisoners in the center.

"So far so good," Sue shouted to her knight.

"Yeah," he agreed. "One more cut-back, then you're up."

As if on cue, the fourth group of bikers rounded a large mound of gravel, cutting off the Sabretooth's flight. Hardcore kicked the car into a 180-degree reversal spin. Two groups of bikers were now between him and the group guarding the victims. The group from the mound, now behind the Sabretooth, were closing in fast. Counting down a "3—2—1," the Cryo-Jaeger fired a smoke round from his grenade launcher just as the three groups of bikes merged on his location, hitting his steering column thumb switch for the "Dragon's Droppings" canister at the same time. Two and a half seconds later, the Sabretooth emerged from the smoke, the brightness of the phosphorous cloud glaring through and even igniting the haze of the smoke, the sounds of screams and multiple secondary explosions confirming his timing was true.

… …

Darkshark was enraged beyond madness. His fixer's deal was that the bikers rode in and kept one corporate suit from getting away from an ambush. The seventy-five grand the Johnson was paying them would keep their bikes charged for a long time. The null-head hadn't told him the suit was a wheelman with a teammate. Then the chick in the red sports car, and now this Sabretooth. He just glared at the fixer, who insisted he himself come for the exchange. Either the drek deliberately set up his gang, or worse, the idiot hadn't done his homework and was just as surprised by the mark's team as he was. He took one look at the poser's face and saw the anguished expression of confusion—the choob *was* just as surprised as he was. "Frakkin' Johnson!" he almost audibly cursed.

When the flame cloud blew a fifth of his gang away, Darkshark went into a frenzy. "Get him!" were the only words he could say. "Get him," were the only words he could think. Eighteen bikers still in pursuit of their latest enemy reacted as though they had somehow felt rather than heard Darkshark's command. Each caught in his own berserk fury, the pack roared its response, howling a bestial glee at the thought of the carnage they would inflict on the occupants of the Sabretooth.

....

Hardcore gunned his car to within twenty feet of the gangers surrounding the victims, then skidded into a sharp left power turn, spraying dust and gravel into the guards, forcing them to shield their eyes—which gave Sue her chance to jump from the car, still sliding sideways in mid-turn.

Hagerstown had changed Susan. Although she'd already possessed a developed talent for gymnastics and had been trained in self-defense since her youth, she had always been one of those that others watched after. While she was growing up, her family and friends protected her from bullies. Her town defended her from biker gangs. When her town, friends, and family were lost, Corey somehow appeared from out of nowhere, stepping in and filling the gaps left by all three.

Then Hagerstown happened. It was true that Samantha somehow replaced a sense of normalcy for her, and the town did protect the pair of wanderers from Iron Mike and his Steel Jackals.

But in Hagerstown, she also became part of the solution, not just a girl needing others to defend her. She defended herself as well, and had transformed from merely Corey's charge to his teammate. Then, being initiated into the Cryo-Jaegers like they were? How cool was that! It was time Susan started paying her rescues forward, so she jumped from the car. But while it was Susan Blakeslee who jumped from the Sabretooth, it was Lady Blackwolf who landed.

... ...

Lady Blackwolf hit the ground blithely, executing several forward rolls in her full body armor to expend the momentum of the jump from the moving car. Even as she rolled, she noted in her gymnast's peripheral vision that most of the bikers were still pursuing Corey.

"Clear on ground, go get 'em, Hardcore!" she radioed through her helmet microphone.

The biker nearest her was still distracted, rubbing grit and gravel out of his eyes. She cut the bound woman loose, but through her helmet's synthesized communications system told her to play dead. Then she covered the woman with blood to try to make the girl look the part. Maybe that would buy her time to free the others.

The ganger was beginning to recover from the gravel spray Corey kicked up while dropping her off—she needed to take him out. She leaped to the attack from behind him, cracking the base of his skull against the butt of her M16A2. He crumpled without a sound. Another ganger spotted her and moved in for a knife thrust, but the Lady Blackwolf parried it with the rifle. Still holding the weapon, she then powered upwards with her left hand, slashing the raised front sight of the weapon across the man's face, tearing a slice in his cheek that began to bleed profusely. Crying out in pain and reflexively grabbing at his torn face, he allowed Lady Blackwolf room to snap her right forearm forward, smashing the stock of the weapon against his left temple with a sickening crunch.

Seven gangers guarding the victims were left. Too many! As they edged towards her, she decided she had to do something she had hoped she would never have to do. Pointing her autorifle at a ganger that was about ten feet away, she squeezed the trigger. Seven rounds raced to the man, who was wearing some sort of chest armor. The first two rounds hit the man's body armor. While the rounds deflected off his chest piece, the impact of the rounds lifted the man in a half-twist, sending him into a spin. The third and fourth rounds missed him completely, but the fifth, sixth, and seventh rounds caught the ganger in the left arm and side. He was dead before he hit the ground.

"Kill him!" bellowed the large-framed, bearded, muscular man nearest the victims. Blackwolf recognized this gang's version of Iron Mike as soon as she spotted him. She launched into a sideways roll to avoid any sudden bursts of gunfire that may have come her way in response to the raging gang leader. She squeezed off a few rounds into the direction of the leader, then slid backwards into a pile of wrecked vehicles. There was nothing more she could do at the moment except hide.

… …

Well, the coast seems clear—I guess it's now or never, she thought to herself, mustering her courage. Rounding the corner of the abandoned quarry building, she jumped the two guards who were distracted by some sort of fight that broke out near Monica. No time for subtlety, she grabbed a fist-sized rock in each hand for a set of impromptu brass knuckles. She sucker-punched the first guard in the back of his head, then followed up with a three-punch volley to the man's kidneys. He went down hard, alerting the other. The new guard tried to melee against her with a length of pipe, but she blocked his blows by parrying against his forearms. Her mind began counting cadence—*Block - and - block - and - step-back, draw-in, KICK!* enunciating the last by sweeping her left foot between her and him, swiping up and launching her booted foot into the man's left jaw. He staggered but remained standing, grinning evilly. *Not as easy as I'd hoped,* she thought. He was dazed—what could she do with that?

So, with an underhand throw, she tossed the rock she held in her left hand to him. Shaken by the kick, he reflexively reached to catch it. Her left arm then shot out, grabbing at his extended hand, yanking him in to add additional force to her right jab at his chin. She hadn't dropped the rock from her right hand, which added to the impact along with the additional yanking force of her pull. The blow popped his jaw out of socket. A flurry of jabs and a roundhouse kick completed the man's journey to a long lapse of unconsciousness.

She leaned over the male prisoner who was now bound, head covered by a black piece of cloth. She removed the hood, cut the cords that bound his wrists, and pronounced, "Sir, I'm here to get you two out of here! This way!" She then led the prisoner around the corner of the quarry building to his several rounds of grateful thanks.

Justin Martinez finally cleared his eyes of the sudden sunlight, just in time to see a petite-looking black-haired female in somewhat ragtag body armor jump into a red sports car, firing it up and squealing into a reversal, pointing twin machine guns into the likely approach of any additional guards. There were none, but she spotted several bikers chasing after a black muscle car that was blasting some kind of music from it. "Well, the enemy of my enemy, and all that," she muttered to herself. Then, after assuring Mr. Martinez was safe, she took off after the bikers.

··· ···

Once Hardcore got clear of the victims, he rotated the turret rearward and began firing intermittent recoilless rifle blasts. Several bikes went down, but now they were no longer surprised. They

209

split up into two groups and pursued him on each side. *Smart,* he thought to himself. While it still wouldn't have been easy, he would have had a better time tracking both groups if Sue had been with him. The Sabretooth was starting to take a beating. The Hagerstown mechanics and armorers had taken special care of his Sabretooth and enhanced its armor, but he didn't know how much more it could handle.

"Lady, this is Hardcore. You got them cleared yet?" he asked over his helmet comm. *"I don't know how much longer I can keep this up."*

"I got Justin clear, but I wasn't able to get to Monica. You looked like you needed a hand first."

Corey was perplexed—*"Uh, this is Hardcore—who just responded? And who are Justin and Monica?"*

"I'm a friend—what do you mean, 'Who are Justin and Monica?' Never mind, no time to chat. Swing that blaster of yours left, I got your right."

With that, a confused Hardcore heard a blast off to his right as a stream of machine gun rounds walked through a motorcycle's frame. The bikers on his right wavered in their pursuit, then some of them split off altogether. Suddenly, he saw some red flickers on his left and watched as several bikes on that side went out of control and crashed. He was mystified until he saw a yellow and black Dominator come into view from around one of the quarry slag piles.

"Glad you're okay, Hardcore," that professional-sounding voice said somewhat matter-of-factly. *"That's some good bit of driving you're doing, so I thought I'd join the show."*

"Thanks for coming to the party, Rickshaw."

"Yeah well, you set a good example."

Corey grinned wide inside his helmet. If Rickshaw was as good as he sounded, they might win this!

"No!" he heard the female suddenly cut in, jarring him from his reverie. *"They're heading back to the hostages! Come on, we need to stop them before they get back there!"*

The defender of Hagerstown glanced to see where the communication was coming from and concluded the girl was the driver of the red sports car. But why wasn't Sue answering? Suddenly panicking, he spun another reversal and gunned the car to get back to where he had dropped her. Going full throttle both in speed and firepower, Hardcore, Melissana, and Rickshaw managed to take out seven of the ten bikers before they made it back. Then they stopped their cars, engines idling. Corey and Melissana locked down their weapons. Their fight was over.

A greasy mobster type was standing over three kneeling hostages that had hoods over their heads. Swaggering and almost carelessly waving his Uzi at the three hostages, he began to slowly clap after they had stood down.

"Well done, and I must repeat myself, *well* done! I must admit, I was not expecting all of this! I mean, wow! I hired the Road Ragers as a backup in case my commission took off on me, but this? Oh, what a show! Now, I really gotta say this, and I hope you guys don't mind…

"Get out of your vehicles with your hands over your heads," the cheesy-looking gangster ordered as he continued to wave his Uzi over the heads of three kneeling hooded hostages.

Melissana was out of her car before Corey could even register what was happening. "Don't kill him!" she pleaded. "Don't you know how important he is—to all of us?"

"Indeed, I do. But my, oh my, who are you?" He leered upon seeing Melissana. "Bonus day for me, I suppose. You know, I thought I was going to retire from the video business, but I think I'm going to enjoy making a few movies with you." Then, returning his attention to the Sabretooth, he said, "Fancy paint job, fancy driving." He dismissively followed with, "You're done. Get out of the car. Helmet off."

Corey dismounted, hands in the air. He didn't know who the victims were, but he wouldn't be responsible for their murders, even if he died trying. The number of bikers was severely reduced, but there were still about twenty-seven left. Glancing in the direction of where the woman had been staked down, he saw she was completely limp and covered with blood. As his new partner removed his helmet, Corey got his first glimpse of Rickshaw. The man was solidly built and toughened, his slightly greying hair cut short but not tight-cropped. His tanned and weathered face made it difficult for Corey to guess the man's age, but he appeared to be between forty and maybe early fifties. Corey never really followed the wheelman circuits closely, but he guessed from the man's skills that Rickshaw was either full pro on some lesser circuit or maybe a test driver for one of the manufacturers—or, he thought suddenly, the man had the look of a bounty hunter. The man's eyes either seemed to naturally squint in the sunlight, or maybe he was still sizing up his opponents.

"Well, see that, kid?" Rickshaw addressed to Corey. "Anyway, I gotta give you credit. I told you ya got heart and guts, kid—heart and guts" he repeated with a sigh, as he raised his hands in surrender. Then, just as he was turning his head back to face their victors, Corey thought he saw the grizzled road warrior give him the slightest sign of a grin, and let out a final under-the-breath utterance in closing that Corey barely heard: "Honor and Courage…"

"Well now, I am surprised again!" the racketeer began, after Corey and Rickshaw removed their helmets and faced him. "It seems our savior has bodyguards of both genders after all. I must say it's almost refreshing—I was beginning to think our friend here only hired women. But, now we have you all. So, come *out*, Mr. Martinez—*NOW!*" the gangster shouted. Then the three hostages removed their hoods and stood up. Two of them were wearing leathers, but it didn't seem to be bike gangers. The third one was big enough he could have been Iron Mike's brother.

A man in vehicular combat armor limped slowly from around the corner of the quarry building. His left hand was fumbling with his helmet strap. His right arm hung limp, evidently wounded badly enough that it could not be raised despite the man's struggling to do so.

"That's right, come right on up here. I want you to see where all your antics got you." The man was now grabbed by the crook and harshly spun to face Corey and the girl in the sports car. "You see? All you did was get all of these others killed. First your girlfriend over there," he said, pointing to the limp, blood-splattered Monica. "I mean, don't look at me, I didn't do it. It happened during your rescue attempt. And now all these others. You really should have come alone like I told you to. So now, death comes to them all.

"Look at you! Everybody worships you as the man who saved the world, and you can't even manage your helmet! I told you, nobody takes one of my girls away from me." As he began to lift the Uzi at Corey, the bikers started laughing.

"NO!" a synthesized voice shrieked from inside the helmet, and suddenly the right elbow of the struggling helmeted figure shot up into the gangster's jaw as the left hand produced a five-inch straight knife from inside the helmet that arced into his ribs. He went down with a gurgling moan. The big biker made a grab for the limping armored man, but he did a back flip out of reach, spun, and vaulted into one of the fake hostages. Rickshaw visibly started and let out a "What the—" but quickly recovered and seemed to grin. Without warning, a red dot appeared on the bike gang leader's torso, and a flicker of red light from Rickshaw's Dominator later, a cauterized hole appeared in the big biker's chest. Corey gaped at Rickshaw in complete surprise. Then surprise turned to abject fear as he stared, not comprehending exactly just what it was he thought he was seeing. Over the next four seconds, Rickshaw glimpsed at six other gangers who were readying their weapons to fire at the captives. Six more red dots appeared in series, each on a different ganger. Corey's jaw fell as the Dominator's laser whined, almost silently, six more times, each producing the same cauterized hole in the other bikers.

Rickshaw glanced Corey's direction. Recognizing Corey had actually caught what happened, he simply smiled and winked. For all that he and Susan had been through with Iron Mike, Corey finally knew what complete terror was.

"Mr. Martinez" removed his helmet, exposing long flowing golden blonde hair, somewhat matted from being tucked under the helmet.

"Sue! You're okay!" Corey shouted.

"Sir," Susan called into her helmet's microphone, "it's clear. You can come out now."

Another man came out from the corner of the quarry building aiming an M16-A2 at the remaining gangers, running to the woman who had been staked on the ground. "Monica! Monica!" was all he could say. "Monica, I am so sorry. I didn't think any of this was going to happen! I wish there was something I could do."

"Mind helping me up?" she replied with a smile, offering the astonished executive her arm. "I thought you kept this quiet, Justin. You didn't tell me you were bringing an assault squad."

"Really, Monica," Justin began, "I truly have no idea who these people are."

The real Justin Martinez finished helping Monica up when an unmarked black helicopter appeared from the northern edge of the quarry. The zipping sound of a Vulcan machine gun was heard, the entire area between the group and the helicopter turned to a dust cloud, stinging everyone in the area while the chopper's public address system blared, "Mr. Martinez, that's far enough. You've put on quite a show here. I see you have eliminated many of our 'contract staff.' I commend you; you've handled most of our payout for us. Now please step to the helicopter."

"What is this about?" shouted Martinez. "Who do you think you are?"

"It should be obvious enough by now, Mr. Martinez—I'm with the Human Acquisitions Department for your new employers. Yes, in fact, the blackmailing *was* a ruse to get you out of town, so we wouldn't have FoodTech security forces getting in the way. I don't know who these others are, and quite frankly I really don't care.

They will soon cease to exist, and nobody will know where you disappeared to."

Emboldened by the helicopter's arrival, the few scattered bikers again began to form up, carefully aligning themselves behind the firing arc of the helicopter's Vulcan. The company man acknowledged them with a curt, "Your payment will be in Martinez's car when I leave. Thank you for your services."

"Now, Mr. Martinez, I think enough people have been involved in this little venture. Come along."

The group was defeated, and Justin knew it. He had no idea who his attempted rescuers were, but there was nothing they could do against the helicopter with its Vulcan. He had heard of corporate kidnappings and Talent Acquisition Teams, but he was usually protected by a small army of corporate security. So, some rival corporation heard about Elaine, and used her past to draw him out. He only wished he could at least tell her goodbye. The black-haired girl was starting to cry, but it surprised him when she said she was sorry to him. She was crying more for him, not herself. He wondered who she was, who these others were. Looking at them, he told them, "I am truly sorry. I don't know any of you, and you have all risked so much. I guess I'll never know how you all got here, but thank you. I am deeply sorry for you all. I am in your debt, though I don't think I will soon be able to repay it." With that, he stepped towards the helicopter.

Corey and Sue held each other. Melissana stood by Monica, watching. There was nothing more they could do, and soon their lives would be over.

Without warning, a white helicopter with the blue and red logo of the Roanoke Media Channel rose over the hills of the quarry. Three other news helicopters swiftly flew around the first, getting video coverage of the crew in their first helicopter. Multiple public address systems from the media helicopters were broadcasting their voice cutovers, presumably to make it more exciting, and so more "realistic" for their viewers.

"AND HERE YOU HAVE IT, WRMC VIEWERS! MURDER AND KIDNAPPING OF NONE OTHER THAN JUSTIN MARTINEZ! OUR OWN LIVE ACTION REPORTER, JOSANNE SINCLAIR, UNCOVERED THIS STORY OF INTRIGUE AND CORPORATE ESPIONAGE, BROUGHT TO YOU LIVE IN ALL ITS SAVAGERY! BUT WHO WOULD KIDNAP THE MAN WHO SAVED THE WORLD? LET'S SEE IF WE CAN FIND OUT!"

The kidnappers swung to fire the Vulcan at the first WRMC helicopter, but the three other news crews were on the air televising live. If he fired, or if they killed anyone below while on camera, WRMC would sponsor a bounty that would ensure they would not survive long enough for them to land and make a break for any ground vehicles. If they were caught on camera and identified, they would be tied to their parent company, and their own employers would make them wish they *had* crashed. Further, if they dusted Martinez, they would lose their chance at grabbing the asset for their own company permanently.

Swearing, the unknown antagonist turned tail and flew off before it could be identified. If their faces didn't get caught on those cameras, maybe they could somehow live long enough to talk their employers into letting them try again.

"THEY'RE GETTING AWAY..." a female voice shouted over her microphone. Scanning the crowds on the ground, she stated, *"BUT THEIR VICTIMS ARE OKAY, ROANOKE! THE VICTIMS ARE ALL SAFE!"* She sounded genuinely and extremely relieved. *"MR. MARTINEZ AND THE OTHERS ARE REALLY OKAY!"* It sounded like she was going to start crying. A male voice cut over...

"GREAT JOB, JOSANNE, AND THANK YOU FOR RISKING YOUR LIFE TO BRING THIS EXCITING STORY FOR OUR VIEWERS! AND NOW A BOUNTY UPDATE ALERT. THERE ARE FIFTEEN BIKERS ON SCREEN NOW." Close-up images of each of the remaining bikers appeared on screen. For some reason, the black-haired girl sat down, laughing and crying at the same time. The helicopter lowered, dropping Josanne off for a moment,

then took off again without her. The male voice continued. "*OUR ACTION REPORTER, JOSANNE, HAS DISCOVERED THESE ARE THE SAME BIKERS WHO NEARLY BEAT TO DEATH A WRMC TECHNICIAN LAST WEEK.*" That was all the bikers needed to hear—they started to make a break from the trap they themselves had laid. The last sentence they heard was, "*AND I'M COLLECTING IT, AND HEREBY PLEDGE TO DONATE ALL PROCEEDS TO THE CHANCE WHARTON RECOVERY FUND, STARTED BY THE WRMC FAMILY.*" The WRMC helicopter's camera cut out as its own Vulcan cut in. The voiceover faded out with, "*THIS IS WRMC, AND HAVE A GREAT SATURDAY MORNING!*"

······

The battle was finally over. Corey warily shook Rickshaw's hand. "Uh, thanks for coming and helping out."

"My pleasure, kid. Thanks for standing up and taking on the odds. But why'd you risk your lives like that to help someone you don't even know?"

"Right thing to do, you know?" was all Corey could respond.

"Well, the media made themselves the heroes, small wonder, but these guys would have been gone if you hadn't put up the fight you did."

"That's some tech you got," Corey said, still disturbed by what he had seen. "I've been around a lot of cars, and I've never seen anything like it. You somehow targeted the bikers from outside your vehicle—how'd you do that?"

"Had a lot of practice, I guess. Do something long enough, and eventually you get better at it. Well, listen, it's been nice meeting you, but I gotta run. You two take care of yourselves." Rickshaw simply turned and left.

The reporter approached with the male hostage as Rickshaw left, conducting a round of after-action interviews like it was a post-game show. "And here you see the pair that Mr. Justin Martinez himself is calling the man and woman of the hour. Mr. Martinez, I understand you have a few words you would like to share with this couple?"

Corey and Sue were stunned. Before, they had been too concerned with survival to focus, but as the man drew near, they could finally recognize him. "Wait—you're *the* Justin Martinez?" Corey's eyes went wide.

Justin smiled and, intimately familiar with the media, began: "Thank you both, for your outstanding selfless service and excellent show of skills. You did a superb job of drawing out these vermin, and on behalf of FoodTech ICC, I want to thank you for your assistance working with the FoodTech Security Forces." As he shook their hands, he palmed a business card into Corey's hand. "I eagerly anticipate reading the details of the matter in your report."

Having made her round of interviews, the reporter was wrapping up her show. "And so there you have it, WRMC viewers. Corporate warfare, kidnapping, hostages, and rescues! It's a *great* Saturday morning in Roanoke!" They could all tell when the camera was off. The reporter ran up to the girl with the red sports car, hugging her and asking if she was all right. For her part, the black-haired girl was still laughing, and crying, and laughing. Finally, she was able to talk. She stood up, hugged her friend back, and managed, "And I thought you weren't cut out for this!" Then she sat down and started laughing again.

Corey and Sue were making introductions to Monica. Eventually, Mr. Martinez called the entire group together. "It won't be long now until FoodTech Security Forces arrive. The public story must be that you were working with FoodTech the entire time. I would be remiss not to reward you in practical terms, but I would also like for us all to meet over dinner. I have already made these plans with my assistant driver," he added, smiling wryly her way. She returned his smile with a mock scorning. "You'd better believe you did!" Now that Melissana had met Monica in person, she liked her instantly.

Observing the again dented and chipped hood of the Sabretooth, he added, "Hardcore, Lady Blackwolf here introduced herself while getting ready to take my place. She mentioned you're travelling south at the moment. If you happen to need anything, please let me know. Your type of valor and heroism is rare these days—a valuable commodity indeed. In fact, after our standard background checks, I could use somebody with your integrity and skills as my driver— both of you, if you are interested. I regret to say I have a feeling FoodTech will require me to have a driver soon."

Then he studied Melissana, puzzled. "Young lady, I owe you a great debt. It appears that you know me somehow, and yet I cannot place you. How did you come to be here?"

Melissana looked at her friend. "Josie, can you give us a couple minutes?" Then she turned her attention back to Justin and his partner. "Mr. Martinez? Monica? We need to talk."

… …

Karen, coming off her night shift of monitoring the city's defense grid, was watching TV to wind down after a long night. She was catching a weather report from WRMC when the program was interrupted with a live telecast. Shrieking in delight, she was on the phone to Handsight in seconds. The two hometown kids had made good.

23

RELATIVE PARADISE

IT HAD BEEN a good month. Sue introduced Corey to her relatives. They openly welcomed the man who had rescued their beloved niece and cousin from the fate of the rest of the Blakeslee line. The Blakeslee's had been very warmly regarded in Asheville, so while they still mourned the rest of their family members who had been killed, they were delighted that Susan was finally safe.

After everything the young couple had been through, the relatives gladly took them in, providing peaceful shelter, good food, and much needed rest with family, all of which the young survivors had been deprived of and craved more than they knew. Even so, as much as they liked their stay in Asheville, after a few weeks of the relative paradise, Corey and Sue felt they needed to move forward with their lives.

Corey had passed the FoodTech ICC background checks, and due to Justin Martinez's pull, he had a cushy job offer with a cushy salary at the ICC waiting for him. He was aware of the risks that came with being Justin's driver, but he was now equally aware of his capabilities. Interrupting a kidnapping attempt by some guy with a Vulcan-toting helicopter had been a large part of his interview process, after all. So, they packed up and headed back to Roanoke, looking forward to their new start together. They were also eager to meet again with Monica, Melissana, and Josanne. Justin had made arrangements for their reunion at a restaurant called The

Golden Chalice. Neither of them had heard of the place before, but it sounded expensive.

… …

Josanne's career was starting to take off. While some reporters were jealous of the attention paid to the upstart, everyone had to admit that preventing the kidnapping of "The Man Who Saved the World" was undeniably *the* coolest footage they had ever seen, as well as a goldmine of a story break. A week later, WRMC executives summoned Josanne to The Glass Room, the upper suite atop their high-rise building. They informed Josanne that Justin Martinez had personally requested for her to conduct a series of exclusive interviews that would scoop the nation and possibly give WRMC a position on the global map of media brokers. The station's executives informed her their attorneys were already working on a new production royalty scheme, as well as a publicity campaign, that would be launched as a result of the interviews.

She asked why her, and the executives flashed their polished smiles and simply stated she'd impressed Justin at the quarry. The Martinez's were going public with something private, personal, and big. They told her no other entertainment channel knew about it, and that the Martinez's wanted as open and favorable interview as possible. They went on to mention that enough paparazzi would come out of the woodwork with their own twists on the story within twenty minutes of WRMC playing the scoop. Then, after she electronically signed a small encyclopedia volume of nondisclosure agreements, they passed Josanne a manila envelope with a handwritten letter from Justin Martinez containing the nature of the interviews.

As Josanne read the letter her jaw dropped. *Melissana, what in the world had you gotten yourself into?* she wondered, being careful not to vocalize her thoughts.

The Martinez's were coming clean. In her youth, Elaine Martinez had been groomed by a sex trafficker. By the time she knew what was happening, it was too late. About eighteen months later, Justin Martinez came along. At first, he was just a college mark for her trafficker, who threw Elaine his way to seduce him and take all his wheelman winnings. But Justin somehow learned the truth, and after several dates, he spirited her away in the trunk of his car, allowing her to escape both her master and her old life.

Somehow, her former master discovered Elaine's identity and sold that information to one of FoodTech's rival corporations. The rival used the story to draw Justin away from his security details so they could kidnap him, and had it not been for the small group that miraculously turned up at the quarry that morning, they would have succeeded. Now that the truth was known, Justin and brave Elaine were going to make a public announcement. While there would undoubtedly be a period of pain and criticism, they knew that as long as they had each other, they would find paradise together. The period that Elaine had merely survived for so long would finally be behind them, for good.

…… ……

Melissana tried to melt back into the streets. She'd never had a lot of friends. Mostly what she had were acquaintances augmented on occasion by a temporary ally. Josanne was a rare exception. Now that Josanne's career was starting to take off, it was Melissana's turn to have to leave messages when calling. The young detective wasn't interested in media attention, although she had immediate access to it through Josanne.

She had over two years' worth of her normal income, slipped to her by the grateful Elaine, but she somehow felt a little empty. She had the credits, but somehow more important to her was how Justin had reacted when she told him what had led her to learn about the quarry. She was ecstatic that they were growing even closer by their decision to come clean with Elaine's past. The trouble was, spending so much time intently studying Justin's and Elaine's relationship, she began to wake up to the possibility that such a relationship was possible. She had never come close to experiencing something like what they had. That other couple, Hardcore and Blackwolf, had the same kind of thing. Now Josanne had her career, and maybe that Lisben guy. Everyone else had their lives to live, so she resolved to try to go back to hers. Only now she knew what she was missing.

Sure, she spent some of the creds, had a good time. Her car was repaired for free by the Martinez's, plus upgraded some. She upgraded her body armor and got some new tech spy toys as well. After a week or so, though, the fun of the money was already starting to wear off. Dying for some friendships to share her good fortune with, she again reached for the vid-phone to see if Josanne was around. Just as her hand was about to touch the receiver, the phone rang.

"Uh, hello? Focus Investigations here."

"Melissana? Is that you?" a familiar female voice asked in her ear.

"Uh, hi, Elaine. How are you?"

"Well, I haven't spoken to you in a couple weeks. Justin told me all about that conversation you had with him."

"Yeah, sorry about that...I never told anyone about a job before—and I never told Josanne, honest! She figured it out on her own somehow! I just saw what you guys had, and how far each of you went to keep it, and just felt he had to know. I'm really sorry. A decent private investigator would never have done that."

"You're right, and that's why I called. I've been thinking about why you did that, despite your impeccable sense of professional discretion."

"And why's that?" Melissana asked.

"Because you did cross the line. A decent private investigator would never have told, but a great one might have. Added to that, a decent friend couldn't have left that quarry without telling."

"I—I don't understand," Melissana stuttered.

"Melissana, you have saved my marriage, my husband's life, and now, my freedom from the nightmare of someone finding out. I've researched your background a little before I hired you, and you and me share some pretty tough life stories. You stuck with me in the darkest point of my entire life, and I would like to consider you my friend. I mean, I don't really know you that well, but you were there like a sister for me."

"Uh, okay," Melissana hesitantly replied. Then she smiled, as though a weight had just lifted. She really liked Elaine, and while having family of any sort was new to her, it felt good. She broke into a full grin. "Yeah, sure, Elaine, let's give this a shot!"

"Okay, Melissana. Justin's working late tonight, so how about you and me get some girl time in? We need to shop to get you ready for our reunion dinner!"

"Yeah, at The Golden Chalice! Did you tell him about where we met?"

"No, he came up with that on his own, unless it had something to do with some bet he said he had with Monica. You'll really like Monica, she's a blast!"

"I can hardly wait! Where do we start?" Melissana asked eagerly, excited about her upcoming evening with her new friend. Elaine seemed just as excited as she was as she listed a few of the salons and shops they would visit. This, Melissana decided, was going to be fun!

<CLICK>

24

WAKE-UP CALLS

FOR THE FIRST time in almost a decade, when Jack opened his eyes, he couldn't see a thing. He jerked upwards to attempt a sitting position, but fiery stabs of pain clawed at his back and ribs where he had been hit, forcing him back down. Still trying to push past his agony to reach for his eyes, he realized he was bound to the horizontal surface he was laid out upon. He lay still for a moment, breathing, listening, thinking. Slowly the memories returned—his last memory was shoving that ganger out of the way of the sniper. What happened after that he had no idea. A sudden sickening feeling came over him—what happened to Chrome and Arañé? If they were okay, why was he bound?

He fought off panic, thinking, praying. *God, You're all-knowing. You knew this would happen way back before You said, "Let there be light." I don't know where I am, or what is going on, but You do. Help me to believe You are in all of this.*

Jack performed a self-check. He had a throbbing pain where he had been hit, but he felt little pain elsewhere, so he concluded he had been treated. By the clean smell and cool air, he was obviously not in Roanoke, at least not anywhere he was used to being—maybe a medical facility. And if he was at a medical facility, then he was being monitored.

"Okay, I'm up," he announced, probably uselessly. Any medical staff would have recognized when he was conscious.

"Yeah, I noticed," a familiar voice returned.

"Chrome? What's going on? What's wrong with my eyes—I can't see a thing!" The uneasiness started to return. He had somehow over the years begun to take his sight for granted. *How was that possible?*

"Relax—we had to cover them for you before the transport. Didn't want you staring at surgical lighting while they were operating on you. We weren't sure if you would overstimulate yourself and burn through your anesthesia. Then you started twitching and rolling around, so we strapped you to the table for the surgery and kept you bound afterwards so you wouldn't roll off the bed. Now that you're up, here…" Chrome undid the straps, allowing Jack to undo his own eye bandages.

"Pretty thick eye pads," Jack noted with a grin. "I guess they'd have to be. Wait—transport? Where are we?"

Chrome smiled mirthlessly. "Facility," he replied. "Like we said, Simon wants to talk with you. Didn't want it to be this way, though. Oh, and before you ask, your gangerboys are fine. We told them we were medevacking you outta there. Arañé's got the neighborhood under watch. You know the run. Arañé reports any trouble, we'll go back. He misses reporting in once, we send in two full teams until we find him. So far things are running like clockwork."

Raising himself on one elbow, Jack grimaced, feeling the bullet wound. "How long have I been out?"

"Week and a half," Chrome replied.

"And the shooter?"

"Arañé got him—some German-sounding guy. No ID. We're running DNA on him. We got a name, no affiliations yet. Decent bang on him. He tagged me, too; he actually managed to punch a hole, but the round was pretty much expended. After that, the bullet didn't hit anything that couldn't be hit." Chrome paused, then continued. "Different story with you, of course. You were gonked pretty good."

"How bad?"

"Let's just say that with the parts we had to replace, you'll never have to worry about drowning again." Chrome hesitated, considering whether to pursue the conversation any further. Finally, he committed. "So, why'd you do it? You almost died to protect that sewer rat who still doesn't even care. Spider says you always have your reasons, but this doesn't gig."

"He'd have died, Chrome. Even if he doesn't care, that doesn't mean that I shouldn't. At least if I die, I know where I'm going, and I know where he's headed. I couldn't just watch that happen."

"Well, maybe. Still doesn't make sense to me, though. You ready to move around a bit?"

"Yeah," Jack replied, grimly, "I'm ready. Guess it's time to talk to Simon. One question before we go."

"What's that?"

"How far would Simon go to get me to talk with him?"

Chrome openly smirked. "Not enough to drill you without talking first. Besides, the way I remember it, you jumped into the bullet's path. The shot wasn't intended for you. Relax, get something to eat first, make yourself relatively at home. Simon can wait."

"Yeah, guess you're right," Jack replied. A nurse brought in a tray of food, and Chrome left. Jack spotted a room camera rotate slightly as he was taking his first bite, then sighed.

Simon wasn't waiting at all; Simon was observing.

··· ···

The conference room was bigger than he remembered, probably because of the emptiness currently filling it. He had often frequented this room in the past, almost every time with at least six to eight others. The ghosts of their memories writhed before him for a second, watching him as he stood in the doorway. Were those ghosts longing for him to return, or still feeling bitter betrayal that he had left them in the first place? Even now that he was here and recognized that the ghosts lived only in his own mind, he still didn't know.

The room had retained its opulence despite the ruination of almost all it had once stood for. A large mahogany table topped with black marble rested on black marble floor, all polished to a reflective sheen. The sole source of light at the moment was a large digital map, which occupied the entire far wall, currently displaying the outline and geo-political boundaries of North America. On a raised dais before the map stood a polished mahogany lecture podium flanked on one side by a United States flag, on the other by the flag of his former organization. Jack blew a brief sigh, said a quick mental prayer to gather his courage, and stepped into the once-familiar room.

He no sooner got situated into one of the equally luxurious black leather executive conference seats than the digital map shifted to form an over-pixelated image of a fortyish man in an expensive tailored business suit. He was half-standing, casually leaning on the front of his desk in his paneled office. Behind the man's desk was another United States flag, an old-fashioned one that still had fifty stars in its blue field.

"Good afternoon, Mr. Mathews," the image began, upbeat. "I do hope you have found our accommodations suitable, if not amenable."

Jack began to reply, but decided upon a simple, guarded, "Good afternoon, Simon. I heard you wanted to talk. It's been about six years since I left. Why now?"

Simon glanced briefly at his wristwatch, another immaculate antique. "It's been five years, eight months, six days, two hours, seven minutes, and forty-three seconds from the time I started this sentence, Mr. Matthews. Five years, eight months, six days, two hours, eight minutes, and twenty-nine seconds since you left CYBER."

Jack had briefly forgotten Simon's uncanny fascination and awareness of time, probably on purpose. It had always unnerved

Jack a bit. Stifling a slight shudder, he decided to change direction. "Still hanging on to that name after all these years? Don't you think it's a little...antiquated?" He smirked, now caught up in the cat and mouse of the conversation.

"Why not?" Simon replied. CYBernetically-Enhanced Response Force is entrenched in its members, it fits, and few outside our agency are aware of it. Why, the very act of changing our name may draw attention to our existence, unnecessarily complicating loyalties, among other things."

"You still do the whole 'shadow-ops' thing, don't you?" Jack said, beginning to anger. "You want to play God but stay out of the light! Why is that, Simon?"

"Really, Mr. Mathews, you are already intensely aware of why that is," Simon coldly replied. "Every child who has ever read a comic book or watched a hero movie knows the answer to that question. We operate in shadow to protect ourselves and those important to us. If we exposed ourselves publicly, the dark would snuff us out completely so it could grow unchecked. There's something else that secretly every cop knows. Every artist knows. Every preacher knows, or should at least be aware of it. I certainly don't need to explain it to you, if you took even a single moment to contemplate it. It's the same at any level—any scene, any setting, any soul. We operate in shadow because that is *exactly* where light meets dark. It's a very finite space, and yet it's everywhere. Evil is ever-invasive by nature, so we are there to snuff the dark before it gets a chance to grow any further.

"But really, you already know all of this. Why don't you tell me the real reason you are so angry right now?"

"I'm out!" Jack shouted. "You claim you don't want anyone to know about you—I've done everything I could to forget, and I was at least partially successful! So why bring me back?" he said, now emotionally spent. "Why bring these memories back?"

"We brought you back to offer you a choice. We currently have opportunity to bring a new team on-line. They are each, of course, capably stellar in his or her own right. They are all ready now. We can offer them training, enhancements, and equipment. What we are not able to offer them is a leader. We've had our eyes open for some time now. New recruits don't have the skills, expertise, knowledge, or experience. The other teams are too tightly integrated and involved in other matters to split up. As you fully know, our teams bond tightly over time, and we have found that long-term loyalty to be an asset.

"We ran vector analyses on technical skills, loyalty, strategy, budgetary, team-building, administrative, integrity, and leadership. One name manages to turn up in every match list. No matter what protocols we use or variables we interject—especially in the areas of loyalty, integrity, and leadership—one name comes up consistently. Jack 'Greyscale' Mathews. You.

"I know your past. You were an exceptional team leader even in your early days. You became a Christian, eventually started checking out whether to go into ministry. Then you had that run that went very badly, lost a team member who was very close to you. As I mentioned, teams bond. After that you left on good terms, so we deactivated most of your active enhancements, left you your eyes.

"Over the next several years, you got involved with three churches. Despite your work, two of them fired you after you told them you were, 'borged,' I recall was how you phrased it. They felt you somehow cheated on God—didn't see your service as the obvious sacrifice we know it to be. They kicked you when you opened up to them, when you made yourself vulnerable to them, and when, in doing so, you needed them the most.

"Now you're in the Roanoke ghetto formed by the outzones of FoodTech ICC, Integrated Media, and Matsua Enterprises ICC. By all reports from Chrome and Arañé, you actually are starting to make a real positive difference there. Correct so far?"

Jack sighed. "Yeah, that's pretty much it."

"We have some dossiers, backgrounds, histories, and profiles on the prospective candidates. We know you're doing well where you are, although of late there seems to be some—complications—developing. But review these people's profiles, Jack. They need you, too. If you don't help them, who will?

"We'll work this just like before," Simon continued. "You have three weeks to decide. If at that time you walk away, no harm, no foul. Will you think it over for us? For them?"

"Yeah," Jack reluctantly agreed. "I'll think about it."

"Glad to hear it," Simon offered. A small disc gently slid out from one of the computers mounted in the conference room table. "I'd like you to stay at Facility for a day or so while you read these, so we can monitor your health to make sure you are okay before you leave. We owe you that much, and admittedly, more."

Jack turned to leave. On his way out the door, he heard the projection of Simon's voice call out, "Jack?"

Jack paused and turned. "Yeah?"

"Think about it." A pause, then Simon offered, "Pray about it. To the capacity I can, I have."

Jack turned with a shudder and left without reply. What Simon had just stated was so alien it unnerved him deeply.

… …

It was 4:29 A.M., and Jack was still awake, reviewing the profiles Simon provided the previous afternoon. These kids were definitely the types of people that CYBER would recruit. The implementation plan was sound. Jack could see the implants and enhancements initially selected for each one was a good fit. And, *Dear Lord*, their backgrounds were simultaneously heart-wrenching and inspiring. But Simon was right; without a leader, they could flounder and be lost.

Lost. Lost like the teammate he'd once had with him on a run against an ICC that was planning on poisoning the water supply of an entire city to kill one of their competitor's executives. The team had gotten in, two deckers to hit the computer system to delay

233

the poisoning long enough for the rest of the team to intercept the canisters. Jack and his protégé went in. His teammate caught some black ICE, which kept him from jacking out while pouring so much electricity into the apprentice he went comatose. Then a full squad of corporate soldiers hit their location before the rest of the team could counter-attack. They saved the city but lost one of their own.

Jack really liked the kid, and he felt personally responsible. After all, Jack was the one who'd planned the mission, took the kid on the run with him, and sent the others out instead of covering them while they executed the hack. That the others said there was no other way to save the city felt like so much consolation speech. He left CYBER shortly after that. He laughed bitterly. "And they want me back to do that to someone else? I don't think so."

… …

Jack left Facility three days later. Chrome was never much of a conversationalist, but the ride back to Roanoke was worse than usual. Finally, Chrome voiced it. "You comin' back?"

Chrome and Arañé had been on his team before he left. Jack considered his words carefully before responding. "Chrome, it's not that I don't want to help," he began. Chrome cut him short.

"It's just that you don't."

"It's just that I *can't*! I tried the whole 'secret agent' thing—but I'm spent! I'm doing good where I am!"

"Come on, Jack." Chrome scowled. "You 'did good' with us. You did good for us! Why throw all that away?"

"You know why, Chrome? As a cop, as a firefighter, as a CYBER agent being both, I can put off someone's death. Doing what I do now, I can actually save someone's life!"

"You once 'put off the deaths' of an entire city, and the other day we stopped a gang war before it broke out. That was your CYBER training, our CYBER enhancements, and two of your still-in-CYBER friends helping you out. Saving a life? Yeah, you done good

234

so far, but good luck with that Diamond stuff starting to trickle into your little community.

"Besides, you've seen what those kids have gone through. Makes me sick thinking about it, because we're the only ones who can really keep that kind of stuff from happening in the first place. And you know what else? We're going to go ahead and recruit those kids, because we *need* another team—and they've got the heart to up and join, and for all the right reasons."

Chrome hit the brakes hard, screeching the car to a halt just outside of Roanoke. He shot Jack an angry glare. "So, tell me. Who's going to save *their* lives, huh, Jack?" He then hit a switch, opening the passenger door. "You need some time to think about all this before you get home. I think you should walk from here, maybe clear your head a little. I can pick up Arañé on my own, then we'll both be out of your hair."

Jack had no sooner exited the vehicle than Chrome hit full throttle, disappearing into the city. Jack sighed and began the long walk back to his corner of the Roanoke out-zone. The last thing he wanted to remember was Simon telling him to pray about it, so of course that thought never left him for one step along the way.

…… ……

Simon received another hourly status check of the CYBER team members. His top priority was the integrity and safety of his teams and the success of their missions. One of the traces raised an alert—something was out of acceptable tolerance levels. Odd, it was one of the perspective recruits—and not a primary, but an adjunct, a secondary recruit. Simon traced the communication referencing the subject's name, then accessed the communications records of the ICC that the contact had come from. Next Simon scanned the entire recording to contextualize the message. Evidently, Josanne Sinclair's brother, James, was no longer content with his sister's banishment from their joint-owned corporate archology. Now that she was making it on her own and drawing attention to herself, he wanted her further out of the way. He had just put a contract out on her to have her killed.

Simon reviewed Josanne's file and calculated the options.

Item: The bounty is significant.

Item: Josanne Sinclair is merely a secondary-level recruit.

Item: She will resist certain elements of CYBER's methods.

Item: She will make an adequate member of the team.

Item: She will give the team courage.

Item: The contract provides an opportune moment for CYBER's current initiative.

Conclusion: Josanne Sinclair must be allowed recruitment.

Conclusion: James Sinclair's action was grievously wrong.

Conclusion: CYBER will take Mr. Sinclair up on his offer.

Action Item: Initiate Monitor: Subject: James Sinclair

Action Item: Initiate Defense Protocol: Subject: Josanne Sinclair.

James Sinclair had just crossed a line he had never even imagined existed.

　　… …

"Greetings, lylothien."

"Simon—What can I do for you?"

"A situation has evolved. A contract has been put out on a young woman's life. Please listen:"

A sound byte of a phone conversation played from a virtual speaker in the virtual conference room.

"The young woman's name is Josanne Sinclair," Simon declared flatly. "She is one of our new recruits."

"That's trouble," Iylothien replied.

"Yes, indeed it is—for James Sinclair, the one who put the contract out. As she is one of our recruits, Miss Sinclair falls under our protection. Alert your team. Monitor communications around the subject. Stay under cover, but do not let any harm come to the girl or her friend. I am providing James Sinclair's contract terms. Plant them somewhere the detective will find them, thereby alerting her. I am allocating a second team for support. One more thing. I will be contacting Greyscale on the matter. He has not yet committed, but I am expecting his reply soon. The contract will actually work in our favor to bring him in, but stay out of his sight for now."

"Understood, sir, I'm alerting the team. Who are you bringing in for the support?"

"Blaze's Fist will be en route. They are initially to observe and protect if necessary. Once the new team is recruited, they will assist with orientation and training."

"Yes, sir!" Iylothien almost applauded.

It was rare for two teams to work together, but if Blaze's Fist was coming in, this was going to be *good*!

…… …

Try as he might, Jack couldn't get to sleep. It had been two weeks since he'd left Facility. In another week, he would need to inform Simon of his decision. He didn't want to go, but he couldn't get those kids out of his mind. The couple who'd survived that whole biker horde coming down on them after killing off their families. The kid who'd gotten thrown out on the streets when she was in seventh grade, trying to make ends meet, staying honest in the process. *Pretty decent with a keyboard as well,* he thought, smiling to himself. Possibly her friend, who seemed to have the right character—rare enough these days! She seemed capable, but other than that not necessarily proficient at anything to bother much with her. Then there was that other kid, down in North Carolina. Odd, CYBER didn't seem to have much of a file on him. Seemed like he was on the right side, but other than that, his character was pretty much the opposite of that other girl from the media. His reports were incredulous—almost to the point of looking faked, if that was possible. Skilled to the point of being lucky, or lucky enough to be considered skilled, Jack couldn't be sure. The kid sure was intriguing, though.

Unlike most other military units, CYBER teams never really had a standard configuration. The team members either clicked or they didn't, and CYBER never tried to force the issue. Also, unlike most other organizations, they didn't focus as much on the tech as they did the persons who were using, or in most cases integrating with, the tech. CYBER was the most effective organization Jack had ever seen, but it wasn't because they enforced any doctrine or policies. It was because they recruited people who shared the same values. CYBER was also the most technologically advanced organization he had ever seen, but Simon was right when he summarized the

CYBER initiative. It wasn't the metal in the agents that made them so special—it was the mettle within. These guys had the makings of a good team. Simon was right—they had everything except a leader.

Jack's conflict was that despite all of the ghetto's problems, he loved the people in his community. He finally felt like he had a home. Upon his return, he held a meeting with his church. Scissors and Beast, his closest friends from the Razors, came as well. Reigis and Zip were there because the night of the near gang war they had seen everything from their perch. The meeting began like the ones he had held in his former two churches. He thanked them all for coming. He offered a special thanks to Scissors and the Razors.

"What's this all about?" Scissors had asked.

Jack told them the whole story. He had been born legally blind—corrective surgery couldn't help. He hated computers until he went to an old virtual reality exhibition. Since then, he'd gotten into Computer Science, Engineering, and Operations. He did so well that a deep-cover government agency recruited him after extensive personality testing, background checks, and capability simulations. They had developed a theoretical solution for his eyes, and CYBER resources could turn that theory into reality. They borged him for free, provided he join the agency as an operative. So, he joined—got his eyes and several other enhancements.

Evading the details of any particular missions, Jack explained that he and his team performed several of them together. Each one was executed against a serious threat to people who had lost all other government protection after the collapse. It was as though their agency was the federal government's apology for all its short-sightedness, failings, and flat-out corruption of its members. The missions were going good for a while, running in the shadows. It was cool, exciting, fun, and best of all, it was for a good cause.

"So, how'd you get into church work?" The question came from Not-Nuff.

"Good question," Jack replied. "I 'found the Lord' while driving around with an auto-rifle under my seat, looking for trouble. I was trained by a guy named 'Hawk,' who turned out to be an evangelist. One night we were riding together, and Hawk was just real quiet. I started kind of praying—you know, just throwing out a silent, 'Hey God, it's me.' But I felt like he was really listening, so I kept going. 'I know you died for me—but you know I'm not worth it, never will be.' Then I felt like he was talking to me, saying, 'You're worth it to Me, but you know, if you don't come to Me, then in your case I would have gone through all that trouble and pain for nothing.'

"I didn't want that—He had gone through too much for it to be wasted. Then I get this thought from out of nowhere, real harsh, like someone butting into a conversation. 'Yeah, He died for you. Sounds real good. But I know you—you never kept any of your commitments, and now you're going to do the same thing to him. You'll get real buddy-buddy, then after a year and a half to two years, you'll quit on him, and it's going to hurt him more than if you never started.'"

"That was the devil!" Rita Williams interjected.

"Yeah, it was, and I always heard he was a liar, but what he was saying was the truth. He was right, and I admitted it. I started to withdraw—I didn't want to do that to the Lord."

"What happened?" Surprised, Jack recognized it was Scissors who asked.

Jack permitted himself a dry laugh. "The Lord spoke to me again. He told me, 'Maybe you're right. Maybe you'll only stick a year or two, and then quit. I already know. But I know something else about you.' 'What's that?' I asked. 'That year or two is going to go by anyway,' he said, 'and if you don't try?' 'Yes?' I asked, and he responded, 'Then you're going to look back on this day and wonder if you would have made it. And that's going to *bug* you.'

"What could I say to that? If He was willing to take that risk, already knowing my track record, I was willing to commit my life to Him. Wild ride after that, but I started thinking about going into ministry. Eventually I got out of CYBER and was at two other churches before I came here."

"Wait." Scissors interrupted. "You mean all those times we, you know, when you were new to the 'hood, and we gave you all that—"

"—Instruction?" Jack offered with a smile.

"Yeah!" Scissors continued. "And you or those joeboy friends of yours could've put it down on us any time? And you didn't? How come?"

"Because I really care about you guys. I wanted you to hear what I had to say."

"Man, nobody's ever took hits like that for me, not when they could help it."

"Yeah, there was, Scissors." The gang leader was confused until Preach continued. "That's *exactly* what Jesus did when He let them put Him on that cross."

Jack wanted to give Scissors some time to contemplate that, so he paused for a moment before continuing from where he'd left off. "So anyway, I ended up here, which is actually fine by me, and things were going good. Which brings us up to Chrome and Arañé showing up."

"Yeah, Preach, who are they? What do they want?" This time it was Beast.

"They used to be on my team. They came to invite me to come back. They helped out with Crack City that night for old time's sake, but after I got pegged, they took me for treatment, and to give me the formal invite."

"What'd you tell them?"

Jack sighed. "I agreed I'd pray about it, but I was pretty clear I didn't want to.

"So that's what this meeting's about. I wanted to be open with you all. We've spent a lot of time together, and I've never mentioned any of this before. To be honest, I was kind of scared to. But I have about a week to go until I need to give my final answer. I really want to stay here—if you'll still have me—but I'm not sure I have that answer yet, and I'd really like for each of you to help pray for my direction."

Jack paused, looking at them. Here was the part when the other churches would get their horrified expressions because of what an abomination he was. But the group did something Jack hadn't expected. They all gathered around him, accepted him, and began to pray for him, each in his or her own way asking the Lord that He would put it in Jack's mind to stay, so they could keep him there with them. Even Scissors and Beast offered their prayers. The group prayed well into the night.

... ...

He heard their requests, heard them all. They were all in agreement, and He loved when that happened. He sympathized with them. But they didn't see the things that He saw, what would and wouldn't happen if they didn't get what they were asking for, and what would and wouldn't happen if they did. Like a caring parent of a struggling teen, an honest cop turning down a payoff from his partner, or the popular kid at school sticking up for someone getting bullied in the hallway, He would risk his popularity by making the right decision. He would rather jeopardize the relationships He had with them than taint their integrity. So, He gently, kindly, and deliberately told each one of them, "No."

... ...

Jack went to see Not-Nuff two days after their prayer meeting. "Hey, Preach. You're leavin', ain't you?" the youth sadly surmised.

"Yeah, I guess I am. I don't really want to go, but I can't tell you guys to obey the Lord while I'm ignoring Him. I admit I don't know where this is going, but I do need to trust Him through it, y'know?"

"Well, what are we gonna do without you?"

"Well, this sounds crazy, but the first thing I'm going to do is change your name. That 'Not-Nuff' tag has to go. From now on, I'm calling you Mo'Nuff. You've been like a Timothy to me for years now, and you have a lot of influence over what happens here. I talked it over with the others, and they'd like to see you step up to fill in for me, if you're up to it."

"Me? I'm just..."

"One of the things Paul wrote to Timothy was to let no one despise his youth. You're old enough. You just got tagged with that 'Not-Nuff.' Well, now you're Mo'Nuff. Keep trusting and following God. It's your turn, now. Even your brother approves. By the way, he has a great head for organization—I never really gave him credit for what he has. It's okay to ask him for input once in a while. He's starting to come around, and will probably appreciate being asked. Now, I'll be around a few more days, then I'll be in and around the neighborhood for about a month. I hope to see a lot of you, okay?"

"*Deal*, Preach. Thanks...for everything."

"Actually, Mo'Nuff, thank *you*. I wouldn't be able to do this if you weren't ready." With that, Jack turned and left. It was his fifth meeting of the day; so far, everybody had already known before he arrived what his answer had been.

The rest of the week had gone by quickly. Preparations were made, farewells said. Mo'Nuff held the farewell service. No details were given, only that God had called Jack to another service. "True enough," Jack conceded.

It was good that the church took up support for Mo'Nuff. Though Jack wanted to stay, he could see he might be holding the youth back if he did. They were a tight church, and having one of their own leading them would bring them tighter still. The church was packed for the service—the Razors were out in force along with several other visitors from the worn-out ghetto whom Jack had befriended during his stay. Jack was proud of how his little church made everyone feel welcome. He could see now that, even in his leaving, the church was continuing to grow.

The next morning, Jack called Simon. Four hours later, Chrome and Arañé showed up. After a few farewells, they were on their way.

243

"We're keeping a check on your streets," Arañé informed his former leader. "We're kind of curious where that Diamond is coming from."

"Oh yeah," Chrome added, "Simon wants to see you. Jack-in through the car. Oh, and Jack?" Chrome continued, getting Jack's attention. "Before you plug in—well, welcome back. We all missed you when you left."

"Yeah, thanks," Jack replied. "Anything else?" Jack had been a part of this team for a long time. Chrome making polite conversation and Arañé not making polite conversation was way off baseline. Arañé looked away, remaining silent, then he sighed. "Yeah. He wants you to meet someone in 'net. Just prepare yourself."

"It's been a while since I've jacked, but I was our decker once upon a time," Jack reminded him. All the same, Jack winced when he plugged in the electrode cord into the port in the back of his neck. Skin had overgrown his socketing—it really hurt plugging in again! Past that, he reached forward and hit the switch. The car disappeared...

and Jack was sitting alone inside Simon's office. Ten seconds later, the air shimmered behind the large desk and Simon appeared, immaculate as always, wearing an impeccable executive business suit that could be described as acute classic.

"Good morning, Jack. I am glad to see you here. Thank you for reconsidering."

"You wanted to talk?" Jack said, challenging him.

"Actually, no, I did not. But someone else did. I do agree it is important, so I made arrangements for you to meet here. It only seemed appropriate."

"Well then!" Jack continued in his challenge. He couldn't let off steam in front of just anyone, but he didn't think God would mind him telling Simon off. "Since when were you such an expert at value choices and what is appropriate? And when did you start to pray so much? And you're going to tell me you're sorry for all the hardship I've gone through, like you even know what that means! Okay, so I came back from a life in a poverty zone, but it was a good life, but I want you to know I'm doing this for those kids, not for you. So, I'm here, where is this mystery person?"

The lights behind Jack waivered slightly, but before Jack could turn, a voice from behind him said,

"Jeez, Grey, you sure are turning crotchety in your old age."

Jack froze, then slowly turned. He recognized the digital signature of the construct's voice immediately but was scared to believe he'd heard right. Yet there he was, the professionally-dressed, twenty-something young man with blonde hair too long for the office, wearing flip-flops, throwing Jack a grin that was undeniably authentic.

"Yep, boss, it's really me. Man, it's good to see you back!"

"Iylo?" was all Jack, completely overwhelmed, could say—and that was barely a whisper.

Inside the car, Chrome and Arañé knew exactly when the meet occurred, when Jack started openly sobbing.

The rest of the trip was uneventful.

25

TRIGGERS

"Hey, Iylo! What's kickin'?"

"Blaze! Good to see you! The Fist all here?"

"All five fingers! The General's on the roof a block away from 'Chalice—got his drones floatin' around doing counter-sniper ax-tivities. Menagerie and me checkin' street goins' on's until dinnertime. Foxfire's their hostess to cover the front door and main floor access. That leaves Fuser, and me an' him are gonna be havin' dinner with Greyscale at the table next to theirs."

"You think they'd make their move at the 'Chalice?"

"Maybe not, but then again, she and Martinez are both known targets. Somebody might go for a two-fer, not realizing that for the Martinez hit they want him alive."

"Yeah, guess you're right."

"So, Iylo, whatcha runnin' these days?"

"I'm keeping with 'Ultimate Fantasy.' I'm getting pretty high-level ranger right now. You?"

"Not runnin' any net-warez right now—doin' street duty. Got a combat sim waiting to load if something hits, though," she said, with that electric smile.

"Oh yeah? Which one?"

"Dance Floor," she related with such teasing delight it sounded to Iylo she had sung it. Iylothien let go with a metallic chuckle.

"Well, if ya gotta kink it, try to bring 'em into a street camera or something so I can watch."

"You got it, definitely. Well, I gotta kick. I miss you, Iylo." She sighed and gave him a virtual hug.

She jacked out, wiped a tear from her eye, and went back to covering the streets that the General's drones couldn't get into, looking for the nearest street cam, hoping for a tussle before dinner.

…… ……

The meal had gone well. It was really fun getting together with Elaine and Justin. Josanne and the Martinez's were trading jokes, obviously very comfortable together and familiar with each other. Monica and her boyfriend/fiancé were a blast. Monica's all-out-there personality perfectly balanced with Jim's quiet straight-man. That other couple—Corey and Sue, she reminded herself—had evidently just returned from an extended honeymoon and were just basking in the evening together.

Melissana had tried to discuss the threats to Josanne's life with her. The young detective stumbled across the file in one of her searches on another potential client. She didn't really understand how the file had been picked up as a search result, but the evidence inside was pretty clear. James Sinclair, Josanne's own brother, had put a bounty on the young reporter's head. The problem was that Josanne would simply not believe it. The next best thing Melissana could do was to keep a special eye on her friend, and hope to be able to defend her if anything happened. Once a direct threat was revealed, Melissana would have her proof.

Now that she was thinking about it, the group at the table next to theirs seemed a little off. There was just something different about them—the way they took their time, talking about nothing. Nobody else seemed to notice, but nobody else was a street-trained private investigator, either. Maybe it was time to draw them out?

"Susan, I think I need to use the powder room. Care to join me—that is, if you two can be separated for about five minutes?" she added as a polite gesture.

"Sure," Susan said. Then, leaning over to Corey, she purred, "Now, don't you go away. I want you right there when I get back."

There was nothing for Corey to say, so Jim and Justin helped him out. "Oh, don't worry. There's not a man on the planet who knows why that restroom herding instinct happens. You'll get used to it," Jim added with a gentle laugh, earning himself a love-tap from Monica's purse.

A few minutes later the girls returned. After another fifteen minutes, Sue began to tire. After profusely thanking their host, she asked if they could be excused. Corey wanted to stay, but she gently insisted, so they got up to leave. The restaurant hostess approached and asked if everything was alright. After multiple assurances that everything was, the hostess cheerfully escorted them to the main door. As soon as they had left, Melissana reminded Josanne that they needed to be going as well, as they had arrived together and Melissana had an early morning assignment of some type. Then they, too, thanked their host and, after passing through the same questionnaire—no they could not possibly try a dessert, as the real food was already rich enough for them both—they made their way to the Zimata. As expected, Justin, Elaine, Jim, and Monica remained behind.

Once inside the car, Melissana spoke clearly. "Josanne, that group next to us was there for you."

"How can you say that? Is this about my brother again? Why should I believe you?"

"Because it's the truth!" Melissana argued back. "They were not who they were pretending to be. I'm a *P.I.*, remember?"

"So where are they, then?" Josanne demanded. "Wouldn't they be out here by now?"

"That'd be too obvious, but I've got a plan. We're going to drive off, then our spotters will let us know if we're being followed.

"Our 'spotters'? And who are they?"

"Corey and Sue. They're going to follow a couple car lengths behind us. We're going to just drive around a while. If Corey and Sue see anyone trailing us, they'll let us know."

"And then what?" Josanne demanded.

"And then you get to find out who hired them."

A tiny drone silently floated fifteen feet above them, capturing the entire conversation.

… …

- *"The detective made you." The sub-vocal came from the General to the team at the table.*

- *"Okay, let's try to find them," Greyscale responded. Either he was rustier than he thought, or that private investigator was sharper than he thought. Or both.*

… …

Melissana, Josanne, Corey, and Susan played vehicular cat-and-mouse for some time. Finally, they decided to call it a night. They met in front of Corey and Sue's hotel, where the young couple pointed out their seventeenth floor suite inside a high-rise building just outside the FoodTech archology. Somehow after they had left the restaurant, they had found time to get into full armor. The fact that they had taken Melissana's concern so seriously did manage to cause Josanne to reconsider the warning, but there had been no activity all night. After saying their goodnights and hugging farewells, the couple drove into their parking garage.

"Well, Melissana, I hope you enjoyed wrecking our evening. We were having *fun* for a change!"

"Hey, I was having fun, too! I never ate real food before—not like *that*! But I know what I saw Josanne, and I know…"

Melissana's sentence was interrupted by an explosion that blasted through the night with a deafening boom that rocked the earth, tearing open plasteel walls, shattering several windows, and throwing debris for a half-block radius. Josanne and Melissana were both thrown to the ground. Stunned and horrified, they noted the blast had come from the seventeenth floor of Corey and Sue's hotel. A body landed in the street with a sickening crunch, still burning. The armor was burnt and twisted, but Melissana recognized it as Corey's. As flames escaped from the now open-air area that was once the hotel suite of Corey and Susan, the young private detective fearfully grabbed Josanne and ran for the car.

… …

Melissana knew Josanne couldn't dare go home that night. The only thing she could think to do was to go to a safehouse she had recently acquired with some of Elaine's credits and put both Josanne and herself up until they could get help. Josanne was beaten, burdened because she had doubted her friend. If she had believed Melissana, would Corey and Sue still be alive? Melissana was also feeling the heavy weight of involving the couple, so much in love, into a death-trap. Neither one felt like talking, neither one much felt like anything.

Josanne watched Melissana enter the room to clear it before Josanne followed. As Melissana turned on the light, Josanne heard an airy *thwip* and a small something that sounded like someone swatting a mosquito against their neck. Melissana yelled, "Josanne, *RUN!*" and attempted to slam the door shut, but a fist enclosed in black cryoplast emerged from the room and grabbed the edge of the door before it could close. A man in a full suit of jet black B.D.A. cryoplast armor appeared from behind a small couch at the far end of the room, aiming a handgun at Josanne. A second puffy *thwip* sounded as Josanne was drawing her laser pistol from her purse, and she felt a sharp sting in her abdomen. Josanne saw Melissana slowly sink to her knees and hit the floor with a non-eventful, distant-sounding thud. The reporter tried to flee down the hallway, but her legs were moving in slow motion. She, too, slowly sank to the carpeted floor, the poison seeping through her system with each pulse of her heart. The last thing she heard was synthesized voices talking to each other through the B.D.A.'s helmets. The voices sounded strangely muffled, but she hazily figured that was just the effect of the poison.

"It's about time. I thought they'd *never* show up!"

"It was easy enough," the other said with indifference. "Bag 'em."

PART 3

SYNCHRONIZATION

"I learned a long time ago that if you cannot get along with the team, you cannot be on the team."

— Eddie Windsor
Increasing Your Personal Capacity

"Your level of leadership is determined by size of the problems you either cannot or will not solve."

— Dave Minton

26

THE GLADE

THE YOUNG WOMAN opened her eyes, taking in a scene that made her feel as if she were still dreaming. She was dressed in a leaf-green gown that stopped somewhere above her knee. Suddenly, she sat bolt upright, shaken. She had never worn this dress before. It seemed like it was made of all-natural materials, but it fit kind of funny. Looking about, she gasped. If she felt shaken about the dress, she was frightened by what she saw now.

She had been sleeping on a straw mat suspended in the branches of an oak tree about fifteen feet above the ground. The tree itself was in the middle of a wood. From what she could see and hear, the forest must have gone on for miles in every direction. There was no trace of city anywhere. Birds chirped, insects hummed. Trees and flowers bloomed. Somehow her anxiety passed though, and she felt a sense of peace and belonging despite her earlier fears. She still felt somewhat dreamy, but per her nature, she soon had a small list of questions.

"Where am I?" was at the top of the list, followed by, "How did I get here?" and "How did I get into this outfit?" She had never seen or experienced any place like this; perhaps she *was* still dreaming? As she saw it, determining where exactly *here* was might give a clue as to how she had gotten to wherever it was. There was only one answer she could think of concerning the dress; she tried to put it

255

as far from her mind as possible. The birds and insects never paused in their chorus, and the girl once again calmed.

She reached for a tree blossom, but it was farther off than she thought. Overextended, she fell from her matting but landed so gently and naturally that she felt no harm. "Where am I?" she wondered aloud to herself. The only response she received was the continual chirping of the birds combined with the occasional insect hum from the environment.

At her feet, she noticed tiny golden, blue, and purple flowers. Intricately and delicately formed, they almost appeared iridescent in the soft glow of the world's day around her. "Why, hello!" She smiled, stooping down to gather a few. "I've never seen anything quite like you before." She started as the petals fell off at her touch, disintegrating into wisps of tiny sparkles as they softly floated to the earth beneath her feet. She noticed the air about her shimmer. She was alert now.

"All right, where *am* I?" she shouted. She had a sudden sense of being watched, and she knew they would hear.

"Hello there!" she heard from a cheerful male voice that came from above and behind her. Startled, she turned to the direction of the voice. She spotted a young man, slim but with the athletic build of a trapeze artist, wearing a green tunic and leggings similar to her gown. He had yellow-blonde hair of medium length that would have hung straight down, except—he was hanging upside down by his knees from an oak branch some 25 feet above the ground. He wore a wide grin on his face so big, and projected a boyish innocence so infectious, she was almost immediately disarmed. On all accounts, he sounded and appeared friendly, but she wasn't quite buying it just yet.

"Who in the world are you?" she asked, but smiled in spite of herself.

"Please, allow me to introduce myself," he responded. To her surprise (not her first since she awoke—was she awake? And if she *was* still sleeping, her dream was certainly taking an interesting twist!), he suddenly let go of his perch with his legs and dropped out of the tree, doing an aerial somersault on the way down. He landed lightly and surely on his feet. It was then that she noticed he carried—a bow? Where was she?

Extending a hand and bowing with dramatic flair, he proclaimed, "I am Iylothien, Barde de le Nêone, and Master of this Realm. For my part, I have the finest pleasure of speaking with the Brave and Clever, the Absolutely Charming, Melissana—and please allow me to say, now that I have finally met you, you are Completely Beautiful."

Melissana didn't exactly know how to respond—she felt herself blush. "The Neon Bard? Master of the Realm? Where *are* we? And what makes you the master?" Noting the forest that seemed to stretch for miles in every direction, she quizzically added, "Is anyone else even here?"

"Please, allow me to show you. I promise I will answer all of your questions.

"First, I mean you no harm, and no harm shall befall you here. That is, of course, not true everywhere, but it is true here. Walk with me, if you care to. There is much I'd like to show you."

Not fully making sense of any of this, but somehow trusting he meant her no harm, she followed. Reaching a bright and sunny clearing, he stopped. She paused a moment, basking in the warmth of a summer day.

"Here's a good spot. See those flowers, like the ones you tried to pick up earlier? Really look at them."

Melissana focused on the patch of tiny flowers just outside her shadow's reach, and saw they actually were somewhat iridescent. "How do they glow?" she asked in wonder.

Smiling, Iylothien responded, "That's not the real question. We're in a clearing, Melissana. Look up.

She looked into the brightness of the sunny sky, instinctively raising her hand to shield her eyes from the…shock hit like a Taser.

257

"*What?!* Where is the sun? *Where am I?!*" she demanded to know, an edge of panic cutting through the fabric of her tone. Her pulse was rising, her breath getting shallow.

"Easy, Melissana, easy," he stated, concerned. "Just relax, I'll explain. Examine the flowers more closely. You don't have to bend down or anything, just mentally focus on them."

As Melissana studied the flowers more closely, she was able to magnify the petals in both size and definition. Narrowing her eyes and concentrating, she was soon able to discover that not only did the tiny blossoms slightly glow, they were actually composed of trace patterns of light that seemed to flow like...

"These are data patterns!" she exclaimed, finally understanding and allowing herself to get caught up in the thrill of what she was experiencing.

Iylothien laughed. "I knew you'd like it! Melissana, you've seen video games before, you know networks. You're aware of the early virtual reality research and work? The best way to really answer your question was to first show you. You are now in a tutorial level of a highly advanced virtual reality system we call an Environmental Module—E.M. for short: Randolph and Emerson's 'Ultimate Fantasy.' I helped perfect it, and it remains one of my all-time favorites. You like it?"

The only response Melissana could give was to gaze about in wonder.

"The world here, everything," Iylothien explained, "is a virtualization of the network we are connected to. With practice, you will see that everything has a flow to it, everything has a certain thinness to it that represents various interfaces with the various objects. You and I are different. Our avatars are solid, because the density of information in our constructs is vastly greater than the network elements, which we normally interact with. That's why the petals disintegrated—you haven't yet developed the knowledge of how to interact with the flowers, so you violated their integrity, in a sense, breaking them."

Melissana was grinning in spite of herself, but shaking her head. "It's really cool. Zero cool," she admitted. "But why show it to me?"

"Okay, here goes." Iylothien exhaled in a sigh. "Try to brace yourself." Iylothien looked out into the sky and declared, "I think she's good, and Simon says she's ready. Slowly reduce the drip."

"What's going on?" Melissana asked. She was beginning to get used to Iylothien, but she was regaining that sense of panic, along with a sense of evasive memories put off by whatever dream-inducing relaxant she now knew they must have been pumping through her system. Memories of explosions, soldiers in black body armor as they entered their apartment, shooting— "Josanne! Josanne! Where are you?!" she shrieked. Suddenly furious, she broke out at Iylothien. "Where's Josanne, you son of a…"

"Easy," Iylothien exclaimed, dodging her attacks, his movements so smooth he seemed to be made of liquid. "Listen, I'll show you—come here and touch the rune on that rock formation."

Seeing there was no way she could actually connect a blow against him, Melissana calmed down long enough to reluctantly touch the rune, revealing a portal to a view through a hospital room camera. Gathered around a bed were two doctor types, some musclebound guy with a tight crewcut and sunglasses, a Hispanic guy with slim to medium build, and Josanne. The person in the bed was Melissana, fully clothed, her head in some kind of skullcap helmet with a couple dozen wires connected to a bedside computer system. The Hispanic guy nodded, then tapped Josanne on the shoulder. He said something to her, then pointed at the camera. Josanne looked somewhat confused. She then nodded, wanly smiled, and waved a little sheepishly at the camera, adding a private jive that everything was okay.

Melissana relaxed. Turning back to Iylothien, she said, "Okay, so what happened? Why all of—this? Which one of those guys down there is you? And why show all of this to me?"

"To cover a lot of ground quickly, I'll go as fast as I can. You and Josanne attracted some very favorable attention from someone who builds independent teams to help society out of the mess it's in. The resources available to this someone are astounding." He waved his arm and bowed with an exaggerated flourish, indicating the environmental module. "Case in point."

"The teams operate independently, autonomously, to avoid detection. More importantly, we also manage to avoid the ability of crooked governments or megacorporations to manipulate these teams for their own behalf. We seek out individuals who are highly capable, courageous, and above all, who show excellent character in how they do what they do. You, Melissana, are being recruited for such a team. As you and Josanne are inseparable, and since Josanne herself shows considerable promise, she is also being accepted into the team, as long as you are willing to join.

"We are aware of her brother's activities, which is why we acted when we did. I was the one who dropped James's files into your search results. We faked your deaths and brought both of you here, buying you time to accept or reject our offer. I will work with you as your mentor for the next three weeks. It will feel like a lifetime, trust me. During those three weeks, you will do all your E.M. training wearing what we call the Hood, like you are now. At the end of those three weeks, you make your decision one way or the other, and we make our decision whether you've passed the first phase of the training period. If you decide not to follow through, you will not be harmed, just simply returned to the life you left behind. Our profile shows you won't betray us, or you wouldn't have been here in the first place. If you do decide to continue with us, we will physically implant the E.M. interface, and you will become one of the quintessential cyberdeckers that hackers have dreamt of becoming since computer networks were first created."

"So, I don't lose either way?" Melissana asked.

Iylothien shrugged his virtual shoulders. "In truth, it's more a matter of you are free to choose what you will lose with impunity. This is a tough decision, Melissana. Like all choices of any importance, there are repercussions either way. You will both gain and lose opportunities no matter which way you go from here."

"Do I have to wait three weeks to decide?" Melissana asked.

"No, not at all. You can decide either way as soon as you'd like, although you would still need to undergo the first three weeks of training before final acceptance if you decided to move forward with us. Also, I think it would be wise to consult with Josanne and the other recruits for your team before making your decision. The core of the new team is almost all gathered."

"And which one of those guys down there is you? The Spanish guy?"

Iylothien chuckled. "Nah, you'd be hard-pressed to find a nicer guy, but he can barely work a school computer. Not his skillset."

He chuckled again, then covered his mouth and briefly averted his focus.

"No, I'm not down there. For your virtual environment training, I think it's best for you to just get to know me here first. Someone else will be taking you through your other training. You okay with that, Melissana?"

Melissana grinned, extending her hand. "Call me Vixenn," she stated.

"Iylo, then." He bowed. "I gotta run. They're going to bring you out in about ten minutes. Just walk around while you wait. If you have any basic questions, draw a question mark in the air and tap the trace."

"You mean you're just going to leave me in here with all this?"

"We hear you like to explore," he replied with a grin.

"Yeah, but what if I break something like those flowers?"

"You won't," he assured her. "Wouldn't be much of a tutorial level if you could just break stuff, now would it? Listen, I gotta run. Been cypher great having this time with you, and I'm looking forward to the next couple weeks. For what it's worth," he continued, "I meant what I told you in the introduction. You are brave, you've got a very sharp mind, I do find you quite charming, and," he hesitated, focusing on the virtual ground and grinning awkwardly, "you are Completely Beautiful." He looked back up at her and beamed. "There! I said it! Gotta run!" With that, he somehow hailed a giant grasshopper, hopped on its back, and with a wild shout, rode it off somewhere into the distance.

Alone in Randolph and Emerson's Ultimate Fantasy Environmental Module, Melissana paused for a moment, gazing at the electronic forest, trying to grasp the vast number of lines of code to model the global network to such a level of detail. She gave up when she recognized that even this tutorial level was beyond her. She was bewildered by the situation, but she had to admit, she was enjoying the rush and newness of it all. She then began exploring the world of the tutorial level around her, excitedly tracing question marks and touching every individual thing she could.

27

KICKSTART

THE AIR WAS tense as the group sat in some huge conference room that spoke of more wealth than Susan Blakeslee imagined still existed. The huge marble tabletop featured a black touchscreen monitor embedded flush into the table surface for each black leather chair. Centered on the table was a stylish setting consisting of various hot and cold beverages and a large display tray and bowl of—was that *real* fruit? She had now seen real food twice in her adult life, both times in the past week. She suddenly wondered how much of the whole food shortage was corporate-sponsored myth.

They were all physically safe, at least for the moment. Glancing around the room, though, she could tell each one recognized they had experienced some variation of being drugged and kidnapped. From what she could see, they were all in great danger posed by an extremely effective, methodical, and overwhelming force. Well, not all of them.

The streetwise private detective from the quarry seemed genuinely thrilled to be here. Odd—the night they had all been kidnapped she had been the most fearful. Had that been a ploy? Had she lured them into the kidnapping that night? Susan did not know a whole lot about the world of private investigators, but from what she'd heard, they were not an especially loyal breed. Whatever it was she was thinking, Susan didn't think it was shared with her reporter friend. Josanne just kind of hung her head and appeared sad about the whole thing. *So she did sell us out,* Sue concluded. Well, at the first chance she got, she would need to introduce Melissana to the Blackwolf, she thought to herself with a certain amount of pleasure.

She tried to reach out to hold Corey's hand, but he withdrew it. She risked a glimpse at him, hurt by his rejection. He was almost completely withdrawn into himself, tense, eyes darting in every direction, frantically seeking a way out without tipping off anybody who might be watching them. He was afraid. She remembered how he had berated himself the night the Jackals caught up to them while they were camping, and even then they at least had had a chance to resist. But these guys? The attack was all over before either Corey or Sue even sensed it was going to begin. She wanted to hold Corey's hand and tell him everything was going to be okay, but in his current state of mind the gesture would only provoke an argument. So, she withdrew her hand and held it herself for the both of them, keeping her fears, doubts, and thin wisps of encouragement to herself. For the first time since she had met Corey, she felt truly alone. Still, they waited.

After several more minutes, the main conference room door finally opened and the Hispanic guy entered the room followed by the thug with the crewcut—"Spider" and "Chrome," she reminded herself. There was a third guy between them she hadn't seen before— kind of young, slightly taller than average and just on the thin side of a medium build. Wiry, confident, good-looking, she admitted to herself. At first, she presumed he was a part of their group, but then she realized they were "escorting" him as well. Spider patiently led, Chrome *im*patiently hurried the newcomer to his chair. Susan knew two things. Spider really was just that nice—he wasn't playing "Good Cop." That was important, because that meant Chrome probably wasn't playing "Bad Cop," either—and that *really* worried her. Despite the muscled cyborg's presence, however, their charge seemed to almost swagger with an air that was a balanced tension between aloof and wary. They were told that each of them had a special skillset or talent that qualified them to be recruited for some government agency team. Susan wondered if the newcomer was being recruited to impersonate cats.

"Welcome to the Hall of Imprisoned Heroes." It was the reporter who came out with that statement, earning her ten "chutzpa" points from Susan, but losing three "wisdom" points. "I'm Josanne, this is Melissana, Corey, and Sue. What's your name?"

Susan noticed the guy watch her as she reached for—well, she thought they were called pears, but she wasn't sure, and she almost dropped her jaw when she saw his deep yet sharp hazel eyes framed by his black hair. *Man,* she thought, *this guy* is *good-looking!*

"You the guys I saw on TV with that rescue? I thought you guys all died," he responded.

"Yeah, so did we," Josanne offered, stabbing Chrome with a glare. Susan figured she would have to recalibrate her point-ranking scales for the reporter.

"Cool," the new recruit said dismissively, then paused. "Name's Johnny." Another pause, then he offered, "Never been on TV."

"Where are you from?" Josanne asked, trying to draw him out a little.

"Just been around," Johnny half-replied, picking up a plate and felt marker from the conference table. He glanced at Susan, causing her to pause as he started disinterestedly scribbling something onto the plate. Corey snapped out of his withdrawal, studying the pretentious newcomer with disdain. A few seconds later, Johnny flashed a smile Sue could only call winsome.

"Sorry," he said. "Nervous habit." Then he grinned and showed his scribble to everyone at the table, beginning with Susan. It was a picture of the five of them, plus Chrome and Spider around the edges of the plate, looking center; in the center of the plate was a near-perfect rendition of Snow White about to take a bite from an apple.

"Enjoy the fruit," he said, in a mocking tone.

Susan angrily returned her piece of fruit and Johnny grinned. "You've got to think about these things," he said. Part of her thought the warning made sense, but most of her was aggravated that Johnny had ruined the moment for her.

The conference room doors opened again, and a cheerful blonde with a knockout smile entered the room. Susan thought she seemed familiar but couldn't place her.

"Hi, everyone, and welcome. Feel free to eat what you want—it's all here for you." She talked like an upbeat flight attendant or a store greeter. The woman, approximately twenty-three years of age, was attractive—super attractive, Susan noticed, and then she had it.

"You're that super-model, Lyn!" Susan exclaimed. The Martinez's, media execs, reporters, and now Lyn. *How did I get here?* she wondered to herself.

Lyn cocked her head to the side, brought her hands up under her chin as though they were a frame, and flashed an extremely friendly smile. "That's right!" she said, with a combination of friendliness and excitement. Then she pointed to Susan, "But you can call me Foxfire. By the way, I love your hair!" she declared with that famous smile. "Fruit!" she exclaimed, heading to the bowl. "Got any pineapple slices?" If Susan had not been so won over by her smile and demeanor she would have been concerned about Corey. She was almost forgetting where she was. Even Corey was starting to relax. Melissana and Josanne were both staring at the celebrity, but where Melissana seemed to be enjoying the moment, Josanne was radiating skepticism.

"I recognize you, too," Josanne finally said, sounding accusing. "You were our hostess in that restaurant. I thought you looked familiar then, but it didn't connect. What were you doing there? What are you doing here?"

Foxfire rolled her eyes, then sat down in one of the chairs. "Well," she responded matter-of-factly, "I'm on one of the other teams you are being asked to join. I was brought in to help protect..." she began circling her finger in the air, "*you*," she declared, suddenly pointing at Josanne.

"Protect me?" Josanne protested, her voice beginning to grow in volume. "Protect me by jumping us and kidnapping us? Protect me from whom?"

"From him," another female voice cut in from the doorway. A pony-tailed blonde, not quite as tall as Lyn, but resembling her enough that they might be mistaken for twins, paced into the room. If Lyn was friendly, this one was all business. Wearing a functional shirt and pants outfit with knee-high boots, she practically marched straight up to Josanne with a folder containing some documents and photos. When she got to Josanne's seat, she bluntly tossed the folder onto the table, allowing some of the contents to slide out. The top document was a photo of a young man who bore a striking resemblance to the reporter.

"Your brother, James. Your friend tried to tell you, but you didn't want to listen. We've been watching your back for the last month and have in fact intercepted three assassins who were on their way to collect your brother's reward. If we hadn't intervened and faked all of your deaths, the hit would still be on, and you'd probably be dead by now. I'm not trying to be rude, but that's just the way it is. We did what we had to do to save your lives. So, let's quit playing dumb, okay? We've got business to attend to." Sue's mind strayed for a moment as she pondered which of the two would win if this girl got into an argument with Chrome.

The woman strutted purposefully to the mahogany podium in the front of the room, turned to face them, and just studied them for a few seconds. She folded her arms, her right hand cupping her chin. Evidently in deep concentration for a few seconds, she pursed her lips, her right boot jutting forward and resting on its heel as though the sole of her foot was wagging accusations at the group in front of it. Then she exhaled a quick sigh, as though she had just made a decision she was not quite yet sure of. Moving forward, her face changed to a half smile, her eyes going a little wider, as she began to address the group.

"Well!" she began. "First of all, I do apologize for how you were brought here. We would have approached you differently, but our hand really was forced by the contract. If there had been a different way, we would have used it."

Susan raised her hand, feeling kind of foolish for doing so, but afraid of upsetting the speaker.

The pony-tailed woman edged her head forward in greeting and said, "Yes? Questions are welcome here, by the way."

"So where are we, who are you, and what exactly are we being 'recruited' for?"

"That's fair," she replied. "You are in a government facility, a base of operations, so to speak. Hardly anybody knows about us, although word is getting out in certain law enforcement circles. You're not all that far from Roanoke, and after we talk, you're all free to leave if you want. I'm betting, though, that after hearing what we're doing, you'll all want to stay—at least to check us out and give us a chance.

"Our organization's name is CYBER, which stands for the CYBernetically-Enhanced Response Force. Yes, Johnny, go ahead and roll your eyes, I did when I first heard about it. CYBER's different from most government or corporate agencies, including most law enforcement entities. We're integrated into teams of about five to seven or eight. Each team has a leader who is responsible for training and provisioning the team. So far, not much new there. Where it gets interesting is what we are capable of doing, what we do, and how we operate in doing it.

"My name is Blaze, and I am a CYBER team leader."

"Are you going to be leading us?" It was Melissana who asked.

"No. My team, 'Blaze's Fist,' was brought in to provide backup for your primary team until we were able to talk with you. Each team operates almost exclusively independently of each other, but with you guys not yet recruited and scattered, and the hit on at least one of you, the situation demanded another team get involved. Now that we're here, we're to assist in training you. It won't cut the training time in half, but it will get you prepared much quicker. That turnaround time is important for a couple reasons. One of them is that, in case you haven't noticed, the people in this country by and large are in one severe amount of drek. Before most of the government collapsed, CYBER was created and given authority to conduct clandestine operations to protect our citizens where no other agencies would or could. There is some ongoing funding that keeps us in operation, but as I stated the teams mostly operate autonomously."

"How does that work?" Susan inquired.

"CYBER provides the initial investment of time, materials, gear, and training to get you started. Once fully trained, each team operates within the 'Spoils of War' clause in your contracts. For example, suppose you discover a mob operation that is raking in a million credits per month. Say your team takes out that operation, and in the process are able to seize assets from that operation worth 100,000 credits. We can't return the credits; the money has been removed from our economy via black markets. So the team keeps the credits, using the money to support the team, future operations, or whatever it needs. They can give it away, we don't care. In fact, we encourage that. The point is, the credits get re-inserted into our economy, the team gets provisioned, and there's no direct trace back to CYBER. Everyone wins. Team leaders know enough about how to finance and budget the team that there's no need to limit yourselves to take on only rich criminals. The real question is whether someone else could or should step in to protect the people so we can redirect the team's efforts elsewhere.

"So, let's get started. This is my Fist," Blaze began. "We'll answer any questions we can, and hopefully you'll stick around and we train you. Each of us has a set of specialties; all will work with you."

She paused a moment. Lyn stood and walked to the podium beside Blaze, more serious and proud than her earlier conversation would have suggested she could be. Lyn believed in her cause, that much was certain. The doors opened once again, and two guys and another, younger, girl entered the room. Except for the proud way they carried themselves, and that they somewhat resembled each other, they all looked like normal adults in their early twenties.

"You've already met Foxfire." At this, Lyn flashed a smile and did a quick curtsey gesture. "Foxfire is an advanced expert in handguns, operations, and human information extraction. Next to her is J.D., also known as 'the General,' who specializes in long-range firearms, drones, and has a singular talent in military strategy and planning." As she finished her sentence, the General smiled and offered a quick bow, revealing two small drones floating silently behind him. As he stood back to full height, the drones darted out to the opposite walls beside him and cut sharp turns to face the back of the room. They then each shot forward along the room's perimeter and cut sharply at within centimeters of its corners to meet, almost touching, at the conference room door. The General extended his arms forward, palms downward, and the two drones slowly and gracefully combined their flight paths into a helix weave, landing to rest on the backs of his extended hands.

Even Johnny was impressed. "How did he do that?" he asked aloud. "He wasn't working any remotes!"

Blaze smiled with satisfaction. "It gets better. As I've mentioned earlier, where things get interesting is what we are capable of, what we do, and how we operate when we do it. I've given you the high-level view of what we do, and I've also touched on how we operate. We are now going into the realm of what we are capable of."

Melissana was so excited Susan thought she was going to jump out of her chair. "Wait, you guys," she exclaimed. "Wait 'til you see some of this stuff! I only got a glimpse before I came to, but this is buzz!"

"What do you mean, before you came to?" Susan asked.

"It's true," Josanne confirmed. "They had her wired into some computer before she woke fully from the sedative. She was the first one who really got introduced to these guys." Then she paused and hung her head, focusing to the table so she didn't have to see their faces. "What Blaze told you is also true…about my brother and me. I didn't want to believe my brother would go that far. Melissana tried to warn me, but I put her off, which jeopardized all you guys. I'm really sorry. It was all there. I just didn't want to really admit it. Some reporter I turned out to be."

"Didn't hurt me any," Johnny retorted. "Anyway, we got Miss Too Hot and Miss Too Cold. So, who's Miss Just Right?"

If they would have been in an old western saloon with a piano player in the room, he would have jumped under the counter. Blaze and Foxfire glared at Johnny. Two drones popped into view over the General's shoulders and pointed towards the black-haired youth. Chrome stood up, shoving his heavy leather chair backwards about three feet. Spider placed a restraining hand on the musclebound tough's shoulder, but he appeared like he would be conflicted if he had to choose whether to let go or not. The other recruits all thought Johnny was going to get carried out in a bag.

"No guys, it's okay," the girl said, with a smile so friendly it would have disarmed a bear—which she had just done six times over as the CYBER members stood down. "Hi, I'm Menagerie." Susan was again struck by just how innocently cute this one was. She had the same blonde hair as Blaze and Foxfire, only hers was fashioned in kind of a pixie cut that hung just below the top of her shoulders. Wearing jeans covered with boots and a black t-shirt covered by a denim jacket, she had a look all her own despite the similarity to the others.

"And what's your specialty?" Johnny said, sneering, evidently having missed his earlier clues to be careful. "Baking cookies?"

At that, Menagerie just glanced up to Blaze and asked, "Can I show them?"

Blaze provided an approving smile, then simply shrugged. "That's up to you, M. Go for it."

A small tube the length of Menagerie's forearm appeared from the cuff of her jacket sleeve. A snap of her wrist and barely audible click later, the tube snapped to the full length of a quarterstaff. A flick of Menagerie's forearm later, the staff sailed over the table in a blur, striking the arm of Johnny's chair with such force it knocked the chair out from under him. He fell onto the floor with a thud. Somehow the staff rebounded back to Menagerie's hand, whereupon she somehow just as quickly collapsed it back into its tube form and returned the weapon under her sleeve.

"Menagerie is our resident expert on melee weapon combat," Blaze said. "She favors the staff for its reach and flexibility. She's also a genetics expert and does great with animals. Menaj, they need to see just what it is they are being recruited for. Call Rachel."

"Rachel! Come here, pretty lady!" Menagerie called, like she would a child.

The newcomers started. "I don't believe this!" Susan exclaimed, but none of the recruits heard. They were too stunned.

A Doberman Pinscher all of 29 inches high at the shoulder pranced into the room and nuzzled up to Menagerie. On its head was a cryoplast half-helmet with eye slits covered with what Susan figured was dark, rose-colored bulletproof glass. "That's a good girl, Rachel" Menagerie crooned, showering the dog with affection. "Rachel," she continued, "the man in the black coat is Johnny." Everyone in the room shifted their attention to the recruit, wondering what Menagerie was up to. "Johnny wants a kiss. Go on." With that, the freakishly large Doberman raced around the table in a blur of unnatural speed and jumped on Johnny before he could think to move. Everyone, including the reluctant Johnny, began laughing as the giant dog started licking his face despite his objections. No one had a clue how the dog understood that it was Johnny in the black coat. *Good girl, Rachel!* Come here!" she called in a cheerful lilt. Rachel returned to Menagerie's side and faced the group at the conference table. "Show teeth." Rachel's lips curled back as she obeyed. Menagerie took a small pen light and flashed it into the mouth of her pet. The recruits observed the light brightly reflect back. Rachel's teeth were lined with metal. This dog had a *serious* bite.

Blaze continued. "The helmet isn't actually worn, it's implanted. Besides the obvious protection offered, it is chipped to enhance Rachel's already gifted intelligence. It also augments her sensory capacity, including vision, hearing, and sense of smell. An advanced cryo-treated polyfiber lines most of her entire body. For all practical purposes, she is both blade and small arms bulletproof. Her muscular-skeletal system is chromed, and we've taken care of some genetic disorders brought on by irresponsible breeding in her bloodline. Rachel was a prototype, a test of some of the surgical procedures we use for ourselves after we saw it worked on some lab rats. Yes, I said surgical procedures. We're on the ultra-tech side of cutting edge, and we have all been augmented in some way. We wouldn't be CYBER without the cyber. By the way, the metal lining Rachel's teeth is a titanium alloy, sharpened to a near-molecular point. Johnny, you *are* lucky. Menagerie could have asked Rachel to fetch."

"Point taken," Johnny replied.

"And, to complete the introductions—Fuser."

The tall, somewhat lanky young man about the age of Johnny strolled off the platform and around the room, matter-of-factly scanning the recruits. His steps sounded heavier than he should make. His focus lingered as he passed Corey, then with a quiet, "Hm!" to himself, he continued, but Corey couldn't tell if it was a scoff or approval. He acknowledged Chrome with a slight nod and stopped when he got to Spider. "How's the grapnel working?" he asked, again so matter-of-factly that Susan almost didn't recognize he had spoken.

"Great!" Arañé replied. "Excellent design. Thanks for sharing."

"Yeah, I always wanted one myself, so since it worked for me, I thought, well, hey…you would find good use for it."

Without another word, he extended his right forearm and pointed his fist down, firing a nearly invisible micro-line from the forearm grapnel gun he had designed a few years earlier into the wall behind the rest of the Fist. Retracting the cord at breakneck speed, he zipped to the podium. He ejected the anchor from the wall and reeled it back into his arm while he performed an aerial somersault to land back with the others.

Blaze picked up her narration to bring the room of startled recruits back into focus. "Fuser is our gadgeteer, as well as a close combat specialist and wheelman."

Corey leaned forward in amazement. Susan, overloaded, looked away. Josanne thought she was going to be sick. Melissana had a grin that seemed to be double her face size. Johnny sat, trying to be impassive, and failing. While Blaze was talking, Fuser rolled up his sleeves and began electronically opening and exposing various compartments and devices in his arms like an aircraft checking flight controls before takeoff.

He followed that by retrieving an inch-wide piece of steel from behind the podium, bending it by hand into a self-supporting stand. He brought his hands forward and caused an electrical discharge that arced between the palms of his two hands. Addressing the recruits like he was giving a classroom lecture, he added, "Now apply the magnet, and…" In grand finale, the arc shot forward to the metal stand he'd created, which began glowing red and throwing sparks of its own. Fuser cut his current when the steel began to melt, smiling at his now completely captivated audience. Rolling his sleeves back down, he shrugged his shoulders as he quietly stated, "You gotta love your applied 1890s electrical science."

After some time of stunned silence, as the group processed what they had just seen, a hand hesitantly rose.

"Yes?" Blaze asked.

"So, if you're our backup trainers, who's primary?" This question came from Corey. Sue was relieved he was beginning to participate. She offered him her hand, and this time he took it with a gentle squeeze.

"Glad you asked!" a man declared, entering the room with the brisk pace of someone used to authority. "I'm Jack 'Greyscale' Mathews, and I'll be leading your team, by which I mean, 'our team.' Your primary trainers are my former crew. They came highly recommended," he added with a smile. "Besides our own track record, which was extensive, we trained Blaze's Fist. Actually, you've already met your primaries in one way or another. Front and center, Hounds!" he called. "You're on."

No one was surprised when Chrome and Spider walked onto the platform. Then the door re-opened and a man who seemed vaguely familiar to Susan entered the room. Corey smiled and visibly relaxed. As the man approached the front of the room, he heartily clapped Corey on the shoulders twice, grinning.

"Hey, how you doing, kid? Really glad to see you here." Corey was speechless. Sue vaguely remembered him from somewhere, but she saw Corey clearly trusted this man. His grey eyes acknowledged Susan. "Young lady, that was quite a stunt you pulled when we first met." He chuckled. "I gotta admit, you surprised me, and that doesn't happen all that much anymore." And with that, Rickshaw took his place on the platform. Then Jack slowly joined them, almost shyly, like he was seeking a shared camaraderie he wasn't sure would still be there.

Susan noticed they all seemed somehow transformed, just standing there together, waiting for something, lost in some distant group memory. She wondered if she would ever feel what they seemed to share in that moment together. Spider put off his usual demeanor and grow taller. Chrome wasn't as scary as he was— *proud*. Rickshaw looked like he was in his element here—that he just somehow fit. Their leader seemed to be basking in it all, like he had missed something for a long time without knowing it and was now just glad he had it back. She would have thought they were at an awards ceremony receiving the Medal of Honor or something, but they were just standing there, simply being themselves, and yet so much more. These men had willingly gone through extensive and probably painful surgeries, maybe sacrificed their very arms and legs, to protect the people of their country, people they had never even met, people who might well regard them as freaks because of those very sacrifices. Yet they willingly exposed themselves and took on things most people went through their whole lives trying to avoid even hearing about.

She glanced at Corey and knew by his rapt attention that he saw it, too. She leaned into him, and he wrapped his arm around her. She stood, offering a weak, "Excuse me." Then she continued. "I'm sorry. I don't know what to say, or how to say it, but...

"Thank you. Thank you for all you have done for us. I don't know how you could do it—I don't know what you think I might have that merits the sacrifices you all have made. But thank you." She slowly started to gently applaud them, not caring what the others thought. To her surprise, most of the others joined in. Josanne stayed seated, slowly shaking her head. Johnny sat back in his chair, stuffing his hands deep into his black duster pockets, adjusting his scoff.

Those on the platform felt a little awkward. They knew what battles, street-fights, crime, terrorism, despotic machinations of mega-corporate executives, and rejection because of their augmentations looked like. But outside of their own groups, even from the very people they helped, not even Jack with those eyes of his, often saw true appreciation for what they did.

Suddenly, the wall-sized screen came to life behind the two teams on the platform. "Good afternoon, teams. Good afternoon, recruits!" The speaker was a man in his mid-forties or fifties, smartly dressed in a sharp, dark navy blue business suit and tie, distinguished enough that he could have been a vid actor. His office could only be described as opulent, with two different versions of the United States flag behind him.

"Welcome to CYBER," he continued. "I am Simon, and I am the head of this elite and illustrious Agency. I want to tell you myself that I am delighted to see you all here. Many people may have the skills we require, but what we really need are skilled candidates who also have integrity and character. I believe I am seeing a group of people with that unique blend of skills and character. Yes, even you, Johnny, even you!

"You see, I became secretary of CYBER at a time when all other systems and organizations were failing. I saw that we dare not fail! I began a thorough examination of every organizational, historical, psychological book, treatise, and document I could find to discover what we would need to guarantee our success. Over the years of my researching, I stumbled onto an old book. In that book was another book, and in that book, was a chapter and a verse. As I read that verse, I found something that I knew I could use to anchor the success of our endeavors here: 'The wicked flee when no one is pursuing, but the righteous are bold as a lion.'"

Jack started at that. Simon had mentioned the verse from the Biblical book of Proverbs to him when he was leaving CYBER, but Jack dismissed it as Simon just trying to keep him in the agency.

"I've been monitoring you all since certain of your 'activities' initially drew my attention to you. Spectacular as some of them were, it was your display of character that earned you the opportunity to join us. Our teams operate independently, so it is essential that we safely trust you. Make no mistake, you will face times of grave danger. You must also have absolute trust in each other. And the only way we can ensure that will happen is for each of you to first trust in yourselves."

"So, what's the Master Plan, movie-man?" Johnny said, interrupting.

"The Master Plan," Simon returned, "is fairly simple, which is itself a lesson: most effective plans are fairly simple. 'Simply simple' often means too many details are unaccounted for, while 'unnecessarily complex' is just as often too intricate, lacking the flexibility to work in the field.

"To the point: You will spend the afternoon in a group tour of this facility followed by a physical fitness event. This evening, you will review history and current events with your trainers and discuss where CYBER fits in to all of this. You'll then be left to discuss amongst yourselves where each of you see yourselves fitting in. You will be our guests for the night. Each morning after exercises and breakfast, you will be completely free to leave if you wish. If you do leave, you will return to your life exactly as you left it. The news will report that in fact it was intruders found at the scenes of your deaths. Be warned: Josanne, your brother is likely to act out again. Johnny, the corporation you fleeced of their ill-gotten gains are likely to resume their retribution.

"The next three weeks serve for both training and mutual evaluation. For those who stay and pass the three-week evaluation period, you will be offered a position on the team suited to your individual skillsets. Accepting a position carries a commitment with it so we can count on you, and so you will know you can count on each other. Inductions follow, and on the following day, you begin your surgeries. After that—"

"Our surgeries? What surgeries?" Josanne broke in with a raised voice that showed more anger than concern. Jack had been expecting this, and Simon must have known her outburst would happen sooner or later.

Simon continued with not even a hint of impatience other than his choice of words. "—after that you will have a six-month period of training in your new capabilities and team integration before going on your first mission. Josanne, I believe Miss Blaze has already answered your question. To quote: 'We wouldn't be CYBER without the cyber.' The surgeries are a great risk, they are a tremendous sacrifice, and they are an absolute necessity. I will be completely frank with you. If you stay with us, there will be many days you will wish you had decided otherwise. From what I know about you all, however, each of you in time would deeply regret any other course of action. Let me be clear—you are at a fork in the road, not a crossroads; there is simply no going straight forward as though nothing ever happened to you. If you pass the three-week evaluation, you may freely decide which path to take, but the two paths are mutually exclusive. So please, whatever you decide each day, choose wisely. Ask your leader, Jack." At this, Jack visibly winced. "I am sure he will have much more to say on the matter."

Simon glanced at his watch, more for effect than needing to check the time. Simon always knew exactly what time it was. "I must be going. Does anyone have any other questions for me before I leave you with your trainers?"

"I do!"

"Yes, Melissana?"

Melissana pointed out the various agents on the platform. "Chrome, Spider, Rickshaw, Greyscale…"

"Yes?" Simon asked, drawing her out.

"Where's Iylothien?"

Jack cut in before Simon could get the words transmitted. "Unfortunately, Iylothien couldn't be here in person today. Although we all would have liked to see him here, he's running a critical surveillance right now. I promise you, Melissana, you will see him in person before the three-week period has passed."

- *"Jack! What are you doing?" Chrome almost sub-vocally shouted over his throat mike.*

- *"I'm leading my team, and I will not start by keeping critically important information from them. I'm telling them the truth—all of it."*

- *"Jefe, you sure that's wise? That wasn't part of the program," Arañé joined in.*

- *"Simon brought me in to lead this team. If Simon didn't want me to lead it, he should've picked someone else."*

- *"You sure you're not just dumping your trash their way?" Blaze added. "Dumping your guilt on them so you don't have to do this?"*

- *"I'm telling her because she needs to know! They need to know the risks! Don't start kicking me because I'm trying to do what is best for my team."*

- *"Um, guys? They're all looking at you weird."* This was Foxfire. *"Think you want to rejoin them instead of coming off like you're all having seizures? I thought we were recruiting these guys. Save it for the gym!"*

The group disengaged from their sub-vocal discussion and refocused on the physical scene in front of them. The General was talking with the recruits, smiling, explaining the capabilities of the sub-vocal systems, using the argument to instruct the recruits. At that particular moment, he was stating that, while the usage was not detectable to others and used for communications in all of their operations, the sub-vocal systems could distract the recruits from their mission if they weren't careful.

Josanne wondered what the obvious dissension had been about.

··· ···

"The wicked flee when no one is pursuing, but the righteous are bold as a lion." Simon had heard the whole conversation. Just because he'd shut down the video didn't mean he'd stopped monitoring the meeting. Jack's caring forthrightness would jeopardize recruiting the candidates, but his logic in telling them was correct. In time, this might become one of the strongest CYBER teams of all.

··· ···

"Oww, my *back*!" complained Corey, getting ready to turn in for the night. "I thought I was in shape!"

"You all right, honey? You took quite a spill out there when Chrome passed you the ball."

"Yeah, I'll be all right. How about you?"

"Who would've thought a supermodel could be so tough?" she groaned.

"Well, you gotta hand it to CYBER—they know how to do physical training. No wonder that Simon called it an event. Who plays basketball like *that*?"

"I guess these guys do," Susan said, moaning. "Wow, I am beat!"

... ...

"What do you mean, this is buzz? Melissana, this is crazy!"

"Josanne, think about it! How cool is what they're offering us?"

"What? The chance to get your arms replaced with machines so you can get shot up better? Like that Chrome guy. He's more machine than he is human, and he acts like it, too. I bet he can't even feel emotion anymore!"

"There are lots of all flesh-and-blood people who have no emotions! Why have emotions if there's no hope? Josie, think about what they've already done for us—for you! Don't you even feel a little indebted to them? They risked it all, just to give you this chance. Are you going to throw that in their faces? Besides, Arañé is just as wired, and he's got plenty of humanity to go around."

"My body works perfectly fine, and I *don't* want their invasive limb replacements! What happens when they get upstaged by last year's model? Send them on a trip to the dump?"

"Well, I'm staying. You can leave in the morning if you want."

Josanne was upset. "Damn it, Melissana, why are you so bent on this? Is it because of that guy you haven't even met yet? Can't you see you're getting in way over your head?"

"That's just it, Josie. Look, I know this is way weird, but maybe that's why they're giving us the three weeks. I think they know we're in over our heads, but they want to give us the time and the tools to teach us to swim."

"Well…okay. We've got the three weeks. But did you see that argument they had at the briefing? They're hiding something. I'll stick around to watch out for you, but I don't like it."

"Thanks, Josie, for staying with me, and for watching out for me. Any idea what positions they might have for us or what their plans are? Obviously, I'm in training to be a decker; do you think they'll match everybody up like that?"

"I don't know, Mel—I just know I don't want to get all my limbs replaced like those guys. Don't you know what I mean? I want to be able to *feel*."

… …

The other recruits had all turned in for the night, but Johnny was sitting in the kitchen, drinking a Soy-da when Blaze walked in, casually opening the refrigerator door.

"So, sittin' all alone in the kitchen. What's Johnny thinkin'?"

"Johnny's thinking Blaze is trying to pick his brain about now. Stay out."

"Yeah?" she replied, closing the door hard. "I'm thinking Johnny got game, but he's too busy tuckin' in to be any use to the team."

"What, 'cause I ain't like your bot-girlz and joy-boyz? I don't know what biz you're trying to work, but this little operation's got more kinks than Levi. Your 'fist' couldn't handle streets if they were dropped in a Jersey 'burb, and you all coming off like you're Town Game. Speaking of which, I didn't hear how *you're* tricked. I'm guessin' bot-girl ain't your gig. Want me to guess?" he said with a leer.

"Oh, Johnny baby, I'm mostly all natural me, but I do be kinked, all right. Null sheen to that! Wanna find out how lucky you can get?" Blaze purred, gently stroking the back of his hand.

"Heh, now you're talking, street-girl. Whatcha say you an' me—*hey!*" Blaze grabbed his wrist and threw him onto the kitchen table so hard a loud crack was heard. At first Johnny wasn't sure if the sound had come from his back or the table, but when he hit the floor, he figured out it must have been the table.

"You coulda broke my arm—or my back!"

"You had it coming. *That* was for Menagerie!" She came at him with a flurry of arm movements so fast he could barely track them. He jerked right just as her kick came. It missed him by a quarter inch. "What the—? What's *wrong* with you?"

"*That* was for the 'Miss Too Hot' crack at Foxfire!"

By now the surprise was over, and Johnny was gaining his rhythm. "All right, you wanna go-to?" he said, challenging her. "Let's play."

The fight began in earnest. They both knew they would not use the silverware and cutlery, but anything else was fair game. Johnny used a combination of kung fu and street. Blaze fought with her own brand of martial arts. Each countered the others advances and blows.

"I'm impressed, Johnny—you are good," Blaze offered after about a minute had lapsed. "You still want to see how I'm tricked?"

"Baby, I can keep this up all night," he replied amidst the blows they were still trading.

"No you can't. Warning: three, two, one, and…*Party Time!*"

Blaze kicked a chip-skill, allowing the program wired to her neuromuscular systems to do what it was created to do, overclocking her movements. She still decided where she wanted to make contact, but the system rerouted how her limbs would get there. Up until then her movements had been professional, well-timed, smooth, artistic. Once the "Party Time" program kicked in, she became a blur of erratic asymmetrical movements that Johnny could only describe as freakish. The shock alone was enough to throw off the rhythm he had achieved in the fight. He was thrown off his game, and he knew it. A sudden sharp pain stabbed him in the right side as the back heel of her right boot connected after extending past him and coming back in as her knee jerked shut. Less than a second later, her right shoulder jammed upwards into his chin, followed by her right elbow smashing into his solar plexus, her left hand simultaneously grabbing the neck of his shirt and pulling him forward for a second ram of her right elbow. For the next minute after that, she used his body to move furniture. He was just short of blacking out when she stopped and bent over him.

"Johnny? You hearing this?" He barely nodded. "Good boy. Now stay with me, Johnny. We're an intensely loyal bunch, Johnny. Don't diss my Fist—it ain't polite. We're gonna work together, we all same-side in this, got it? Teams don't diss on each other. Now you're good, you're the deal, chip truth. You could take maybe five, seven, maybe even ten normals. But you'll be going against more, an' the choobs we dance with ain't normal, one way or 'nother. You're skilled, and I swear you do got the luck. We know what you're fighting for—we can help you, take you farther than you've dreamed. But it's a team gig, Johnny. They're all stronger than you think they are. And they'll back you, too, if you let 'em. Yeah, Simon thinks they need you, or you wouldn't be here. But good things ain't never a one-way street, Johnny—you need them just as bad.

"Sleep on it, Johnny," she said, just as he lost consciousness.

- "Chrome? Blaze here. Found Johnny sleepin' in the kitchen. Mind putting him to bed for me?…I can hear you laughing, you know!"

20

WORK AND PLAY

"GOOD MORNING, EVERYONE." Jack greeted each of the recruits as they came to breakfast. Most of them still appeared worn out from the training event from the day before, but Johnny looked like a truck had run over him. He'd have to talk with his teams about that later.

- *"Blaze, we're supposed to be recruiting the kids, not driving them away," he said, sub-vocally reprimanding her.*

- *"He had it coming, and besides, he had to be humbled a little to open up to the team. 'Tough love' I heard some chummer call it once," she replied, giving him a wink.*

So, she remembered! Blaze had been a handful in her day, but Greyscale couldn't be prouder of how she was doing. He could savor the memories later, but this team was waiting for him. Best to simply get the day going.

"Let's just hang out around here in the living room area. We're hardcore, but we don't need to be overbearing. I know you guys all had a rough night last night, so we can afford to take it easy this morning and just hang out. This is the moment you've all been waiting for. I know you've been wondering what your roles will be on this team of ours. I've watched all of you since before you got here, and CYBER was able to put a pretty good profile together. I promise you, no secrets between us. It's a standard rule I've had with all my teams. Yes, that goes for me, too. As proof of that, inside the folders Blaze is passing out is a copy of the same profile I read on each of you. If you want to take the time to read it, you will know what I know about each of you.

"Over the last month, I've analyzed these profiles and drawn up a proposed fit for each of you on this team. I have also paired you up with at least one of the instructors, who will go over your augmentation and training programs with you. Adjustments to the plan can be made, but please be aware I've been doing this for a long time. I have a pretty good eye for this sort of thing, no pun intended. Further, I have reviewed the plans with Simon. Simon agrees that while this is near-optimum, it won't work if you're not comfortable with it. So, consider it. Think about it. Of the entire three weeks, fine-tuning this plan is by far one of the hardest things you will do. What we've said before is true—you can simply return to the lives you've led before. But it is also true that you cannot simply go back to the *way* you were before. Any deliberate choice is a commitment, and saying no to the commitment is in itself a commitment.

"And now for what you've been waiting for. Everybody get comfortable—I'm going to show you some people who are really impressive."

A wall screen came to life, displaying a satellite image video zoomed in to show a massive battle between a bunch of cars going against a ridiculous amount of bike gangers. Everyone leaned forward to catch the action, as miraculously the cars seemed to get the better of the biker horde. Footage then cut to a group of seven cars facing the bikers alone, one parked in front of the leader's entourage, just staring them down while the cars raced around the city, whittling themselves down in number until the only two left started blowing up some kind of equipment arrayed against the city. The camera zoomed in closer on the pair staring down the bikers, showing a de-helmeted Corey and Sue. The footage cut to a large rocky area where Corey and Sue were again taking on a bunch of bikers. A remote camera caught him dropping off Susan while on the move and her going to town on the bikers, and again the ruse when she pretended to be Mr. Martinez. The vid showed Sue back-flipping in full race armor after nailing one of the bad guys. The other recruits turned and stared in awe at the couple.

"Corey," Jack began, "your driving skills are exemplary, as is your commitment and sense of duty. Sometimes a team gets in a tight spot, and we'll need a heavy who won't ditch on us if he's not already in the thick of it. In short, I figure you to be our wheelman. You will be training the next three weeks with Rickshaw and Fuser. They'll explain the rest to you. You okay with that?"

"I'd be honored, sir," Corey replied, looking up at Rickshaw.

"Music to my ears, Corey, but I'm not a sir. I'm just Jack, or when we're on the street, Greyscale.

"Sue, with your gymnastics skills and that fighting expo you did in full body armor, you've got close combat written all over you. It gets messy, and I don't want to put you in danger, but protecting your team sometimes means taking out bad guys. Like that guy you dropped in the vid. By the way, you may not know this, but that was one of the lead organized crime cartel underlings you managed to pop. I hear Chrome and Arañé are jealous," he said with a smile. "Your trainers will be Arañé and Menagerie."

"Not Chrome? I mean, I thought he was your muscle guy."

"Glad you're thinking, but no. Your fighting style is too different from Chrome's, but very similar to your trainers'. Yes, we can make it so your fighting style can change, but we really make every effort to accommodate who you are, not take you over. You're already quite adept with your current style, and I wouldn't tamper with that. By the way," he said cupping his ear, "Chrome just passed on his thanks for thinking about him."

More footage from the quarry rolled, showing a red sports car taking on overwhelming odds. "Melissana, every team needs at least one decker, and you're it. I know it's not a surprise to you or Josanne. But since it's hard to show a video of your activities…" He was interrupted by stifled chuckling from not only the recruits but also the established team members. As he completed his thought, the screen abruptly changed to show network diagrams tracing out the connections Melissana laid out during one of the Martinez phone hacks. As the sequence ended, Iylothien flew by on a giant grasshopper, paused to wave to the viewers, then flew off into the distance. As the laughter continued, Jack turned to see Iylothien just before he faded from the screen.

"Yes, everybody, that was Iylothien. It was Melissana who put together that Justin Martinez was going to be kidnapped, and having no other resources at her disposal, took it upon herself and went out *on her own* to try to help. That pretty much epitomizes the core of what CYBER is all about. Melissana, I know where you came from, and I deeply regret all of that. But you will no longer be alone. Whoever sticks around and passes their three weeks will be your new family for life. Your primary trainer is Iylothien in 'net, with myself and Blaze to a lesser extent."

Footage resumed, showing three well-armed helicopters flying with swift purpose out over and away from a city, then rolling desolation. Josanne's pre-flight phone conversation with Mr. Lisben played as voiceover while the helicopters were en route. The scene then cut to video shot from one of the helicopters, coming over the quarry lip and facing down the mysterious black helicopter.

"Josanne, you were the wild card that saved not only the life of Justin Martinez, but also four of the people in this room right now. You found a way to acquisition your op to save your friend when you had nothing. You came up with and executed a solid plan while under significant duress. You played your conversation with Lisben well, *and* you managed to do all of that without compromising yourself in the process.

"What we have in mind for you is a little unusual. If you stay, you will be our 'conversationalist.' You will also serve as team medic.

CYBER tries very hard to keep our teams from getting hurt, but it happens; when it *does* happen, we can't wait for the deli truck."

"Wait a minute—I don't know anything about doctoring, let alone whatever you replace their parts with!" Josanne protested.

"In six months, you'll know both," Jack countered. "And in less than three weeks, you'll understand *exactly* how this will happen. CYBER is not just about sticking metal and plastic stuff into people. Our training techniques are as radically advanced as our tech. If you agree, you will have some very non-invasive modifications that will assist you in that capacity. You'll be working with Foxfire and Fuser."

"Whoa, maybe you forgot, but I am dead set against what you guys are doing to yourselves. I mean, seriously, why would anyone do that to themselves?"

"I didn't forget. In fact, that makes you the perfect candidate for the job. When CYBER first started, we had a team that got addicted to the tech. Their game changed from how they could help to how they could wire themselves more. The Agency was somebody's political baby, once, before Simon got ahold of it, and they just had to have more from their teams. It got ugly. You will *not* let your team go over this edge. I know you're not on board with this, and I expect you to be reserved in your judgment. What I am asking is for you to help take care of the ones who are on board with this, because they're taking those risks to help others who cannot help themselves. I believe the woman who did this," he said, pointing to the wall screen, "will be very capable in doing that."

"Which leaves me," Johnny said, almost as though it was a challenge. "Do I get a movie, too?"

"Which leaves you," Jack said in agreement. "And no, not directly." Then he called "Roll it." The mini-documentary started out as news vids of an impoverished city area that had been gassed by a weapons manufacturer to demonstrate its new product to a potential buyer. Out of the entire area, the voiceover continued, there was only one survivor: an eight-year-old boy with black hair. The image at this point was inexplicably grainy. The video cut to a train wreck a few years later, telling the story of two trains, which collided on a bridge over a large body of water. The impact was enough to shake the bridge, collapsing both trains into the water below. "No one survived," the reporter stated, "except a fifteen-year-old boy who happened to be in the train's tiny restroom, which minimized the secondary collisions. Footage showed a black-haired youth on a stretcher being loaded into an ambulance, but a transporting E.M.T. was between the camera and the boy's face. The boy was rushed to the hospital but released, as he had no other injuries other than some heavy bruising. The videography of hair-raising escapes continued, eventually revealing footage from a warehouse security camera. A buy was occurring between a black-haired young male organized crime figure and an arms manufacturer.

"Hey, the logo on the crates matches the logo from the first vid," Josanne observed.

The conversation was interrupted by a Yakuza assassin squad. Evidently the Yakuza were promised they had exclusive rights to the same goods. The mobster claimed he had no knowledge of any of that, and that, of course he would honor the agreement the Yaks had made in good faith. As a gesture of apology to the Yakuza who may have been offended at his intrusion, he offered his briefcase of purchase credits to the Yakuza squad leader along with the combination. After opening the briefcase and showing the squad leader the credits inside, he reclosed the briefcase and left it on one of the crates. He apologized again, and asked if he could leave, as he knew the Yakuza would wish to continue their conversation with their supplier in private. The Yakuza leader politely stated the man's actions proved he meant no offense to his organization, and his offering of apology was accepted. Yes, he could leave. He was advised he would need to find a different supplier to work with in the future, which the man received by bowing and thanking the Yakuza man for his generous advice. The video ended with another news story about an explosion at a warehouse owned by a weapons manufacturer. Found at the scene was a company executive and a crew of his bodyguards.

"So, Johnny, that was clever. Infiltrate one mob to get another to turn on a weapons manufacturer. The follow-up was impressive. The Yakuza figured the other mob hit their team, which started an all-out war between the two. Meanwhile, the weapons supplier was no longer trusted by either, so they lost two lucrative clients."

"Yeah, went well," Johnny said. "Actually, better than I planned. The Yakuza showed up at just the right time."

"Well, where was the bomb?" Melissana asked. "The briefcase was the only thing you brought into the warehouse, and you showed them all that was in it were the credits."

"The briefcase was the bomb. Opening it primed the device, relocking it set the timer to the numbers I selected for the combination."

"Your profile reads 'So skilled you pass as lucky, or so lucky you pass as skilled.' I'd say both. Johnny, your 'luck' factor is proving quite hard to analyze. Simon has been working on quantifying it but has been unsuccessful so far. That, in itself, is a laudable achievement. Trust me, it's the first time I've ever seen Simon stumped. You are fairly unique, young man. We don't want to tamper with what you've got. At least for now, you will be totally unmodified."

"What?" Johnny and Josanne cried out in unison. Josanne cut in first. "Why does he get out of the surgeries, but I don't?" she said.

"And Muffin here," Johnny added in protest, referring to Blaze, "pretty much sold me on the 'You're not good enough; we're gonna make you better' bit last night. Now you're ditching the plan?"

"Never was the plan," Jack said, correcting him. "We'll augment you, sure. With training. With support. But we will proceed very slowly with any implant augmentations, because we don't know what it is about you that makes you so lucky. Do you really want us to tamper with one of your greatest assets, potentially destroying it for good? *I* don't, and neither does Fuser or Simon.

"So, everyone, from here on out, you will be spending the day with your trainers, having evenings for physical training, then have the rest of the evening to relax together, compare notes, work out any questions, and discuss any issues."

… …

"So, how does the E.M. work? I know the basics; I move, I touch stuff, but how do I use it?" Melissana was in another training session with Iylothien. The training wasn't always intuitive, but she was completely enjoying the cool, definitely top of the line stuff she was learning about. It was like being inside a vid, only there were times she'd be able to interact with real objects in the real world. She had always liked learning about computer tech, and she thought hacking was really cool, but she had never heard of anything that came even close to this stuff. The fact that she was starting to develop a crush on Iylothien didn't hurt anything, either. She wondered when she would meet him in person. He said that would have to wait, that he wasn't able to be there in the real world just yet. She caught herself being distracted, so she again focused on what he was telling her.

"Randolph & Emerson's 'Ultimate Fantasy' is a fantasy type E.M., where you're a Knight, Barbarian, Wizard, Priest, Ninja, whatever. From your hacking style of hitting sites as remotely as possible, I originally placed you as a Ranger. Watching you in here, though, and seeing how you're really drawn to learning completely new tricks rather than staying with tried-and-trues, favoring glass cannon tactics, indicates you might actually prefer playing a Wizard."

"You mean I get to pick which one? Like a game?" Melissana asked, incredulous.

"That's exactly what I mean. You'll also have your pet, a daemon program useful in a variety of ways, from assistance with SYSOP requests to helping defeat various forms of ICE. We developed the E.M.'s as an experimental way to improve our inner-space performance. Flat-screen hacking eventually always came down to typing and work. The E.M.'s actually serve to boost our reflexes, do longer runs, generally be both safer and more effective at the same time. Besides, why should hacking be dull?" he added with that smile of his.

"The Ultimate Fantasy module renders target systems as dungeons or towers. Gold and gems represent real-world data files, evaluated according to street value parameters you set before you jump. Once inside, each system is displayed as a path through a dungeon-type setting, with more of the floor plan revealed as you go farther into the system. Gateways into other departments and system machines are stairways, gateways to hidden nodes are secret doors. The target system 'level' is the number of node hops from your current location back to your point of entry. Usually, the deeper levels are more dangerous due to the higher security measures and more difficult access pathways to get there. The ICE gets more difficult to defeat, and the results of failure are more drastic.

"ICE is rendered as monsters, interpreted in terms of the relative threat imposed to you and your connection to the system. Levels 1-5 are usually the white, 6-12 is grey. Anyone having more than 12 levels in the same system is advanced enough to field black ICE. Black ICE kills. Remember that. This ain't a game to the ICCs. While relatively rare, other hackers, target system admins, and cyber security teams appear as wizards, paladins, and berserkers, respectively. Blue chip bet that if they're not us, they're hostile.

"Now bring up your character menu, and we'll go over that really quick. The E.M. also provides an interrupt vector override, which blocks lag alarms for a short period of time. This is relayed as hunger status; if you starve, you've been detected and get kicked from the system, or worse. 'Food' allows a refresh of those vectors, allowing the 'decker more time in the system. While we're on the subject, the more you have loaded on your deck, the more you 'carry' with you. The more you carry with you, the larger the rift in operating cycles will have to be to fool the system. So, the more you load onto your deck before each run, the more 'food' you're going to need if you plan on being a while. Run out of food, and they'll eventually detect you and send everything they've got against you.

"That icon's the 'Rest' button. 'Resting' allows your deck to restore and repair your pathway and refresh your counter-ICE, displayed as restored health and spells. However, resting too often increases the likelihood that a random system check will detect you on their grid, which means more ICE to purge you from the system. Trust me, you don't want that to happen. Rest when you need to, but it's not a free pass; you'll still burn food rations while resting.

"Now for the bottom of the display: Hit points are gained by resting, 'gaining experience' occurs by achieving goals and overcoming ICE. If your health goes down to zero, as a minimum your construct is ejected from the system. It can get far worse than that. When you're fully jacked in and ICE fries a system to shut it down, you can go with it. The 'trodes we use now to connect us to our decks dampen some of the signal, but it's better to not get hit than to test how well they work. ICE can kill, or otherwise turn your day all southbound if it hits you.

"Remember, this isn't really a game. Don't take on what you can't handle, no matter how tempting the target. Got it?"

Melissana's avatar nodded as she tried to keep up. He wasn't kidding when he'd told her the three weeks would feel like a lifetime!

After a while longer, he emitted a strange metallic sound: a virtual sigh, Melissana guessed. "I have to go. We've been runnin' now for six hours today. Keep playing with the help system; there are a lot of different constructs, each denoting real-world objects or files. I'd really like to stay, but I'm needed elsewhere. I gotta admit, though, you're the most fun student I've ever had in here. There, I said it again," he declared. He somehow managed to get his avatar to wink. With dramatic flourish, he again bowed and performed his favorite exit: mounting a giant grasshopper and riding off into the virtual sky with a wild and exuberant whoop.

And, every time, Melissana just stayed for a while and stared after him, wondering where he was going, how he could be so experienced yet so boyish at the same time, and asking herself when could she finally meet him in person.

... ...

"So, you have a good car, with a really good configuration. Your father definitely knew what he was doing. But if you decide you want in on this, your Sabretooth won't hold up. And by the time the guys like you and me get into the wet work, we are *always* outnumbered. As good as the deckers are, at some point it usually comes down to guys like you and me getting into the wet work."

"Will I need to replace it?" Corey asked Rickshaw, disappointed.

"The short answer is no. Here, take a look at the Dominator." Rickshaw picked up a sledgehammer from the shop floor and swung it at the car with full force. The hammer rebounded off the car, forcing Rickshaw to catch himself to avoid falling over backward. The Dominator was not so much as smudged.

"The Dominator's stock armor, which I had already reinforced before I joined CYBER, has been overlaid with a super-compressed ferro-kev polymer applied under hyper-pressure and inductively sealed. The extra armor is light enough that it doesn't affect handling, but a two-millimeter coating of the stuff will stop most bullets. Your Sabretooth will be lined with a centimeter of it. Trust me, boy, you won't often have to worry much about that paint job. We'll line your glassware with a substance that is not quite as tough but transparent. Added to the bulletproof glass, and the only thing you'll have to worry about from anything under a direct rocket hit to the windshield is controlling the urge to flinch.

"We'll add some radar, IFF, and other sensing equipment. We'll also go over some of the weapons layouts. I prefer the lasers to rockets, but with some additional weapons miniaturizations the engineers are capable of, you may be able to add additional weaponry and keep your recoilless. Any questions so far?"

"I've got two. First, me and my dad researched trying lasers on cars. Doesn't using lasers suck the battery dry? Second, I know what I saw at the quarry. You saw that I saw, because you winked. How'd you do that?"

"Both are a little off topic, but fair game, and I guess there's no better time to tell you. Let's pop the hood." With that, the Dominator's hood opened as if by itself. "You're right. Lasers with the power rating my Dominator's got would kill a battery in no time flat—I'd get maybe six to ten shots before I'd have to call a tow truck—*if* I used an electric battery. So, I don't use a battery anymore. Check it out."

"Oh my…I don't believe it!" Corey said in an awed whisper.

"CYBER's resourcing tends to open up new ways to solving problems—much like Josanne and her three helicopters.

"Miniaturized fusion core!" Rickshaw boasted. "The only way to go. Completely shielded, I know that for a fact. If I held the laser down continuously, the laser itself would melt out before I lost power. The core powers everything in the car. I won't have to replace it for decades."

"Wow! We never thought that would have been possible! Man, I wish he could see this…" He paused, then cleared his mind. Like Handsight, Rickshaw just allowed Corey the time. "And then…" Corey resumed, shaking off the memory. "So your car is voice activated, and you used your sub-vocal link to fire the lasers when you were out of the car…"

"Very close on that one, Corey, but not quite. If it was voice-activated, how would it aim?"

"I hadn't thought of that—I don't know."

"A good driver knows his car, right? The driver and the car are a team, the two become a unit. We both *know* that happens. And you know *when* that happens."

Corey nodded his agreement.

"Now, suppose I was to tell you that, in a sense, a car is like a suit of armor. You put it on, you wear it, you move, the suit moves. Got me so far?"

"Yeah, but you've got to control the car, it's got physics all its own."

"Do you think you 'control' body armor? Consider Fuser or Arañé. You think Fuser 'controls' his arms?"

"Well, that's different."

"Why?"

"Well, I guess it's because I wear armor. I don't have to steer it. And Fuser's arms are attached. They're somehow directly connected to his nervous system. All he has to do is think about it, and his nervous system gets it to his arms. From there his arms just—follow—through—with …"

"From there his arms just follow through with what his brain told them to do. Bingo. I'm connected to my Dominator like Fuser's connected to his arms, like the General connects to his drones. CYBER Wheelmen don't just drive the cars—we *link* to the cars. We *become* the cars. When I'm in the Dominator, I *feel* the tires. The reactor is my heartbeat; the camera sensors, my eyes; the radar and all the other sensory devices become my expanded consciousness. The Dominator reciprocates the relationship. Look at my eyes closely, Corey."

Corey intently peered at Rickshaw's eyes, starting upon his observation of tiny etchings of targeting reticules arrayed in his irises. "The car fired, not when I told it to, but when I *thought* it to—using the interface built into my eyes. That's another reason I like the lasers, I guess. Running a highway chase at a hundred miles per hour, it's pretty much a WYSIWYG—What You See Is What You Get. No delays while the rockets are in flight. Big booms are sometimes important as well, but I like the real-time fire-and-hit you can only get at the speed of light.

"For the next three weeks, we'll connect you to a simulator using a specialized body armor helmet. If you do well and decide to really join, we will make the modifications to the Sabretooth and hardwire the implants into you. The surgery will hurt like a bear for about a month, and you'll have headaches and vertigo for about two months. After that, if all goes well, things will stabilize, and your Sabretooth will truly come to life for you. You'll have a connection to that car that your dad never imagined, though I'm guessing you both dreamt of it for years."

"Side effects for months? And it might not work?"

"The neural implants are the riskiest of surgeries. I also have to warn you—when your car gets hurt, you will feel the pain, though not nearly as intensely as if you yourself were to get hit. We just need a way to let you know that car's taking damage, and pain is the best way of doing that. Any other questions?"

"Just one," Corey responded, a smile forming on his face.

"What's that?" asked Rickshaw.

"Where's that helmet?"

300

... ...

"Let me get this straight. You guys are going to do some kind of surgeries that will take months, and there won't be scars all over the place?"

"There won't be scars because your skin will grow completely back, unlike scar tissue that normally occurs with most surgeries."

"And do I turn it on and off, or is it always there? If I shut it off and I'm all wired up, how would I be able to move? And won't there be any wires bulging out and stuff?"

"Here, take a look," Arañé told Susan, holding out his right arm. "Notice anything unusual?"

"Yeah," Susan replied. "I don't see anything unusual! Are there any side effects? What about long-term affects like cancers, allergies, and stuff like that?"

"We screen for any susceptibilities before we operate. In addition to the protective layer of tissue-sensitive protectorate around the wiring and other emplacements, we also line tissues around the wiring with a layer of amino acids, which forms a type of shrink-wrap around the tissues for an extra layer of natural safety for the individual."

"You said they shut down when my brain waves go into sleep state. What about nightmares? I still have some issues from—home."

"Trust me," Arañé said, reassuring her with a gentle smile, "you couldn't have a better team leader than Jack to help with that in long-term. But once you get out of surgery, it would probably be safest to sleep alone for a few months. During that time, we'll be able to dial in the control factors, and after that you should be fine."

"So, I get a lot faster, increased agility, a little stronger. Anything else?"

"We have several options here, but most of that depends on you."

"And I'll have additional training so I can pick up an egg without breaking it or something?"

"No, that's more of a Chrome-type training event. We do have something similar to that, though. With random gunshots going off nearby, you will be required to pour several cups of coffee without splashing."

"When do we get to check out this combination gym/training room/obstacle course?" Susan asked, eager to begin.

… …

"So, how much of you is real?"

Foxfire rolled her eyes. "Whoa, hold on, there one sec. I was recruited *after* I started modelling, thank you. How much of *you* is real?"

"What do you mean by that?" Josanne replied indignantly.

"I know the newsvid business," Foxfire argued. "Like you just wake up and go on the air without make-up, or a wardrobe consultant, a hairdresser, and a script for you to read."

"Well of course I do—it's media!"

"Exactly! You do all that for your fans—trust me, I know. It's the same thing here. Let me put it this way—if someone needed a heart replacement, would you object?"

"No, of course not!"

"And if someone had liver disease, would you object to replacing their natural liver with an artificial one?"

"No, but that's different, and you know it! Those people have no choice."

"They have the same choice we do. Have the surgery or die early."

"It's not the same!"

"Yeah, you're right. These days, the guy who needs the new liver probably inflicted it on himself doing drugs or something. We need the replacements because we're trying to help and protect people. No offense, but you've led a pretty sheltered life. Not everybody has had it that easy."

Josanne stopped there—Foxfire was right on that point, and Josanne had nothing to counter it with. "So, what does a team conversationalist do, anyway?" Josanne asked, trying to change the subject.

"We try to get people to see things from our point of view."

"Like now?" Josanne asked.

"Not really," Foxfire returned. "That's more like steering them into a course of action. This is different; I'm just trying to get you to understand it a little bit."

And since Josanne figured that Foxfire was, in fact, trying to steer her into a course of action, she pretended she accepted Foxfire's response as the truth, which was actually the exact reaction Foxfire expected Josanne would have. Of course, Josanne switched to the subject of her current decision when confronted with the pain of her recent past that led her here; it allowed Josanne to regain some sense of control. But Foxfire was pleased Josanne had made the topic switch fluidly, displaying neither anger nor pain. The model-turned-agent continued the discussion, drawing the reporter further into her explanation, continuing Josanne's conversationalist training for another three hours. When she was done, Fuser entered the room to talk with Josanne about the possibility of learning medicine, electronics, and mechanical engineering.

… …

Jack was watching all of this via monitors and was now convinced he was on the right path. Corey's relationship with Susan was his biggest asset—and his greatest liability. Susan's displaced mistrust of Melissana, Melissana's over-eagerness, Josanne's reluctance, Johnny's constant antagonization of the group…each of them on their own had great portfolios, but without some serious training to meld them all into a team, there was no way they'd survive their first mission.

29

TRUTH AND DARE

"Well, here we are. You've all made it past your first two weeks, and you're doing well so far," Jack began. He was genuinely proud of how they were doing individually. He enjoyed their evening discussions, watching them grow together, if just a little. They were not only concerned about themselves, but they had learned enough about the rest that they were beginning to care for each other as well. Even Johnny had tempered down since that first night. Would they commit, though? He promised he would give them all the information they would need to make a judicious decision. Tonight he would fulfill that vow. He wouldn't want any one of them to quit, but he felt he would be failing them all if he didn't follow through with his intentions. He sighed to himself, offered up another mental prayer for strength, and began.

"Now comes the hard part. You all know what's ahead. By the end of this week, you will wake up and be on your way—either to your surgeries, or back home. I presume since you're all still here that you're planning on joining. I commend each of you for having made it so far, and especially for your dedication to helping others. I've got two last items we need to go over before you make your final decisions. Any final questions before I get started?"

"I have one," Melissana said.

Of course you do, Jack thought. He saw it in her eyes, how charged she got whenever she talked about jacking in. All he vocalized was, "Yes?"

"I thought you said I'd meet Iylothien in person before the three weeks was out."

"I did, and I meant it," Jack responded. "In fact, Iylothien is in the building right now, and you'll all meet him. I wanted you all to be able to meet him in person before you sign up. Any other questions? All right then, let's go."

Jack led the group down a hallway to an elevator. Once they boarded, Jack pressed the Hold Door button followed by a seven-digit sequence of the floor buttons. After he pressed the Hold Door button a second time, the elevator began a quick descent.

"Okay, I never saw that one coming," Johnny admitted to the air. The elevator stopped, and the group stepped out into what must have been a technical floor of a hospital wing. "Take a good look," Jack announced to the group. "For those who stay, this is where you'll be for the next four to eight weeks."

"We're going to have our surgeries here?" Josanne asked incredulously.

"Where else would you have them? To be a doctor on this floor, you need to have a doctorate in biomedicine, genetics, electrical engineering, and computer science, as a minimum. We believe this to be the most advanced hospital in the world."

"Doesn't look like much," Susan stated. Even Corey seemed a little apprehensive. "I pictured something a little, I don't know, brighter?" he conveyed.

"This serves as our hospital, engineering wing, and other sundry functions CYBER needs to stay operational."

"Oh! He works on the networks from here, then," Melissana chirped. "I'm really excited to finally meet him in person!"

They got to the end of the hall and made a left, then continued for another minute or two. "Geez, how big is this place?" Melissana asked.

"We're almost there," Jack assured her. "Why don't the rest of you wait here for a bit. Melissana? You can come along with me."

A few paces later, they entered through a set of double doors. They were in a critical care room with a single bed. On the bed was a young male, gaunt, severely scarred from burn wounds that seemed to cover his entire body. His left arm was missing, and both legs were amputated at the knees. A heart machine was beeping in rhythm to an artificial respirator. An EEG showed almost no brain activity at all. Behind the patient's grotesquely burned head, robotic hands extending from a pair of metallic arms tapped on a keyboard. A camera rotated to focus on the visitors, the lens shutter suddenly going wide as it spotted Melissana. The arms stopped for a moment, then started typing so fast the keystrokes made the whooshing sound of an air current rather than a series of clicks. In less than three seconds, the screen filled and began scrolling with an infinite count of a single three-character repetition:

NO!NO!NO!NO!NO!NO!NO!NO!NO!NO!NO!
NO!NO!NO!NO!NO!NO!NO!NO!NO!NO!NO!
NO!NO!NO!NO!NO!NO!NO!NO!NO!NO!NO!
NO!NO!NO!NO!NO!NO!NO!NO!NO!NO!NO!
NO!NO!NO!NO!NO!NO!NO!NO!NO!NO!NO!
NO!NO!NO!NO!NO!NO!NO!NO!NO!NO!NO!
NO!NO!NO!NO!NO!NO!NO!NO!NO!NO!NO!
NO!NO!NO!NO!NO!NO!NO!NO!NO!NO!NO!
NO!NO!NO!NO!NO!NO!NO!NO!NO!NO!NO!
NO!NO!NO!NO!NO!NO!NO!NO!NO!NO!NO!
NO!NO!NO!NO!NO!NO!NO!NO!NO!NO!NO!
NO!NO!NO!NO!NO!NO!NO!NO!NO!NO!NO!
NO!NO!NO!NO!NO!NO!NO!NO!NO!NO!NO!
NO!NO!NO!NO!NO!NO!NO!NO!NO!NO!NO!
NO!NO!NO!NO!NO!NO!NO!NO!NO!NO!NO!
NO!NO!NO!NO!NO!NO!NO!NO!NO!NO!NO!

NO!NO!NO!NO!NO!NO!NO!NO!NO!NO!NO!
NO!NO!NO!NO!NO!NO!NO!NO!NO!NO!NO!
NO!NO!NO!NO!NO!NO!NO!NO!NO!NO!NO!
NO!NO!NO!NO!NO!NO!NO!NO!NO!NO!NO!
NO!NO!NO!NO!NO!NO!NO!NO!NO!NO!NO!
NO!NO!NO!NO!NO!NO!NO!NO!NO!NO!NO!
NO!NO!NO!NO!NO!NO!NO!NO!NO!NO!NO!
NO!NO!NO!NO!NO!NO!NO!NO!NO!NO!NO!
NO!NO!NO!NO!NO!NO!NO!NO!NO!NO!NO!
NO!NO!NO!NO!NO!NO!NO!NO!NO!NO!NO!
NO!NO!NO!NO!NO!NO!NO!NO!NO!NO!NO!
NO!NO!NO!NO!NO!NO!NO!NO!NO!NO!NO!
NO!NO!NO!NO!NO!NO!NO!NO!NO!NO!NO!
NO!NO!NO!NO!NO!NO!NO!NO!NO!NO!NO!
NO!NO!NO!NO!NO!NO!NO!NO!NO!NO!NO!
NO!NO!NO!NO!NO!NO!NO!NO!NO!NO!NO!
NO!NO!NO!NO!NO!NO!NO!NO!NO!NO!NO!
NO!NO!NO!NO!NO!NO!NO!NO!NO!NO!NO!
NO!NO!NO!NO!NO!NO!NO!NO!NO!NO!NO!
NO!NO!NO!NO!NO!NO!NO!NO!NO!NO!NO!
NO!NO!NO!NO!NO!NO!NO!NO!NO!NO!NO!
NO!NO!NO!NO!NO!NO!NO!NO!NO!NO!NO!
NO!NO!NO!NO!NO!NO!NO!NO!NO!NO!NO!
NO!NO!NO!NO!NO!NO!NO!NO!NO!NO!NO!
NO!NO!NO!NO!NO!NO!NO!NO!NO!NO!NO!
NO!NO!NO!NO!NO!NO!NO!NO!NO!NO!NO!
NO!NO!NO!NO!NO!NO!NO!NO!NO!NO!NO!
NO!NO!NO!NO!NO!NO!NO!NO!NO!NO!NO!
NO!NO!NO!NO!NO!NO!NO!NO!NO!NO!NO!
NO!NO!NO!NO!NO!NO!NO!NO!NO!NO!NO!
NO!NO!NO!NO!NO!NO!NO!NO!NO!NO!NO!...

Melissana started to gag, then she looked up at Jack and, through tears, simply said, "I don't understand."

Jack sighed. The screen continued to scroll, while the mechanical arms continued their flurry of activity. "Melissana, this is Iylothien."

... ...

The team was sullen as they occupied a corner table at The Lounge, an on-site facility where CYBER technicians and other staff could socialize freely without worrying about security leaks. It had been off-limits to the recruits before, but Jack had not only cleared them, he also made sure they were the only ones there besides Grey's Hounds and Blaze's Fist. The other teams had known Iylothien intimately, so it was only appropriate that they all be there. Jack bought the first round for the group, then the second. Nobody felt like a party—flat out, nobody wanted to feel at all. Finally, the silence, only broken by Melissana's sobs, got more oppressive than anything Jack could possibly say.

"It happened about six years ago," Jack began. "Simon could tell you exactly how long ago, down to the second. Iylo was one hot cowboy—played the wires like a guitarist even before he was chipped. When he was in a system, well, you really can't describe it.

"I was his mentor. We started working on something that would make decking less tedious."

"The E.M.'s," Melissana mumbled.

"Yes," Jack said, nodding. "They were his brainchildren; I was helping with some of the designs.

"Then we did a run against a certain ICC. They found out that a rival corporation's senior executive in charge of releasing a new product line would be visiting a corporate office they had in 'Frisco. Our targets felt financially jeopardized, so they decided to stop the product release by killing him."

"And they decided to do that by poisoning 'Frisco's water supply," interjected Arañé.

309

"Yeah. They try not to mention that too much in their advertising campaigns," Chrome added bitterly.

"They're still in business?" Melissana asked, enraged. "How could you let them?"

"The ones who were responsible are no longer employed there, or anywhere else, if it makes a difference," Jack replied, more coldly than he would have liked.

"Anyway, we were hitting the cache of the poison. Iylo and I both went in-line to find the canister locations and cause delays in the deployment process. Chrome and Arañé would make the actual grabs, and Rickshaw was on perimeter and monitoring backup deployments."

"Just the *five* of you? Against an ICC?" Johnny shook his head. "What the hell were you guys thinking?"

"They were thinking what we all would have thought, although myself and Blaze hated Jack for it for years," Foxfire offered. "They were thinking nobody knew they were coming, and that if they didn't at least try, 'Frisco would go toxic. There was no time for backups; they had to go. We don't do odds like that all the time, but it happens."

"Better put on your big boy pants if you want to sign up," Blaze added. "'Cuz we're the biggest kids on the block, an' sometimes there ain't no seatbelts for this ride. And 'sides, don't you ever get curious as to how lucky you really are?" she added with a smile that, for the first time, revealed she actually felt a kinship for the group.

"All right, I get it. There was no time, no one left but you. *Drek!*" Johnny bitterly declared, downing the last of his beer. Jack nodded to the bartender, who replaced it with another.

"So, what happened?" Josanne asked, experiencing an empathy for Jack she hadn't before. She conceded to herself that although she had been trained as an investigative journalist before, she had learned quite a bit from her two weeks with Foxfire. She was really feeling his emotions, his psyche.

"We were thirteen nodes deep. Long and tense hack. We were tag-teaming each other on the ICE. Iylo found the canister location and felt so relieved that for one second, he forgot where he was and got careless. Any idea how long one second is in-line?

"Anyway, he tripped an alarm. ICE reavers black as death started coming down on us, while the system alerted security. Chrome and Arañé had to go for the canisters first, while Rickshaw was tied up keeping reinforcements at bay. Meanwhile, we were trying to keep the ICE off us long enough to jack out, which we knew we had to do quick because the meat-layer guards were on their way. I got out just in time to take a bullet in my leg and smell Iylo's deck getting ICE-burns—except keeping the meat security off delayed my getting Iylo unplugged. His brain was frying before I could get him out, which I had to do by cutting the melted wires from his cyberdeck.

"While I was doing that, their flex-joes set off some phosphorous rounds. I was able to avoid the splash, but Iylo caught some before I was able to get him out of there. There was no heartbeat, no breath, his head had been cooked by that ICE. Up until three weeks ago, I thought he was dead."

"Whoa! Wait a minute!" Corey said, jumping in. "They had him down there in the basement the whole time and they didn't tell you? What if it was me, or Susan!"

"It wasn't quite like that," Rickshaw said. "Grey had to move, cover for the team, wrap up the mission. We brought Iylo back with us, but there were no life signs. About a week later, Jack quit. The only one who had a trace on him was Simon, and Simon wasn't saying where Jack was—no matter how much we asked—probably trying to honor Jack's desire to leave.

"We kept Iylo on life support. Shortly after that, Simon wanted Iylo hooked to 'deck, telling us it was a longshot experiment. Guess he read some old reports about people talking to comatose patients, and Simon thought maybe there's activity, but the patients can't respond in a way we know how to measure."

"But the cyberdeck could bypass almost all of that because it's wired directly to the brain," Melissana concluded.

"Correct." It was Chrome's turn to reply. "Simon somehow got a link to Iylo, and the two of them designed and developed the Waldo's so he could hit keys again. From there, they continued to develop the E.M.'s, both as a decking tool and also as therapy to help him."

Josanne went off. "So, you're telling us that Simon is able to trace Jack when no one else can, runs this entire Agency, predictively analyzes macro- and micro-threat activities, *and* has time to sit and go deep-tech with a comatose hacker when no one else can even find any brain activity? Yeah—I have a question of my own!" she shouted, breathing heavily.

"Who in the hell is this mystical Simon?"

The room went quiet. Members of the Fist and Hounds glanced back and forth between each other.

"And stop sub-vocalizing!"

Foxfire smiled. "You pick up quickly!" she stated, trying to defuse the situation a little.

"I had a good teacher." Josanne falsely smiled back to show Foxfire the trick hadn't worked. Then she fixed her stare on Jack. "So? Who is Simon?"

Jack raised his hands in defense. "Okay, okay—I was going to tell you tonight anyway. I really *want* you to know everything so you can make informed commitments, if you decide to stay."

"You're telling the truth!" Josanne declared, suddenly realizing just how effective Foxfire's training had been.

"Yes, I'm telling the truth, thank you! But I can't really answer your question."

"Because you don't know who Simon is either, isn't that right?"

"No, that's not it," Jack said.

"It's just a simple question, Jack. 'Who - is - Simon?' So why don't you answer?"

"Because it's the *wrong* question," the bartender said, interrupting. The room went silent. Everyone had forgotten he was there.

"Whoa! You're Simon?" Josanne guessed.

"You don't look like him," Johnny countered.

"Brother," the bartender replied, looking up from his polishing rag, "nobody looks like Simon. *Especially* Simon!" he said, with a puff of a laugh.

"What do you mean?" Josanne asked.

"He means 'Simon' isn't a name," Jack admitted. "It's an acronym."

"What?!" Josanne retorted, in a staccato shout.

"Get the popcorn," Johnny said, "cuz here we go…"

There was no stopping now, so Jack continued. "Simon's an acronym—stands for "Synchronized Independent Interface Monitoring and Observation Neuronet." He paused, drew a breath, then concluded. "Simon's an A.I."

"Simon's an A.I.? Simon's an *A.I.*?" Josanne's voice was starting to rise again.

"Artificial Intelligence," Fuser offered.

"*I know what an A.I. is!*" Josanne yelled. "But I never thought they were real! And now our very own Simon is an A.I. *Great!*"

"An A.I. in charge of a secret government agency," Johnny reminded them. "A secret government agency with cyborgs as its agents. *Frakkin'* drek!"

"An A.I. who wants us to be its next set of minions," Corey thought out loud.

"I'm going to be sick," Susan added.

"I'll be honest with you, Jack-O," Johnny complained, with extra disgust. "You sure know how to throw a party! When are you serving the brainicide?"

"First Iylothien, now this?" Melissana languished. "You're kidding about all this, right? Is this some kind of a test?"

"Yeah, it is," Jack answered, feeling suddenly deflated. "It's a test for me, to see if I really had the integrity to let you know all of it before you made your commitments rather than wait until after you already had your surgeries. It's a test of CYBER, to see if what we saw in you will come forth. It's a test of your consciences, whether they will be worthy of our continued effort." Jack sighed, defeated. "Also, it's a test for me again, to see if you'll still want to follow me after what I've told you tonight.

"I promised you when you first started, no secrets. I have kept my promise. Now I am making another one. Up until now, you have been confined overnight and given every opportunity to leave in the mornings. A lot's changed from your perspectives, but in reality, nothing's changed at all.

"But there's no way you're going to believe that. So tonight, you can all go now if you want. You're free to come back in the morning, but you don't have to. CYBER was *always* a voluntary option for you. We got you here to hear us out. You've heard all we have to say, so now you can go. You're off old I-95. Roanoke's about two hours southwest by car, if you're not going all that fast. That reminds me—here you go, Corey," Jack said, fishing a set of car keys from a pocket.

"You're just letting us go? How do you know we won't say anything?" Corey asked.

"We trust you," Jack offered. "Even when you might not trust us." He gave Sue a quick nod, adding, "I'll never forget you applauding us, even if you don't feel the same way now. Thank you."

With that, Jack tossed Corey the keys to the Sabretooth, turned, and left the room. After a few brief farewells just in case, the Hounds and Blaze's Fist left, too. The bartender looked at the group, finished polishing the glasses, and said, "Tell you what, kids—I had a long day, you had a long night. Just lock up behind ya's when you leave."

Then he, too, was gone, leaving the group by themselves to talk and think about what to do next.

After some murmured and hesitant conversation, Corey and Sue left first, offering Josanne and Melissana a ride. Josanne would have accepted, but Melissana wanted to talk to Iylothien, and she could only do that through the hood. There was room for Johnny, but he declined going farther than Roanoke, saying he'd made his own way so far, he could do it again. With final farewells, the group split up and went their separate ways.

… ……

Jack watched each one as they disappeared into the darkness for as long as he could. He hadn't been part of a team like that since, well, since he'd left Grey's Hounds six years earlier. Their leaving hurt more than he thought it would have.

Jack's room phone rang, but he just let it go. A message began, interrupting his thoughts. "And just what did you think you would accomplish?" the digital voice of Simon asked.

"I just wanted to let them know the truth," Jack said defensively. "I thought maybe, just maybe, at least some of them would have stayed."

"Jack, Jack, Jack. Luck is Johnny's department, not yours." Jack was about to demolish the phone when Simon added, "I regret the night went badly for you. But you are going to need that strength again. You have other resources you rely upon. I suggest you prepare to use them."

"You telling me to pray about all of this again? What do you want from me this time?"

"Not *from* you, Jack—*for* you," Simon responded. "Your night is about to get worse."

"And how can that possibly happen?" asked Jack.

Simon paused, a flat sound over the phone's reception. "Best you hear it from Arañé. He's on his way to tell you now."

A knock sounded on Jack's door. "Yeah, Spider? Simon told me you were on your way up. So, what's so bad it's going to make this night worse?"

Arañé sighed. "It's Angie, your waitress friend in Roanoke," he responded. "She's dead."

315

30

RETURN ERROR (304)

"Jefe, You need to get down here. We got a problem," Arañé announced when Jack picked up the call.

"What now?!" Jack exclaimed. It had been a long night. He watched as his new team each went their separate ways. Only Melissana had stayed in the end. She spent the rest of the night talking with Iylothien, hooded up in the critical care room. Josanne told them she'd had enough and left on her own. Now Angie was gone, too, the life drained from her like a dead fly after the spider was done with it. Some suit showed up at the diner and said he had a credstick from Jack. It had a spring-loaded needle in it that injected her with Diamond as she was stuffing it into her pocket. She just went out walking—and was found dead in an alley the next morning. Simon was right. He would have to do something about the Diamond before it got any more out of hand.

"Lord, who am I kidding? What am I even doing here? I lost the whole team!" Then he sighed, long and heavy. "At least they knew before the surgeries. I kept my promise, Lord. If nothing else, I kept my word." He then dressed and dragged himself down the stairs.

"What is it?" he complained to Arañé.

"Listen, I know you had a really rough night last night, but your troops are hanging around with nothing to do."

"What do you mean—" Then Jack saw them—all of them—lined up in their morning formation. He ran a quick diagnostic check of

317

his ocular systems to make sure they were functioning correctly; he thought he was seeing things, but Arañé's voice confirmed his eyes. "What the—what?" he asked, suddenly relieved and uplifted, if only a little.

"I need to stay," Melissana explained, shrugging her shoulders. "Iylothien and I connect, and this is the only place I'll ever be able to talk with him like that."

"And she's hopeless without me, you saw that in your vids," Josanne offered, adding, "I'd be dead by now if it wasn't for you guys. I figure I can stay a couple more days and try to make sense out of all this before I just quit."

"Sue and I got to talking about how you received our applause," Corey began. "Between what happened with Iylothien and then hearing about Simon, we forgot how human you all are. You mentioned something once—it's not the metal CYBER puts inside us that makes us CYBER, it's the mettle within that makes us who we are. Simon's an A.I., but maybe that also means he's—it's—not as susceptible to corruption or the whims of politics, right?"

"So, we came back, at least for this week," Susan finished for him. "If this A.I. would have wanted his mind-controlled battle minions to attack us, it would have done so by now."

"Even you, Johnny?" asked Jack.

"I admit, last night messed me up. Went to Roanoke to get a feel for where you were coming from. That Diamond operation run by that corp is just flat jacked. The suit's gotta burn."

"It was Johnny who called 'em all back," Arañé added. "Evidently, he somehow found out about the Diamond issue in Roanoke—and what happened to Angie. He called all the others. They'd like to take a crack at bringing the whole Diamond operation down, if it's okay for them to choose their first mission. They want to know if you'll still want to work with them after they bailed on you last night. They want to do it, for you."

"After—after last night?" Jack stammered.

"Was a hell of a thing you did there," Johnny offered, "showing us all that, telling us all that. I haven't been trusted like that in a long time. I've never had anybody be that up front and honest with me before—not before they already got what they wanted from me, anyway. So yeah, I'll follow you anywhere you want to go. Besides, this is where the game is—this place *is* the Game. If there's anybody to keep the choobs in check, it's you guys. So how about it?"

"Simon cleared the op, if you want to take it," Arañé announced. "Family gonna bring a little *rain* on the goveks."

"Okay," Jack agreed, feeling a sense of purpose and direction he hadn't felt for weeks. "And every one of us is in on this? Because once the rain starts, it's a hack of a thing to try to stop it. The way this works is we either all agree on the run, or there is no run. Are you all *sure*? This is that point of commitment; this is the choice." Fixing his gaze on each of them, he saw the same look of resoluteness he himself was feeling about taking the Diamond operation down.

"*Acid* rain," Johnny added.

"Those are my streets, too," Melissana stated, showing her support. "Ain't much, but nobody kickin' Hometown if I can help it."

"I can't believe they would be that cold," Josanne added. "Someone has to stop them."

Corey and Susan exchanged nods. "For Honor and Courage," he declared for them both.

"Hounds and Fist are in," Arañé reported.

CYBER was family more than anything else. The new recruits would form a new team, and their first op was taking out a new killer drug operation before it spread any farther. They would be trained by some of the best: two veteran teams Jack himself had previously mentored. Individually as well as a group, the three teams all knew that the next target had just practically challenged them to be removed.

"All right then, we've all got a long road ahead," Jack declared, taking charge of the operation. Despite his time away, he just gravitated to the central role; now that he was committed, he was in all the way. "Let's get to it."

PART 4

EXECUTION

"I think having a great idea is vastly overrated. I know it sounds kind of crazy and counterintuitive. I don't think it matters what the idea is, almost. You need great execution."

— Felix Dennis
How to Get Rich

"It's time to quit bein' a jawbone and start bein' a backbone."

— Tim Minter

31

BRINGIN' HEAT

QUEEN VIXENN HAD heard of hot before, but this was *insane*! Chrome and Spider were taking hits as she jacked into the Matsua remote link connecting to its local server farm. Even this substation was guarded by more Matsua flex than some banks. She flicked the power switch on her Mitsushi 2049, and the lights from the World started to fade around her. The last thing she saw was Johnny turning the latest round of Matsua muscle into random chunks of lawn ornament, and Hardcore dropping off Lady Blackwolf as he spun to take on the approaching Matsua Tigerpaw.

Good! she thought. Maybe that would buy her enough time to be able to pull this job off!

Another, softer light took the place of the lights from the World, and she looked through the sylvan glade to spot a narrow cleft in a hillside. She pulled a branch of a nearby tree, and the hillside swung partway open, exposing a narrow stairway leading upward. She chose her icon, launching her daemon program Dogpet, took a deep virtual breath, and entered her cyberdeck's version of the Matsua computer network. She involuntarily shivered as swarm-clouds of grasshoppers and locusts started to blot out the virtual sun.

"Bard to Queen: Substation's cut from the rest of Matsua. All you gotta worry about now is local ICE," Iylothien reported. "Now sling spells and run this grid! Time to prove you're the Queen. Now GO!"

Queen Vixenn ran up the darkening pathway, the daemon's electronic aural glow providing enough light for her to see the climb was a dead end. Dogpet sniffed out a back door into the base of a tower, then Vixenn used a Lockpick spell to get in. So far, so good, she thought to herself. A glimpse over her shoulder later, and she suddenly became afraid.

"Grey, the door's open, but it's starting to close already!"

"On my way in," Greyscale acknowledged. He did a half-roll and screamed in sideways through the closing gap in the vortex Vixenn had opened. His environmental module was an aerospace fighter sim. Though the systems worked the same way, each rendered its own version of the environment differently on the client; where Queen Vixenn had hunger, Greyscale had a fuel gauge. He saw her now, a slower, more vulnerable plane than his A/F-179 Corvus.

"Incoming, Queen—seven bogies on your left. I'll take 'em, you go ahead." With that, he streaked across the sky, and in a series of three barrel rolls, he took them all out before they even knew they were spotted.

"Geez, what the?" Vixenn had no idea anyone could be that fast. Greyscale the Magnanimous had just teleported to the seven goblins that came up on her left, bone shards firing from his fingertips into each of their throats before any could scream for help. She thought it odd, though, that when she complimented him, he commented something about "Just Messerschmitts."

She shrugged it off as some old-world name for goblins and proceeded on her hunt for the location of the vault. She wondered how things were going in the real world...

... ...

- *"Hardcore, you got three more inbound coming from the North Gate," the General reported sub-vocally. "I'm running interference to delay them, but I'm not sure I can stop 'em."*

In the substation shipping lot, Chrome was returning fire with his twin .44 Magnum automatics, with Spider providing close support with his shotgun. The General was keeping the high ground clear of any Matsua activity. Lady Blackwolf took out a group of four Matsua guards as they were maneuvering to get behind the Hound gunmen, but then she got pinned down by a fresh Matsua Armed Response Team, who opened up with an LMG660 light machine gun. A blast from one of the team's grenades caught her and blew her into the side of a freight bin with a harsh thud, and she blacked out. The Matsua vehicle and seven ground troops in heavy armor approached the downed member of the new team.

"*Susan!*" Corey, who heard her cry of pain through the Sabretooth's radio, started to leave his assigned area to protect her but found himself trying to navigate through the maze of shipping containers and starting to get stuck himself. Cursing, he had to give up and backtrack to where he had gone off course. Fuser had been performing recon sweeps of the ground level from his motorcycle, weaving in and out of the warehouse shipping containers, being as mobile as possible. He started to rescue the downed Lady Blackwolf, but had to turn off to support Corey, who was beginning to have some trouble getting out of the mess he had gotten himself into in the crate maze.

- *"I was on my way to help Blackwolf," he announced over their comm channel, "but I need to turn back or there's going to be two of them down!"*

Meanwhile, a hail of bullets rained down upon the cove, protecting the downed gymnast from the dismounted response team that was now supported by an additional Tigerpaw. They had seen enough of what their attackers were capable of. Now that one of them had gone down, the Matsua ground forces would keep her down. Distracted for the moment by the sheer volume of fire they were laying to keep their acrobatic assailant pinned as they advanced on her position, they didn't notice the black and rust form racing through the darkness of the night until it was upon them.

The first screams over their helmeted radios signaled that the hunters had become the hunted, as the seven shock troops found themselves face to face with a fiendish creature, which with tooth and claw was rending them to shreds despite their combat armor. Dozens of rounds were pumped into the snarling mass of incarnate nightmare with little effect. Blade and baton would not deter the ferocity of the beast that was wreaking havoc upon them.

The team inside the Matsua vehicle recognized that in moments all seven of their comrades were neutralized, torn by the freakish creation that was now eerily glaring at them through the ruby red eye slits in its helmet. They were about to open up on the creature with their heavier vehicular weaponry when Fuser, returning after helping Hardcore get unstuck, jumped onto the roof of the vehicle, sinking two curved blades that extended from his forearms into the joint where the turret was mounted to the vehicle roof. The turret whined against the metal anchors that held it lodged in place, then screamed its death cry as Fuser's electrical arcs fried the circuits through most of their car. Panicked by the heat and dangerously arcing terror inside their vehicle, the crew forgot about the monster outside and hastily retreated from the shocking sparks, only to be knocked unconscious by a series of rapid cracks from a metallic quarterstaff.

"Good girl, Rachel," Fuser said as he gratefully patted the Doberman. "I owe you some." Rachel's short hair ruffled and stood on end from the residue of Fuser's electrical arc, but she happily wagged her tail like she enjoyed the sensation.

"C'mon, Rachel," Menagerie called out. "We need to provide some cover for Greyscale and Queen." And with that, they were off.

… …

"I'm not gonna lie, this is getting a little tense. You guys about done in there?" Foxfire asked, knowing Greyscale and Queen Vixenn couldn't hear. She and Josanne were providing close cover in the real world for the two on-line deckers.

"Where did these guys all come from?" Trigget asked.

"Well, let's be glad for small favors," Foxfire called back. "They stopped their wave rushes and are now content to contain us inside this perimeter of theirs."

"And that's good? How?"

"Because perimeters only work in one direction at a time," Greyscale responded, unplugging his 'trodes from the base of his skull. Vixenn was doing the same, although she seemed a little disoriented.

"You okay?" Trigget asked. "Your flushed, and you're a little out of focus."

"Yeah, I'm okay. Whoa—we did it! I *got* it!! Whoo–*hooo!*" She screamed so loud it caused the Matsua perimeter forces to recoil for a second.

Greyscale was already on the comm channel.

- *"All teams, all teams, Gold Light! Gold Light! We got an inward-facing perimeter in here. Can we get an exit, please?"*

327

- *"Copy, Gold Light,"* Arañé acknowledged. *"All teams, we are now in recovery mode. Hardcore, Fist, provide egress for the internals, thank you."*

And in less than a minute's time, the Matsua guards who had enclosed Greyscale, Queen Vixenn, Foxfire, and Trigget inside their perimeter surrendered when they found that they themselves were surrounded by Rachel and Menagerie, Fuser, Chrome, Spider, Blaze, and a still woozy Lady Blackwolf. The security group could only watch as two of their "prisoners" strolled past and got into a midnight black Sabretooth and the other two casually got into a yellow and red Dominator. Then the rest of the team left under the overwatch of three of the General's armed drones, Trigget silently gathering her diagnostics of Blackwolf's injuries as they withdrew to Hardcore's vehicle.

As soon as the cars pulled away, the drones fired sleep gas canisters into the room. As the vapors took effect on the remaining Matsua troopers, the CYBER team faded into the same nothingness from which they had originally appeared.

32

THE SACRIFICE

THE GROUP WAS back at the Facility Conference Room, Jack addressing them all.

"All right, CYBER, time for review. What happened last night?"

"We hit the Matsua substation that had the link to the Matsua mainframe," Johnny replied. "We thought we'd grab the Diamond formula, but all we were able to get was the location of the facility that produces the Diamond. Said location also houses the main server where the Diamond formula is kept. Something wasn't right about it, though."

"All right," Jack said, nodding. "Let's talk about that. Wasn't right exactly how?"

"The guards were more aggressive than normal," Josanne suggested. "I mean, normally they'd try to steer us away first, you know, company image and all. These guys were almost asking for a fight the second they saw us."

"You think maybe that was just you?" Johnny asked.

"She did, until I mentioned it to her myself," Foxfire said in support of Josanne. "They were way too trigger-happy."

"Something else..." Blaze offered. "How many megacorps would be sloppy enough to store a new product line at the same place they store the formula? When the formula isn't even on the corporate mainframe?"

"You think maybe this Mahlon is doing this on his own? Like maybe he's got a side gig goin' on the company's dime?" Spider theorized.

"Or maybe they're keeping it quiet and just playing it close, like a pilot project," Chrome countered.

"So, we have some things to chew on," Jack summarized. "Either Mahlon's acting on his own, which would be good, or this is some kind of Matsua pilot program to start testing drugs by selling them on neighborhood drug markets. That would be bad."

Johnny countered with, "Wouldn't be the first time, though. I remember the headline from when I was eight years old: 'ICC Uses Masses to Demonstrate Product Line.' Everyone I knew was a part of that."

"What are we going to do if it is Matsua?" Josanne cut in. "We had enough of a time handling that substation, let alone wherever the location codes point to. We had *three* teams out there, and we struggled."

"Right, let's talk about that," Jack began. "First, yes, we had three teams. We were the primary, with the Fist and Hounds to cover for us. So, what happened?"

"I wasn't expecting it to go so hard so fast," Susan began. "I mean, when we fought against the Jackals, we knew what we were up against. I thought maybe these guys were just, like guards, employees, but they weren't. I was hoping they would—"

"Not fight back?" Chrome asked. He almost sneered. "These are the brute force of the ICCs. They're hired out to protect corporate assets, not corporate image. The only difference between the gangers you've faced before and these guys is that the training and equipment just got better. ICCs often recruit goveks out of prisons and embed 'em with controller chips to blow 'em sky high if they cross corporate loyalties. They'll fight back against anything at the first chance they get."

"Then what are we supposed to do?" Corey asked, almost pleading. "These are people! Are we really just supposed to go out there and shoot up anyone who gets in our path?"

"Corey's right," Sue admitted. "I had a hard enough time shooting someone in self-defense, in the heat of the moment. I was just someone trying to stay alive—I don't think I can do this."

"Which was a major reason why Simon chose you two," Jack replied. "Because you weren't out to just blow somebody away. This is the real sacrifice. It's not the body parts, as Josanne originally thought. It goes deeper—it's our selves. Susan—everyone—this is important. This is the 'why' behind what we do."

"Listen," Arañé began, "we all get where you're coming from. It's easy to think you know what to do, before the surgeries. Then a run goes like this one, and you think, 'Am I doing the right thing?' The whole point of this is," Arañé continued, "we have to fight this out for two reasons: One, if we don't, the bad guys will do whatever they want with nobody to stop them."

"What's the second?" Josanne asked, leaning in. She was seeing an all new humane side of the elite force. She wasn't fully convinced yet, but at least she could catch a glimpse of what they were really about.

"If we don't fight it," Chrome continued, "others less well equipped will have to."

"So, tell me, Susan," Arañé asked, as he fixed his eyes directly at her. "If you had a choice between you or someone's thirteen-year-old little sister fighting off those bikers, would you turn and walk away?"

"No! How could I?" Susan protested.

"Or you, Josanne?" Chrome continued. "Would you leave your niece in an alley alone with those guys at the substation?"

"No," Josanne admitted.

"Well, CYBER has given each of us that same exact choice. The bad guys are all out there, and if we don't stop them, we'll be forcing some poor wage slave stuck in a cubicle or some kid who has enough trouble just trying to survive in a crate in some ghetto to deal with it. We fight to give them a chance. *We* fight it out so *they* don't have to."

"We deal with the pain of their fight," Jack added, almost to himself. "And that's the real sacrifice. That's the reason why everyone on the CYBER team agrees to the run, or there is no run. We can't afford the toll on our consciences."

"Tell me something then, Jack," Josanne began. "Are you the only one who's ever gotten out?"

"Voluntarily? No. There have been a few over the years, but it's been rare. But to be completely open, I am the only one who's been called back."

"And why is that? Why would Simon call you back after all those years?" she persisted. Even Blaze was beginning to get annoyed at the line of questioning. Foxfire was focusing on Joseanne, trying to scry where the former reporter was going.

"Because Simon figured the team, all of you, need me in your game. He tried to find someone else, but everything always came back to me. I didn't know exactly why at first, but I think I'm beginning to understand."

"And what made you want to come back?" she asked.

Jack looked at her and smiled. Somehow, she had triggered a memory of him talking with the Razors. Suddenly, he was calmer than he had been since he'd agreed to leave Roanoke. "I didn't—want to come back, that is. But I knew I would be betraying everything I had done in those years in between if I didn't."

"Oh?" she asked, almost drooling. She could smell she was getting near some pay dirt. There was something different about Jack, something he was still holding back from telling them, despite his open-door policy. She appreciated Foxfire's training— now he was openly telling everything. Their leader would come clean, confessing his involvement in some extreme government or megacorporate power plays. "And what exactly was it you did during those 'off years'?"

"I was a pastor," he said, so simply and openly she knew it was the truth, "in a small church in a Roanoke ghetto."

"A pastor? Like in a church? In Roanoke?" she exclaimed so loud it was almost a shout. "Where?"

"The ghetto in the sprawl formed by the Matsua, FoodTech, and SyncTec ICCs. Known as the MFS Outzone to outsiders, we knew it as something else."

"And what was that?" Josanne asked, her attitude changing from callous challenge to curious interest.

"Razor turf," Jack declared, casually, confidently, almost proudly, with an underlying tone of affection. At that point, she knew he had truly considered it a sacrifice to leave there. That ghetto had become his home.

"And you were a pastor? There?" She knew he was telling the truth, but the enormity of it hit her all the same. "And now our leader on this cyborg team, recruited by an A.I., no less, is a pastor of some urban ghetto street mission? This is too much!" She scanned the others for some sort of support, but all of the newcomers except Johnny, who seemed bemused by all of this, were in the same state of stunned silence she was. Finally, she jumped up, waved her arms in complete exasperation, and cried out, "Oh, for the love of God!"

"Exactly," Jack responded, with a wink at Johnny.

"You must get that a lot," Johnny replied, with an uncharacteristic smile.

"Let's just say it's not the first time."

"And of all people, you knew about this?" Josanne asked Johnny. It was almost an accusation.

"Yeah—well, not at first. But my augs were nothing like any of yours, so my surgery and heal time went a lot quicker. So, while you guys were sleeping off your surgeries, Jack-O here took me on a recon in Roanoke to find out more about where that Diamond was comin' from. We weren't in those woods for three hours 'fore some street ganger crew shows up. Nasty joe's and chikas in that pile. So I get ready for a go-to, an' Jack tells me to stand down, asks where some rucker named Scissors is. Guy's eyes go wide an' he 'bout goes nuts seein' our boy here. They tagged him as 'Preach' once upon a time, if you can believe it. That's when I said the exact same thing you just did, and got the exact same response.

"Anyway, so we meet Scissors, he gets us news'd up an' current. Evidently, they've got a turf cold war goin' on with some rival choobs, but the choobs are geared from whoever's punkin' the Diamond. Jack tells Scissors we're removing Diamond from the equation, all of it. Scissors gives us keys to the kingdom, so to speak. Says cops can't touch the ICCs, but Diamond's bad press—startin' to cause problems in other areas of the city, only a matter of time before it's outta control. The badges put up a bounty on whoever is makin' and punkin' the stuff, but people are afraid of Crack City Brotherhood, a.k.a. Razor's rival gang. Scissors says some nulls they picked up in a fight said they were getting fed from a Matsua suit, but the suit didn't come with a name tag."

Jack picked up the narration. "Iylothien began running surveillance on Matsua, grabbed some traffic about a new pharmacy line they're trying to develop. They ran into a schedule delay, so they decided to experiment on humans to gain time. Project Director's name is one Mahlon Atchins. Atchins has only recently been on Matsua's payroll; originally, he was on contract for their Biological Assets division. For some reason, he's been hired full-time for directing pharmaceutical projects. He's efficient, but the civilian casualties of his projects have been high—almost like he enjoys it. Besides his involvement introducing people to hopelessly addictive drugs, he's also quite the predator. According to our intel from disgruntled Roanoke cops, he likes his girls sweet, innocent, and drugged. It's his thing."

"Human shark," Johnny commented.

"Hey—don't insult sharks," Fuser said.

"So, Jack-O and me go down to Matsua archology," Johnny said. "Between his wire-dance and my smooth, we end up actually inside. Hung out at a popular restaurant in one of the mall sections as new employees in their Biological Assets department—nobody anywhere messes with H.R., Jack-O says—and I happen to hear Mahlon on his phone jokin' about why pay human test subjects for new drug lines when you can have lines of streeters payin' you?"

Jack smiled this time. "Johnny even had the nerve to interrupt him and tell him that while Matsua Assets division is pleased with his opening the new revenue streams, he is warned not to discuss those things over the phone in such an insecure setting. Atchins actually thanked us and apologized."

"So that's how you got us to Matsua," Melissana realized. "Then when I came to from the neural interface surgery, Iylothien had me doing practice runs on Matsua."

"Yes," Jack agreed. "Only they were never simply practice runs. We knew it was Matsua, but we didn't know where their Diamond facilities or formula were located. You were able to figure out that the substation held the records of that location and a link to their mainframe."

"So, we hit the substation," Josanne said, tying it all together.

"Yes again," Jack said. "*We* did," he stated, taking the time to look each of them in the eye. Then he added, "Now, do any of you know of anyone else who could have done that?"

After a respectable silence, Jack smiled. "Neither do I."

"Okay, we got some kinks to work out." Jack picked up the pace of the conversation, getting back into the business. "I for one think having three teams on the ground worked against us. We got careless because of our numbers. Not saying the numbers were bad, but we can do better." He made notes on part of the wall screen that turned whiteboard. "Anything else?"

"Menagerie, Rachel, and Fuser really covered for me when I went down. I was in serious trouble there," Susan volunteered.

"No worries, Lady Black," Menagerie returned. "We all get into spots where the biz is more than we got the creds to pay for."

"You'll pay it forward couple times over before you're done, I betcha," Blaze added.

"Yeah, about that," Jack started. "Corey, you have got to trust your team, and that includes trusting the plan the team comes up with. You could have gotten both yourself and Fuser into serious trouble. Plus, you actually delayed the help Susan would have gotten because Fuser had to turn back to rescue you. We can't afford to let our emotions control our reactions when we're on a run, got that?"

"Yeah, got it," Corey replied, feeling the full weight of his error.

"You kids all did good, 'specially for your first run," Rickshaw said. "You'll be prime time before too long," he added. "That's why we're here now, to get you guys up to speed."

"Okay," Arañé said, changing the subject, "it was an overall good first run, but the job ain't over yet. What's comin' up next?"

Jack sighed. "Unfortunately, Arañé's right. Matsua's not a light run in any arena, and you can bet your farms that they're running analytics on what we hit and why. We can't assume they'll buy that our hit last night was a one-night stand or a simple grab for pharmaceutical creds just because we also hit their ordering system as a cover. We need to hit 'em again, and hit 'em quick, before they figure out what we're really after. To do that, we need to get into the archology itself."

"What?" Corey asked, surprised. "What ever happened to remote access and hacking?"

"Remote hacking still exists, Corey," Jack responded, "but if we just hack their formula, they'll still be able to reverse engineer it from whatever product they already have. We need to go in and get rid of it all."

"So, what'd you guys find out? What's the run look like?" Johnny asked.

Jack responded with, "Iylo? Queen? Go ahead and run it."

The far wall showed a 3D display of a vast complex the size of a small city, with the animated Bard de le Neon providing highlights and voiceover. The purple, silver, and mauve of the Matsua ICC flag billowed on the screen for a moment.

"What? Who thinks up these color schemes?" Johnny said. "Man, that is horrid—can we take them down and make them change to something decent?" He was immediately shushed by several parties. With a final, "I'm just saying, I thought we were about doing *good* for people!" he settled down.

"The Matsua archology is laid out quite differently than its neighboring ICCs. Surrounded by a plassteel wall ranging from 14 feet high on its public facing side to 30 feet high facing the outzone, and topped with three loops of concertina wire and rusted but still solid sharpened metal spikes, it somewhat resembles a fortress town."

"Or a high security prison," Chrome interjected.

"Or a high security prison," Iylothien agreed. "Hardened cameras and mini-turrets are spaced 20 feet apart, each set to pan its field of surveillance at slightly different rates of movement. In addition, the outer wall is patrolled by security forces on foot equipped with M16A2 assault rifles, automatic pistols, and military grade combat armor. As if that isn't enough, there are no less than three corporate-grade combat vehicles on alert at any one time, with the promise of more available if anything actually starts going down."

"Their corporate line for all of this is that they're a wealthy pharmaceutical company that happens to border upon not only two potential competitors," Iylothien's construct chirped, "but also the neighborhood miscreants, freaks, and low-lifers just beyond their walls."

"Works both ways, though," Arañé added. "It also means that anyone who might try to quit the company would probably never make it to the street outside. These days, sometimes you don't pick a single corporation to work at for the rest of your life. Depending on the ICC, you're making a trans-generational commitment."

"And the wall's only the first main barrier," Iylothien continued, rotating the display to prominently showcase each feature he was currently discussing. "The approach to the wall from the inside is a minefield 30 yards deep, with an inner electrified security fence and a grid of laser trip beams that cover everything but the authorized approaches. These approaches are themselves covered by an armed security force delegated to the main approach, plus an automated Vulcan machine gun for each of the tertiary approaches. Access to and from each is controlled by its own security station where only those with proper authorization for that station are admitted."

The display swept the viewers though a simulation of the fence line and inner security perimeter, then panned out to a broad expanse of flower gardens and outdoor park areas. "Once past the inner perimeter fence, there's another 20-yard-deep security zone park area that surrounds the archology building. Between the security zone and the main entrance, there's a 100-meter area that is divided between a park for employee dependents and an extensive flower garden." At this, the entire complex rotated with a wild sweep that left the newer viewers with a sense of vertigo. The view it now settled on contrasted sharply with the public-facing front grounds. "On the back side," Iylothien said, maintaining his oratory, "well, that's the side that faces Jack's old hometown borders. Nothing to see there except the vents and dumping pipes that spew into your backyard, if you crane your neck high enough to see past the 30-foot-high wall."

The video cut over to focus on the archology structure as Iylothien maintained his narration. "The Matsua building itself is a near-pyramid, with a base approximately two miles square and extending up approximately 500 floors and down eight. Above ground are the shops, auto dealers, offices, and other forward-facing Matsua enterprises and media; followed by the local Matsua academy and other higher education facilities; then by their residential areas, convenience markets, theatres, and pre-college school system. Above all that are the corporate research and executive office suites. Adorning the rooftops at every tier level are local algae farms and security stations, and the top roof is a fully functional heliport that can support flight operations for up to six Aztec-class helicopters."

Iylothien continued his briefing. "Matsua's production and product storage facilities are in the eight subterranean levels of the archology itself. Here's where this gets interesting. The location where Queen Vixenn got off the substation points not to the archology but to an old pharmaceutical processing plant complex against the south wall of the grounds that's got no Matsua usage designations. And if there's one thing an ICC is good for, it's cataloging its stuff. The complex has its own security forces, perimeter, and equipment. From what I can tell, the special security and regular Matsua grunts really can't stand each other, like they're working for rival companies. Evidently the security regular grunts think the special guys are a bunch of low-life criminals."

"Well, there you go," Johnny dourly cut in. "It really does take one to know one."

"Formula's kept in an off-line mainframe inside the production facilities," Iylothien continued, "but there are network log file traces of a backup that was run to a personal computer in one of the residential areas on the 454th floor. I'm guessing that'd be Mr. Atchins's personal rig." Except for Iylothien's image, the giant wall screen went dark. "Well, that's all I got," he announced. "Any questions?"

"Why the special security zone? And why all the bad blood between the two security forces?" Josanne asked.

"Happens a lot," Johnny commented.

"Actually, in this case because the special security actually *is* a gang of criminals," the voice of Simon cut in, the familiar rendition and office filling the screen. Iylothien's video was replaying in the upper left corner of the wall screen as Simon continued. "I've cross-referenced the Matsua staff schedules against the names referenced in some voice communications about who was pulling the special security details. I do hope you don't mind, Iylothien, but you have been busy with your research as well as your tutelage of the young Queen Vixenn."

"What'd you find?" asked Jack, wondering exactly how much of the evening's conversation Simon had been listening in on.

"They are not Matsua employees. In fact, they are organized crime. After that discovery I ran a global check on a reconstruction of the face of Arañé's German friend. Evidently our Mr. Atchins had him on retainer from the 'Organisierte Kriminalität,' old Germany's organized crime."

"So, there's an organized crime operation going on inside an ICC. Nice—makes it cop-proof," Johnny summarized.

"Which is exactly where we fit in," Arañé said.

"But what's their angle?" Fuser asked.

"Matsua wouldn't let someone else in on their lands if there wasn't something in it for them," Chrome said.

"Free drug development?" Corey guessed.

"I don't think so," J.D. offered. "Initial profit margins would be tempting, but an ICC openly developing street chemicals would risk an unwinnable publicity campaign waged by the other pharma corporations."

"The trouble is," Melissana offered, "even if we hacked every one of their communications it would take too much time to wade through the millions of calls to determine exactly what the connection is."

"And that's assuming they're using plain-speak and not codifying any of the discussions," Blaze joined in. "I'm with the new kid—it could take years."

"We just don't have that time to figure it out," Fuser concluded, "unless they come out and just tell us."

"Well, this may sound just a little pessimistic," Johnny began, just to break the foreboding silence that descended over the group, "but it's not going to make a difference. There's just no way we can assault that place. They've got enough bang to hold off a full megacorp ICC assault."

"So how *do* we get in?" Susan asked, completely perplexed.

"J.D.?" Blaze asked the twenty-something young man who was still staring intently at the replaying video. "This one's yours. How *do* we get in?"

Everyone stopped as the General ran through a multitude of strategies and scenarios in his mind. Several times he asked Iylothien to replay sections of the demonstration and voiceover. Clearly he was in his element, but the task seemed to be a stretch, even for him. He withdrew even further into himself. After forty minutes, he approached the screen which, at the touch of a few buttons, converted to a giant digital whiteboard. Two hours later, the whiteboard was filled with circled stills from the video, recorded sound bites from the presentation, and looping videos.

And then he stopped, almost looking confused for a few seconds. Or maybe he'd remembered something? He replayed the sound from before Iylothien began his presentation, then replayed it four times more. Searching further into his thoughts, he pondered an idea. Then, in a moment of decision, he returned his attention to his now spellbound audience and smiled.

"We actually *are* going to assault the place," he announced. "But first we're going fishing."

And so their meeting continued, discussing their first operation together, and planning their main run against the facilities located inside the Matsua archology itself.

33

SHARK FISHING

COREY REVIEWED THE plan in his mind once more. The high-level plan was simple. Find out when Atchins was going to be at the Matsua facility that produced the Diamond. Deck the facility and grab the formula before it could be uploaded anywhere else. Once that was complete, acquire Atchins so Foxfire and Trigget could extract where any Diamond not at the production facility would be. In the process, trash the facility and any traces of the Diamond still at the site. Trigget and Foxfire would also find out if Atchins was working on his own or if Matsua was conducting the operation. Had to be careful there, Johnny warned. Just because it might not have been their original idea didn't mean Matsua wouldn't like it once they heard about it. In a megacorp way, it was good biz.

But to find out Mahlon's schedule, they had to get to Mahlon. Foxfire, Trigget, and his own Lady Blackwolf were working on that right now. Corey was waiting in his Sabretooth, leaned back in his seat with his eyes closed. To anyone passing by who could see through the reflective window glass, he looked like he was taking a nap. He thought of those months and the intense pain as his body accustomed itself to the new wiring and sensory interfaces the CYBER surgeons had crammed into him. It was almost unbearable—by far the toughest thing he had ever gone through. He missed Susan, who had to be held in a separate area so they wouldn't hear each other's agonized shrieks and cries as their bodies adjusted to their new systems.

But Jack and Rickshaw were there almost every day. In one of those waking moments, Rickshaw confided in him how he'd gotten his name. He shared that he had been born Richard Dwight Shaw, and the guy who trained him was a wheelman of Japanese origin whose sense of humor couldn't pass the opportunity to tag his apprentice with a new handle. Corey couldn't keep himself from laughing no matter how much it hurt. Rickshaw told Corey later that he was sorry he'd told him, which only made Corey laugh again. Both times he passed out from the whiteout sensation of pain. Remembering all this caused him to briefly chuckle again, this time with no pain at all.

He saw Lady Blackwolf glance his way, and he flexed his right eye, giving her a wink. The front right turn signal flashed once at the honey-blonde woman who was madly in love with him. She giggled and winked back. *Man, I love my life!* he thought to himself with a lazy smile.

His smile faded as he saw Atchins approaching through the Sabretooth's concealed rear camera, one of the standard CYBER add-ons. His sighting was confirmed by the General, who had a quintet of hand-sized drones in constant surveillance. Corey liked the General. Despite the guy's total sense of dedication, and the way he could control multiple drones with such precision, he was completely just, well, *friendly*. Corey wondered once again how the Fist had formed. Their connection to each other was so deep it was almost symbiotic. He was sure they were already closely related before they joined CYBER. Close family, he guessed. Like him and his dad.

The memories still hurt, but he was doing something he knew his dad would approve of. Handsight came back to his memory then, and Corey felt a twinge of guilt that he hadn't reconnected with Hagerstown since the recruitment. He vowed that as soon as he could, he would get back in touch with the Hagerstown Defense

Commander. If Jack could let the Razors know he was alive, he would surely be able to let Handsight know.

- *"Hardcore! Wake up!!"*

The car engine revved as Corey was jump-startled from his daydreaming. It was Jack—*Greyscale*, he had to correct himself. What had he missed? Atchins had made his approach. The girls were pretending to do a street-side photo shoot, totally believable seeing how one of the models was Lyn in full regalia. Trigget was working the camera, with Susan posing as an up-and-coming model being trained by the more experienced Lyn. Blaze was helping Trigget with the equipment. Corey adjusted the car radio volume so he could hear the conversation play out better. *Brother,* he laughed to himself, *if you only knew!*

"Hey!" Lyn called to Trigget as Mahlon walked by. "I've got an idea!" Tugging on Mahlon's arm, she drew him close to her. "Excuse me, sir. We're working on a shoot, and I just had an idea. Can we use you in a couple photos? I promise it won't take more than five or ten minutes. Please?"

"Well, I'm in kind of a hurry," he objected, but then he began to recognize something familiar about the girl. "Say, do I know you?"

"Well, not yet." Lyn pouted, then flashed that dazzling smile of hers. "But that doesn't mean you can't get to know me." As if on cue, a giant billboard across the street suddenly burst into a full close-up photo of Lyn with that same smile, with a voice-over chanting the brand of a high-end cosmetic product. "But you've probably seen me before—see?" she said, pointing out the billboard with that smile in her eyes. She was in her element, she was gorgeous, and she knew it.

"Wow! A real celebrity here! Now, how could I say no to that! Yeah, let's get to know each other, sure," he agreed.

345

Lyn smiled, but inside her stomach churned. Some things a girl just never gets used to—and soliciting attention from guys like Mahlon was one of them.

"Okay," Trigget began. "Here's what we do. Sir—can I get your name? Mahlon? Great!" She half-pushed Lady Blackwolf into his arms. "Mahlon, you and Felicity here hold each other kind of close, like you're dancing. Great, perfect!"

- *"I owe you for the billboard, Iylo," Foxfire sub-vocalized.*

- *"Marvella Cosmetics owes me for the billboard, Fox," Iylothien replied.*

- *"Yeah, but they owe you something you'll want," she said through gritted, smiling teeth.*

Corey didn't like Trigget's idea of perfect. He felt the car weapons tingling in the tops of his forearms. "Easy," Rickshaw said. The two were linked through their car interfaces until Corey had more experience on his own. "You don't want to accidentally fire off a couple rounds."

"Yeah, you're right," Corey admitted, then added, "not accidentally."

Trigget continued. "Okay, now Mahlon, look back over your shoulder, yeah, and look longingly at Lyn. Yeah, pretend like you're really interested in her," Trigget said.

"Yeah, like that's hard!" he joked. "And how 'bout you, babe?" he asked Susan, who almost blanched. "Do I get the pleasure of getting to know you, too?"

"Good!" Trigget interrupted. "Now take off your coat—it's an evening out!" At the former reporter's suggestion, Mahlon obediently removed his suit jacket, handing it over for Blaze to hold while he posed.

"I'm Felicity," Susan said, recovering. "I'm just learning all this, but of course I'd like to get to know you a little better." To herself she was thinking of how correct Arañé was about sacrifice at the review. Mahlon was a suit, but she hadn't felt so leered at since Iron Mike. Had Corey not been just a block away fully armed, she would have bolted right then and there. She also knew Blaze was cracking Mahlon's smart comm frequency while he was distracted between her and Lyn. Blaze and Queen Vixenn would plant the appointment at the facility later.

"Hey, relax, darlin'," Mahlon said. "We're dancin' here!"

And, recognizing Susan was going to express it anyway, Josanne said, "And now Felicity, look like you are really angry that Mahlon is paying so much attention to Lyn!"

"*Perfect!*" Trigget announced.

Corey liked *that* perfect much better.

… …

"Okay, time's up for Mr. Mahlon—we don't want to hold you up," Trigget said. "So where can we send the developed images to?"

"What? Oh yeah, just bring them by yourselves to my apartment later on. It's inside the Matsua archology. You, too, honey," he offered to Blaze. "Never a problem with the more the merrier, is there? Here are a couple passes to get inside to the residential area. Just bring the prints up to my place, we'll all go through them together." His smile was far more slick than sincere.

"Sure! We'd love that!" Lyn said, pretending to be excited. "What's your address?"

The bait was swallowed, and as Mahlon handed the archology passes to Foxfire, the shark was hooked.

34

MAIDEN VOYAGE, MOTHER RUN

THUNDERCLOUDS HOVERED OVER the outzone slum, threatening to dump rain on rats of both rodent and human origins. The oncoming thunderstorm didn't matter to Scissors and the rest of the Razors. The storm that did matter was the meet they were about to have with the new Crack City Brotherhood leadership.

Thirty Razors marched into the Crack City section of the ghetto, armed more for a gang battle than a political meet. There had been bad blood between the two gangs for some time, and it had only been aggravated by Mahlon Atchins meddling in their internal affairs. Scissors hoped the meet tonight would heal some of that. The former Brotherhood leadership was no longer a threat. Preach ghosted Krellick and Broze off somewhere, and within a week, the fight was taken out of them. After that they talked some, but all they really knew was their contact was from Germany and worked with a local ICC. Then they were sent to some prison in a different state. The Crack City Brotherhood made a few other attempts at punking Diamond after the showdown between Preach and his two friends, but the Razors found them and shut them down. Now that Crack City was no longer useful to him, Mahlon abandoned the leaderless group to their fate. Still, it was a meet with the Brotherhood on Crack City's turf—if there was going to be trouble, it would happen tonight. Scissors smiled. Even without the aces up their sleeves, the Razors could handle trouble.

... ...

Thirty meters above the heads of the Razors, the General's drones were maintaining their sweep of the Matsua archology maintenance tunnel systems, while two miles and an entire world away, a classic black limousine slowly approached the Matsua main gate.

... ...

Inside the western perimeter of the archology, ten rats implanted with tiny neurohelmets similar to Rachel's skitted up the outward-facing side of the wall, barely a chitter to give away their presence. Upon reaching the top they paused, resting on their haunches, rubbing their forepaws, awaiting their next command.

... ...

"Welcome to Matsua Pharmaceuticals ICC—your health is our way of life," an automated voice said to Melissana, who was driving the limo. "I do not recognize your vehicle. Please state your name and insert your Matsua ICC pass, or press the Call button to speak with one of our professional security representatives."

After pulling into their parking slot on the ground level and being verified and scanned by the Matsua security, Lyn, Blaze, Susan, and Josanne wordlessly made their way to the executive elevators for their ascent to Mahlon's suites. At this point, there was not that much left to say, so they would save their banter for when others were around. The group of friends turned all business. "Femme Fatales reporting—we're in," was all the conversation they needed.

"Mr. Atchins? We brought our pictures for you!" Lyn cheerily announced into the elevator call box. "Of course, Mr. Atchins, we're all here. You're having a party so some of your friends can meet us?" She made sure she was physically smiling while mentally rolling her eyes. "Well, would it be okay to bring my driver up as well, then? I don't like her just sitting in the car the whole time by herself. Really? Great! We'll be right up!"

- "Hey, Iylo, whatup?" *Foxfire cheerfully asked over the sub-vocal circuit.* "He deleted the fake appointment and decided to throw a party. Got any idea who's on the invite list?"

- "I got nothing," *Iylothien replied.* "Wait—there it is. I see some texts to some mid- and lower-level management types, some researchers, and a small cadre of security muscle-boys. One of the replies says something about fine dining on choice meat. Another says they wouldn't miss it for a week's pay, and one of the security joeboys made a crack about super-models loving Diamonds. Lot of LOL responses on that one. Umm, I think this is, like, the wrong party to get invited to."

- "Or the perfect one," *Blaze responded.* "Sounds like he might be rounding up his crew for us. Thanks, Iylo."

Blaze then fixed a meaningful look at the group of ladies.

- "We're going to find out if all those people at the party are in on the Diamond gig," *she silently radioed.* "Then we find the whereabouts of any diamond-heads that aren't at the party."

- "And what happens then?" *Susan asked, hoping there would be no more violence.*

- "Then we keep any more Angie's from happening," *Blaze responded, with unmistakable finality.* "Gear up," *she added, slotting two chips into the base of her skull.*

351

The elevator arrived, and the girls entered. "Level 438, please," Lyn requested, pressing her pass against the card reader. "We're here to see Mahlon Atchins."

··· ···

As the elevator began its ascent, Iylothien cloaked himself with a ranger Camouflage spell. He invisibly slipped through the portcullis bars of the security subsystem controlling Matsua perimeter cameras along the southern wall. Now inside the castle, he grinned and, breaking into a spirited electronic jog, launched his assault against the Matsua fortress in earnest. By the time the elevator reached level 20, Iylothien had gained full control of the cameras on the level where Melissana had parked the limo. When the elevator reached level 57, he gave an all-clear signal.

··· ···

Johnny acknowledged Iylothien's signal from his current position in a hideaway underneath the limousine's trunk, opening the hatch to the pavement surface below. His objective was securing the main gate so the girls, now calling themselves *The Fatales*, would have a way out once they got to the car. Glancing around to make sure no one had spotted him, he stood to full height and adjusted his jacket.

- *"Purple, silver, and mauve!" he sub-vocally muttered. "You all owe me!"*

He continued his survey of the parking area surroundings. He could only wear the bare essentials of a Matsua security uniform to pass any weapon scans at the gate. He'd have to acquire a helmet, weapons, and other gear from a real Matsua security officer.

....

Scissors stopped the Razors 30 yards from the parking lot where they were supposed to meet with the Brotherhood. "Listen," he cautioned those closest to him, "they could have anything out here—stay sharp."

Jack silently prayed for the success of the night's operation and even more for those who depended on him for their leadership. He scanned the area telescopically first. He then switched to starlight, ultraviolet, and finally infrared. Halfway through the process, he caught himself subconsciously flexing his newly-reactivated enhancements. He willed himself to stop and continued his vigil. Arañé sent a series of radar and sonar pings, receiving an outline of almost everything in the area. What Jack couldn't see, Arañé could sense via detailed analytics of what those pings revealed. Between the two of them, they spotted a lot of Brotherhood.

"I don't get it. Nothing?" Scissors asked Chrome, who was currently both bodyguard and CYBER liaison to the Razor leader.

"Oh, they're here," Chrome stated flatly. "Move your guys up. Keep it tight."

Thirty steps into the parking lot, a group of shadows stepped out from their cover. Jack saw they were all armed, but he also observed that while Crack City Brotherhood still had some effective firepower, they didn't seem to have access to the same level of tech they'd previously enjoyed.

"You goveks way outta your turf, comin' here," a tall youth with slim build practically growled. "We got yo's covered all the way down back to yo' woods, so too late for runnin' that. Whatchas want?" he continued, dropping his voice to an intimidating whisper.

"Just wanna talk, Wraith, like we told y'all the other day," Scissors said.

"About what?" the new Crack City spokesman said, raising his voice in both volume and pitch, effectively mimicking the shade he was named after. Some of the Razors twitched. Despite being

353

new as the Brotherhood's leader, Wraith wore the title competently. Scissors, though, appeared unimpressed.

"Krellick started a war against us on our turf," Scissors began. "We're here to end it."

... ...

"Wish I was with them," Corey said to Rickshaw.

"You'll get your turn soon enough, Hardcore," Rickshaw replied. "Your hooks set?"

Corey nodded they were.

"Good, let's get started."

... ...

"Mr. Atchins! Good to see you again!" Lyn had to shout to her host to be heard over the noise of the party. "Wow, there are a lot of people here!" she said, her smile flashing to mislead Mahlon into believing she genuinely enjoyed being there.

"Yeah, well, I had to invite some people over when I found out you were actually going to come," Mahlon said, laughing.

The Fist's conversationalist detected a distinct touch of hidden malice in Mahlon's reply. She laughed an effortless and completely fictional laugh. "And are these all friends of yours, or did you charge admission?"

"Are you kidding? Baby, if I would've charged admission to see you or any one of you friends, here, I could've retired tonight. Even your driver, *wow*! I gotta admit, I'm a little surprised."

"Oh? And why is that?" Lyn asked him, leaning in just slightly to draw him out further. His overtone was brutishly obvious, but there seemed to be a secondary undertone that didn't seem quite right.

"Well, I was expecting that a doll like you would go around with a bunch of apes and arena boxers for protection," he half-joked, with just a touch of eagerness. Lyn surveyed the room for her friends.

Each was separated from the others, surrounded and engaged in conversation with about five to seven of Mahlon's friends.

····· ·····

"Suits been playin' you, Wraith. Been playin' the Brotherhood, and us. Tryin' to edge us to war. Near did that, 'cept Preach got involved."

"Yeah? I was there when it happened, Razor. Saw those choobs jack up Krellick an' Broze. An' that panzerguy with Anchor, cuz Brotherhood was gonna make you pay for musclin' in on our turf. Suits were gearin' us to hold our own against you! So, you tell me who's playin', cuz I see the face of a gamer all over you!"

"Wraith, what? Suit's tellin' you *we* were invading? They been pumpin' killer blow they're callin' Diamond into our hood, usin' your guys to take the heat. All we been doin' was stomping the punks sellin' it on our side. They weren't even sellin', just slipping it into people to watch 'em die so they don't have to waste byproduct until they find out a way to line up a bunch of addicts who'll pay and keep paying 'til they're dead. And once they had no use for Krellick, they turned and tried to kill him off!"

Wraith's eyes flared. It was common knowledge that the corporations were really no different ethically from the street gangs except in one area. The street gangs typically shared an intense sense of internal loyalty. Renegotiating a deal was one thing, but to break a deal with another gang member was to court disaster. Trying to kill a gang leader you had brokered a deal with was inviting a death sentence that would be executed with passionate fury.

"Prove it," Wraith finally uttered.

Scissors nodded and took a step back. Jack, Chrome, and Spider stepped forward from the rest of the Razors who stood silently behind.

"Whoa, whoa, whoa! I recognize y'all! Been a year since that mojo yo's worked up on Krellick and the bros. Then ya's up and

355

whacked 'em. We owe you blood vengeance on dat, my friends. We been hopin' to see yo's back in our hood so we can give street just for what yo's done."

Scissors stepped forward. "Let 'em at least talk first, Wraith. They're not the ones you want. Was your suit chummers that tried to off Krellick."

"Scissors, you'd sell your own mother to protect your gang!" Wraith said, challenging him.

"Wraith, Preach stepped into the bullet and took the hit for Krellick. The guy who popped Anchor took a second round. This guy Spider here caught the choob, some corp ghoster from Germany or somewhere."

"Yeah? So where's Krellick, then?" Wraith demanded to know, his voice again raising to a near wail. A fourth figure detached himself from the group of Razors, grinning at first, then quietly began to let out a slow drawl of a laugh, just under his breath.

"Dag, Wraith, you been workin' on that ghosty-voice of yours fo' sho! Sorry, dawgs," he said to those standing next to him. "I was holdin' back there, but I never could hold it straight when Wraith started crankin' his squeals." The tall figure stepped into the light given off by a perimeter wall floodlight and faced the Crack City Brotherhood leader, the large spiked mohawk unmistakably confirming his identity.

"Anchor? That really you, man? They—they said you was all killed!" Wraith exclaimed, dropping his voice act. He no longer needed to mimic a ghost—from what he had heard, he was looking straight at a real one.

"An' who told you we were deaders?" Anchor asked, suddenly very much like his old dispassionate self. "Was the Matsua suit, wasn't it?"

Wraith nodded and started to explain, but Anchor cut him off. "Scissors is talkin' chip truth. I *saw* Preach push Krellick out of the way and take the hit. They're legit. The suit hired the shooter.

Krellick an' Broze are up river, the stars locked 'em up. Anyone question whether I'm lying to my own colors?"

No one spoke. Either everybody thought Anchor's word was unquestionable or they were too scared to challenge him. After an extended silence, though, Wraith steeled himself and finally raised the questions that many of the other Brothers had wanted to ask but were too afraid. Nobody ever questioned Anchor before without getting a beating for the effort.

"So how come you're back? And where you been?" Wraith was inwardly shaking but stood his ground.

"I been upriver myself, an' after tonight I'll be goin' back for a while. But they let me come with 'em so I could tell you myself that the scammin' choobs in all this is the suits.

"Now, we know we can't hit the corps for payback, neither can anyone we know. But Scissors and his crew think they got a way to rain drek justice on the baggers, an' they wanna let us in on settlin' score as a peace offering. Personally, I want in on representin' Brotherhood Uppance on the suits." He gave a suddenly wicked grin, then let the expression fade. "But it ain't my call anymore, Wraith. You're leadin' Brotherhood now, an' by all I see here you're runnin' good code. Just listen these chummers out, then decide right by the Brotherhood."

… …

"Well, we like to be free from all that, you know, live our own lives," Lyn offered, maintaining her light conversational tone as they continued chatting.

"Yes, well," Mahlon said, offering Lyn a drink, "don't you think that can be dangerous, given your celebrity status?"

"Oh, I don't know," she said in the midst of a sip. "I think the status itself protects me. Who would want to risk the—"

"Status didn't seem to help with Justin Martinez," Mahlon cut in. "You'd make quite the tempting target—you know, the guy who wants to get the girl everyone wanted. Yet you travel with just these girls? Your little group here could hardly fend off a pack of determined assailants. Status doesn't protect you, Lyn. Power does." Lyn caught Mahlon allowing the wolfishness in his smile to escape for a second or two. "And I've got power."

... ...

"Hey, you! Get your sorry hands up!"

- *"Drek!" Johnny called in over the sub-vocal while raising his hands. "I've been spotted before I could grab a helmet."*

"I wanted to warn you, but I got some problems of my own," Iylothien whispered in a quiet, deliberate tone.

- *"Iylo, not like you to complain. What you got?" Jack demanded.*

"Not much now," Iylothien quietly returned, while notching a greenish-bronze arrow into his electron bow. "Just a couple wizards, their pets, and a raiding party of trolls. They were camouflaged, I almost missed 'em. These guys got some nova security around their perimeter and interior control systems. It's gonna be a serious Mother Run to get into their system R&D databases. Now if you'll excuse me for a minute or so, I've got some hunting to do."

... ...

A distant lightning bolt flashed, its thunder bellowing across Roanoke's horizon. Matsua Perimeter Camera MRP-34 started picking up a disturbance outside the exterior wall. Moments later, a radio call came across the Matsua security network, more bemused than concerned. "Ground level units, south wall, be advised: Rival gangers are tussling. The Razors and Crack City Brotherhood are fighting over a block or two like freakin' rats fighting over a piece of stale cheese." The voice over the radio laughed. "So, if ya hear any gunfire from over the wall, it's just our illustrious neighbors going at it. I'm calling dibs! I've got Razors over CCB at three to two odds. Any takers call in. Replays after work if anyone wants to shell creds for the viewing. Perimeter clear."

Johnny smiled to his captor. "Hey, man, I'm sorry." He raised his hands. "Jimmy DesCartes, new guy, transferred from 'Bama. Wanted to check in early so I can walk the map and get a little lay of the real land before I have to start. But hey—maybe we can catch the rumble over the gate monitor screen before the central jockeys lock down the view. We might be able to catch a few rounds to see how the fight's goin' and get some smart bets in on the action, eh?"

The guard confirmed Johnny's cover story with the desk, smiled broadly, and lowered his weapon. "You're on! Name's Larry," he said, while extending his hand. "Let's go," he added, turning to the gate station. "I'll introduce you to some of the guys."

"This kind of thing always go down 'round here, Larry?" Johnny asked.

"Nah, not really. Last couple months two of the local gangs been stirred up against each other. Don't really know why. Guess they figure it's time for a showdown."

"Sounds like you got that right!" Johnny exclaimed. "Can't wait to see it!"

"And linking in to camera MRP-34, and…" Larry laughed. "Oh, ho-ho! Look at that! They're gonna burn down half their own neighborhood! It's Crack City Brotherhood's home turf, though. I'm betting on them."

"My hunch is that they'll both come out ahead," Johnny said. Larry started to ask how that was possible, but by then Johnny had put a sleeper hold on him that wouldn't allow the air to pass. After a few seconds of struggling, Larry forgot about the gang war outside as his mind filled with the all-surrounding blackness of unconsciousness.

Whistling to himself, Johnny parked Larry's body in a corner of the gatehouse office. He had to adjust his new gear belt and holster a little and had to tighten the chin strap of his helmet, but five minutes after knocking out the guard, Johnny-Jimmy-Larry left the gatehouse for a quick tour of the assigned parking area.

- *"One down, I'm guessing about fifteen to go, not counting the vehicle crews,"* he reported.

... ...

The decaying brickwork of the run-down warehouse where the rival gangs met echoed the rapid staccato of automatic pistols interspersed with the ear-splitting booms of shotguns and streetsweepers. The sound of glass bottles breaking near MRP-34's microphone interrupted even this noise, and a fire began to rise just off screen of the perimeter camera. From what the Matsua security troops watching the fighting over the cameras could see, it was a bloodbath. The Razors were holding their own, but at the moment, it was anyone's guess who would survive until morning. The cheering from the gate station guards could be heard throughout the parking level; Johnny wouldn't need any help finding *that* place. One of the armored personnel carrier crews wanted to watch the action, too, but since they were prohibited from deploying to the scene itself, they parked at the gate to watch the video.

- *"So far so good,"* Johnny reported in. *"But where's Iylo?"*

... ...

"Grey, it's the storm!" Menagerie yelled. "They can sense it—I can't hold them much longer! Optimohelius is going to lead the others out if we don't get them moving soon!"

"We're almost ready. Bring 'em down on the inside, Menagerie. Then try to have them hold on for just a couple more minutes. Will they wait?"

Menagerie paused, then smiled. "They're on their way! Thanks!"

… …

- *"Hey everybody, I'm back!" Iylothien enthusiastically broke in over the comm circuit. "Miss me?"*

- *"'Bout time!" Chrome sub-vocally yelled in reply. He took a swing at one of Wraith's bodyguards as the ganger swung a chain lined with barbed wire strands that ended in what looked like weighted fishhooks. "I've been shot seven times! You got control of the perimeter yet?"*

- *"Yep, got it, and intercepted the feed from the last 17 minutes, 41 seconds. I can't help it you never learned how to dodge! I found a good place for the loopback. Sequence starting in three… two…one…"*

The flame brought to life by the off-camera Molotov cocktail flickered for a second. The scene of the gang warfare wavered in the light of the fire and smoky shadows, for just a moment.

- *"…annnd CUT! Okay, everybody, you can relax now, but keep the noise coming for anyone on the other side of the wall. And yes, for the uninitiated, it actually does matter that both minutes and seconds were prime numbers—makes the job for their monitoring algorithms to track the looping exponentially harder, if you're interested. It also happens to make it just as hard if you're not interested. Anyway, we're on, Greyscale!"*

The fighting stopped almost immediately after Jack sent the all clear. An unusually odd sound was heard after the gunfire and smashing of bottles, cracking of wood boards and clashing of metal slowly ceased. Scissors, Anchor, Beast, and Wraith all began laughing together. After a few moments, some of the others joined in. Though it was clear hostilities between the two the gangs would not disappear completely in one night, definite progress had been made in ending the war that had been started by Mahlon Atchins.

"All right, everybody. I really hate to break this up, but now that we've all caught our breath, we need to get to work," Jack said. "You guys sure we're all together on this?"

Scissors nodded. "Yeah, Preach, the Razors are in, but it's Crack City's turf. It's their call to use their land."

Wraith paused and thought, then glimpsed at Anchor, who nodded. "You really gonna bring the pain on the suits who set us up, who sold out Krellick an' Broze? Ain't no way we could think of doin' a corp without ghostin' all of us, so yeah," he said, smiling cruelly, "you got our permission. Do it!"

- *"Rickshaw, Hardcore, you heard 'em. General, Operation Drawbridge is a Go."*

- *"Roger, Greyscale!" Rickshaw acknowledged. "Hardcore, our turn. Let's go."*

Corey fired up his Sabretooth, and Rickshaw his Dominator. Between them, they half-towed, half-dragged a metallic structure consisting of a huge section of sheet steel that was half the length of a football field and almost the width of the entire street. The sheet rested vertically on its long side between two frameworks of girders and supports resembling staircases. All of it rested on a flat metal base that rolled on solid metal wheels with grinding screeches that grated against the evening air, competing with the rain and thunder for the attention it felt was its due. The structure easily weighed 4,300 pounds—more than Corey's Sabretooth when fully loaded. It took them nine minutes to navigate the seventeen blocks through the Crack City territory, but at long last Rickshaw and Hardcore got close enough to the wall that they could both pull to the side and detach the tow hooks.

Lightning flashed, briefly illuminating the rain bouncing against the platform. Arañé, Chrome, and the others gathered at the height of the strange structure.

"You sure you want to do this?" Scissors yelled to Jack over the now pouring rain. "You weren't counting on the weather!"

"Neither were the girls, and they're all inside! It's too late now—in fact, this might actually help us! If we wait the storm out, it'll be worse! This needs to be anchored six to eight feet away from the wall if we're going to make it—are we there yet?!"

"Three feet to go, Grey," Chrome shouted. "If I can get a couple Razorboys and Crack City Brothers to give me a hand," he yelled over his shoulder, receiving a few shouts and whoops of affirmation, "we should be ready in about seven minutes!"

"That leaves us with about one minute left before the end of the first loop. Let's go, then! General, we're ready for the drones and tether lines." Jack, now in full CYBER mode as Greyscale, was once again leading his troops. "If that tape loops through too many times, somebody's bound to catch on!"

"*Man,* it's good to have you back, Grey!" Chrome hollered over the storm, echoing what they all felt. After that, Chrome reverted to his typically dour self—he was in mission mode as well. "All right, ladies," he yelled, "get your rides ready!"

Another flash of lightning lit the eastern skyline, close enough that the thunder's report rumbled both the trash cans outside and the new allies' chests inside.

… …

The ten rats had slowly descended the western wall, away from the flashing skylight. They then resumed their wait in the shadows at the base of the wall. Rubbing their forepaws, they consoled themselves with thoughts of the fresh scraps they would feast on when they all got back to their laboratory home.

One of the newer rats, Smallear, was hiding farther back from the rain when its keen ears heard other rats from an under-the-sidewalk rainfall passage behind it. Smallear informed the others of what he'd heard. Optimohelius took in the new information with interest. Thus it happened that, waiting in the rain for Menagerie's command signal, the senior lab rat with heightened intelligence had an idea.

… …

"Mr. Atchins, this conversation is beginning to sound a little, well, kind of creepy." Lyn let out a dry chuckle in the middle of a dance. "I must say that if we weren't with all these people, I'd be a little concerned."

"Well, as it turns out, Miss Lyn," Mahlon responded, with the air of one presenting a fact at a board meeting, "you should be." The song ended, along with their dance and any sense of goodwill. "You see, I recognized your bodyguard detail after we parted company the other day. They're the ones who got Martinez out of his little tight spot last year. I heard they died about nine months ago, so I never thought much about hunting them down." He chuckled to himself. "I don't know how they found me or how they got you wrapped up into their game—did maybe the Roanoke news hire you?"

"What do you—what do you mean?" she said in protest. "We came to bring the photos. Here, see for yourself!" she said, producing a manila envelope.

"Ask your friends, if they haven't already told you!" He disinterestedly grabbed the envelope from her. "It doesn't matter why you came along with them. It's not that I won't enjoy it. I told you, status doesn't protect you, it just exposes you—to people like me. Power protects you. Oh, and for the record, 'all these people' prove my point. They're all friends of mine. And *my* people are going to make sure *your* people don't make it out of here. You see, *I* was the one in the helicopter at the quarry. That operation cost me a bundle. Tonight, I collect."

He broke eye contact with her for just a moment, allowing himself the luxury of a glance at her glass for just a fraction of a second, to bask in the sweetness of a dark secret.

Lyn dropped her glass. Melissana and Josanne responded to the sound, only to see Lyn fall to the floor. As she hit the carpet, hands grabbed for Melissana, Josanne, and Susan. Blaze broke for the door to find the exit blocked by three off-duty Matsua muscle-boys. "You ain't goin' nowhere, sister," one of them said, flashing the smile of a predator.

35

OPERATION DRAWBRIDGE

"GENERAL, GET THOSE tethers anchored, *now!*" Jack commanded.

"Got it!" the General replied. Two microdrones electromagneti- cally gripped a loose end of thin steel cable attached to the fabrica- tion that was now six and a half feet away from the Matsua pe- rimeter wall. The General deftly guided each drone as it looped its cable through or around perimeter turrets and other formations, effectively anchoring the structure to the wall.

"Menagerie, you're up! Go!" Greyscale ordered. Menagerie nodded, concentrated for a moment, and then smiled. "They're on their way. We've got a surprise for you," she announced. Seeing the concern on Greyscale's face, she shrugged and quickly added, "Don't look at me, it was all Opto." Refusing to answer his unasked questions, she simply maintained her grin. "Wait for it…"

Jack considered his options. If CYBER operations were music, "Drawbridge" would be a symphony whose Master Composer was the General, with the Concert Maestro Greyscale conducting, and the orchestra of world-class musicians the team of agents, each playing their individual notes and pauses to form epic chord progressions that no single one of them could have possibly achieved on their own. It seemed as if the weather itself had allied itself with their performance, embellishing and accentuating the score with flashing displays of lightning, echoing booms of thunder, and always the steady background sound of applause caused by the falling rain. The Razors and Brotherhood just watched, amazed.

Greyscale was intuitively aware of these musicians enough to know when to let the performers interject a little bit of themselves into the Master Score—an innate sense regarding these impartations was one of *his* talents. In the midst of it all, the actual concert may occasionally lend itself to certain improvisations that embellished the final overall production, and he knew this was one of those times.

"All right, Menagerie. Go for it." Jack hit a button on the framework, rotating the metal slab and locking it into the staircase supports, converting the structure into a giant ramp. He ran to get into the gunner seat of Hardcore's Sabretooth as the fabrication transformed itself. As if on cue, just when the car door was closing, Jack "Greyscale" Mathews heard about thirty different klaxons sounding along the western perimeter.

"All right, team! We give Matsua and the bad guys eighty-three seconds to start responding, then we give 'em what we got!"

…… ……

It was Optimohelius's finest moment. He understood fully the intents of his matriarch. His forces were to create a diversion so her pack of humans could hit their enemy from behind. His idea seemed obvious once he thought of it—if his pack of ten rats could create a distraction, then a swarm of a hundred rats could create a larger one. He'd get those hundred by defeating the local alpha rat of the burrow Smallear located. The fight for dominance of the swarm itself didn't take much time—he was only fighting normal rats, and the leader had the sense to flee. Optimohelius chose to spare the former head rat, so after the typical three-meter run, the deposed leader turned and rejoined the pack. With his nine lab brothers at his side, convincing the rest of the swarm to join him was simple fare. By the time his mistress called for him, he was ready with his new army. He sensed an urgency in his matron's summons—he would hurry, and his new command would hasten beside him.

As Optimohelius broke from the safety of the wall across the field of battle, he could sense her exhilaration at his cleverness, his success! If he lived through this battle, the rewards would be great. But now was a time for wit and skill, for leaping, and for teeth. It was time to attract the attention of the mistress's enemies.

… …

"We got multiple blips on the interior grid array, sir! Multiple klaxon alarms, too!" the startled Matsua alarm monitor reported. "I swear I didn't see anything coming over the wall! Automated systems didn't report anything either." Had they all really been *that* distracted watching the gang fight? "Yes, sir—multiple klaxons. Ground forces responding, dispatching Remus I and Remus II to the scene."

… …

"General!" Menagerie cried, pausing on her way to join the others to toss a vial to the team's drone expert, "hit one of those APC's with this. And *don't* spill any on yourself!" She left the General for her Yashuba Mystique at the base of the ramp, whistling Rachel to her side as she mounted and revved her bike.

"Whiskey Sector, this is Dispatch, report! What you got?"

"Dispatch, this is Whiskey Three. We got rats—comin' up out of the sewer grates like nothin' I've ever seen before. They're just jumping in and out of the grid beams, setting off the alarms. Never seen anything like it—maybe the storm—GAGHH!"

"What the—?" The dispatcher gasped. *"Whiskey Three, Whiskey Three, report!"*

"Dispatch, this is Whiskey Seven—Whiskey Three was swarmed. I think he's got about thirty of 'em crawling all over him. Nothing

369

I could do—Bill—Whiskey Three is down! Now they're jumping all over Whiskey Two!"

A small drone flew over the first Remus and dropped the liquid-filled vial at the turret. The small glass tube smashed against the tough armor, but nothing else happened. The General was confused.

- *"Menagerie, this is General. Payload delivered, nothing happened."*

- *"Thanks, General, keep your eyes open!" she ended, smiling.*

The General continued his scan of the eastern section. Then he saw it. Menagerie's rats all left their current targets and headed to the Remus in a swirling, leaping horde. In fact, he also saw that Optimohelius's pack—originally ten, now a swarm of a hundred—was being joined by what looked like thousands of other rats, not only from along the walls, but seemingly from every crevice the landscape could offer. Within two minutes, the Remus was covered with layers of the rodents.

"Mayday! Mayday!" a panicked transmission sounded from inside the Remus. Screaming could be heard in the background as the radio operator continued. *"We've got rats coming in through the turret gun and engine compartments, eating their way into the vehicle's hull. Oh, drek, we are screwed!"* The vehicle ground to a halt, lifeless except for the teeming mass of mottled fur.

- *"Menagerie, what did you do?" the General asked in equal measure of wonder and horror. "They're tearing that thing apart!"*

- *"You've got your C4," Menagerie replied. "Behold the power of P4—a concentrated mix of Norway Rat, a.k.a. Common Rat, hormones, estradiol, and progesterone. That's $C1H24O2$ + $C21H30O2$, to be exact. When trying to get to a female in heat, Norway rats 'rump bite'—and with enough rats, their jaws can* *exert enough precise pressure, to enough exposed crevices, to work their way through the entire vehicle. That radio operator was closer to the truth than he realized. 'Amor omnia vincet.'"*

- *"That's just gross!" Fuser exclaimed, wrinkling his nose in disgust.*

Another radio report came over the Matsua comm channel.

"Remus II, this is Watch Command. God only knows what chemicals those rats have been feeding on, but we cannot risk a containment breach. I have clearance from Executive. Exterminate the threat—both the rats themselves and any secondary contamination risks. Do you copy?"

"Watch Command, this is Remus II. Roger, Remus II copy eliminate any chance of containment breach...

"Break—Whiskey Seven, this is Remus II. Sorry, I was looking forward to dinner with you and the kids tomorrow." A sigh, then, "No need to acknowledge, Remus II out."

"Hank, you gotta be—" The whump of an APC short-range canon and blast of an antipersonnel shell fired at Whiskey Seven concluded the radio transmission with prejudice.

... ...

*"**Strike Team - GO! GO! GO!**"* Greyscale screamed into Hardcore's radio.

The Dominator and Sabretooth both hit the ramp at 60 miles per hour and left the top end at 70, clearing the southern wall with a meter and a half to spare. They were followed closely by Arañé and Fuser on their Yashuba Desert Knight motorcycles, then by Chrome on his Morrison-Hayley Bravado-class Highwayman. Menagerie paused to issue Optimohelius's signal for him and the other CYBER rats to return back over the wall, promising an abundance of fresh cheese, meats, and fruit awaiting them at home. Then she urged her Mystique up the ramp and jumped, the augmented Rachel bounding alongside.

Gunfire and radio reports were coming from both sides of the Matsua internal ground conflict while the six CYBER vehicles were still in the air. Rickshaw and Hardcore hit the ground with jarring thuds a scant three meters past the minefield and electrified fence, swerving outwards in opposite directions to cover for the inbound bikes. The lighter bikes landed with bounces that almost took them into the children's playground and its equipment along the inner perimeter wall. Chrome's heavier bike landed well short of the playground, but even with the suspension heavily modified for the jump, the bike wavered upon the impact of the landing and almost gave way completely. A few seconds later, Menagerie's Mystique touched down and took a hard-left skid, Rachel landing to her right, scrambling for traction to keep up with her mistress.

Without the distraction from the rats, they would have been torn to shreds before they hit the ground. As it was, Matsua ground troops not involved in the in-fighting of the eastern sectors started firing at the new threat posed by the CYBER strike team, but the Dominator and Sabretooth provided sufficient suppressive return fire that all six vehicles and their occupants survived the jump. They were in.

…… ……

"I'm not going anywhere? Neither are you, null-brain," Blaze said. "I'm not here to escape. I'm here to lock the door." She paused, holding up her index finger and then winking, cupping her hand to her ear. "One sec…" she told them. Bewildered but not the least bit frightened, they actually complied.

- *"Blaze? Iylo here. You're home free. I'm finally in, security monitors are ours now."*

"Oh, this is gonna be fun," one of the brutes replied while Blaze was momentarily distracted. "Any last words while you can still talk?"

- *"Iylo, you got eyes on?" she asked.*

- *"Yep, got ya's in my sights through the room cameras. Why?"*

- *"Remember back at that restaurant? I owe you a dance," Blaze replied.*

Blaze looked up at the goon with a playful twist in her smile.

"Last words? Just four for you, choob," Blaze said, as she kicked her Dance Floor chip: *"DarkPsy Trance Mosh Pit…"*

The sounds of bodies crashing against the door-side tables let Susan know the party had indeed begun in earnest. She snapped both arms forward, grabbing one of the mercenary-types in front of her by the shoulder blades and squeezing in, protruding the two-centimeter long cryosteel blades from under her fingernails. Digging into his shoulder blades and slicing the muscle underneath, she pulled down sharply. With an agonizing cry, the man went to his knees, enabling Lady Blackwolf to rotate over him like she was doing a routine on uneven parallel bars. Now, on the outside of her immediate circle, she withdrew her blades and kicked back, sending the man into the rest of the circle. Off-balance, they tried to respond to the suddenness of her unexpected attack, but she had already grabbed another one of the group, and with the twirl of a discus thrower, sent the man into the rest, knocking them all down.

"Frakkin' *perverts!*" Melissana screamed, tucking her fists in at chest height, planting her right foot, leaning right and kicking out sideways and up with her left leg. Her booted foot caught an assailant in his throat just under the chin, snapping his head down as his body began its short flight up and away from her. She raised her foot upward as she withdrew her kick, connecting a second time with the underside of his chin, snapping his head back and allowing the now airborne body to sail past her boot.

The augmented detective raised in the pulse of street fighting then dropped into a crouch and whipped both arms outwards, flinging a pair of tethered metal weights into another assailant on either side of her. Bright lights flickered with an audible series of crackles as the weights struck their targets. The two men went down, drooling and twitching, their hair standing on end from the static electricity that had been discharged into their systems. The others were surprised but quickly recovered, one of them laughing. "We'll never let Oxy live that kick down!" he said derisively, assuming a modified Snake style kung fu stance. "Wanna try one of your toys on me?"

Melissana knew she was in trouble—she was wired for the wires, not wet-work stuff like the others. "You betcha, duster," she grimly replied, more out of street determination than confidence. Then she threw a flash-bang pellet onto the floor in front of him to escape.

At the first sign of trouble, Josanne raised her hands in surrender to the men who had surrounded her. She pleaded for a chance to help Lyn, who was beginning to shake on the floor. She began to explain that Lyn had nothing to do with the quarry job, that hurting the supermodel was unnecessary, but three of the men stepped in to grab her. She looked at the stone-cold expressions on each of them as they approached and sighed, arching the back of her tongue as she did so. They drew closer, then hesitated. One coughed once, the other two simply stood unmoving. Within a few seconds, they limply sat on the floor, completely docile in their pheromone high.

Josanne quickly glanced around the room. As Blaze was making sure her targets were soundly "asleep," Susan was wrapping up with her crew. Josanne saw, though, that Melissana was struggling to survive against some guy who was moving like a stunt double for a Vance Parrow action vid.

The detective was on the floor, her face bruised, her hair torn. She flinched as the merc-type she was fighting was about to connect another serious and possibly lethal blow when he suddenly arched back, flailing his arms widely, stunned. He stopped and turned around, a mask of pained shock on his face. He looked like he was trying to say something, trying to ask a question, but the words wouldn't come. As he moved, a sliver of light briefly shone through a small, cauterized hole in the man's chest. A second later, he fell to the floor, dead. Melissana traced his final gaze in time to see her best friend drop her laser pistol onto the thickly carpeted floor of the apartment. It made no sound as it hit, and neither did Josanne, catatonically horrified that she had just killed a fellow human being.

…… ……

Hardcore and Greyscale were using combinations of smoke, sleep, and tear gas to suppress the Matsua ground troops while Rickshaw forged a path to the production facilities. Minimizing Matsua casualties was a strategic goal that the CYBER strike team could not ignore; the obvious problem was that the megacorporate forces, brutal enough under any circumstance, had no way of knowing that, and probably wouldn't care much if they did....

Avoiding the minefields between where he'd landed and his target location, Fuser coerced centrifugal force into working overtime as he raced his bike sideways along an inner security containment barricade, his left arm blade extended, furrowing the ground as he rode to keep the G-forces from hurling his bike over the lip of the wall. The plan worked until the concussion of a grenade blast disrupted the delicate balance he had woven between gravity and speed. The bike lurched upwards to Fuser's right, then downwards, spilling Fuser and sending the bike awkwardly cartwheeling away into the minefield. The first two bounces of his Desert Knight were acrobatic but uneventful. On the third bounce, the bike triggered one of the mines, blasting it another five meters to the side. It rolled sideways once more, and finally settled.

Dang it! Fuser thought to himself. He was shaken but not incapacitated. Still, it wouldn't be long before the Special Security

Forces would be searching the minefield for his body. He quickly fitted a SLAP micro-missile to his pistol, took aim, and fired. With a barely audible pop, the subsonic round slowly arced along its flight path for nine meters before a flight rocket kicked in with a flashless but deafening blast that echoed off the walls of the Roanoke buildings within a quarter mile radius. The missile landed a fraction of a second later behind the searching defenders and emitted a series of high-intensity strobe flashes and bangs that rivaled the flight motor's ignition.

The startled gangsters instinctively went prone to protect themselves; in those seconds, Fuser fired his microfilament grapnel into the concrete wall close to where his bike had landed and silently zipped at seven inches above grass level to his fallen machine. He lay silently to play dead until he was sure his enemies had spotted him. Convinced he had been on his bike when it hit the landmine, they averted their attention to the commotion along their front line, allowing Fuser to slip past and take his position securing the far corner.

Menagerie's Mystique had been shot out from under her halfway to her goal. The indomitable Rachel was at her side to guard her fallen mistress, dragging her to relative safety behind another small barricade. Menagerie revived a few second later, the sound of Greyscale's voice yelling inside her head and Rachel's moist tongue on her face being her first physical sensations this side of consciousness. Clearing her head and establishing her resolve, she retrieved her staff from her sleeve. "Okay, girl, time to show them their mistake."

The first toss from her augmented arm landed a solid crack against her target's cryoplast armored head, stunning the victim and giving Menagerie and Rachel time to close the gap. She lowered her arm and activated her staff's retrieval magnet with another *Kriminalität* soldier caught between her and her favored weapon. The staff flew its path with an eagerness that was not delayed for a second as it made contact with the intervening target's legs. His armor kept his legs from breaking, but the impact tossed him over backwards with enough force that he was concussed. Another toss and retrieval later and she was within melee range of the rest of the squad. Rachel bounded up beside her, some cryoplast held in her teeth.

"Little girl," one said, laughing as the group of soldiers levelled their weapons on the CYBER operative and Rachel, "you and your freak pet are going to regret being born."

Menagerie assumed a combat stance and replied, "My name's Menagerie. I'm normally good with training animals, but you're not worth the time. It's like this: I got a different job to do tonight, and you're in my way…"

Chrome and Arañé made their way across the gardens towards the Diamond production facilities but were starting to catch heavy weapons fire from the defender's ground troops and vehicles. Flickers of red light from Rickshaw's Dominator answered the call, silencing some of the heavier guns. Chrome grinned, launching a HEAVE rocket from his heavily armored Highwayman. The heavy rocket pushed itself along its flight path, first impacting with the wall 25 feet from the facility gate at 450 miles per hour, then exploding with a deafening boom that blasted a gaping hole in the facility's inner perimeter wall. The concussion permanently downed the facility's security forces within 50 feet. The shock wave caused even Chrome himself to wobble, but Rickshaw just exclaimed over the radio, "See, kid? I told you that every once in a while you need a good, solid boom! That one shook the ground so much it tickled!"

… …

Johnny had just subdued the northeast gate and was securing the staff until the raid was over. Knowing Johnny was now in control of the station, Iylothien opened up the monitors in that station so CYBER's inside man could watch how the attack was progressing.

"Oh my Lord, they're actually doing it," one of the older Matsua staff bemoaned in despair. "Oh, those poor children!"

Johnny froze. "What did you just say?" He leaned menacingly close to the older man's face.

"The children," the security man repeated. "Those goveks kidnapped a bunch of the executive's children and are holding them hostage. They said if we ever did anything to that facility, they'd kill them. We couldn't go near the place, or they'd kill them!"

Johnny was stunned. "Where are the kids?" he demanded to know.

"Do you actually think for one nanosecond that if the Matsua Director of Operations knew where her seven-year-old daughter was, a Tactical Asset Team wouldn't have already been deployed to neutralize every one of those racketeer wannabes? They got seventeen of the executives' kids, including the Security Director's son. Their RFID's aren't transponding... We have no clue where they are." He briefly glanced up at Johnny, then lowered his head and sobbed in spite of himself. "One of them is my grandson..."

"Got it," Johnny replied to the Matsua security man. He had to let the team know.

- *"Strike Team! Strike Team! This is Gatekeeper. I know the hold Atchins has over Matsua. They've got a bunch of executives' and security's kids held hostage somewhere. Repeat—Atchins has child hostages!"*

- *"Roger, Gatekeeper. This is Greyscale. We read you, but we're already in the thick of it now. We're committed, can't effectively get out. We stay with the plan and hope to God we find those kids. Iylo, top priority! Scan Matsua's network and try to find them!"*

Jack returned his thoughts to the battlefield. In the eastern sector, he could see the firefight that had broken out between the

Matsua ground forces and the remaining Remus was winding down. The Remus II was damaged but still sluggishly operational. Remus I was completely wrecked. Besides the damage the rats had wrought, the second Remus must have used the flamethrower on it to get the rodents. Just as he started to think the night couldn't get any worse, three more Remus vehicles rolled out from their underground motor pool.

- *"Company!" Greyscale called, as he spotted the third and fourth Remus APC rolling out from the Matsua parking garage.*

… …

"Grey, Iylo here. Not seeing anything so far about the kids." The swoosh of an arrow zipped past, barely missing his ear. "More good news—the board's starting to light up. Matsua must be trying to take back control of their systems." A fireball exploded nearby, the heat scorching his cloak. "Holy Mother Source-Code!" he exclaimed. "They got some hot codeslingers on point. I'm gonna be busy. No time to talk… I don't think the kids are on the Matsua grid. Queen, you gotta find those kids on Mahlon's system." With that, the Barde de le Nêone was gone in a fight for his life.

… …

"*Iylo!*" Melissana screamed in anguish.

A slur of rapid-fire gunshots sounded, the report coming from an auto-pistol fired at Susan. She twisted sideways and back-flipped, surprising herself by dodging the cone of fire with relative ease. By the time she ended her movement, though, most of the joe-boys that remained had firearms drawn and leveled. Susan would be fine, and Blaze probably as well, but Trigget had mentally withdrawn from the battle, and there was no way Melissana would survive the hail of lead that would come her way.

"*Enough!*" Mahlon yelled, pointing a shotgun at Lyn's head. The model just lay on the floor, jittering, her eyes staring at something apparently somewhere beyond the confines of the ceiling. Mahlon openly jeered. "Look at you, babe," he said. "Didn't know you could dance." He spat on her.

With a sudden clarity that threw Mahlon off balance, Lyn sat up and locked her eyes on him in a barely controlled rage.

"I also sing," she almost growled. Before Mahlon could respond, Foxfire threw her head back and opened her mouth wide. A sustained strain of discordant soundwaves flooded the room, engulfing the minds of everyone not prepared in advance for the onslaught of freakish sound. Glass broke from the high octaves while hearts and furniture rumbled from the bass pedal tones, with alto and tenor tones intermixed, all of it at ear-splitting volumes that would crescendo and decrescendo, each at different rates of intensity. Within seconds, the men that were left were too incapacitated to keep hold of their weapons, too busy grasping their heads in pain, affected with severe earaches, headaches, nausea, nosebleeds, and in some cases diarrhea. Mahlon, the closest, had all of the above. The fight was over.

Foxfire ceased her attack and shook her head, clearing the last effects of her daze. "By the way, I have a chipped pancreas, liver, and kidneys. It took a while to process the Diamond, but do you honestly think you're the first person who's ever tried to slip something into my drink?"

Blaze checked the room, verifying it was secure. "Tie them up," she told Lady Blackwolf in disgust. "I don't care how.

"Vix," Blaze added, "you heard Iylo. Find the kids, ASAP.

"Trigget? Hey, *Trigget!*" Blaze called out, clapping her hands in front of the stilled member of her team. "What's wrong with..." Then she spotted Josanne's laser pistol on the carpet, and the fallen man with the hole in his chest. "Oh, drek!" she said, then took a moment and sat Josanne down.

"Hey, Trig?" she said, more gently than Susan or Melissana had ever heard her speak before. "Hey, it's me, Blaze. I'm gonna just give you some time, okay? We might need you soon, but right now I know you're going through a lot, and you're processing a lot. I just want you to know that we're all here, so it's okay that you take this break. You're doing fine." She reassured the former reporter, patting her traumatized team member. "And Trigget," Blaze added, softly looking into Josanne's tear-clouded, glazed eyes, "you saved Vixenn's life, you know that? Thank you for doing that," she added gently. She then did the completely unexpected. There, in front of everybody, like they were the only ones on the planet, in the middle of a mission, Blaze gave Josanne a hug.

… …

Melissana couldn't interface directly to Mahlon's personal computer, so she opened her chauffer's attaché case and withdrew her Mitsuhasi 2049, one of the hottest rigs on the streets. Half paid for by CYBER, one quarter financed by the spoils of war from the substation run, and the remaining amount paid for with the credits Elaine had given her, it was more than she thought she could have afforded on her own for years. A 128-bit n988 processor with 16 slots, it had enough power to concurrently run her environmental module plus several other programs, apps, and subroutines. Of course, she also added her own customizations to adapt the rig to CYBER's special needs, then retrofitted all that hardware into one of her older cases for urban camouflage.

She spoofed Mahlon's IP3 address to hack into the gangster's network, then rerouted back into Mahlon's computer. A few seconds later, she found the Diamond formula, plus a backup copy he had saved onto a ghost drive. "I got the formula!" she announced out loud. "Found a backup copy, too. I don't see anything on the kids, though. I'm going back out onto their net to see what I can find."

"What? The formula? The kids?" Mahlon asked, starting to come back to his senses. "That's what this is about—the Diamond operation? Not Martinez after all, eh? Well, who knew?" He laughed to himself. "Here I thought you were after Matsua's Martinez heist."

"Blaze," Queen Vixenn reported, "I can't find an exact location of the kids, but they're definitely within the Matsua local grid. The *Kriminalität* net ICE is popping goblin raiding parties at me. Nothing I can't handle, but nothing indicating the location of the kids, either."

"Heh, keep tryin', sister." Mahlon, still dazed, chuckled to himself. "You'll never find the kids that way."

"Oh?" Foxfire said, tilting her head to the side. "And why is that?" she asked, donning a calculatedly cheerful smile. Trigget had received the same pheromone implant modelled by Foxfire, and Foxfire figured that the spray she had just infused Mahlon with would take effect in a few seconds. Instead, Mahlon just sniffed the air and shook it off. "Heh, you think we'd store that on the net somewhere for the Matsua cowboys to figure out? And is that the best you got to get me to talk? Some perfume? Forget it, I'm onto you." He grimaced.

Foxfire looked at Blaze and shrugged. "He's a sociopath. He's blocking the pheromones."

Blaze was both desperate and furious. She strode towards him, filled with a vengeful wrath. It took her three steps, which ended when she stopped just short and planted a kick into his side that sent him crashing into the heavy table of food behind him. The secondary impact moved the table two feet. "I have had *enough* of you!" She bent low, slapping his head so hard it rocked on his neck. "*Where are those kids?!*"

Mahlon just raised his face, now bloody, and spat at her. "Good Cop didn't work," he said, chiding her, "so bring on Bad Cop?" He laughed, a wheezy tone that reflected his condition. "Yeah, go ahead, beat it out of me, that's the way! I've never been beaten before, you stupid…" Another slap ended the insult before Mahlon could begin to phrase it. "You think I never been hit before? Go ahead! But you'll never get the information from me in time, and if I don't make a phone call in thirty minutes, the kids are dead. So how much time do you really want to play, 'cuz I got all night!"

"Glad we agree this is fun," Blaze said, backhanding him, causing him to groan despite himself. "But I do agree with you—we don't have time for this. Stay put!" Stepping on his leg with her heeled boot for good measure, she crossed the room and went back to Josanne.

… …

"Greyscale, Iylothien here. Just letting you know things are getting quite saucy in here in Castle Criminalia. The problem with bad guys is they have stuff they're not supposed to. Experimental virus code, new versions of black ICE, you name it."

- *"How you holding up, Iylo? Do you need to jack out?"*

"What, and lose my title? I don't think so—wait a nano—I just spotted the treasure. Huge trunk, glowing, in the middle of a hoard of loot, jewels galore. Almost there… Oh, that's weird; the system wizards all backed out. One second and uh-oh … Oh, drek, I don't believe this."

- *"Iylo, this is Greyscale, what is it? Respond now!"*

"Grey, you're not going to believe this."

"NOW what?" exclaimed Greyscale. He was in the middle of a firefight with Hardcore against a Matsua Remus on one side and one of the criminal tanks on the other. The girls were having trouble

getting Mahlon to tell them where the kids were, and now Iylo was going cryptic on him. *Lord, help us!* he silently prayed.

"They're cutting off the system from the Matsua gateways. That's why the wizards backed out. They're not winning, so..."

- *"So, they're quitting. Get out, now!"*

"No way I'm leaving now, Grey! I just got their locks picked, and I'm just about to start the download. It could be years before we get another shot at this much of their organizational data. I'm telling you, Grey, it's that hot, and I'm staying."

"What's he doing?" Hardcore asked.

"They're shutting down their gateways to the outside systems."

"So, what's the problem?"

"The remaining hackers and admins will all be inside the gangster's system, but Iylo is connected via a pathway through one of the gateways. If they shut down the gateway before Iylo jumps through, he could suffer severe brain injury. In his condition, it'll probably kill him."

"But he sees the pot of gold, so he's staying to take the shot," Hardcore concluded. "Anything we can do to help?'"

Jack looked at Hardcore. "Only one thing from here," he said. "We can pray." The blast of a tank gun's neat miss lifted the vehicle for a second, the jarring impact of the landing causing Hardcore to wince. "Dang! That one *hurt!*" the CYBER wheelman complained. "Not much time here to do any praying, Grey."

... ...

"Hey, Trig?" Blaze spoke gently. "Hey, it's me. You're hearing what's going on here, yeah?"

Josanne almost unperceptively nodded, still withdrawn.

"Well then, you know those kids are gonna die if we don't find them in the next half hour?"

Again, Josanne slowly shook her head yes.

"Okay, so it's like this. Vixenn can't find where they are, and neither can Iylo. Seems like the only way we can find out is to get Perp One over here to start blabbing, yeah?"

Once again, Josanne nodded.

"Now Foxfire tried, but the guy's brain's wired perp screwy, so she's stuck. Also seems like the guy likes the pain, so my way ain't working either."

For the fourth time, Josanne nodded.

"We need you, Trigget," Blaze confessed. "We're stuck, and I think you're the only one here who can get him to talk."

"You need me?" she asked Blaze, confused. "You guys are all the super people. All I can do is the talking thing, and Foxfire's better at that than I am."

- *"Trigget," Greyscale cut in, "can you hear me?"*

Josanne nodded again, still withdrawn.

- *"Listen, Trig, you are an important part of this team. You saved the lives of many of us at the quarry, and from what I heard you saved Vixenn's life again tonight. We need you again, Trig. We're counting on you to save the lives of those kids. Blaze is right. You're the only one who can get Mahlon to tell us where they are in time."*

"But how?" Trigget asked out loud, still withdrawn but beginning to respond. "He won't respond to the pheromones."

- *"Diagnose him," Jack said, his heart breaking. "Analyze his symptoms. We need to make him talk, Trigget, to save the lives of those kids. You're the only one who can."*

- "Okay, I guess," she feebly ventured, as though the effort to focus took all her faculties.

She then said out loud, "I'll try…"

Engaging medical protocols… A transformative calm almost instantly came over the young reporter's face as the medical programming engaged, almost as though she wasn't there at all. For a few seconds, she said nothing, then the program kicked in and she began a monotone chant:

"SUBJECT: One Atchins, Mahlon H. Lived a relatively sheltered life, hints of megalomania at age thirteen. Animal cruelty turned to bullying and victimizations of peers at age sixteen. Evidence of psychotic schizophrenia established at age twenty, especially towards females and those he regarded as power figures…

"DIAGNOSIS:," she continued. *"Subject will not divulge location of children, whom he regards not so much of a shield as a way of striking at targets he could not reach otherwise. Subject has been subjected to sodium pentothal often enough in the past to have built up some resistance to the drug. Hmm, subject has developed a history of trypanophobia—the one thing he is afraid of is…needles.*

"PROGNOSIS:," Trigget said, her former withdrawal giving way to effectively treating a condition that would save the lives of seventeen children. *"Subject will not disclose location of children willingly. Prescribe three milliliters of sodium amobarbitol tripentathone combined with one milliliter of oxytocin."*

She shook her head to clear the last of the shock caused by re-entering her own mind. "And for good measure," she said looking up at Blaze and wiping tears from her eyes—how long had she been crying?—"add another bourbon to whatever else he's had."

"Yeah?" Mahlon said. "And where you gonna get all the juice, huh sister? But yeah," he added, "I could use a drink. Get me a bourbon."

At that Trigget stood up, walked over to Mahlon, and checked him over. He still wore the same mocking grimace. "You really do deserve what's coming," she said, with a resigned sigh. "Blaze and Blackwolf, can you please hold him still for a couple seconds?" To Mahlon's horror, she opened a small pocket in her left arm and withdrew a tiny syringe kit. She then lifted the left side of her shirt, exposing a tiny nozzle tip with a pinch to her abdomen.

"Our bodies produce most of the chemicals and enzymes required, and our immune and other systems typically filter out the others," Josanne informed Atchins. "So yes, in a way we are chemical supply facilities. I just have a way to access mine."

A few seconds later and the syringe was filled with a slightly yellowish liquid. She gave it a nurse's flick twice, then with the skill of an anesthesiologist, administered the dose into the side of his neck. "I could have done this almost anywhere on you," she told him, "but this way you get to watch it."

He shrieked and struggled against the Fatales that were holding him in place. His struggle fruitless, he settled into a docile whimper. "And for the record, we don't really need to give you the bourbon, just the ethyl alcohol it would have contained."

The injection done, she turned to Blaze and declared, "Just hurry and ask him what you need to know. In less than thirteen seconds, he'll be completely out."

"Where are the kids?" Blaze demanded to know, but Mahlon just laughed again.

"Forget it, sister. Your horror show's done. I can hold against this stuff for thirteen seconds! By the way, your time's up." His smile faded as Mahlon lapsed into unconsciousness.

"*Now* what are we going to do?" Blaze asked. "What just happened, Trig?" Trigget smiled and held her index finger to her mouth in a shushing motion.

-*"You forgot that Trigget's a conversationalist," Foxfire sub-vocally replied with a smile. "Now his brain thinks he's safe from telling us what we need to know, so his subconscious has no reason to think he should hold anything back from us. Ask your questions. He'll tell you whatever you want to know. We've got to find those kids, and we only have eighteen minutes to do it."*

...   ...

"Got it!" Iylothien cried as he pierced the lock and despoiled the treasure chest of its contents. "This is my last transmission. I deleted the formula from their mainframe and wiped all backups. The secret's safe. Whole world's going dark here, though. My connection's cut. Queen Vixenn, if you can hear this, I love you."

And Iylothien, the Barde de le Nêone, simply stopped fighting, sat down, and watched as his instance of Randolph and Emerson's Ultimate Fantasy environmental module began to collapse into darkness around him.

Suddenly, a flash of reddish light burst from behind him, and an orange-red globe of energy illuminated the remaining landscape. Surprised, he looked behind him to behold Queen Vixenn, arms flayed wide, holding a glowing staff, black hair blowing wildly in the howling wind of summoned electronic mana.

"I love you, too—now come on!" she ordered, grabbing him and holding him close against her. A bright yellow flare of light flashed, blinding the orcs, trolls, and even the other wizards who'd crept up on the deadly ranger once he'd resigned from the fight. A nano-second later, they were gone.

The pair flashed for a second before a dungeonesque lair that Iylothien knew must have been her connection to the criminal network in the archology.

Queen Vixenn's deck monitor flashed bright yellow against a wall mirror, jolting Trigget from her withdrawn stupor. For a second, she caught an image of her friend in a flowing mage's gown, being held tightly by a golden-haired guy with a bow. They were both smiling. Then the screen flashed a second time, and they were gone…

And bounced back into Iylothien's Ultimate Fantasy, just before the entrance to the Matsua network. The globe faded; the ethereal gale died. Still, they held each other closely.

"I don't understand," Iylothien finally said. "How'd you do that? Hell, I'd settle for knowing what it was you did."

"What I had to," she admitted. "Your connection was getting cut off, but I had a separate routing through their internal network that was still good. So, I jumped to the node you were in and bounced your signals through my connection—"

"And back to the IP address from where I entered the Matsua system, effectively restoring my persona before it was cut off. Man, that was EPIC!"

"I take it milord is pleased?" she asked, with a curtsy and a smile.

"He is the Barde de le Nêone, not some oafish lout!" he returned with a bow. "He is most pleased. Thou art Wizardess Royale, indeed!" he declared with a smile.

… …

- *"STRIKE TEAM! STRIKE TEAM! This is Foxfire. Mahlon talked. The kids are in level 237 of the archology. It was once used for education, but it's getting renovated for chemical storage. We left Mahlon tied up and unconscious in his apartment and are going in to rescue the kids. General, if you can, we're requesting backup. Foxfire out."*

Greyscale now knew the kids were not in the production facilities, so the strike team was free to resume the assault. The fighting was fierce, but eventually the criminal element was no match for the joint CYBER team task force, especially since the criminals had severely crippled their own systems when they cut themselves off from Matsua's network. Making matters worse for the defenders, whatever Iylothien and Queen Vixenn had done to their mainframe severely disrupted the building's electronic control systems, not only hampering automated defense systems but also throwing climate and air control systems in complete disarray. Chrome and Fuser were the first ones to punch through, and shortly after the transmission from the Fatale element, it seemed like the Matsua forces were pulling back, freeing Hardcore and Rickshaw to worry about being rearguard and join the frontal assault. The facility fell quickly, resistance rapidly scattering. The destruction of the underworld organization's Diamond supply was complete; the subsequent CYBER-induced fires annihilated any other evidence that the killer drug had ever even existed.

"Thank God not all Diamonds are forever," Arañé muttered, as he watched the spreading conflagration. "Your team's done good, Greyscale. All they need now is a name. We're keeping 'Grey's Hounds,' if you don't mind, so I guess you'll need a new moniker yourself. I somehow don't think you'll mind leaving some parts of you in the past."

… …

The CYBER strike teams emerged from the facilities to find themselves hemmed in by the Matsua forces. Five Remus APCs, two tanks, and a field gun were awaiting them, all guns levelled at the entrance to the facility's lower level. "What the—? You gotta be kiddin' me! What now?" Chrome said in exasperation. They were tired. Their vehicles were beat up and low on ammo. Rachel was limping, Menagerie was leaning on her staff, her Mystique reduced to a wreckage that as far as she was concerned, Matsua could keep if they wanted to. But they had won, and Diamond was now irrevocably lost to anyone who might wish to resurrect the compound. They would go down fighting, if they had to, but they had no real desire to needlessly fight the Matsua troops just because the megacorp was trying to defend itself.

The Matsua troops just held, unmoving. Jack didn't like the stand-off, but something in him told him to wait. Most of the Hounds had been with Jack in situations like this earlier and had grown to trust his instincts. The recruits, however, were on edge.

- *"Easy, Hardcore," Rickshaw said, cautioning him. He noticed Corey starting to race his engine ever so slightly. "Grey knows what he's doing, even when it feels otherwise. Trust him."*

Moments later, an armored personnel carrier approached. The troops just held their places but stiffened as a squad of troops in gloss black heavy body armor debarked and swept the area. A few seconds later, an impeccably dressed suit with an air that deafened the immediate area around him stepped out of the command vehicle, the air of authority he exuded as acutely real as the creases of his Panatti suit.

He glanced at them indifferently, as though appraising them. After a moment, he turned a slow circle once to review the damage, then scrutinized them more intently. Nobody else moved.

"I am Mr. Johnson," he began.

- *"Of course you are," Chrome sub-vocally jibed, causing a few of them to grimly smirk.*

"Executive Director Mau wishes to congratulate you on your successful venture," Johnson continued. "You have some very unusual connections, it appears. Connections we would wish to know more of. For instance, your Simon somehow contacted myself and Director Mau on our *personal* comm links and informed us your teams were dispatched in good faith to help us resolve the situation with the missing children.

"We are most curious as to how your Simon happened to find Director Mau's link code, which is in fact a number I myself do not have." He pronounced the words with emphasis, straining against the self-control he was enforcing upon himself.

"Mr. Johnson," Jack began, as he stepped out of the Sabretooth, "with all due respect, I don't know how Simon got the numbers. We had no intention of going over your head."

"Yes. Well, I immediately dispatched our T.A.T. forces to the compound on the 237th floor. They arrived in time to watch your team—the Fatale team, I believe they called themselves—escorting the children out of that...*prison*. I watched the feed as some of the children were carried, others snuggled against their rescuers in a way that confirmed to the strike squads that your team was friendly.

"Inside, of course, was another matter entirely. Our extraction teams confirmed the complete success of your rescue operation, a true testament to the skill and efficiency of your team. Now, looking at all this," he said, surveying the ruined facility and wrecked defense stations, "is truly remarkable. I dare say our own T.A.T. squads could not have effected a better outcome, even though they are intimately familiar with the archology grounds.

"In fact," he concluded, "I really must insist that you stay. I believe Matsua engineering and development teams would profit greatly from the experience of, shall we say, *examining* the members of your team. You're their leader, they'll do as you say. Consider your response very carefully," he said, with the unmistakable tone of finality.

A tense silence ensued as Jack silently prayed.

Lord, we can break out of here, but at what cost? We didn't come here to wage war against Matsua, but I don't believe we should surrender ourselves to their experiments, either. What do You want us to do?

"*Tell them that...*" Jack thought he almost audibly heard. He sighed. *Here goes nothing,* he thought to himself.

"Mr. Johnson, we came here to help, not to wage war against Matsua. Now that we've done what we came here to do, I don't believe we should surrender ourselves to your experiments."

Johnson was about to respond but was interrupted by a call. A few terse nods and three "Yes, sir's" later, Johnson put his phone away, squared his shoulders, and almost politely smiled at the CYBER teams.

"That was Director Mau. Evidently your Simon has informed Mr. Director that he has a number of other teams at his disposal that would make a vendetta against Matsua their highest priority if your teams are not immediately released unharmed. Director Mau has weighed the consequences of his various options and has agreed that you may be released. You may proceed, under escort, to the east gate of the archology grounds."

"Thank you, Mr. Johnson," Jack replied, relieved. He didn't want to accrue any more casualties, on either side.

Johnson just started climbing back into his transport when the first mini-missile struck, missing Hardcore's Sabretooth by only a few feet. The blast hurled clouds of dirt and shrapnel into the air along with two more of Matsua's ground troops. A black helicopter appeared from around the southern wall of the archology and hovered over the procession of Matsua and CYBER vehicles.

"You're all *DEAD!*" a voice screamed over the helicopter's bullhorn. Mahlon's voice! Only then did radio reports come in that the remnant of Mahlon's supporters had somehow freed him, helping Atchins escape to the helicopter gunship he'd used when he tried to kidnap Martinez at the quarry. After a surprise assault on the Matsua helideck, Mahlon's forces crippled Matsua's other helicopters, allowing the crime boss to wreak his vengeance by rocketing the Matsua and the CYBER vehicle teams before he left for good.

Hardcore and Rickshaw tried to get into position to return fire, but they were caught in the open and could at best try to draw the helicopter's fire. Reliant on their helicopters for air defense, the Matsua Remus vehicles were not equipped for a surface-to-air fight. Deaths mounted as Mahlon's helicopter fired salvo after salvo onto the ground troops below, the chin-mounted Vulcan II machine gun spewing added destruction. Every square inch of a football field-sized patch of ground was pocked with leaden death every second the Vulcan fired.

"Enough of this!" Mahlon shouted. "You think you're safe, living in your steel and concrete towers?" Mahlon turned and levelled the helicopter, threatening to expend the remaining rockets on the archology building itself, the deadly Vulcan trying to devour the civilians inside. It would be several more minutes before other air support would arrive, and there was nothing the strike team could do that would stop the heavily armored gunship.

- *"I've got an idea!" the General called over the CYBER frequency. "I didn't want to risk crashing the chopper against the building, but civilians are definitely going to die if we don't try something! If I could just…"*

As he was speaking, one of the two drones still connected to the ramp tethers disengaged from the perimeter wall and flew upwards into the helicopter's flight path, towing the tether cable behind it.

- *"General, there's no way that micro drone's gonna take down that gunship itself!" Greyscale said.*

- *"No choice—my other drones are still in the maintenance tunnels. Have some faith!"*

The tiny drone flew up past the cockpit but was smacked aside by the heavy rotor blades of the gunship. Broken and smashed, it crashed to the ground in a spinning whirl, the tether cable looping outwards like a lariat as it trailed, drifting to the ground.

The helicopter fired a missile that blasted away at the Matsua building. Despite the solid construction of the archology, glass shattered into a thousand shards, concrete and durasteel crumbled and bent to the blast.

- *"Almost had it!" the General exclaimed. "I've got one try left…"*

Jack caught on to what the General was trying to do. Silently he prayed, not for Mahlon's destruction but for the safety of the civilians. Almost immediately he felt an awareness of his mistake in jumping on the General the way he had.

- *"Go ahead, General! You got this!" he said, encouraging the young drone pilot.*

The General withdrew deep inside himself to focus. The five drones in the Matsua maintenance tunnels collapsed in the ductwork with a clanging, echoing crash that was heard in the adjacent floors. The General didn't care. Pouring his entire waking consciousness into the remaining micro-drone, he saw the approach of the spinning blades, sensed the heat of the engines he was nearing, felt the tug of the air resistance against the length of steel cable as he lifted up, up, and…*through* the small whirlwind of the rotors as the tiny drone passed between the blades.

"*YES!*" the General cried, cutting the magnetic grip on the steel cable, now caught fast by the helicopter blades. Incurably tangling in the rotors, the steel cable slapped against the air, the rotors, and the body of the aircraft. Within moments, the helicopter blades jammed completely, causing it to sharply dip in a violently skewed spin. The tail rotors collided first against the building, then against the ground itself, killing all on board in an electrified firestorm. As the initial smoke cleared, it was obvious that very little damage had been done to the structure from the collision. No additional civilian injuries were reported.

As emergency crews responded, the strike team proceeded the rest of the way without incident. The Fatale team left in the same limousine in which they had arrived, waved through by a young, black-haired gate guard who winked at them as they passed. Before dawn began its ascension over the horizon, he was the only CYBER team member left on Matsua grounds.

… …

Johnny spent the rest of the night watching replays of the gang fight, hanging out with a very grateful grandfather and the rest of the Matsua gate guards, who were elated to finally be rid of the despised criminal organization's 'Special Security.' At the end of the shift, he shook hands with them all and simply walked off the archology grounds into the sunrise, hopefully never to return. He truly hated the Matsua uniform colors, but he inwardly grinned as he decided it had been worth it.

Around the corner, the limo waited. He smiled, remembering that fight with Blaze his first night. She was right, he concluded. He wondered how CYBER knew, but then he just accepted that they did, and really didn't care how. After desperately searching for almost his whole life, at last he had found what he was really looking for. For the first time since he was eight years old, he finally had somewhere to go.

EPILOGUE:

IT WAS A good day at Facility, where the three teams had gathered for their after-action review in the conference room. Blaze and Arañé were making an announcement.

"We, Blaze's Fist and Spider's Hounds, officially welcome and celebrate the genesis of our brand new team," Blaze began. "Each of you was making positive impact on your own—including you, Jack. I'd say you were all lone wolves, but you were stronger—you were *lions*. But you each lacked one thing—physically," here she looked at Josanne, "emotionally," she continued with glances at Corey and Sue, Johnny, and Melissana, "and even spiritually." She ended with her eyes resting on Jack.

"Now comin' up with these names is tough," Arañé confessed. "Believe me, I spent solid days reading through dictionaries and more than one thesaurus. But I think we finally found something that fits. You were lions, you needed family, and now you have one. Without further ado, we hereby dub you, *Preach's Pride*."

"So, our little family has a name now, eh?" Johnny mused. "Not too bad."

Blaze continued. "And now that you have a team identity, we present to *Preach's Pride* the opening deposit to the team's account."

"*Man!*" Melissana gushed, trying to comprehend the amount of the deposit as it flashed on the giant digital wall screen. "Where did all this money come from?"

Jack laughed out loud. Even Chrome allowed himself a chuckle now that the tension of the mission was past and the recruits were working out okay.

"Finding the money's never been the problem for CYBER," Jack said with a ready smile. "Finding the people who can handle it with integrity is.

"Matsua offered half the victim's life insurance payout for getting their kids back, but I turned them down—that's not why we do what we do. Besides, I don't trust them—Mau wouldn't offer the payment if he wasn't going to get something in return. FoodTech ICCs different. They were paying for the capture or demise of the person responsible for the Justin Martinez kidnapping plot. You and Iylo found several of the organized crime's money laundering franchise accounts, netting a couple million credits before the franchise even realized the accounts were compromised. By the way, the franchise was further hurt by the 'brain drain' caused when said organization purged the incompetents who failed to recognize we'd hacked them. All in all, it was an excellent deal for us."

"So, what are you going to do with your share, Chrome?" Susan asked.

"Oh, I'll get my bike fixed, maybe upgrade to something bigger."

"I'm just going to take some time off," Arañé contributed.

"I'm gonna upgrade my Dominator," Rickshaw offered. "Maybe add some of those HEAVE rockets, or just upgrade to a luxury sedan. Y'know, you can really load up one of those babies!"

"Well, the Fist is going to go on a trip to the beach, then just go back home to the mansion," Lyn declared. The rest of the team eagerly nodded in agreement.

"I think I'm going to make a sizable donation to a small church in Roanoke," Jack divulged, and then with a chuckle added, "and maybe fund an air-conditioning plant." He then paused for a moment, considering the seed of an idea. Then he more reflectively added, "Or maybe some other company to cool down the neighborhood…"

Josanne and Melissana smiled. "Speaking of Roanoke, we're going out to eat with Justin, Elaine, Monica, and Jim. We owe them a dinner, and this time *we're* buying. How about you two lovebirds?" Josanne asked.

"Oh, we'll think of something," they said simultaneously, sharing a smile.

… …

"It's been a long year, Jimmy" Handsight complained to his long-time assistant and friend, sighing as he did frequently these days. "I don't know—you ever thought you've lost too much to even try to get it back? After Sam and I lost our kids to the raids, I thought I'd never have that kind of feeling again. But then those two kids showed up with all hell on their tails, and we both felt it." Some days, it all hit rougher than others. He'd need another beer.

"Yeah, they were good kids. Remember when Karen called you when they were on the news? We all had a soft spot for 'em. Then that hotel mess happened. Doesn't seem right. I guess I know how you feel," Jimmy responded between swigs.

Both men paused, lost in the moment of their memories, until the town's banker entered the bar and interrupted them.

"Mr. Jenkins, I'm sorry to bother you, but someone stated they wished to make a donation to the town defense fund account. But they have one condition."

"You need to talk about that now, Daniel? I'm tryin' to have a drink and relax a little here! Tell 'em we're still workin' down the line. If they want us to fix their house before all the others, that's not the way this works. If they insist, tell 'em to keep their 100 credits."

"Sir, the donation is for three quarters of a million credits, cleared, and the only condition they have is they want to personally hand it to you and your wife."

"Well then, tell 'em they're crazy! Nobody in this town has that kind of money!"

399

"Mr. Jenkins, they've already showed me the credits—literally! We're bringing Samantha here now."

"Sir?" a female voice asked.

"Now you, too, Karen? What are you doing here?"

"That hacker, Iylothien, came on-line again today, told me to meet you here—something about them being unavailable because of a series of surgeries and extended operations."

"And you left your post on takin' the word of a hacker?" He was getting upset; his quiet day off was not going as planned.

"I got someone to cover my post, sir, and when has that hacker ever done us wrong?"

"Your wife is here, sir."

Handsight stood up as his wife entered the room. "Sam? I don't know what's goin' on here today, but all right, Daniel," he said, with a sarcastic bow, "show in our illustrious donors."

He fell back into his chair as Corey and Sue entered the room and presented Handsight with the credits.

... ...

Guy walked into Vince Prentiss's office. "Vince, your next client is waiting. He apparently has need for our services."

"What specifically does the gentleman need, Mr. Reigis?" Vince asked with a smile.

Guy smiled wide, relaxed, and laughed in spite of himself. "You know, six months have passed since Preach helped get us patched up with the CCB and off the street, and this still cracks me up!

"Okay, sorry—Ahem!" he said, trying to clear his throat, and breaking into one more brief spat of laughter. "Sorry, Vince. The guy's got problems with some uptown choober tryin' to stong-arm him outta business. Not makin' much cred, but he's on the level—a good guy. I like him."

"Okay, your judgement's never let us down, we'll help him," Vince Prentiss agreed. "Oh, I'll be leaving the office after this—I've got a meeting in an hour. Then after that I'm going to head over to the church for a while to visit my brother. Show Mr. Parionte in."

Vince extended his hand to offer his client a reassuring handshake. "Welcome to the Roanoke Azonal Regional Security, Mr. Parionte. My company and I have helped several clients with their security risks and issues. How may we help you?" he asked. Vince smiled as he glanced over his desk setting while he regained his seat. On the desk was his favorite keepsake, a hefty decorative paperweight with an open pair of golden scissors mounted in its base.

… …

Quietly, by himself in his prayers, Jack thanked God for his new calling, his new family. He took some time to reflect on each of them before God. He thought of Josanne first. Jack deeply regretted any loss of life on a mission, but he felt especially remorseful for her. Outside of Jack, she was their moral compass. She needed to get past what happened in Mahlon's suite, but at the same time Jack really didn't want her to, if the alternative was for her to get too used to it. Then he noted Johnny, who was starting to soften up, if just a little. Corey and Sue were young and in love, but life in 2048 put strains on relationships like theirs—a life in CYBER without sound guidance could easily destroy their relationship from the inside out. And Melissana? For someone who grew up in such a harsh environment, she was still so much like a kid in so many ways. But how long would that last before she got jaded by everything she would see?

He knew now and gratefully accepted that he really did need to be here for this team. He was *their* pastor now.

… …

401

Simon reviewed the operation, the team, and the re-integration of Jack. It was pleased with the results. It then intercepted a communication between James Sinclair and one of his operatives:

- *"Shame about your sister."*

- *"Nah, she'd never be worth anything, and we needed to make sure she never came back."*

Simon listened in on the rest of the conversation with growing interest. No wonder James Sinclair wanted Josanne out of the picture. Simon concluded a decision gate had been reached and its threshold crossed. Something would need to be done about James's activities.

FINI

Coming next in the CYBER series...

ANGELS

NIGHTTIME IN WITCH City was nowhere to be on the run. She continued to push though, half-skipping, half-hobbling, wincing with each step, fires of agony flashing in her eyes. She couldn't let herself cry; they would hear her.

She stumbled and fell as heavily as her undernourished frame would allow. At least she was getting closer. Closer to her freedom. Closer to being reunited with her family. *Family*—just the thought of the word brought renewed strength of purpose. She crawled onwards through the dirt of the littered alley, no longer able to walk. It just hurt too much! Earlier in the chilled Witch City evening she had gritted her teeth, picked up the piece of metal she found in the alley, and gouged out the RFID chip they had implanted deep in her right heel. The excruciating pain was almost unbearable, but if she didn't do it, they'd just track her down like they did the others who tried to run—and she didn't want to end up like them...

ACKNOWLEDGEMENTS:

IF I WERE to write a list of all those I would like to acknowledge in this book, I would have filled enough pages to have my second book! There are a few who have been especially helpful, though, and deserve special thanks.

To all those mentioned in the dedication, I truly thank you, even if (in the case of the authors) we may have never actually met. Without you I would have had neither the strength nor the conviction to start, let alone complete, this work.

I would like to thank the management and staff at Steve Jackson Games, FASA, and other RPG companies who have fueled my imagination over the years.

A huge Thank You goes out to all the staff and family at Capital Christian Center. I restrict my use of the word "awesome" to its truest sense. You guys are truly amazing and, well, *awesome*!

I sincerely thank Krista Dunk and Debbie McClain of Creative Force Press for helping me get started on the path to publishing. Eric Schroeder of Westbow Press greatly contributed to the success of this project by thinking outside the box and connecting dots. Thanks also to Dave Triplett, who provided the phenomenal cover art—a true artiste, indeed. Lastly, I thank Stephanee Killen and the staff of Integrative Ink for all the work they did getting this story into shape for publication. I am *highly* honored to have worked with each of you.